ERIC LEWIS

THE HERON KINGS' FLIGHT

Book Two of the *Heron Kings* Series

This is a **FLAME TREE PRESS** book

Text copyright © 2022 Eric Lewis

FLAME TREE PRESS
6 Melbray Mews, London, SW6 3NS, UK
flametreepress.com

US sales, distribution and warehouse:
Simon & Schuster
simonandschuster.biz

UK distribution and warehouse:
Marston Book Services Ltd
marston.co.uk

Publisher's Note: This is a work of fiction. Names, characters, places, and incidents are a product of the author's imagination. Locales and public names are sometimes used for atmospheric purposes. Any resemblance to actual people, living or dead, or to businesses, companies, events, institutions, or locales is completely coincidental.

Thanks to the Flame Tree Press team, including:
Taylor Bentley, Frances Bodiam, Federica Ciaravella, Don D'Auria,
Chris Herbert, Josie Karani, Mike Spender, Cat Taylor,
Maria Tissot, Nick Wells, Gillian Whitaker.

The cover is created by Flame Tree Studio with
thanks to Nik Keevil and Shutterstock.com.
The font families used are Avenir and Bembo.

Flame Tree Press is an imprint of Flame Tree Publishing Ltd

flametreepublishing.com

A copy of the CIP data for this book is available from the British Library
and the Library of Congress.

HB ISBN: 978-1-78758-700-7
PB ISBN: 978-1-78758-698-7
ebook ISBN: 978-1-78758-701-4

Printed and bound in Great Britain by Clays Ltd, Elcograf S.p.A

ERIC LEWIS

THE HERON KINGS' FLIGHT

Book Two of the *Heron Kings* Series

FLAME TREE PRESS
London & New York

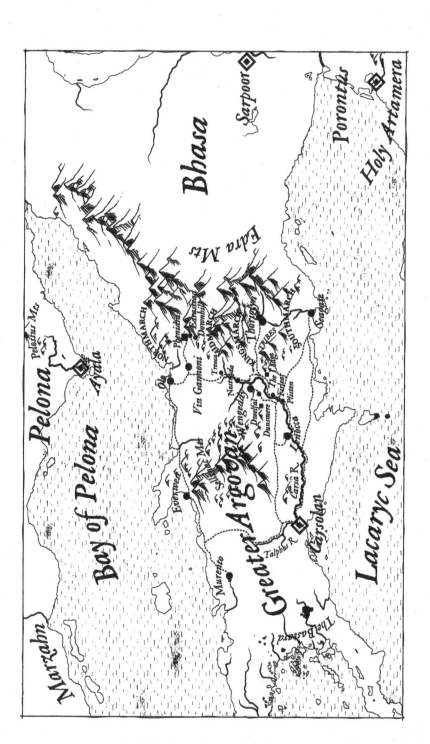

PART ONE

CHAPTER ONE

Justice Enough

Linet strode through the twilit halls of the Lodge of the Heron Kings, gathering bits of gear, moving from one chamber to the next and through the long-remembered routines of lacing her leather jerkin, hooking a quiver of arrows to her belt and stringing her bow. There was some small comfort in these familiar acts, but she knew they were only a distraction from the worry gnawing at the back of her mind.

Where are they? she thought.

It was just a routine skirmish, another Marchman tribal incursion meant to test Lord Osbren's resolve, no more. What had begun a century ago with a desperate band of peasant guerrillas lived on in the deadly rangers, a forest refuge for those born with no place in the civilized world and who exchanged freedom from it for service from the shadows. The task of the Heron Kings had been to block the woodland paths while Osbren's men did the dirty work of driving the barbarians back into the mountains. But the twenty sent to do the job were late in returning. They were proficient fighters in any setting of course, but they were most dangerous among the rocks and trees in the dead of night. Tactics that availed one little on an open field.

Linet was late herself, should already have been out on her nightly patrol around the perimeter of the Lodge. But she itched to steal a horse and ride out into the night to make sure nothing had gone wrong. She came to the entrance hall just as the last drops of sunlight fell into shadow, casting a dimness over the valley and leaving the opening to the underground complex, difficult to find even in the noonday sun, as good as invisible. It was almost empty tonight, with everyone of fighting age out on patrol and only a staff of fledglings and elders remaining.

The hall was the only open space in the Lodge, with ornate double doors opening to a concealed access tunnel. A domed ceiling curved down to corridors connecting the system of subterranean chambers that were part natural cave, part carved from the rock. It was a minor marvel of engineering that could house a hundred in perfect secrecy, situated beneath both a natural hot spring and waterfall and suffused with pipes and ventilation shafts. Years of improvements had given the underground fortress a little home-like quality at least, including a stone hearth at one end of the entrance hall. Two high-backed chairs sat side by side before it like faithful old hounds, padded and upholstered and worn deep in the seats with much use. Passing by on her way to the exit, Linet cast a glance in their direction, a last look at a piece of civilization before the wildness of the night forest, and then screamed.

Or rather, she screamed as much as her lifelong training would allow. A shrill yelp of surprise before she recovered into a fighting stance, her short recurved sword halfway out of its scabbard and eyes trained on the odd figure sitting in one of the chairs. It was covered in dirt and leaves, its wild and tousled hair prickly with twigs.

"Identify yourself!" Linet demanded. The figure started, rose and turned toward her. A face flickered in the low hearthlight. Linet breathed a sigh of relief as she dropped her blade back into its scabbard. "Aerrus! You ass, you frightened m—"

"Lin," the young man croaked hoarsely, running forward and clapping dirty hands hard on her shoulders. "Has anyone else made it back yet? Tell me they have!"

"Made it back? No, not yet. What do you mean? What's happened?"

Aerrus's brow wavered. "No. So I'm the only one. Lin, it was a *trap*. Somehow the Marchmen, they knew we were gonna be there. They ambushed us with torches, set fire to the whole godsdamned forest it seemed. Went up like a thatch barn in autumn. We never had a chance. They…they cut us to pieces."

Linet's voice caught in her throat, her knees suddenly weak. "*What?* But…how?"

"Someone betrayed us," Aerrus growled, looking like some forest wight out of legend, filthy as he was. "Told 'em right where we were going to be. Someone who in the near future is going to become a corpse. Very. Slowly." Fury boiled in his eyes. "And I know just where to start. Is anyone else about?"

"No, everyone's either out on patrol or…with you."

"It'll have to be just us two, then," he said urgently. "We can do it, they're only six. Come on!"

"Wait, where are we going?"

★   ★   ★

They rode double through the hidden bridle paths on one of the sturdy, shaggy horses the Marchmen favored, downhill from the Lodge and toward the road that followed the Carsa River. Linet held on to Aerrus from behind, the stench of earth and smoke from his clothes strong in her nostrils. She fought to process this news of the slaughter of nineteen of her fellows, and in the dark she let tears fall without shame. "Tell me," she demanded as they rode, "tell me all of it."

"Osbren's troops were doing their part, we ours. Just before the battle, Bolen spotted six men riding into the Marchman camp, but we didn't think much on it. Then they fired the woods and came at us from the side. Knew exactly where we were. I got brained with a torch, and I guess knocked out." He ran a hand down the back of his head where the hairs were singed. "When I woke up our dead were all over the place. No survivors. I was hoping I'd miscounted in the smoke, but…."

Linet still couldn't believe it. "None? Bolen, Curswell, Gastere, Ellandi?"

"All dead. Savages! The Marchmen didn't even press their attack, just ran off before sundown like always. Found one of their horses wandering around. I was on my way back to the Lodge when I came up behind those same six riders from before, headed north in no kind of hurry. I turned onto the high hill path and came home, just sat down to catch my breath a bit when I spooked you. Figured we could return the favor, ambush them and maybe get some answers. Six against two and we only need one wagging tongue, so I ain't too inclined to mercy. I *know* they had something to do with this."

"How can you be sure? Just because—"

"Didn't get a real good look, but I'd swear at least one of 'em was wearing sable 'round his neck."

Linet knew very well what that meant, and it changed everything.

★   ★   ★

A silvery moon shone down on the forest road, marking out the well-worn path. Six riders nudged their skittish palfreys on two by two. Quietly enough now, though they'd wrought pandemonium only hours ago. With that business behind them and their mission fulfilled, they now rode in silence. But the old rumors of this forest, of what happened to the unwelcome here…the nervousness weighed so heavily that even the horses whinnied every few yards.

Linet crouched in the brush three paces off the road, her bowstring taut. The bow was a small treasure as well as a weapon, crafted out of fine yew from the forest around her, carved to fit her own hand and tipped with polished ramshorn nocks. The fletches of a broadheaded arrow tickled her finger as she held it half-drawn, waiting for the agreed-upon signal.

One of the lead riders halted. Or rather his horse did, though at no command. With annoyance the rider adjusted his rich furs and dug spurs into the animal's hide. Once, again harder, again. It just stamped and snorted.

A raspy whisper from behind. "Oi, what's the hold-up?"

"Ssh, listen! D'you hear...?"

"I ain't heard nothing 'cept that yer horse is fracted in the noggin. Kick it on!"

The lead rider tried again, and the horse began to buck.

Snap. A twig breaking. It came from somewhere in the trees. A soft sound, but it echoed loud in the all-consuming dark. The horse stilled again. A pause. "Oh, shite...."

Linet raised her weapon, drew and loosed. An acid *thwung* rang out from the string until it was drowned by the hard slap of the shaft hitting flesh. Both lead riders screamed and fell, as though struck by two unseen blows. The horses neighed in terror as the other riders shouted curses. Another arrow already drawn, she turned in the other direction. *Thwungslap!* A rear rider went down, clutching his chest.

Two horses bucked in panic and threw the remaining riders to the ground, breaking the neck of one. The last managed to kick hard enough to spur the animal on, trampling writhing bodies, and down the forest road with low branches whipping his face into bloodied bits. An arrow lanced out from across the road, but it missed the fleeing target.

The other thrown rider stumbled to his feet, dying comrades groaning in agony about him. A movement. Dark and obscured by the cover of the forest growth, but there nonetheless. Fury overcame fear, and the rider drew a long war sword and rushed toward the movement, shouting bloody murder. He swung wildly but the long blade bounced off the thick branches, useless. A gleaming short blade leaped out of the gloom like a serpent, and he jumped back just in time to avoid a killing thrust.

"Gyah!" Dropping the longsword, he drew a dagger and charged ahead. The shape before resolved out of the dark: no demon after all, but a man. A short one, at that. He swiped left and right, but the wiry frame jumped away each time. With a cry he drove a kick into his midsection. He flew back and down, a great blow of outward breath proving his enemy mortal.

The rider glowered over his attacker to deliver the killing blow, raising the dagger high. The man on the ground suddenly turned, spun in an arc with his own short sword in hand and with a sweep opened the rider's throat.

A groan, a gurgling spray, and he fell to the side, his last sensation the cool wet earth against his face.

Aerrus rose, breathing heavily. Where the rider had been now stood another, more shapely figure outlined in moonlight.

"One got away," said Linet.

"Gods fuckitall! Any others still alive?"

She looked down at the carnage they'd wrought. Not all of their shots had been killing ones, but the bucking and stamping mounts had added to the score. "None that'll live long enough to tell us anything."

Aerrus kicked a tree. "I was too hasty!"

"Search the bodies," Linet suggested. "Maybe we can still learn something."

"Yeah," Aerrus answered, broken by fresh weariness and a grief that hit them both all of a sudden. "Yeah...."

As the blood flowed at their feet, the pair fell into a mournful embrace and wept.

★   ★   ★

The two figures flitted through the forest like ghosts. The moon now hung low in the sky, but if one happened to look at just the right moment, a shaft of light down through the trees might reveal a hint of movement, but that's all. In a blink it'd be gone, leaving any spy not really sure they'd seen anything. Neither spoke, thanks not only to a lifetime of training but simply because nothing needed to be said. Linet and Aerrus came at last to a place where the trickle of water over rock whispered a soft welcome home. They hunkered into a crouch and disappeared into what at first glance would seem a solid stone outcropping. The forest left no trace of their passing.

They trudged into the Lodge's entrance hall, followed by a few others now returned from night patrol and demanding to know where the pair had been, where the rest were. They ignored all this to collapse into the chairs before the hearth, except to allow fledglings to take their weapons and gear away to be cleaned and mended. "There are horses stashed in the usual place," Linet said wearily, "and...some bodies that'll need to be cleaned from the road." Even in disaster, secrecy and security had to be maintained. Especially in disaster. "And—"

"There you are!" The Lodge came to life now at the news of their return, and a tall redheaded man entered the hall from one of the side passages, then nodded to one of the fledglings. "Tell Perrim they've returned. She'll want to see them straight away."

"I'll tell her myself, Vander," Aerrus said, standing again slowly.

"We both will," Linet answered.

They crossed the hall to another passage, down and around toward a council room that contained the Lodge's single waterfall-shrouded window, and lanterns set into the walls. A tired-looking woman, made older than her sixty or more years by worry, and a man of similar age sat at one end of a long oak table worn smooth by a century of pounding fists.

The young pair waited while their older counterparts regarded them. There was grief in that waiting, no less palpable for its being silent.

"I have been sitting in this chair," said the woman at last, "for far too long to have to guess what you're about to tell me. Something terrible has happened."

Aerrus told the story as he knew it, and when Linet entered it she took over. Perrim's frown grew deep and deeper, yet no tears fell.

"So," said the man next to her angrily, "it was a bit of revenge you were after, then?"

"No! Lom, you know us better than that." Linet glanced briefly at Aerrus, his face a mask. "Well, you know me better than that."

"Yet you failed to take any of these mysterious men alive! And one escaped to tell the tale. Would you care to enlighten me as to what you did accomplish to salve this bloody catastrophe?"

Aerrus held up something he'd been clutching tightly like a magic talisman. "They had these on 'em." He dropped a folded package onto the table. "Letters of friendship and alliance in a couple different languages. From the adventurer-despot Phynagoras to Ordovax, our not so friendly local Marchman chieftain."

"Alliance?" Perrim's mouth hung half open. "Phynagoras is busy conquering the corpse of the Bhasan empire. What business has he with Marchmen?"

"It looks like he might aim to invade Argovan next. The letters offer Ordovax a petty kingdom in exchange for their help. Along with what would seem to be, erm, a bribe." He held out a handful of jewels and coins.

"That doesn't make sense," said the older man.

Perrim turned to her trusted adviser. "Lomuel?"

"The Marchmen are savages. They neither read nor use money. What value a bribe? Or letters, for that matter?"

"Well…" Linet began, swallowed hard. "We think those riders were just middlemen, and the bribe was to keep them quiet. What they did made it justice enough to cut 'em down, but…." She glanced at Aerrus, not wanting to be the one to say it.

"We've reason to believe that it's not just tribesmen involved with Phynagoras. That there's a third party acting as mediator."

Perrim frowned. "What reason?"

Aerrus reached into a haversack slung over his shoulder and pulled out something else, long and soft. It was a black sable neck wrap, splashed with mud and a thin bloodied slice running down its middle. He tossed the unmistakable badge of office onto the table and it slid to a stop in front of Perrim.

She quivered with barely suppressed rage. "Marcher lords."

CHAPTER TWO

A Higher Priority

The warm, crowded taphouse was the social center of the sleepy old garrison town of Vin Gannoni, and the lone rider to escape what was already being called the 'Marchwood Massacre' was currently the center of the taphouse. Not a soul spoke while he related the story of the carnage, told after a week of hard riding back northward to the nearby border fortress Phenidra.

"…and bodies, everywhere, all over the road! Arrows flew outta the dark, too quiet for any mortal hand to've shot!"

A few gasps. Then a cleared throat. "What do you mean by that?" Captain Coladdi. Of course.

"You *know* what, old man. We all know what folk say about that forest. Demons, spirits, whatever!"

"Stories," the captain snorted as hearthlight danced across his frown, "hundred-year-old stories! Don't be stupid—"

"You wasn't there, I was!"

"Yes," said Coladdi with suspicion, "just what *were* you doing so far south, anyway?"

"What's that matter? Carryin' out the Lord Armino's business!"

"And have you reported this to him? Or was the taphouse brewer a higher priority?"

"I—" The man cast a furrowed brow downward into his cup. "I'll go up the hill tonight, soon as I drink up enough courage. Don't know how I'm goin' to explain all this…."

The spell of rapt silence broken, a measure of normal chatter slowly returned to the place. Coladdi sat back down to nurse his last beer of the evening, shaking his head.

"So?" The young soldier sat next to him leaned in closer, his imagination racing.

"So what, Eyvind?"

"What do you think about it all?"

Coladdi sighed. "About our evening's entertainment? I think those men stopped off somewhere after their task was done. They were likely halfway drunk and easy prey for bandits, and he imagined or concocted that story to cover his arse. Demons! Don't tell me you believe that nonsense."

"Well...no. Consider m'self a thoroughly modern man and all that. It's just...the stories go back a long time."

Coladdi nodded. "Aye, back to the time of the civil wars, when peasants fed up with the slaughters sacrificed children and virgins to the ancient Chthonii like savage Marchmen, raining down blood and vengeance on the noble lords what tormented them! Whoo-hoo!"

Both men laughed, but Eyvind's laugh was just a touch less convincing. "All right, all right! Still, Lord Armino's own officers, butchered? Something's going on in the southern Marchwood."

"There's a mountain of difference between *something* and what our friend there was on about. Besides, the nobles are all but gone now, except for border lords like Armino."

Eyvind grinned. "Then the demons must be especially hungry!" He tossed back the last of his own drink, then set the cup down hard. "Eh, whatever. A good tale to tell and hear on the last days of garrison duty. It's back up the hill for us too, sadly. For another whole season!"

Coladdi grunted. "Don't like Phenidra much, do you? Is it the cold, the food, or the cold?"

"Yes," Eyvind replied.

"You're a paragon of the peacetime soldier, my boy, and don't ever let anyone tell you different."

"Why thank you, Cap'n!"

"Time enough for some sparring tomorrow though, before we head back up. You game?"

"Aw...."

"Come on, a little old-fashioned sword and buckler work'll do you good! Take your mind off those demons."

Eyvind nodded, acquiescent to the old man's entreaties as always. "Fine, fine."

"Good. Still…what *were* those men doing so far south?"

*   *   *

Garrison duty in Vin Gannoni was just about the plummest of plum assignments a soldier of the Northmarch could draw, so there was the usual grumbling when it came time for the company to pack up and make the trek back up into the mountains, to Phenidra. The string of border fortresses from the north of the Argovani Peninsula to the south was meant to protect the country from the interminable machinations of Bhasa to the east, but long years of relative peace had led to a slackening of that vigilance. Now, with the assassination of the last Bhasan emperor and the rise of the charismatic Phynagoras, those manning the old stronghold suffered no shortage of anxiety.

None more than Lord Armino, Eyvind thought. Phenidra was a great ugly lump of stone situated just above the treeline. Beyond, the snow-capped Edra Mountains loomed with their thousand hidden passes. As Eyvind marched through the gate, a glance upward gave a familiar sight: the dark sable-clad form of Lord Armino pacing the battlements, gazing often at those ominous mountains. Less familiar were the two grim fellows carrying crossbows who followed two paces behind.

"Right, lads," bellowed Coladdi as his command column snaked in and around the courtyard, "you know the drill. Stow your gear, find a bunk, and get stuck in for the duration. Seems we drew the cold season." An old joke, but the column laughed anyway – it was *always* the cold season at Phenidra. "And pray the last bastard in your rack didn't piss all over it every night in fear o' the wind howling through the watchtowers!" Vin Gannoni's replacement garrison hurled the customary insults at the newly arrived soldiers before beginning its own march down into the valley, glad to be quit of the place for the next quarter of a year.

Eyvind shivered at the chill he never quite got used to. "Hey, Cap'n," he said, catching Coladdi when he'd finished giving orders, "what do you make of those two?"

"Eh?"

Eyvind pointed up at Armino, still pacing. "Them crossbowmen mother-henning the lord. That's new."

Coladdi gave a sour sneer. "Mercenaries. Bodyguards, most like. That news about the riders must've spooked him more than I thought."

"Mercs for bodyguards? Here? Hasn't he any faith in his own soldiers?"

Coladdi shook his head. "That's a question far beyond your pay grade. Or mine. You just get your bunk squared away."

"Yes, Cap'n."

*　　*　　*

A week after Eyvind's return, Phenidra received a visitor. Which itself wasn't unusual, but what *was* unusual was the direction from which the visitor arrived: east. A small figure clad in the bright blue robes typical of eastern emissaries and leading a packhorse by the bridle walked right up to the walls over a frosted gravelly path. It was a woman. She'd been seen a mile or more off, and the guards on the watchtowers stared at her the whole time. Long after she rounded the walls to pass through the front gate and into the central keep, tongues wagged and gossip flowed like wedding wine.

"Whatever her business is, it's none of our concern," said Coladdi between blows of his blunted training sword, though he didn't sound very convinced to Eyvind.

"I know, I know," the young man replied, trying with his usual mixed success to deflect the strokes with the old-style buckler shield. Clangs and crashes bounced off the courtyard walls. "It's just...I can't put it outta my head, y'know? The whole bloody mess, and the lord's taking it poorly, those mercs, and now this foreign filly come out of nowhere – *aieee!*"

"Move your feet!" snapped Coladdi as he rapped Eyvind's insufficiently gloved knuckle for emphasis, "and remember your wards. Better yet, *learn* 'em so you don't have to remember!"

"Aye, aye."

"I know it's all about halberds and massed pike-work these days, but poles break, and your sword hand might be all that stands between you and a mud nap someday. I tried to teach your father that, but...." Coladdi looked older all of a sudden, and tired.

Eyvind dropped his guard, tucked the trainer under one arm and clapped the old man on the shoulder. "I know, Cap'n. That weren't your fault, I've told you a thousand times. And I know your lessons are worthy, even if I run my mouth the whole time."

"Hey now," Coladdi said with a rough, embarrassed laugh, "I'm allowed to get sentimental in my old age. You, not so much." He let out a long, wheezing cough that gave Eyvind a twinge of alarm. "Gyah, but enough for today. Let's haul these antiques back up to the loft."

"I'll do it, I can handle it all. You go lie down."

"Don't you be givin' me no orders, boy! Still...maybe some rack time...do some good."

Eyvind gathered up the practice gear and climbed an outdoor plank stair to the storage loft located just above the keep's main hall. It was a dark, mostly forgotten space reserved for the least useful of supplies, including the old sword and buckler tradition favored by Coladdi. Eyvind stumbled through the gloom to the boxes where they were stored and gently laid the gear inside. He turned to leave, then paused at something.

In the farthest corner of the room, near a stone bust of one of the long line of lords that had ruled there for so long, a single ray of light pierced upward through the floorboards. He'd never noticed it before, but now idle curiosity led him to investigate. He stepped slowly so as not to trip over anything, then he knelt and peeked through with one eye. He gasped.

Most of the space below was indeed taken up by the main hall where Armino would receive official visitors. But for unofficial ones there was another, smaller chamber. Armino's private chamber. The one Eyvind now spied down into. And the current visitor was almost certainly very, very unofficial. It was the foreigner, the one come from the east. She and Lord Armino sat before a hearth, arguing over something. Every muscle in Eyvind's body screamed at him to come away from that hole, to mind his own business. But something held him fast. Some morbid curiosity, some need to peer into the hidden world of high lords and foreign ambassadors, perhaps. He strained to hear, and Armino's gruff voice rang out.

"...changes nothing! The message was delivered and the agreement made. Those men served their purpose, and the survivor has been dealt with. Permanently. We proceed as scheduled, and you just tell your master *that*."

The foreign figure inclined her head slightly, her ordered calm a stark contrast to Armino's tantrum. She spoke in a thick accent, almost unintelligible.

"I will tell my lord Phynagoras anything you wish, but I promise that will not quiet his concerns. The documents your officers carried could prove bothersome in the wrong hands. My lord has placed a great deal of trust in you and your part of the bargain, satrap."

Armino slammed a fist onto the low table between them, setting the wine cups placed there to shudder. "And he'll not be disappointed! When your master comes over those mountains he'll find no resistance, not here nor in any corner of Argovan. Until word spreads by other means, of course. But by then—"

"By then," the foreigner said with a sinister grin, "it will be too late. King Osmund has no armies of consequence nor nobles to command them in time to stop us. Then, and only then, the Northmarch will be yours to rule as you see fit, just as it was in the old days. Of course they won't be the Marches anymore. We'll all be one big, happy empire, with a million souls and more, keen to make these green western lands their new home."

Armino nodded. "That's all I want. *Then* you can call me satrap."

"Make no mistake, Phynagoras does not wish to repeat the errors of the old emperors, nor of your king. Direct rule over so much of the world is impossible. His offer of peace extends to all who draw breath; merely bend your knee and swear undying faith and obedience, and you may order your domain as you like. Mostly. His rewards are lavish, but his punishments for betrayal are equally lavish."

"Then we understand each other very well." Armino raised his cup in salute.

"But I strongly recommend there be no further accidents like that which you just related. Sloppiness and betrayal often converge to the same unfortunate result – the withdrawal of my lord's offer of peace. And that is something I promise you do *not* wish to experience."

Armino just nodded.

"Good. Then, as a demonstration of your fidelity, I have brought something which my lord has entrusted to me." The ambassador stood, pulled something from a pouch. Something shiny that glimmered in the firelight. A ring. She did not put it on, but extended the face of it toward Armino and waited, expectantly.

Armino snorted. "Are you serious?"

"Oh, yes. Absolutely."

Sighing, Armino bent his lips toward the ring, but the ambassador drew back. "Ah," she said, jerking a pointy chin to the floor.

"Why you hook-nosed, mud-skinned...."

"Insult me as you like, satrap, I am only the vessel of my lord's commands. This is one of them. Take care – my lord does not extend a hand that has once been slapped away." She nodded once again at the floor, where a rich rug showed scenes of battle sewn into fine embroidery.

Armino rose with a growl, then slowly knelt to one knee.

"Both, if you please."

Eyes flaming, Armino obeyed. On both knees, he touched his lips to the device adorning the ring.

"There," said the ambassador, "now that that's done—"

Eyvind had watched all this in growing shock. Having forgotten to breathe, he huffed loudly and lost his balance. A slip, a stumble, and he crashed to the wooden floor that was also the ceiling of the chamber below. At the noise, Armino shot to his feet.

"What in the nineteen hells...?"

The ambassador glared upward in fury, then pointed at the dark hole above them. "We are not alone here!"

Armino howled for guards, bellowed orders to seal the entire keep, prevent any from leaving and to storm the storage loft. Heart racing and head swimming, Eyvind dashed out of the loft and down the stair to ground level. But a frost had put a sheen on the wood, and he slipped.

After Eyvind tumbled to the bottom of the stair, a guard caught him. "Here! I got 'im!"

"What's this all about?" asked another soldier.

"Dunno, the lord said to arrest anyone tryin' to escape the keep."

They dragged Eyvind into the main hall where Armino and the ambassador waited. He was tossed at the lord's feet. "This is him," said the guard, "he was runnin' like a madman outta the storage, m'lord."

Armino grabbed Eyvind by the neck and lifted him with surprising ease for someone of his age. "You spying sneak, what did you hear? Answer me!"

"I...." Eyvind fought to breathe. "I dunno what you mean, lord. Nothing! I was just—"

"You're a bad liar, boy." Armino drew a dagger from his belt. "Hold him while I spill his intestines." Eyvind struggled.

The ambassador stepped between them, an olive-toned halting hand held out sharply. "Wait! We don't know if he was alone. He could have an accomplice who escaped capture."

"What about it, boy?" growled Armino. "Who else are you

working with? Who're you working *for*? Who's paying you to spy on me?"

"No, please, no one! I was just putting the trainers away, I swear it!"

"Lock him up," Armino commanded, "in the defaulter's cell. We'll get to the bottom of this. Where's the torturer?"

One of the guards swallowed nervously. "Um...."

"Well?"

"He's just been rotated down into town garrison duty, m'lord. After all, it's mostly a ceremonial title, not much call for actual torture these day—"

"Well bloody recall him! Now!"

"Yes, m'lord."

Armino turned his venomous scowl back onto Eyvind. "Put that faithless snake in irons. Make sure he lives long enough for me to bleed the lies out of him."

CHAPTER THREE

Knowledge Applied

"The deal is, we leave the world alone and the world leaves us alone. When it doesn't, we kill. But we need to keep up our end – we don't get involved in wars."

Perrim scowled at Linet's pronouncement. "That 'deal', as you so eloquently put it, is with the Argovani crown, and a tenuous one at that. If Phynagoras truly means to invade with the numbers we think he has, there could be no crown to deal with at all!"

"We're already involved," said Aerrus. "We ambushed his messengers, after all."

"They deserved it for what they did," Linet retorted. "That's part of the peace we keep—"

"We all know the credo, my dear, no need to remind us." Lomuel had said little all morning, and glared out the Lodge's only window, which looked westward. The Lodge had been put under constant guard, and an unlucky few detailed to collect the bodies of their fallen and clean up the mess left on the river road. They'd continued the meeting after letting Linet and Aerrus get a bit of rest, with strict instructions from Perrim that the specifics of what they'd learned spread no further than the four of them.

"Not," Linet continued, "that there's like to be any peace to keep much longer, now that one of the Marcher lords is plotting against the king. Maybe more than one. He's partly brought this on himself."

"I got no love for Osmund," sneered Aerrus. "I don't bend my knee to no one on this earth, same as any of us. But at least he's a devil we know, one we got leverage with."

"I visited Bhasa once," Lom said. "It's poor, flat, hot and crowded. The deserts advance year after year, taking what little farmland there is with it. We're green and empty by comparison, and to be honest I'm shocked there've been no invasions for this long. It seems they lacked only a unifying leader. Phynagoras has woven a cult around his own personality, and if he's decided to move now as these documents imply, with the people who follow him...it won't just be another war. It'll be the end for us. For all of Greater Argovan."

"But what can *we* do?" Linet almost pleaded. "This isn't some pack of bandits we're talking about, or Ordovax's raiders."

"I don't know," answered Perrim, frustrated. "There's too much we don't know."

"Like who sold us out," said Aerrus. "I told no one but Chancellor Essimis. Who else could know we were going to be there, in the forest?"

"Lord Osbren, obviously," said Lom, "and of course his brother, King Osmund himself, if he cared to notice."

"I doubt it's Osbren. His men fought hard as they always do. He hates the Marchmen deep in his guts. And those six were riding north, not east. That implies Valendri or Armino, but it's no proof."

"Then there's this." Lom took a patch of hide from the unruly pile of documents before him. It was rough, dry, scraped and rescraped multiple times to use as a cheap writing surface. "It was found on one of them, while the bodies were being stripped for disposal." He laid it on the table. It showed a crudely drawn sketch still recognizable as the area of the skirmish. A flat plain with hills to the north and south, a forest, and a river farther west. A series of Xs and Os in lines approximated the positions of Osbren's men and Ordovax's warriors. And along one little stretch of forest at the base of a hill....

"That's right where we were!" exclaimed Aerrus. "Those crosses! I knew it."

"Yes, there's no doubt," Lom confirmed. "Those marks were made hastily, as an afterthought it seems." He almost sounded insulted.

"You're cultivating an intelligence network all up and down the valley, yes?"

Linet nodded. "It's still a bit of a new project, but we've got a few people I trust with their ears to the ground. Some of our retired fellows, folks we've managed to put in our debt, a few paid informants. I'm helping B— Uh, I mean, I *was* helping Bolen with it."

"Then you're to go north as well, see what you can find out. Aerrus, I know you have something of a rapport with the king's chancellor."

"Not sure *rapport* is the right word, but I've given Essimis the impression that I'll cut his throat if he doesn't tell me the truth."

"I hope that's only an impression," Perrim said with a raised eyebrow.

"Eh, details."

"Well, I want you to go find him. To Carsolan itself, if necessary. Find out what in the nether hells is going on, and what the king intends to do about Phynagoras."

"That won't be difficult. Osmund couldn't take a piss without Essimis to hold his prick for him."

Normally Perrim might have chided Aerrus for his rude language, but not today. "We're operating in the dark here, and I don't like it. This massacre of our family will *not* stand. Knowledge applied is power – so bring me some!"

That evening a hasty funeral was held. Nineteen bodies wrapped in sailcloth were laid in front of the entrance to the Lodge atop the overgrown stone cairns that held the remains of some of the founders. But the newly slain would soon be laid to final rest in disparate places throughout the Marchwood, buried in secret beneath the roots of strong oaks that would serve for their monuments. About half of the hundred or so rangers were present, the others away and about some vital task or other. Linet and Aerrus stood in silence next to their four closest remaining fellows. All shared in the grief, but the weight of righting this wrong weighed on them in particular.

"How could this happen?" Vander mumbled wistfully. "How?"

"Any of a hundred ways," said young Drissa. "Two can keep a secret, they say, if one is dead."

"Sounds good to me," a grim man named Haskell growled.

"Starting with them cocksuckers at the palace. I say we track 'em down and get some answers."

"That's my job," Aerrus said. "And Lin's. The others'll need you to keep the Lodge secure. Cut any throats that get close will be the order of the day, I imagine."

"Done."

Kanessa choked back a bitter, teary laugh. "Bolen could've solved the mystery."

Linet nodded. "Aye. But I guess we'll have to do now."

Perrim stood before them in the dark, without lamp or taper or torch to reveal their presence from afar. "We give up a lot to live like we do. We come from the unwanted of the world, the orphaned and forgotten. We take no wife, no husband, we beget no children. But while we live, we live free!" Perrim glanced briefly at Aerrus and Linet. "We bend our knee to no one, in a chain unbroken for a hundred years. Tonight we lay nineteen links in that chain to rest, their service concluded."

The names were called out, followed only by the whisper of the wind through the trees. A rare bottle of sweet icewine was passed around to salute them with, happy memories and tears were shared, and when the memorial ended the hunt for those responsible for it began.

★   ★   ★

Eyvind paced the tiny cell as much as was possible. How had this happened? How could his luck turn so suddenly? And how could Lord Armino betray king and country? It was too much even to think on. And now his stupid curiosity was going to get him disemboweled. He hadn't even known Phenidra *had* a torturer.

The corner tower they'd locked him in had two window slits. One looked out across the chilly highlands, and far in the distance a tiny tendril of smoke marked out Edrastead, his home village. It might as well have been across the Western Ocean now for all the good it did him. The other window showed the courtyard and keep of Phenidra, and a small crowd of gawkers gathered at the foot of the tower. Wondering no doubt what their unassuming comrade had done to get imprisoned, what fate he might suffer, and whether they'd get to watch.

Snap! A bolt being thrown back. The entrance to the cell was from above, from the top of the tower and battlements, making escape a near impossibility. Eyvind took a step back as the trap door swung up and open. His stomach turned in fear when a ladder was lowered. Could he make a break for it? No, the chains on his legs kept him from any sudden movement. And there were probably guards every two steps up above. He was two seconds from vomiting into the rancid floor rushes when the most unexpected figure shambled down into the cell.

"Cap'n! Thank the gods, I thought you were the torturer!"

"Aye, so did they," Coladdi replied, jerking his thumb upward, "mostly because I told 'em I'd taken over the job. What is going on, boy? Rumors say all manner of crazy things, not the least of which is high treason!"

"I'm not the one committing treason, Cap'n. I...I can't believe I'm saying this or that you'll believe it, but Lord Armino's the traitor. He's going to help Phynagoras invade Argovan!"

"Wha...you're fracted in the noggin, son. Must be. You took some head injury and now you're confused—"

"It's true!" Eyvind recounted what he'd seen and heard through that damnable hole in the loft floor, word for word and in as much detail as possible. Coladdi listened in silence, then remained that way for a time afterward.

"It...it makes sense. When you think about it, I must admit it makes sense. All the facts fit. King Osmund's gathered absolute power to himself, dissolved most of the nobility that could oppose him. He'd do away with the border lords too in time, replace them with his own bought-and-paid-for creatures. The armies are a shadow of what they once were. There's no better time to invade, and no better inducement to the remaining lords to turn on him."

"Cap'n, I didn't know you followed high politics. So," Eyvind ventured, "you believe me?"

Coladdi frowned sharply. "Of course I believe you! What'd I just get done sayin'? You were just in the wrong place at the wrong time. I'm so sorry, my boy, if I hadn't insisted on my stupid sparring...."

"You couldn't have known, no fault of yours. But is there any way out of this for me? They think I'm a spy, and the real torturer is on his way!"

Coladdi reached into his pouch and pulled out a roughly made leaden key. "Well, for the irons, I nicked this copy years ago, never thought I'd have use for it. After that? Hmm...." He rubbed his chin, glanced at the ladder still leading up and out of the cell.

★   ★   ★

"Get back!" The guards did get back, probably more out of uncertainty than Eyvind's threats. After all, they were peacetime soldiers, more accustomed to spending long hours on sentry duty staring at nothing than the sight before them: Eyvind had emerged onto the battlement from the corner tower with Coladdi in a firm grip, the old man's arm twisted behind him and a knife hard at his throat. Coladdi's eyes opened wide as if in terror, lip trembling above that sharp blade.

"Please, do what he says," Coladdi whined in a manner most uncharacteristic of the hard-bitten soldier. "He's crazy, says he'll cut my throat!"

"I will, too," Eyvind snarled, putting on his best act as though his life depended on it. Both of their lives now, if that copied key was discovered. "Back, I said! Back!"

"What do we do?" one guard asked another.

"The lord said he ain't to come out under any circumstances, you heard 'im."

"But he's got the captain!"

"Well...well...." The guard lowered a halberd and made a pitifully hesitant move toward the pair. "Now come on, you just let him go and go back to your cell—"

"I said get back!" Eyvind pressed the blade harder into Coladdi's neck, and the tiniest trickle of blood streaked over the steel. *Gods forgive me*, he thought, *but I got no choice*. He pushed Coladdi a pace ahead of him, and on the narrow walkway there was no way the halberd could get to him without going through the captain as well. "I'm getting out of here and taking him with me, and that's all there is to it! Now for the last time, get ba—"

"*What in the blueballed fuck is going on there?!*" The cry came from halfway across the courtyard, and it almost made Eyvind jump. Armino strode from the keep, flanked by his crossbowmen and the foreign ambassador. He pointed up at them, gave an order Eyvind couldn't hear, and both mercenaries raised their weapons. These two had absolutely no hesitation, and loosed their quarrels up at Eyvind and Coladdi. As they dove backward, one of the guards, perhaps seeing his chance to gain favor, lunged with the halberd but only managed to get in the way of one of the shots. He fell screaming from the walkway and into the courtyard, where the sound of shattering bone echoed among the shouts.

Eyvind and Coladdi stood apart now, and unimpaled. Which now meant that their farce was over.

"Uh-oh," Eyvind said. "What now?"

"Now, run!"

"Where?"

The crossbowmen reloaded, and more soldiers began to converge on that section of the parapet from both sides. Sweating heavily, Coladdi ran back into the tower and hoisted the ladder out of the cell. He threw one end of it over the fortress wall, secured only by the round edges of the topmost rung and Coladdi's strength. "Go, climb!"

Eyvind shook his head. "It ain't near long enough!"

"It'll have to be. Roll when you hit ground, then run."

"Cap'n, I can't leave you—"

"Go!"

Thwackthwack! Two crossbow bolts hit Coladdi in the back, and his eyes bulged wide for true this time. He exhaled sharply.

"Cap'n! No!"

Coladdi collapsed between two merlons, still grasping the end of the ladder. "Go...not...losin' both of you! Tell the king, tell the whole world...what that monster...."

Tears streaming, Eyvind scrambled down the ladder even as Coladdi's dying grip weakened. He made it halfway down when the ladder fell free, and suddenly Eyvind was dropping straight down through the air.

The ladder snapped when the bottom hit the ground and sent a painful shock through Eyvind's limbs. He kicked against the wall, and the remaining bits of wood swung him outward. He landed hard and forgot to roll. Bruised and bloody, but with nothing broken, he rose to run into the thick growth beyond the wall.

More shouts from above, and arrows loosed from longbows bit into the cold earth around Eyvind's feet, but he kept running. In more military times the land around Phenidra would've been kept clear of even the barest shrubbery to deny cover for any sneak attack. Now peacetime neglect shielded him as he scrambled away from the place with no time to mourn the captain. His last sight of the fortress in the fading daylight was of Armino standing once again on the battlement, peering after his lost prisoner.

As day waned, Eyvind burned to run home to Edrastead. But he dared not, knowing that would be the first place they'd look for him. If he was caught again there would be no waiting for the torturer this time, no last-minute rescue. Instead he prowled the outskirts of the village, near its own nominal garrison – a dozen or so billets mostly set aside as an excuse for old soldiers nearing retirement to serve out their terms in better comfort than Phenidra afforded, and a luxury Coladdi had always scoffed at. *Half of them will be asleep already*, Eyvind thought, the shock of events blessing him with a kind of cool-headed logic, *and the rest busy at cards.*

He sneaked along the low stone wall surrounding the ramshackle barracks, into the stable beside it. While he was in the clumsy process of trying to tack and saddle a horse in the dark, a dry wooden creak screamed at him from behind, and he jumped.

"Who the hells is...Eyvind?"

Caught paralyzed between attacking and scurrying for some dark corner to hide, he stood fixed, squinting to make out the intruder. "Is that...Aunt Tess?"

The middle-aged woman was not really his aunt, but had had such a hand in raising him she might as well have been. Now she looked on him with a mix of delight and concern. "Eyvind, it is you! Finally get some away time, did you? But what you doin' sneaking about the stables—"

"Tess, I can't explain right now, but I'm...in some trouble. Actually, a lot of trouble. I need to get a horse and get out of here, fast. I don't want you near if they catch me."

"Catch you? Who? Eyvind, what's wrong? Have you got too far into gambling debts? Your poor father had the same—"

"No, nothing like that! It's much worse. Please, just help me get away from here!"

To her credit she helped him without asking anything more. Before riding off into the night he tried to tell her to watch out for Armino, for invaders from the east, but he wasn't sure she fully understood, and he knew he didn't have the time to explain.

Bare minutes later he heard cries of alarm behind him – Armino's men already on his heels. He rode hard as far from Edrastead as possible, down the mountainside. *But where to now?*

CHAPTER FOUR

Some Unseemly Criminality

Linet rode north in a foul mood. The rain had started just after midnight, and with no wayside shelter to be found, she'd decided to make some progress rather than try to sleep in the mud. Wind blew under her cowl, matting wet hair to her cheeks. And since she didn't trust the billowing clumsiness of cloaks when unexpected situations arose, mud from her horse's hooves spattered her legs.

Useless, anyway, she thought with a sour frown. None of her contacts in Nostrada or Trenca had heard anything of consequence. Even if they did uncover proof of faithless Marcher lords, what could be done about it? Their small band of free rangers, made even smaller now, had little hope of stopping or even slowing the kind of invasion Perrim feared.

Though isolated in the wilderness, Linet already felt the outside world moving past them, past the post-feudal chaos that'd birthed the Heron Kings, molded desperate insurgents into the lethal fighting force they'd become. A force best suited, perhaps, to the last century. Many of their older members retired into the world, joining the knee-bent society at last yet remaining eyes and ears of the Lodge, and the news from them grew ever stranger. New ideas, new inventions, governments, new ways of living and of dying – who could keep up? Linet hoped the contacts she now rode toward had better news, but she rather doubted it.

So lost in these dour thoughts was she that Linet almost didn't notice the commotion that bore down on her until she was nearly run over. She'd ridden through Trenca village the day before, passing from the forestlands of the Kingmarch territory and into fair green Midmarch farming counties halfway to Vin Gannoni, when hard gallops on the road drew her attention. Through the fog and early dawn gloom an apparition of horse and rider took form, the latter slumped over the mount's lathered mane and holding on for dear life. This was no fast courier keen to win a bonus.

"Look out!" Linet shouted, wrenching her own horse out of the way. Horses naturally shy away from each other, but this one was exhausted and half blinded by mist and mud. The animals collided side-on and Linet's more sensible mount let itself be nudged off the cleared roadway, but the clash sent the other rider – a youngish man sporting a nasty bolt protruding from a blooded thigh wound – falling into Linet's saddle, and she fought to hold on. "Gods, what—?"

"Phy...Arm...Cap'n..." he muttered, delirious. "Save...."

"What? What are you—?"

"Phy...nagoras...."

Linet took in a sharp breath. "What did you say?"

"After...me...Lord Armino...Cap'n, no! Help...." He collapsed into near unconsciousness as another set of hooves thumped from further down the road. No, two sets. She'd never believed in the supernatural foresight that Marchmen and ancient Argovani legends spoke of, but in that moment something told her that this was a situation that she absolutely *should* get involved in. "Come on," Linet said with a grunt as she hoisted the wounded man fully onto her horse. He moaned in pain as she turned about and set them to full gallop back southward.

Two large men on war chargers emerged from the fog in hot pursuit. They wore no armor except open-faced bascinet helms, and bore heavy crossbows slung from their saddles. Leaving the wounded man's mount forgotten, they tore after Linet, slowing only enough for one to raise his weapon and shoot. It went wide, ripping a hole in Linet's clothes before embedding itself in a tree beyond. Linet urged the animal on harder and harder, but it was no match for chargers bred for speed.

Then, out of the corner of her eye she spotted a fork in the road. Barely more than a deer path, easily missed. At the last possible moment she wrenched the animal toward it, and the horse neighed in protest. The chargers tore past at full speed, and in the precious seconds before they could turn around Linet drew rein and brought the horse to a stop. In one fluid motion she unslung her bow from her shoulder, drew a gray goose-feathered bodkin-tip arrow and had it nocked and ready. The light weapon seemed a feeble thing in comparison to the powerful crossbows, a relic of a bygone era. But it did the job when the first rider came into view and she sent him tumbling to the ground, writhing in agony at the shaft in his side.

The second came just after, and didn't take the time to unhook his crossbow but charged toward Linet with a blackened steel mace. He swung it at her head, and she only had time to raise her left arm. A sickening crack and explosion of pain announced the result. The bow fell from her grasp.

He swung again, but as the horses drew back from each other the blow went wide. Linet grabbed feebly at the mace with her right hand, and her brute strength wasn't even a fraction of his. Yet the short delay held the two fast long enough for her wounded passenger, not completely insensate after all, to reach for the knife at Linet's waist. With his last drop of strength he drove the blade into the rider's midsection. The crossbowman howled and fell from the saddle, leaving a comet of blood streaming behind.

Rather than attempt capture or interrogation of either of the two attackers, Linet nudged her horse back toward the fork in the road. The agony of keeping both herself and her new charge upright with a broken arm drew a fountain of tears from her eyes and filthy curses from her mouth that would impress even Aerrus.

They rode south as quickly as Linet could manage, which wasn't very quickly at all. It was a sad, shambling sight, and any passersby might've felt as much sympathy for the poor horse as for the two damaged wretches it bore. Eyvind – she'd gotten his name at least through the pained mumblings – rode somewhat side-saddle, cradled in the crook of Linet's shoulder like a swaddled newborn as she held the rein looped around one good arm. Though the other was broken, her thighs hurt almost as much from the strain. Every once in a while a drop of blood trickled along the length of the bolt still lodged in Eyvind and fell to the ground, making Linet wince each time at the notion of leaving a trail. Her bow had somehow fallen around Eyvind's neck and now swung back and forth limply as they went.

When the sun was at its zenith and the heat added sweaty slickness to their list of woes, Eyvind came once more to consciousness. "Ph... physic. Need...."

"I know," said Linet, "but we're far from any that I know of. Should've brought a kit with me. Stupid!" Though no simple kit would mend the hurts they'd taken, and certainly not the simple medicinal phials she carried at her belt for minor hurts.

"Where...are we?"

"About half a day north of Trenca, I think. But I daren't stop in such an open place if there are any more of your friends around."

"There's a...priory. Lay brothers. Hid in the forest. Path...eight miles north of Tr...." He faded back into senselessness.

A priory of the Polytheon, Linet thought, *hidden away in the sticks? It's perfect.* They would have a physic, too. But would they help them?

Linet rode on, eyes stinging with sweat but straining to spot the path Eyvind mentioned. She almost missed it, and breathed a word of thanks to the gods of that priory when a side path saved them for the second time that day.

The priory was less than half a mile along the path that petered out into almost nothing at some points. And though the undergrowth was sparse, it was the height of summer and greenery obscured the place until they were almost on top of it. A low stone fence enclosed a good whitewashed house and a few outbuildings and gardens.

A robed brother tending one of those gardens dropped his spade at the sight of them hobbling up to the gate. "Wha...?"

"Help," Linet breathed, searching her memory for the words to recite when asking charity from the religious order. "Please. By...

by the Sundered God of Man and the Unnumbered Gods of Holy Artamera, we beg aid and comfort!" And in the manner that one's bladder tends to give way just upon reaching the privy, exhaustion overcame Linet and she slumped from the saddle, taking Eyvind with her.

The gardening brother managed to reach them before they could hit the ground and likely snap two necks at once. But as he broke their fall, both Linet and Eyvind cried out in pain at the irritation of their injuries. The racket brought more brothers, who carried them into the priory's sick house as gently as such rustics could manage. Linet surrendered to the gaggle of stern voices and shouts around her, and at last she perceived a flat surface beneath her, and a frowning visage above.

"Now," spoke the craggy, walking frown, "would you kindly explain yourselves?"

Another voice, high and piping, came from somewhere. "Is...is that a woman? In man's clothes? Is that allowed?" The words carried the excitement of scandal and possibility. *Lay brothers, indeed*, Linet thought through the pain.

"Never mind that. Charity may be one of the gods' commands, but we don't take kindly to mixing with bandits, highwaymen, or whatever you are. These wounds of yours were surely got in the course of some unseemly criminality! You—"

"We're...not bandits," Linet said, shocked at the weakness in her own voice. "Please...in my purse." She motioned to her belt pouch, sweat sticking the coarse bedlinens to her skin. The walking frown – the prior, most like – nodded once, and a pair of hands reached from behind her and pawed through the leather container. "There," Linet said, "the vellum."

The hands passed the rolled document with red wax seal to the prior, who promptly broke it and read. "Hmm. I see, yes. Agents of Lord Osbren, are you? Well, that's different." It was a forgery of course, but a good one. A letter of safe conduct from King Osmund's brother had a tendency to open doors, and Linet always carried a reasonable facsimile. "Wait, is this to do with some sort of political affair? Because we may not involve ourselves—"

"No, nothing...like that. Please...." What did one more lie matter, after all?

"We'll take care of you, then. But I hope this charity will cause Lord Osbren to look favorably on our humble house in the future. Prior Eribert, at your service." The prior nodded again to someone else. "Send for the chirurgeon! That's a foul bolt wound, certain. And as for you, my dear...."

Linet screamed once more when they set her broken bone, but the pain quickly faded when they gave her a few drops of opiphine, more precious than gold. Praying her mission partly accomplished as she sank into blessed oblivion, Linet vowed never again to doubt getting involved.

★   ★   ★

Eyvind awoke to fresh pains, and found the crossbow bolt replaced with a bandage and poultice. "Ech..." he moaned, partly from the pain and partly in disgust at the spongy green stuff poking out from beneath his bandages. "What...?"

"Moss," the strange woman who'd rescued him answered from the adjacent cot. "Supposed to keep it from turning foul." He looked over to see her whole arm done up in bandages, her face pale and tired.

"Oh. What...what's your name again?"

"Linet."

"Well, Linet, thanks for, you know, saving my life and all. Sorry about your arm."

"Wasn't entirely charity. You spoke of Phynagoras. And since you're awake enough to ask questions, you can answer them too. So, out with it. Everything, start to finish." They lay in the priory sick house, man and woman together and alone. Scandalous, but Prior Eribert had acceded to Linet's demand for secrecy. Her gaze drilled into Eyvind and it seemed he now faced a huntress-spirit out of ancient myth, and he did not hold back, however ridiculous it seemed.

"…and that's when I ran into you. Literally." He lay flat, staring up into the rafters as he finished. "I know, it sounds insane. I don't expect you to believe me."

A few beats of silence, then, "No. I believe you. It all makes sense now." Her words echoed Coladdi's enough to bring renewed exasperation.

"*What* makes sense? Who are you? What's your part in all this, and why do the brothers treat us like royalty?"

"I—" Linet began, then stopped. "It's a long story."

"We seem to have plenty of time for the telling," he replied, pointing to her heavy cast.

"I'll tell you, but not here. We have to get back."

"W…we? Back where? We're in no shape to travel—"

"South. My people need this information, and I'll risk both our lives to deliver it. That mercenary you stabbed was done for, the other I'm not sure about. If he lived he might still be looking for you. For us, now."

"Great."

At Linet's insistence they rested only another day at the priory, and then made to depart. Linet exchanged her rounsey for two packhorses with ill-fitting tack. It'd be a slow journey but less aggravating to their wounds. Eyvind winced when he climbed clumsily into the saddle while a brother helped Linet mount up, red-faced at having to hold on to her to do so. Eyvind carried her bow over his shoulder. Though the bow was now useless to her, Linet refused to abandon or even unstring it. The prior bid them farewell and repeated his desire for favor from Lord Osbren.

"Osbren?" Eyvind held his bandage close to keep it from jostling, though the horse's smooth gait didn't upset it much. "Somehow I don't think you serve—"

"What you think is painfully uninteresting to me. Just ride."

They rode, and it was indeed still slow-going, though not so bad as before. Eyvind kept a few paces behind Linet, watching for a chance to slip away if he had to. She must've read his intention, for at one point she looked back and said, "Get up here, where I can keep an eye on you."

He grudgingly nudged the packhorse forward. "Look, I don't know who you are, but I don't have any involvement with this! I'm just a soldier. Now I've told you what I know, why not let me go?"

"Go? Where? Even if you tried to run you wouldn't get far."

"And if you tried to catch me *you* wouldn't get far," he sneered.

"Yes, we're two broken fools! Together we just might add up to a whole one, so we might as well."

Eyvind didn't argue, but neither did he stop watching for his chance.

★   ★   ★

"Argh, get off—"

"Shut up, woman!"

Eyvind was jolted awake by shouts and the neighs of frightened horses. He'd slept like the dead every night of their journey south, to where he still didn't know. Linet had said little since they'd left the priory, and he'd considered giving her the slip in the night more than once, only to dismiss the idea each time.

They'd camped a bit off the road, keeping away from Trenca, Nostrada or other places where they might draw attention, their fire burning low. Now, Eyvind looked a few paces past the last embers to see a snarling man with a dagger hard at Linet's neck and a grip on her injured arm. *The mercenary!* A crude bandage covered his arrow wound. Next to them one of the pack horses stamped nervously. He must've sneaked up on Linet while she was leading it to water.

"Well, ain't this a familiar situation?" he snarled, seeing that Eyvind was awake. "'Cept you're on the other end of it now. Both you'll be comin' wi' me. Merry chase you led me on. I only need bodies, but

I'm guessin' the lord'll be real interested in putting *you* to question."
Linet's face twisted up in agony when he squeezed her broken bone.

"Stop it!" Eyvind held out his hands. "All right, all right.
We'll come."

"There's a good little shitestain. Now you get up, real slow, and I
mean honey in winter slow."

"Okay, just don't hurt her. Just...." The wound in this thigh
gave him no choice but to move slowly, and as he leaned forward
to prop himself up on one hand his gaze shifted downward. In a
flash of one moment he noticed several things at once: the horse's
rein was dangling free, the bridle clearly having been made for
another, bigger animal. The loop at the end of the rein was lying
on the ground, probably knocked out of Linet's grasp. And the
mercenary was standing right inside it. Eyvind committed to his
course of action without much conscious thought, took hold of
the last smoldering branch from the fire and flung it hard at the
packhorse's rump. The animal bolted, the rein jerked, and the
mercenary fell to the ground with a shout.

Even as he fell Linet was in action, twisting the knife away from
her throat and back towards the mercenary. Eyvind hobbled over to
them as fast as he was able and fell atop the man, ripping his bascinet
off and pummeling him with it. The mercenary tried to spit curses at
them through broken teeth, but all that came out was gurgling blood
as the knife rose and fell in Linet's wild grasp. Seconds later he was
nothing but a quivering mass of meat.

Exhausted and out of breath, Eyvind looked up at Linet. She was
dripping red. "Are you...?"

She nodded. "You?"

"I...." After years as a soldier, it was only after deserting that his
first kills came. He'd been barely conscious for the first, so both hit
him at that moment. He tried to stand up, but upon looking down on
their handiwork, he instead doubled over and vomited onto it.

When the pounding in his ears ceased and the killing fever left him,
they retrieved the horse and washed the blood off themselves as well

as possible, which wasn't very well at all. As the little stream they'd camped by carried it away, Eyvind knelt over it and said weakly, "Some warrior I made."

Linet shook her head. "Soldiers aren't warriors. Complete opposites, really. You're neither one now, I guess, so no need to act it. You handled it better than, well...."

"What?"

"Nothing."

Eyvind cupped a mouthful of water, swished and spat to rinse out the taste of puke. "Mercs don't risk their lives like that for regular pay. Armino must've promised them...I don't know what. Just to get me back."

Linet nodded. "And threats if they should fail, I don't doubt. Don't think it truly hit me until just now. This is real. This is happening. And we're the only ones who know anything about it."

"But what can we do?"

"Right now, just keep following me."

They made an early start and clumsily mounted up again. But as they were about to ride back to the road and continue south, Eyvind said, "Wait."

"What is it?"

"I've followed you this whole time without a word of explanation. Stuck with you out of fear of that merc. Now he's crow feed, so if you want me to go another step, it's time to do some talking." He feigned stern confidence when in truth he could barely sit in his saddle, but there were limits even to his cowardice.

Linet's mouth twisted in indignation. "Who are you to make demands? I—" She sighed. "You're right. I guess I owe you some little measure of truth now." She nudged her horse slowly toward the road and Eyvind followed, but skittishly, without commitment. "Listen... how do I begin? Not everyone in the world fits neatly into the feudal order, whatever the laws say."

Eyvind nodded. "No secret there. The old wars mostly wiped out that nonsense. With most of the lords sacked, peasants pay their taxes to bureaucrats sent by the king. There're private army levies, merchant guilds, free cities, even powerful whoremistresses sproutin' up all over these days. What Coladdi called a kind of middling class, gods rest him."

"I'm not talking about the merchants. Look the other way." Confused, Eyvind turned his gaze away from Linet, making her laugh in spite of the ache it caused. "No, I mean socially. Ever since the civil wars and before, there've been folk with even less to lose than the peasant farmers. Whenever someone gets more, someone else always seems to get less. There are always cast-offs. Children, even. Orphaned, abandoned."

"Aye, that's always so, sad as it is," said Eyvind, still confused. "So?"

"So imagine if a precious few of them decided, long ago, to form a kind of guild of their own to survive. No, I don't mean thieves or assassins, though those skills have their uses."

Eyvind frowned. "Such a 'guild' as you call it could put certain folks with a lot to lose at a bit of unease."

"So it should. Best then to keep its existence a close secret."

She looked hard at him and Eyvind stared back, the implication slowly dawning on him. What *had* he fallen in to? "You don't mean… you?"

"Those riders you told me about, the ones who were ambushed? We spotted them meeting with Marchmen. A chieftain, no less." Eyvind's eyes went wide. "We're mostly self-sufficient, but nick what little else we need from the villages. In return we protect them from that sort. An unspoken agreement but a real one."

"Gods, all the stories, the rumors…demons and spirits indeed! And you were born into this…guild? Band, whatever?"

Linet shook her head. "Don't know where I was born or to whom. We renew our numbers as I said, from the unwanted. There are always those. We have no children of our own unless we retire into the open world. Who could bear to send their own flesh and blood on dangerous tasks like these?" She held up her cast as demonstration.

"Sounds like a hard life."

Linet raised an eyebrow. "Hard? My bones were whole until I met you."

"Good point. Does anyone outside know?"

Linet shrugged. "The king knows. His chancellor, a few others. There's another unspoken alliance. Marchman raids, Bhasan petty kings crossing the mountains to make a nuisance, bandit gangs – they never get very far but no one ever bothers to ask why. Amateurs, all. No one's ever found us out."

Until now, Eyvind thought, shaking his head in disbelief. "I never imagined."

"My mentor Perrim says, 'If the world isn't quite as you thought it was you'd better change your thinking, because you can't change the world.'"

"Humph, it seems to be changing anyway. So what's your involvement with Armino? Phynagoras?"

Linet looked away from him, but not in time to hide a pained expression. "We were betrayed. I won't say more than that now, but it's got something to do with this. I have to get what you've learned back home."

"What exactly are you going to do with it?"

"That's up to others than me."

Eyvind cast Linet a nervous glance. "And what are you going to do with *me*?"

"Same answer."

★   ★   ★

Eyvind fidgeted more and more as they approached the Marchwood. At last they came to a spot he'd certainly never seen before, yet knew well enough from the tale. "This is where it happened, isn't it?"

Linet squinted at him with suspicion. "How did you know that?"

He pointed downward. "The ground. It's all torn up, even with weeks of weather. Bucking horses made those marks. And these other...drag marks? I won't ask about those."

"Humph. We'll have to do a better job of covering our tracks. We've gotten sloppy if even a – um...."

"If even a dumb slogger can see it? Thanks."

"Come on, it's not far."

She led them another half mile or so, then abruptly turned the horse leftward off the road and up a barely visible track. The animal neighed in protest at first, but soon found a comfortable gait while Eyvind's mount shambled behind, trying to keep pace.

"Wait, where are we going?"

"Home! Let me do the talking. We don't normally get visitors. Not the willing kind, anyway."

"Whoever said I was willing?"

She looked hard at him. "I mean it. We...how do I say it? We've been compromised. Tempers are bound to be a bit raw, so don't do anything stupid."

"Too late for that."

Up and up, and when it seemed Eyvind's small horse would just quit, Linet drew rein not far from a rocky outcropping where trickling water echoed in the distance.

"That should be far enough. Now," she said, suddenly dead serious, "don't move. At all." She looked away. "You can come out, eyes green, fullwise athwart."

Eyvind was about to ask what in the nether hells she was babbling about when, to his consternation, she started making strange motions with her hand, as if putting an enchantment on the trees.

Nothing happened.

Looking irritated, she repeated the gestures facing different directions, making slight adjustments to the routine each time, awkward with her bound arm. Finally, something dropped from a tree to Eyvind's right and somewhat behind. He yelped in surprise and reached for Linet's knife as the horse neighed and shimmied. "No, stop!" Linet yelled. "I said don't move." He froze, but dared a glance toward the direction of the movement. It was a wild-eyed and grim-faced man with a shaved head and goatee. His brown and rust colors blended perfectly into the surroundings. Then, as if sprouting from the very ground like wood sprites, five other figures materialized in spots he could've sworn were empty, all with bows drawn and ready. Linet turned to the grim fellow and continued her weird signs. The goateed man, who looked furious about something, managed to infuse his anger into the movements he made in response.

A silent hand-language! Eyvind realized. The army had simple signals for communicating over distances, but they were rudimentary by comparison. Here appeared to be a fully developed, unspoken tongue. And by the look of their jerky movements and the expressions, it was quite a heated argument. Between the signs, Eyvind noticed fingers pointed in his direction more than once. Suddenly annoyed at continually having his fate dictated by strangers, he cleared his throat loudly. "Excuse me." They ignored him as though they'd not heard. "Excuse me!" he yelled, as he would trying to be heard across a crowded room. They broke off their fighting and looked at him, frowning.

"Where I come from it's considered quite impolite to talk about someone behind their back. I think this qualifies." Goatee stared at him askance.

"Like I just said," Linet huffed in frustration, "he's not exactly a typical outsider. Now take us to Perrim. We have some knowledge to apply."

CHAPTER FIVE

Black Crow Flies

"*Have you lost your mind?*"

Perrim had just finished setting the orders for the day's patrol, and quickly dismissed everyone else from the meeting room upon hearing of Linet's return. Linet had anticipated her wrath, but that didn't make weathering it much easier. After all, no outsider had even found the entrance to the Lodge, much less been brought inside. She had a terrible feeling she'd put Eyvind's life in danger, but there was no turning back now.

"I know," she said, trying to remain the calm one, "I know it's dangerous, but—"

"Dangerous? It's lunacy! You've endangered the security of our entire family! Where is this pet of yours now?"

"Haskell has him locked in a cellar."

"Well there's some sense at least."

At that moment Lomuel burst into the room, still clad in a robe after being roused from a nap that the aging fellow needed more and more of these days. But he was fully awake now. "Is it true? They told me—"

"It's true," Perrim confirmed, collapsing onto one of the benches along the table.

"My girl, how could you?"

"How? How could I not? He was an eyewitness to the whole thing. Armino's going over to Phynagoras, letting him just walk in and take over before anyone can do a thing about it! He risked his life to spread the word—"

"He ran away," Perrim snorted. "As you tell it, he's no hero. Soldiers, they're all the same!"

"But we can use this one. He knows that country, knows Armino. If we take him before the king it might spur the old goat to action. If we move fast we could even take Phenidra and stop Phynagoras before he arrives!"

Lomuel rolled his eyes. "Listen to yourself. *Take Phenidra?* You a general now, are you? This is *not* what we meant by getting involved."

"Well, that's just too bad. Endangered the security? They plan to bring hordes of people over those mountains, too many to keep any of us secret for long. One slogger will be the least of our worries. Besides...we owe him. I owe him."

Lom's mouth hung open as though Linet had just declared her intention to take holy orders. "You...*owe* him?"

"He saved my life, as I saved his. And he led us to the priory." She nodded toward her sling. "I would never have found it alone. We're joined at the hip now, and he may be a less-than-perfect ally but we're going to need every one we can scrape together."

Perrim eyed Linet suspiciously, seeming only now to notice the blood on her clothes. "Linet, have you become smitten with this man?"

Linet's face went red even in the poor lamplight. "What? No!"

"Oh, I've seen it before. A little shared danger, long nights on the road together, you certainly wouldn't be the first—"

"How dare you!"

"It'd be no business of ours," said Lom, "but if your feelings are clouding your judgment...."

"My feelings inform my judgment." Linet sat down next to the older woman, the lines in her face perceptibly sharper than they'd been before setting out on this quest. She took Perrim's hand in hers, squeezed gently. "You taught me," she said, "to speak only the deepest truth I can sense whilst in your presence. And I'm telling you, this is the right thing to do."

"It wasn't your call to make," Lom said, but weakly. "There are *rules*."

"There are more important rules. The world's changing, you feel it in your bones same as we all do. It's time we changed too. I was wrong before. Hiding in this cave for another century isn't an option. A tide's coming, and we can ride it or be smashed by it."

"Great gods," Perrim said with a wry grin, "I never imagined it until now. You're after my job, aren't you?" Linet opened her mouth to protest, but Perrim waved dismissively. "Never mind, it doesn't matter. I—oh..." She put a hand to her temple and slouched, suddenly weary.

"What is it?"

"Nothing. Nothing, I'm just tired. Get him out of here. Take your damned redoubtable soldier that you're most definitely *not* infatuated with and kill him or do what you like with him, but he's not to see the inside of this place again. We'll speak of it no more; I've more important tasks for you. But have Myrtho take a look at that broken wing first. Mayhap he can improve on those priory hayseeds."

Linet stood, legs weak with the knowledge that she'd actually nearly won an argument with Perrim. "Where's Aerrus?"

"Just left for Carsolan, a few days ago."

"Just left? Why the delay?"

"Well, there's some good news anyway," Lom replied. "Young Thanis has earned his full ranging privileges. As his mentor, Aerrus wanted to be present for the event."

"That's good to hear." Linet smiled and shook her head. "I know we need every blade and bow we can raise right now, but fourteen seems too young for such responsibility. Seems more so the older I get."

"Imagine then how we ancients feel," Perrim said as she slowly rose to seek out her sleeping cell. "You were no older, and look at what you've wrought for us today."

Linet left the room in little better mood than when she'd entered, and by the time she got to the infirmary wished her arm were healed if for no other reason than to be able to hit something. The space was the cleanest in the Lodge, one of only two sources of hot water drawn from the spring. Presently there was a middle-aged or slightly past man bent over a steaming basin, scrubbing at metallic instruments while droplets of condensation hung from his beard. Oil lamps flickered as a cool breeze wafted upward through ventilation ducts set into the stone. "Myrtho," Linet said quietly.

He started, then turned around. "Lin! How many times do I have to tell you, don't sneak up on me when I'm cleaning scalpels!" He pushed a pair of spectacles – likely the only ones for a hundred miles in any direction – back up his long nose.

"Sorry."

"What happened to you?"

She proffered her slung arm. "Battle damage. Bastard merc with a mace. Paid it back though. Anything you can do?"

He looked over the work a moment, then nodded. "Not bad, but I think a better cast would be advisable. Temple work?"

"Priory."

"Uh-huh. Sit down. What was all that shouting just now? Locking horns with Perrim again?"

Linet sighed while Myrtho unwrapped her bandages. She looked away when ugly blue and yellow flesh was exposed. "I don't know if it'll blow over this time. I might've done something really stupid."

"As long as you learned from it."

"That's the thing," Linet said nervously, "I'm not sure if I did, or if it really was stupid or if it was necessary or what!"

"Well I hope you learned one thing at least – don't try to block maces with your arm. Now hold still."

★   ★   ★

Well, here I am, locked up in the dark again. They'd tossed a sack over Eyvind's head, bound his hands, and prodded him down into some subterranean hell of jagged rocks and low ceilings. It would've been slow-going even without the limp of his wound. Round and round it seemed until the silent death march ended with him being tossed forward into some cool space with hay underfoot. The bag was wrenched away and the goateed man snarled at him once more in the rushlit gloom, grabbing a fistful of his bloodstained shirt.

"Make a move, make a sound, and I personally cut out your eyes. Then your tongue, then your balls, assuming you got any. And *then* I start getting mean. Understand, pig?"

Eyvind stared at the brute a moment, took in the seething sincerity of his words, and at the utter absurdity of it all suddenly broke into paroxysms of laughter. "Is…is that so? Well listen, brother, last couple weeks I've had, that'd just about be a bloody holiday."

"What in the nether hells…?"

"Oh, I…I'm sure you mean to do all those horrible things, really, but…at the moment…I just…can't bring myself to actually…*give a shite.*" He broke down uncontrollably.

The goateed man just shook his head in confusion, turned and slammed the door to the cell shut.

In the hour – or had it been hours? No way to tell time in this stygian underworld – Eyvind had surmised that he was in some kind of storage cellar, for the dry air had a salty tang to it. *Not a proper prison cell then.* Folk as these probably didn't take prisoners.

He'd been leaning up against a barrel of something to try to get some sleep, but his hands remained bound and it was an awkward position. So it was only a minor shock when the clang of a door latch interrupted his dozing. He was expecting Goatee armed with instruments to make good on his threats, but the tiny lamp revealed Linet's concerned face instead.

"Stay quiet," she said without preamble. "I've…been ordered to get rid of you."

"Ah. And here I was all relieved you weren't that other unpleasant fellow—"

"But I wasn't ordered *how*. Get up." She cut his bonds, and on closer inspection the lamplight showed her arm sling from the priory now replaced with a new, more elaborate and tightly bound contraption that might've come from the finest University doctor. "What—"

"No questions now. It's the middle of the night. We can be out of here without too much fuss." She handed him a full rucksack with her bow strapped to the outside and led him up, around, down, around again in a seeming maze, the poor light little better than the total blindness through which he'd been interred here in the first place.

Yet it was astounding. In addition to the carved tunnels winding every which way, there were what seemed like snakes made of wood or clay or tanned hide clinging to the ceiling and running through every hall and chamber. "What are those?" he asked in a nervous whisper.

"Ventilation," Linet said, "and water lines. Now hush."

They rounded a corner and passed a hewn doorway hung only with a stretch of fabric. A cool breeze wafted out of it, and they were a few paces beyond it when Linet stopped short with a sharp breath. "Oh!"

"What?"

"I forgot something. It's important. Wait here." She turned back to the doorway and brushed the fabric aside. Past it he could barely make out what looked to be shelves of scrolls, stacks of paper and vellum, desks. The lamp outlined Linet rifling through these, apparently looking for something. She stopped suddenly as she glanced at a small writing desk at one end of the room. Something lay directly in the middle. Documents, and other objects too dim to make out, opened wide as though someone had just been reading—

Linet stood up straight, sighed. "Hello, Lom."

To Eyvind's confusion, she seemed to speak to an empty room. Then, out of the darkness of a far corner, a bulky shape emerged. A labored breath, shuffling feet. The elderly visage melted into view, an incarnation of the ghost of fatigue. "Your skills remain sharp as ever. That at least is good to know."

These folks would make excellent spies, Eyvind thought. *Or burglars.*

"Not really," said Linet. "You still got the drop on me."

"Humph." He turned sharply toward Eyvind, his head peeking through the folds of cloth. "Boy, do you have any idea how lucky you are to be alive right now?"

"I'm starting to get some, yes. Been that kind of day, actually."

"So I've heard. Going on a little trip, are you? Off again already? Perhaps following Aerrus to Carsolan?"

"Come on, Lom, it's just us here now. You know it's the right choice."

"I know nothing of the sort. If, as you so eloquently put it, this wave is coming, we'd better prepare for it. You're needed here." He put a brave face on it, but even Eyvind, who knew these people not at all, could hear there was no fire in the man's assertion. This was just honey to coat a pill already destined to be swallowed.

Linet looked the man straight in the eye. "I'm needed, *we're* needed, out there. And I'm going."

Lom sighed heavily, dramatically, perhaps feeling his role as only a bit player in the farce. "Then, I suppose you'd better take all the proof you can." He waved toward the documents and objects on the desk.

Linet smiled, warmly for once, which was a new thing to Eyvind's eyes. "I will. Thank you, Lom." She gathered up the materials and stowed them in a side pocket of the rucksack Eyvind carried and hugged the old man.

"And take along extra blades! You—"

"I will!"

"And *you*," Lom added, giving Eyvind a hard glance, "look well after her, if you know what's good for you."

Eyvind nodded. "I will."

★   ★   ★

Linet led Eyvind up, up into the entrance hall. The great hearth burned two small logs to cast dancing shadows across the far walls. "A castle below the ground," he mused. "Complete with a great hall."

"It is, exactly that," Linet answered. "Those chairs've been there since long before I was born, and most of the rest of it, too."

Hiking the rucksack higher on his shoulder, Eyvind limped after Linet to the double doors that led to the outside, then stopped for a moment to admire the exquisite carvings that adorned them. Another luxurious incongruence. *Who are these people?* he thought again.

"Qassorian oak," Linet said, "carved by one of the original founders. They all had regular lives before coming here, regular professions. Left it all behind, determined never again to be victims of highborn wars."

"Striking story. Do you believe it?"

"It's as true as it needs to be. Let's go." She pulled one of the double doors open, one-handed and slow.

"To what task that needs doing now? That old fellow mentioned Carsolan. I don't think I can ride that far."

Linet grinned as they made their way through the cave-like exit. "Don't worry, you won't have to. We have our resources."

★   ★   ★

Eyvind was in heaven. Or as close to it as he could fathom after the last weeks of pain, danger and exhaustion. They'd ridden only a short distance before encountering a southbound convoy of wagons, and paid an elderly couple a silver penny to ride in the back with their turnips and sacks of millet. They'd left their horses hitched at a wayside just outside Firleaf village, and Linet had assured him they'd be collected by others later. There was something about the exchange with the wagoners that struck Eyvind as odd. Surely the sight of two wounded folks, one a woman in man's clothing, traveling together and obviously not married should've made the villagers far too suspicious to risk taking them on. But there'd been no questions asked, only a nod, a penny between hands and then the bliss of lying flat on his back as the miles fell away beneath them. Nor, once they were so embarked, did any of the villagers try to make conversation. *They know*, he thought. *They know enough at least not to seek to know more. An unspoken agreement, but a real one.*

When he opened his mouth to ask Linet about it, she must've somehow sensed his consternation, for she just shook her head as she lay next to him, eyes closed. "Just relax and enjoy the ride."

Like a good soldier, Eyvind knew to snatch rest whenever and wherever possible, and he was soon fast asleep. When he awoke again a sliver of moon arced overhead and the wagon had stopped. He tried to sit up, but stiffness and ache had fairly paralyzed him. "Argh!" he moaned, craning his neck as best he could to look beyond the sacks around him.

"You're awake," said Linet from somewhere before appearing overhead. "Come have some supper. It's just pottage, but you must be hungry."

"Thanks a lot," he said, gripping his suddenly grumbling belly. "Didn't know just how hungry until you said that. Help me up, will you? Slow!" They shimmied out of the wagon and toward a blissfully large fire where a group of travelers gathered and gossiped and a pot bubbled. They hadn't quite reached Plisten, but it was safe country so a roadside camp was to be the caravan's stopping point. 'Course, they're not fleeing bloody mercenaries and betrayer lords, he thought, which probably makes for a more pleasant voyage.

After he managed to sit down again, Linet put a steaming bowl in his hands. "Here, I paid enough to feed us the rest of the way."

"Do I dare wonder where you get your funds?" Eyvind asked before shoveling a spoonful of the tasteless but hearty stew in his mouth.

"No." She turned to the man distributing the pottage, one of the wagoners they'd hitched themselves to. "What news on the road, good father?"

The man shook his head. "No news at all. Which is news all itself! No word from the palace, from the gov'mint bureaucrats, from the councilors. Like pullin' teeth to get any word about affairs from anyone outta Carsolan, or even finding any! Only time that lot keep their mouths shut's when they got something to keep quiet about. Mark my words, missy, there's strange things afoot at King Ozzie's court."

With such little news to speak of, someone in the caravan produced a reed flute, someone else an old, out-of-tune long-necked theorbo. They broke into a rustic song that Eyvind had never heard before but

Linet seemed to have, rocking her head gently back and forth to the odd cadence.

Somewhere up there beyond all love or care
Black Crow tears the whole world's heart out
Never comes down
Just sends slaves 'round
Names you know though not so fair

Crow sent the plague for my ma, for my da
Tears on the earth grew twisted branches
High up to the sky
Where the old Crow flies
Laughed out loud with his cruelest caw

Crow sent the lord, to the wars I'm bound
Glory for the crown with my father's helmet
Childhood's dead
The Crow's fed
Haunted eyes on the coldest ground

All your orders
Obeyed I cry yet
In the blink of an eye
Twenty years gone by

All the blood I
Paid yet I cry
In the blink of an eye
Twenty years gone by

Crow sent the bank down to take my home
Taxes owed, got to fill his coffer
Cold under the sky

How my hungry babies cry
Crow sent one to the catacomb

Crow sent the king, it's another damn war
Told him no, I done my service
Not you this time
Eyes on a fresher crime
Crow stole away my only boy

Crow sent the plague back, now I'll go
Take my bones and the dust they'll make
Next the Crow's tongue
Tastes some new young
One of innocence white as snow

All your orders
Obeyed I cry yet
In the blink of an eye
Twenty years gone by

And the Black Crow flies

Some distant day at the end of all days
Black Crow will devour the whole world
When he's all that's left
He'll eat his own flesh
Crow will only mourn his own fate

All the blood I
Paid yet I cry
In the blink of an eye
The Black Crow flies

All the blood I

Paid yet I cry
In the blink of an eye
No Black Crow flies

Black Crow fly.

Eyvind didn't interrupt the song, but when they both retired back to their wagon to sleep, remarked, "There's a charming tune. You'd think they were living through the bad old days."

"I know," said Linet as she curled up under a pile of sweet new hay. "I asked Perrim about it once. She said peasants always worry that way. Always too much rain or not enough, too hot a season or too cold. They know good times never last, yet still think that maybe if they just keep staring misfortune straight in the eye it can't come any closer. Would that that were so."

CHAPTER SIX

Polite Emissaries

Eyvind stood gawking as the riverboat passengers pushed past him. He'd never seen the king's capital before, never been so far south at all in fact. Lenocca had been impressive enough, had put Vin Gannoni and even the northern port of Ólo to shame. But this....

Linet and Eyvind had parted from the wagon convoy in Lenocca, lingering there just long enough to determine that Essimis, the king's chancellor, had indeed left for the capital, and thus they must follow. 'Nocca was a proper city set at the confluence of the Carsa River and another smaller one whose name Eyvind had forgotten, with bridges and rows of streets, markets, guildhalls, trade quarters and brothels, all dominated by the stone compound at the center that had begun long ago as a fortress, then was donated to the Polytheon as a temple by Good King Latimer and was now a crown government hall. Eyvind spent a little coin – Linet seemed to have access to a bottomless purse – at a stall that sold cold cider and spiced sausages on skewers. 'City food' as he thought of it, and welcome after three days of the bland millet pottage of the peasant convoy. Linet meanwhile went to confer with 'associates' in the city. Then it was passage on a riverboat the rest of the way to Carsolan.

Carsolan in turn now made Lenocca seem the quaint country burg. He couldn't even see the other side of it, nor the harbor opening into the Lacaryc Sea beyond the vast network of roads and canals. Three rings of defensive walls, built one after the other over the years as the city grew, obscured much of the interior, but every now and then a glimpse through a gate showed a chimneyed landscape like a field of houses instead of crops, the entirety of his view carpeted in wood, plaster and cobblestone. There was something unnatural about that, he thought. Nearer, buildings lay so close they seemed to hang over the streets like a maze of canyon tunnels. A few even had glass windows. Along some streets were set high lamps to light the way at night, and under them a dizzying rainbow of merchants, beggars and thieves congregated, squeezing against each other all in hopes of wringing some profit out of the great stinking metropolis. Almost forty thousand souls it was said, all crammed into such a place. It boggled the mind.

The endless din of so many human voices talking, shouting and laughing in a dozen tongues all together like the summer hum of beehives had a hypnotic effect on Eyvind, the spell broken only when Linet shoved him further down the gangplank to the river quay where fog danced along the water. "Bit of a sight, isn't it? I remember my first time in the city. Nothing quite like it."

"How…how are we supposed to find anyone in this? It's chaos!"

"From here it might seem so. A god's-eye view would show a bit more order. Walk long enough and you'll end up at the palace, or near it." Linet pointed to a spot on the artificial horizon, and poking above it all only the very top of the highest tower of the palace could be seen, and King Osmund's blue and silver banner of a castle over a bridge with three fishes below. That at least was a familiar sight. "Come on, and watch out for cutpurses!"

He'd taken it for a joke, but Eyvind found no fewer than three sticky hands trying to wriggle their way into their rucksack where the crush of humanity ran thickest. Each time he instinctively moved to thrash the transgressor, stopped only by his wound and Linet's halting glance. "Don't draw attention," she said, pulling him on.

The fish and sewage stink of the harbor grew as they neared the palace, the narrow streets twisting and turning. They crossed arched stone bridges over countless canals where men used poles to guide gondolas filled with passengers or goods. Suddenly the forest of walls and buildings fell away to reveal a broad cobblestone plaza. To the right a line of ships towered over them, each one teeming with crews and dockhands loading crates, barrels and all manner of supplies. Straight ahead lay the palace.

It was underwhelming in a way, amid the great modern city. The palace was an old, ugly, simple stack of blocks and hard angles, much like Phenidra. The irregular hexagon sported squarish towers at each corner, except one that boasted the newer addition of a round one. Three of its walls plunged right into the harbor where wide, flat-bottomed boats drifted in and out of an arched opening. Atop them only a few crumbling crenelations remained, between which bored-looking guards in the king's livery prowled. More guards congregated on the ground near the palace's wide front gates, which were approached by steps ascending to a raised courtyard almost as large as the plaza itself. The whole thing had a patchwork quality to it, a testament to the years and changes it had seen.

"No proper castle, that," Eyvind remarked, "though I don't suppose there's much need with all them walls rounding the city."

"Unless Phynagoras attacks from the sea," Linet replied.

Eyvind looked out at the fleet of cargo ships cramming the harbor and at the windy Lacaryc Sea beyond. "Well now, there's a terrifying thought I didn't need."

"One of our first lessons is that frontal attacks are the way of foolishness. Always flank, ambush, surprise, deceive."

"Is that how you plan to get us inside? Don't imagine folk such as us can walk right in the front door and demand to see the king's chancellor."

Linet nodded. "I still have my false safe conduct. That should get us in. But not here. There's a courier's entrance round the north side."

"You've done this before?"

"Don't ask silly questions!"

Dodging hungry seagulls and more pickpockets, they hugged the narrow alley that ringed the palace wall until they came to a little moss-covered portico jutting out from the stonework. Linet reached through a rusty iron grille to slam a knocker against the oaken door behind it.

After almost a minute and another round of knocking, the door finally opened to reveal an annoyed guard even nearer to retirement than Captain Coladdi had been. "All right, all right! What is it? You know there's a fine for pesterin' the—"

Linet held up the safe conduct. "Courier! I've business with the chancellor. In the name of Lord Osbren I beg entry."

The guard eyed the letter, then Linet, then Eyvind, then Linet again. "A woman courier? Humph. What is the world comin' to? Not like in my day, that's certain. And no livery!" As he complained he slowly unlocked the iron gate, and the grille swung aside.

"Well," Linet said, "some messages are of a certain...*sensitivity*, if you take my meaning. Best not to draw the eye."

The old guard gave a noncommittal nod. "I see. What happened there?" He motioned to her cast and sling.

"Oh, bandits," Linet said with feigned exasperation as he led them inside. "Can you believe it, in this day and age? Thus the hired muscle." She jerked a thumb back at Eyvind.

"Hmm. He don't look like much."

"He didn't cost much."

"Right. Would you mind if I had another look at that letter? My old eyes ain't what they were afore."

Linet visibly tensed for just a fraction of a moment, making the hairs on the back of Eyvind's neck stand straight up. "Oh, uh, of course."

After handing over the fake document, they were conducted to a guard's anteroom. "Just wait here a bit, and I'll fetch a footman to show you up to the chancery. Help yourself to the wine, just please don't tell me captain about it!" The old guard gave an insultingly false laugh and disappeared further into the palace without returning Linet's letter. The door he went through locked behind him with a loud clang.

"Shite," Eyvind spat, "that was too easy. The old man's on to you, I mean us." He indeed considered helping himself to the wine sitting open on a table, then thought better of it in case they had to fight their way out of there.

"I don't understand," Linet said with a frown. "The forgery's perfect, there's no reason for him to suspect it."

"Hired muscle?"

"I had to say something! I usually work alone."

After several minutes of waiting, the guard returned though the same door. He gave another false smile and beckoned them inward. "Everything is now in order. Please, come this way." A worried look passed between Linet and Eyvind, but they had no cause to delay. They passed down a short corridor, the guard following behind.

Suddenly the door behind them slammed shut, echoing along the hallway. Eyvind nearly jumped out of his skin. In front of them, six more guards armed with halberds rushed into the tight space, and they soon found sharp tines leveled at their faces. Linet instinctively reached for a hidden knife.

"Don't!" A sharp voice cracked from behind the wall of iron. A tall, severe woman emerged, wearing no livery but a simple fitted black gown with a silver clasp at the neck in the form of a bird with a serpent in its beak. The guards parted to let her through yet kept their weapons poised. "Lemme see your hands, high up! Don't give these jumpy heroes cause to fear for their lives, now."

"What's the meaning of this?" Linet growled, more angry at their discovery than fearful. "I have a letter of—"

"Yes, I know. It's the second such I've seen in as many days. Both identical, right down to the signature, both borne by rough rogues with neither noble sigil nor retinue. And don't insult me with lies about your limping bodyguard there. Who *are* you?"

"This is all a misunderstanding. We can explain—"

"I certainly hope so. I won't have spies that aren't mine slithering about my palace. I *will* get to the bottom of this. For now...." She motioned to the guards. "Take them!"

★   ★   ★

"I really am getting sick and tired of being locked up," Eyvind said. They'd been stripped of weapons and taken to a cell in one of the palace's towers. A twisting stairway ended in a room blocked by a barred iron gate and a narrow window that looked down on a luxurious inner courtyard with expertly trimmed grass, crisscrossing marble walkways and colorful gardens. The beauty was marred only by several curious black splotches here and there on the ground.

"At least it's not pitch-dark this time," Linet answered. "Damn that Aerrus, he must've used the same letter!"

"I don't understand, surely there can be more than one?"

"Yes, but forgery's a tricky business. Write your signature ten times, and it'll look slightly different every time, though all clearly your own hand. But if you need to fake it, it's harder. Safest is to make exact duplicates. It's only a problem when you have two side by side to compare." She sighed heavily. "Our story was fishy from the start, it raised suspicion. I was sloppy. We've all gotten sloppy! This wouldn't have happened ten years ago."

They passed almost another hour in silence, not sure what fate awaited them. When the shadows the towers cast over the city began to grow long, a gaggle of footfalls could be heard from below. Linet had fallen asleep, but Eyvind just stood staring out the window, taking in the view of Carsolan. He turned sharply when two men, one older and one younger, stopped before their cell, two armed guards and that strange woman behind. The older man was dressed in fine silks and linens, a chain around his neck from which a golden medallion with a device of crossed keys dangled. A small purple bruise adorned his chin. The younger one was more rustic, short but strongly built and dressed in forest colors. They both frowned.

The younger man stepped forward, eyeballed Eyvind with arms crossed. "So who the hells are you?"

Linet jerked awake at that, and was on her feet in an instant. "Finally! Aerrus, you simpleton, you let them keep your safe conduct!"

"They wouldn't let me in otherwise," he said with a shrug. "Said they'd give it back when I left. The cryptarch's a bit of a stick-in-the-ass about the rules."

"With good reason, it seems," the woman added.

"Yes, congratulations, Rinalda, you're a credit to—"

"I don't suppose," said the older man with a voice that boomed despite his age, "you lot considered that falsifying official royal documents is a hanging offense tantamount to high treason? One is bad enough, but now I see you have copies! Do you do this often?"

Aerrus looked sidelong at the man. "Well...only when necessary." The man ground his teeth, seething. "Like, hardly ever."

"Twice in the span of two days?"

"Lord Chancellor," said Linet in as close to a placating tone as she could manage, "if you'd relent and give us a genuine safe conduct from Os— Er, from His Grace's own hand we wouldn't need to manufacture one just to come see you."

"Royal writs of passage are no trifles to be handed out like sweetmeats!"

"That's it," Eyvind said, fed up at last. "That is it! In the last few weeks I've been beaten, shot, chased down like a fugitive, had a forest of metal pointed at me, threatened with torture twice, and tossed in prison three times. I've killed two men, and if I add a few more before following them it'd sit just fine with me! Now it's clear you all know each other, but I don't, so if you would kindly let me out of here I'll explain everything, hopefully before Phynagoras marches in and takes over it all!" He said it all in one breath, and now leaned against the bars to catch it.

"You're a temperamental one, ain't you?" Eyvind almost reached through the bars to strangle Aerrus for his comment.

★   ★   ★

They were shown to Essimis's private chambers, to a room set aside for receiving important visitors away from prying eyes. It was a tastefully furnished space at odds with the palace's spartan exterior. There was another view onto the courtyard, but now accompanied by soft chairs and couches, writing desks and tapestries. A low table sported a castra board with pieces scattered about, showing that a match had recently been interrupted. "Come in, come in," Essimis said when he'd regained some composure, "sit anywhere. Will anyone take wine?"

"I think our tongues are all about to wag more than enough," said Linet without any humor.

It was Eyvind, Linet, Aerrus and Essimis, the others having been dismissed, though in the case of the woman Rinalda with a barrage of whispered instructions from Essimis. Finally, behind locked doors the others seemed to breathe just a bit easier, though Eyvind found it difficult to follow suit.

Linet turned a hard chair backward and sat. "First, before anything, who is that woman? I don't know her."

"That charming specimen of femininity," said Aerrus, "is Rinalda, the king's cryptarch."

"Cryptarch? What's that mean?" asked Eyvind.

"Apparently spymaster wasn't a pretty enough title."

"The office was reactivated after some decades of dormancy," Essimis explained, "when the current threat became more pronounced. Rinalda has served in the king's personal guard for years, has his full confidence. She'll maintain secrecy, I assure you."

Linet snorted. "We'll assure ourselves, thank you very much. Did she know about our plans regarding the Marchman raid?"

The chancellor's jowls wobbled. "No, she didn't even know you existed, though I think that will have to change now. As I explained, I told no one but Lord Osbren. I referred only to 'our old allies', as agreed. I swear I do not know who has betrayed you."

At Eyvind's look of confusion, Linet glanced at Aerrus. He nodded sharply.

"All right, I'll tell you the part of the story you don't know. We were assisting Lord Osbren to turn back a Marchman incursion. It was routine work just to keep their spears sharp. But this time someone told them our position, and it was we who were ambushed. It was a bloody massacre."

"I was the only one to come back," said Aerrus angrily, turned halfway toward Eyvind. "That's why we cut down your precious riders. They were there."

Eyvind's mouth hung open and dry. "I...I didn't know. Truly."

Linet nodded. "We recovered proof that they were mediating an alliance between the Marchmen and Phynagoras." She opened the rucksack that'd finally been returned to them—minus the extra weapons hidden inside it—and handed Essimis the documents for him to inspect. "He's offered them a petty kingdom in exchange for help invading, says they can recover the lands their ancient ancestors lost to...well, to us. To the Argovani."

"Those are the originals," said Aerrus, "of the copies I showed you before."

"Yes, yes. The question," droned Essimis as he looked at the pages written out in a mélange of languages before him, "is who sent them?"

"Armino did." Eyvind told his story yet again. Essimis turned various shades throughout the telling, none of them comforting. A few times it seemed as if he was going to be sick, and Aerrus snatched a vase from a corner of the room to keep handy just in case.

At last Essimis stood, wobbling on his feet like a drunk. "I, erm, need to...confer with His Grace. Immediately. If you'll excuse... the servants can attend to your...excuse me." He fairly leaped from the room.

As soon as the chamber door slammed behind him, Aerrus turned to Linet. "All right, how much of what you just said was true?"

"All of it," Linet replied.

"That's what I was afraid of. So you really brought him into the Lodge?"

"I had no choice, he—"

"You. Brought him. Into. The Lodge." Aerrus eyed the soldier with fresh suspicion.

"I already had this argument with Lom and Perrim, I'm not having it with you."

"That's 'cause there's no argument to make! Have you—"

"Yes!" Linet threw her good hand up. "Yes, I've gone mad! It's a mad, mad world. Can we move past it, please? Tell me true, was it Essimis himself who betrayed us? Because if it was—"

"It wasn't," Aerrus answered with a wave. "I'm convinced of that. You see that beauty mark on his chin? The old coot's an expert at self-preservation if nothing else. I popped him a good one then damn near strangled him before even asking the question."

Eyvind's eyes went wide. "You *punched* the king's chancellor? And he didn't have you executed?"

"Oh, I left him with the distinct impression that should I not return home with a satisfactory answer then another, less polite emissary would follow. Trust it, he wasn't lying when he says he told no one about us."

"I hope you're right," said Linet uncertainly.

"It gets worse, though. You see all them ships out in the harbor? They're loading the whole damn palace. Osmund ain't even going to fight Phynagoras when he comes. The bastard's *running away*."

Now it was Linet's turn to blanch. "Are you serious? He…he can't! He can't just abandon the whole country—"

"He is. He's running off to Pelona to hide under Queen Synophae's skirts. Essimis says he'll try to return in force 'when conditions are more favorable', whatever that means."

"That—" Eyvind had to clear his throat before speaking, his throat was so dry from his mouth hanging open so long. "That makes less than no sense. Dumb slogger I might be, but even I know there's no time more favorable to cock up an invasion than before it happens!"

Aerrus nodded once. "I know. And now we're all caught up. I been trying to winkle out what the real situation is since we got here."

He pointed toward the castra board. "Even played some rounds of his stupid board game to try and smooth it out of 'im."

Linet frowned. "Wait, *we*?"

"I brought Thanis along with me."

"You did? Where is he?"

"He's safe. He's...uh, seeing the city. You know."

Linet cast Aerrus a squinting, suspicious stare. "You took him to a brothel, didn't you?"

"Well, why not? You know what things've been like at home since that awful-ass funeral? Hells, we could all use some distraction. Besides, he got his fletches and it's a...well, a bit of a tradition."

"I never knew about any such trad—" Aerrus gave her a rueful look, and she sneered. "Oh. Right. A *male* tradition."

"Eh, you're over it. If he can kill and die in a fight, surely he can dip his wick. Besides, there's more to worry about going on here." He leaned in closer, lowered his voice. "When we first arrived, there was talk. Gossip from down in the city, from members of the royal court. Crazy talk, something about, I dunno, thunder and lightning inside the palace."

That took Linet aback. "You mean lightning struck the palace?"

"No, coming *from* the palace. On a clear day."

"...have you been drinking?"

"I know, it doesn't make sense. I asked Essimis about it, and he got cagey. That's the real reason I kept Thanis down on Harlot's Row. Safer with the dangers there that we know about."

"You ever hear about anything like that?" Linet asked Eyvind.

"No, nothing. Not outside of a fright-tale."

She shook her head resignedly. "What is going *on*?"

★   ★   ★

Night fell, and Essimis failed to return. But servants did provide the trio with meals and cots to sleep on. "The Lord Chancellor bids you make yourselves comfortable," said one flatly. "He will see you again in the morning."

"He can't possibly still be working at this hour," Aerrus complained.

"There is much to be done." The servants left the chamber, and the hollow *thunk* of the heavy oaken door being locked from the outside echoed loudly.

CHAPTER SEVEN

The Shape of Things To Come

The door didn't unlock until the next morning's sun shone through the open window. Aerrus and Linet were on their feet immediately. Eyvind still slept, for though the cot was of rough straw, it was still the softest bed he'd encountered since fleeing Phenidra.

Essimis strode into the room with vastly more formality and dignity than when he'd left, though his eyes remained bleary and red, as though he'd been up all night. He nodded once at Aerrus and Linet, then frowned. "Would someone kindly wake that soldier?"

Aerrus nudged Eyvind to life, and he yawned and groaned irritation at his first true rest in weeks being cut short. "Aw, what is it this time? We fighting, running, or getting arrested?"

Light footsteps fell behind Essimis, and the chancellor stepped to one side, bowing deeply. Rinalda followed him, standing across from Essimis, and bowed as well. And between them....

None of the trio had ever laid eyes on King Osmund, yet there could be no doubt. The man was near forty-five or fifty, clean-shaven in the current fashion, with dark shoulder-length hair and a long, pointy nose with sunken, owlish eyes above that fairly begged for spectacles. He was of average height, but so thin he could easily be taken for taller. He wore comfortable silks, and a narrow golden circlet upon his brow was the only regal raiment that marked him for a king. His face was an expressionless mask, although a certain grim curiosity peeked out as he beheld the three intruders in his palace. Behind him, two imposing figures in bright new plate armor glowered, armed with swords, spears and mean expressions. No regular guards, these, but the king's personal bravos.

Eyvind came fully awake, and upon realizing who was before them stumbled directly from the cot to kneel, grimacing at the latest insult to his wound. Aerrus and Linet, meanwhile, stood still as statues.

Osmund's gaze rested on them first, as though silently challenging their failure to abase themselves. The two stared right back. A pause. "So," Osmund said at last, his voice a practiced tenor, "our friends of the forest, I presume." He spoke in the increasingly rare aristocratic accent that had once been taught to Argovani nobility. He looked down at Eyvind, still kneeling. "And you are the soldier of Phenidra?"

"Yes, Your Grace," Eyvind muttered.

"You've done a brave thing, though not, perhaps, for brave reasons. We've much to discuss, we two, and I would hear every detail direct from your lips. Rise if your injury allows it, and while we talk my personal doctors will tend to you." Eyvind hobbled slowly to his feet, though could not bring himself to look Osmund in the eye.

Osmund turned to Rinalda. "You shall attend as well, I think. Essimis, conduct these other two to the master alchemist. I'm sure they have…questions about our current plans, and I wish to make the sense of it crystal clear. Then get some rest."

"Yes, Your Grace," Essimis and Rinalda said in unison.

With that, King Osmund of Greater Argovan turned and left the chamber, his bodyguards in tow. Rinalda motioned for Eyvind to follow, and then she herself. Eyvind cast a worried glance backward, and Linet gave a reassuring nod.

"It wouldn't have killed you to show a little respect," said Essimis with irritation when they were alone.

"We told you before," said Aerrus, "we don't ben—"

"Yes, yes, but do you have to be so damned *literal* about it?"

"I think His Fluffy Grace will survive the slight. Now who's this alchemist he was on about?"

★   ★   ★

Essimis shooed Aerrus and Linet down a hallway lit by a shaft of late morning sun. "I only hope he's, erm, *awake*."

Aerrus snorted. "Not an early bird, this alchemist of yours?"

"No, not, uh, exactly. Here, hold a moment." Essimis disappeared around a corner.

"Is it just me," wondered Linet, "or does he get more and more cryptic each year?"

"I stopped paying attention a long time ago," Aerrus replied with a shrug.

Seconds later, the sounds of a door opening and closing echoed down the hall. Two young teenagers, a boy and girl, rounded the corner. They were clad – just barely – in the most cursory slips of silk that left nothing at all to the imagination. With eyes averted they snaked past Aerrus and Linet, disappearing as quickly as they'd come down some previously unseen passage.

"What—?" Linet began to ask when Essimis appeared again.

"Ah, come. This way. The alchemist has made himself…available."

Confusion turned to something else in their stomachs when ushered into a bright, windowed chamber. A nondescript thirtyish fellow lounged at the edge of a huge, canopied bed, wearing only linen braies into which he was presently stowing his anatomy.

"Ah, g'morning to all! I'll just be a minute."

"*This* is your master alchemist?" Aerrus threw Essimis a sour look as he knocked an empty wine bottle away with his toe. "And those two kids—"

"The king has been forced to allow Antero a wide range of… privileges," said Essimis with hands held wide in resignation.

"Right you are," the alchemist said, words muffled by the tunic he now tossed over his head. "And I'm guessing that I'm to provide another demonstration of precisely why that is. That so, Chancellor?"

"It is," Essimis growled.

"Excellent," answered the alchemist, hopping into his shoes. "To the courtyard!"

The courtyard that they'd seen before from a distance was a rare round space in a world inured to the plain sense of angles. Stone colonnades ringed the mostly green sward, supporting a semicircular portico with statues of the reigning dynasty all around. On the ground a network of marble outlined a great eightfold Polytheon star, the center piece boasting a small fountain.

The alchemist Antero led the trio into the yard as though he commanded the palace himself. He motioned to a nearby household guard. "You, go tell the other guards that I'll be performing another demonstration. Tell them to try and not wet themselves this time, and to remember the punishment for speaking of it to anyone."

The guard gulped nervously, then nodded and left the yard. At the same time a servant approached, carrying a box and walking very, very slowly, a look of sheer terror on his face.

"Good," said Antero, "put it here!"

"What is all this drama?" Linet asked with irritation. "We don't like surprises."

"Then I suggest," said Essimis, "that you pay close attention."

"Especially since I haven't much to spare for entertainment!" added Antero.

"Much of *what*?"

Antero pulled a clay bottle from the box and uncorked it. Without a word he held out a hand and the servant pressed a lighted taper into it. Antero touched it to the lip of the bottle and it burned to life. Lamp oil. He raised the vessel, then tossed it hard onto a stretch of marble well clear of the fountain. The bottle shattered a few paces from a statue of Queen Hawisa, and burning oil coated a small patch of stone.

"Oh," said Linet, rolling her eyes, "well that's *very* impressive. Well done, that'll turn back Phynagoras no problem—"

"Would you be patient!" Essimis hissed. "And *watch*."

Antero now carefully – oh, so carefully! – lifted a small glass phial from his box. This one contained a clear liquid that seemed to shimmer almost in the sunlight. He twisted off the stopper, dipped a glass rod into the weird substance, then let a single drop fall into a new, empty phial. When the first was safely sealed again, he held the one-drop vessel aloft.

"Stand back," he said. Aerrus and Linet took a step backward.

"Farther." They took five steps back.

Antero lightly tossed the phial amid the now-dwindling lamp oil flames.

BOOM!

The entire courtyard quaked with the explosion, the blinding greenish flash and shockwave nearly knocking them all from their feet. It was indeed as if lightning had struck the yard, and Aerrus and Linet instinctively tried to cover both eyes and ears at once.

The stone beneath the point of conflagration now stood blackened and smoking, several bricks shattered to bits. Hawisa gazed down in marble disapproval, her prominent nose dark with soot. Aerrus and Linet stood aghast, wordless for many moments afterward. Essimis and Antero said nothing either, letting the pair absorb the experience.

At last Aerrus managed to pick his jaw up off the ground and muttered, "What...what...?"

"I call it *Vrril*," Antero said, rolling the word like it was the trilling of some exotic animal. "Appropriately otherworldly name, don't you think?"

"How...how much of this...*stuff* do you have?" Linet whispered the question, still in awe.

"Well, that was one drop. I've managed to make enough Vrril for, oh, say a thousand such demonstrations. And more by the day, as His Grace commands."

"Gods...."

Antero shook his head. "No, this is the work of men, or men inspired by devils. You understand the implication, my dear antiquated forest rangers? I'm no master alchemist, I'm nothing special. I was about to be thrown out of the University of Murento for...reasons that aren't pertinent at the moment when the king learned of my invention. I happened upon this demonic weapon by sheer luck. *Me.* If I can do this, someone else absolutely will, eventually.

"You see, this is why I drown myself in wine and young flesh. Our world is over." He pointed at the ruin in the courtyard. *"That's* the shape of things to come."

Aerrus and Linet stared still at the lingering cloud of smoke, finding no cause to deny that.

★   ★   ★

They huddled around a corner table in Madame Feynaud's, one of the cleaner brothels on Harlot's Row. To its credit, the place functioned as a respectable inn as well as a whorehouse. Five copper pennies bought one a night's stay in the common room near a warm fire, pottage, bread and beer. A silver one, one of the rare private rooms, meat and wine. The girls were on an entirely separate menu. But at the moment its most valued amenity was that it was well out of earshot of the palace.

At least I hope so, Linet thought as she cast a suspicious eye about. *That Rinalda could have spies anywhere.* The early afternoon crowd seemed more interested in the lunch specials than anything else, but she refused to let her guard down. She noted also that Eyvind sat upright almost normally. "How's the wound?"

"Oh, the king's doctors took good care of me," he said, holding up a tiny flask. "They got more opiphine than I've seen in my entire life!"

"Careful of that, I hear you can get sticky to it."

"Let it be then, I've done my part. His Grace grilled me for hours. I get the feeling he wasn't terribly surprised by any of it. Like he was expecting betrayal eventually, just didn't know who, or when."

"But he is running away," said Aerrus, nursing a cup of small beer. "He didn't deny that?"

"A 'strategic withdrawal', he calls it. There's barely any standing army to speak of beyond his household troops, and the task of raising one would just give Armino advance warning. So no chance of taking Phenidra off him. The court's moving to Ayala to gather allies, financing, and to build up enough of this...what did that filthy alchemist call it?"

"Vrril," Linet replied, not bothering to try the ridiculous pronunciation. "It changes...well, it changes everything! What is it? Is it magic?"

"No such thing," Aerrus said.

Eyvind shook his head. "I don't know. The weird things they do at the University...I've heard stories I was sure were just drunken tales. A ship dropped anchor in Ólo a couple years ago, smuggled a sack of some black powdery stuff from Ghresh that burned and spit, spewed smoke all over the place, and we all thought *that* was black magic. That was a toy compared to this. With a weapon like that alchemist made, you could...." He shrugged.

"Conquer the world," Linet finished.

"Essimis tried to explain it to me," Aerrus said. "Stuff about...ores mined from somewhere in the mountains with their own inborn heat that makes people sick, slimy growths welling up from deep in the sea, some disaster at the University that made it by accident...couldn't really follow too much."

They were interrupted by a new face, and young: a lanky, awkward lad stumbled down from a winding wood stair already gnawing on a hunk of bread and crossed the halfway crowded common room, pausing only a moment before finding the faces he sought. He clumsily pulled up a spare chair and plopped down at the table. "There you guys are!"

Linet smirked at him. "Thanis, I hear congratulations are in order, for a couple of reasons. Enjoying yourself?"

Thanis cast a nervous, sidelong glance at Aerrus. "Uh...."

"Don't let her shame you, lad, that's one of her puppet strings. Agree and amplify!"

"Oh, right. Then, yeah, I am!"

"I see you taught him all the important stuff," Linet sneered. "This here is Eyvind. We can trust him."

"*That* remains to be seen, strictly speaking," Aerrus said, "but for now you can talk free in his presence."

"Thanks for the vote of confidence, mate. Anyway, the plan is to return in force when enough of the weapon is made. Pelonan alchemists are years ahead of ours, and the king thinks they can improve the process, speed up the crafting of it."

"And then Pelona will have this ability as well," Linet said. "Antero's right about that – something like this can't stay secret very long."

"Are you talkin' about the rumors we heard earlier?" Thanis asked with a full mouth.

"Not rumors anymore," answered Aerrus. "The bastards have learned how to put lightning in a bottle."

Thanis almost choked on his breakfast. "Wha— Really?"

"Really. And Osmund thinks, what, that this'll let him retake the whole of Argovan once Phynagoras gets stuck in? And what are we supposed to do in the meantime?"

"It weren't exactly a two-way exchange of information, mate," Eyvind said.

"Fuckin' kings," Aerrus growled. "We're just disposable resources to them, as ever!"

That potentially seditious comment made Linet look around them once again for any overeager ears. "There's still the matter of who betrayed us."

Aerrus nodded. "And I ain't leaving until that's figured. You can do what you want, but there's a snake in the royal court. Well, they're all snakes, but one in particular needs its head cut off. Even if I have to follow 'em all the way to Pelona."

★   ★   ★

They were lent a room in the palace to sleep in, but it was no luxury. It was in the oldest wing, unrenovated and drafty, and had disturbingly realistic serpents carved into the walls and pillars. They spent few waking hours there. When not questioning the entire palace, Linet sat in Essimis's chancery chamber poring over lists and logs to try and see some pattern that might reveal something of value. Nearby, Aerrus played castra with Essimis in hopes of getting the chancellor to slip up and reveal something he hadn't already. "I'm never going to get the hang of this," he muttered.

"Patience, my young friend," Essimis replied with annoying serenity. "Castra takes only minutes to learn, but a lifetime to master."

"I don't have that long." He moved a piece to attack, then rolled the dice. But even with the advantage, the numbers came up against him, and he grunted. "Figures."

"A game of skill with a strong element of luck is always the most frustrating, much like life itself." Essimis collected Aerrus's captured piece.

"Ha! I thought people played games to escape real life." The room echoed Aerrus's derisive laugh, amplified as it bounced off a far wall. He looked up past the chancellor at what'd accomplished the trick. "What is that ugly thing, anyway?" He nodded up at a concave metallic shape mounted on the wall like a shiny trophy.

Linet turned to look at what Aerrus indicated, as did Essimis. "Hmm? Oh, a shield I suppose, captured after some old battle no doubt. Someone must've found it in storage and put it up there."

"Why?"

Essimis shrugged. "I've no eye for decoration. His Grace has undertaken a program of consistency and uniformity of government in all places, and this evidently extends to the furnishings. There's another like it in my office in Lenocca."

Aerrus rubbed his chin. "Huh."

After winning his third straight match against Aerrus, Essimis left to attend to some meeting or other. Aerrus continued to glare up at the strange metal disc.

"What are you thinking?" Linet asked.

"Not sure, just...whooo!" He hooted loudly enough to send another echo bouncing back.

"What the hells?" She put down the lists, having lost her place thanks to Aerrus's racket.

Aerrus turned to face the opposite wall. Above the door and directly across from the shield was hung a decorative grotesque, new in the style of modern sculptors. The monstrous mouth of some hell-spawned Chthonus gaped wide, and within that mouth was darkness. "Hmm."

"Well? What's wrong with you?"

"N-nothing. I, uh...." He looked up at the grotesque once more with suspicion. "I need to go to 'Nocca for a bit."

"Lenocca? What for?"

"Just something I need to look into. And I want to send Thanis home with what we've learned. Be back in a week or so." Aerrus left the chamber, and as he walked past Linet he flashed a few furtive hand signals. *Be patient. Guard your words.*

CHAPTER EIGHT

A Few Whispered Words

"What about this one?" Linet held up the long list of the chancellor's visitors and pointed to a name inscribed in tiny letters. It was one scroll among hundreds, and Linet was determined to scan every one if she had to. "This fishmonger's guild official left Lenocca the morning after Aerrus's meeting with Essimis."

The cryptarch Rinalda shook her head and proffered another, almost identical scroll. "No, can't be. He turned up at the palace a few days later to meet with a Cynuvik ambassador to make a shipping deal. No time to go east."

"Hmm. Then maybe he handed the information to an accomplice...I didn't know the Cynuviks even *had* ambassadors."

"The march of civilization's unstoppable, even among savages."

Linet set the scroll aside in frustration, leaned back in the uncomfortable chair in the cryptarch's office and yawned.

Rinalda smiled. "Not exactly the glamorous job you'd expect, is it? Most intelligence work is just reading until the sun's down and your eyes are red. Sometimes I think she had it easier." Rinalda jerked a thumb up at an old painting hung on her wall above a desk. A woman with fierce eyes and a scarred cheek glowered down on them.

"Who's that?"

"Vinian, the first royal spymistress. A lot more wet work in those days, the wars of the Bergovan Succession. Brutal times, but at least back then you knew who your enemy was."

"How does one became a cryptarch, anyway?"

Rinalda shrugged. "In my case, almost by accident. I was a guard at the Argovani consulate in Porontus. By chance I overheard a drunken boast about a plot to kill the consul. I reported it, but at that time a woman in the guard was still a bit of a novelty, and they didn't take me seriously. So I had no choice but to—"

"To expose the plot yourself," Linet finished with a grin. "Brilliant."

"I slipped away from my night posts to spy on the conspirators, gather proof and catch them in the act. They were idiots and the plan never had any chance, but the consul was impressed with my initiative. Found I had a talent for it too, realized I could do more good with a few whispered words than a strong sword arm. When the king reactivated the position he remembered the reports about me and would have no one else for it. So here I am."

"Well, if we're to survive what's probably coming we're going to need a good intelligence system. I'd love to hear your ideas."

"Certainly."

Linet leaned in close, though no one else was present. "Rin, what do you think of Osmund's decision, truly? Can you really support just abandoning Argovan and putting all faith in that damnable Vrril to get it back?"

Rinalda frowned, looked away. "It's not my place to second-guess His Grace. He has my support in all things. As for the Vrril...I don't know what to think about that. Only that it scares the hells outta me."

★   ★   ★

Eyvind was on a mission of his own, and though it was of a more mundane nature he was no less determined. His wound had almost healed, and he walked constantly about the palace to exercise his leg back to strength. He still limped a bit though, and to spare himself embarrassment his route took him through lesser-used parts of the great compound. Presently he was negotiating a stairway leading down to one of the stone docks built into a palace wall facing the sea. It was a gloomy, smelly passage, abandoned in favor of a newer dock equipped with machines for unloading cargo. Having delivered to the king news of everything he knew, everything he'd seen and done, he wasn't sure what function he now served, and with Phynagoras's invasion imminent his military career was, ironically, finished.

His ruminations were interrupted by a sound echoing softly off the vaulted ceiling of the hallway he traversed. A voice, whispering. The events of the last weeks had instilled a healthy paranoia in him, and Eyvind felt the hairs on the back of his neck stand on end. He pressed himself against the wall and blew out the rushlight taper he carried. The only illumination became the glow at the far end of the hallway where it opened onto the dock. There was an intersecting passage ahead from which the voice – no, two voices now – grew louder and closer, though still whispering. Eyvind pressed himself up against a rotting support beam, and peeking past it he could make out two figures. They stopped right at the intersection and continued whispering in a language unknown to Eyvind, but which had an unmistakable eastern sound to it. *Gods*, he thought, *have I stumbled on the traitors they're looking for?*

It was too dark to make out either of the figures, though Eyvind could see that one wore an elaborately brocaded doublet that shimmered even in the gloom – gold thread? He passed something to his fellow, a folded paper or parchment. A message. The recipient nodded, then turned and proceeded down the hall toward the dock, while the other went back the way they'd come.

Eyvind waited until the footsteps faded away completely, then several more minutes after that before fumbling in the dark back up the stairs as quickly as his limp allowed.

★   ★   ★

"All right, slow down. Who was this again?"

Eyvind sighed, frustrated. On his way up to Rinalda's office he'd found Linet returning from a brief meal break in the guards' refectory where she'd listened intently to their idle chatter while eating, just in case something of value was said. Apparently nothing had been, as she was halfway down the corridor toward the office when Eyvind ran into her. "I told you," he said, keen to get the fruits of his latest surveillance out before some new misfortune befell him to prevent it, "I didn't get a good look, it was dark. He was rich, though, I could tell that much."

"How do you know that?" Linet asked.

"He wore a fancy doublet with some kind of shiny thread. Probably cost a year's wage of a common slogger."

Linet was about to reply when the door to Rinalda's office creaked open. Once again Eyvind instinctively leaned against the wall to remain unseen. They watched as a man in more foreign clothing – that seemed the rule rather than the exception at the palace – emerged, holding something. The dark-haired and dark-eyed fellow looked nervously left, right, then shoved the something into a pouch and skittered the other way down the corridor. "Who was that?" he wondered.

"That," Rin said moments later when they entered the office together, "was just one of my agents, from the old days in Porontus. Don't ask for details." She glanced from Linet to Eyvind, then back again, then again. She was nervous too, though neither of them could tell why.

"Of course not," Linet said. "We have a more pressing tale."

Eyvind told his story again, and Rinalda listened carefully, then pursed her lips in thought. "Hmm. Describe this fancy doublet again in as much detail as you can possibly remember." Eyvind rolled his eyes and began once more. When he finished, Rinalda nodded. "As I suspected. The Thazovi ambassador. He's known for wearing such finery."

"Does that mean he's our traitor?" Linet asked, excited.

"Not necessarily. There's intrigue aplenty throughout the palace."

"But," Eyvind said, "he's clearly doing something nefarious, otherwise why all the secrecy? Meeting in moldy old hallways? You should arrest him, find out what he knows."

Rinalda shook her head. "I don't know, we don't want to cause a diplomatic incident. I suggest keeping a watch on him, see if he does anything else, implicates others—"

"Rin," Linet insisted, "we're running out of time here. Once the palace is packed up aboard ship we won't have access to these records. And if Phynagoras has a spy at court, Osmund will be more vulnerable in Pelona, not less."

"Please," Eyvind said, "let's just check it out!"

With a sigh, Rinalda nodded. "Fine. But if it all goes wrong, you'll be the ones to explain it to Essimis and the king."

A tail was put on the Thazovi ambassador, and when next he was observed to be making his way down to those dank tunnels for no apparent reason, he was followed at a distance. His whispering conversation with his accomplice was interrupted by guards swarming in from all directions, cutting off any possible escape route. The ambassador was incensed.

"Vhat is ze meaning of ziss?" he shouted as halberds faced him everywhere he turned.

"That's precisely what I was hoping you'd clarify for me, mister ambassador." Rinalda descended the stair with a bright lamp, with Linet and Eyvind behind. "You've picked an odd location for a conference, and not for the first time."

The ambassador's face turned visibly beet-red, even in the low light. "Zat is no business of yours, voman. I haff diplomatic immoonity!"

"Not in matters of palace security, you don't. His Grace the King is hemmed in all around by enemies and traitors. Are you one?"

"Rideeculoos!"

"We'll see." Rinalda held out an expectant hand toward the ambassador's more poorly attired companion, who clutched the message he'd been given like it was a magic talisman to ward off the fear so clearly scrawled across his face. "Every second you delay makes these stalwart guards' hands more weary, and who knows where their blades will fall? Quickly now!" The guards all drew a step closer. The man's hand quavered, and Rinalda reached past the guards to pluck the note out of his hand.

"Ziss is an outrage!" His droopy mustache wiggled with each spat syllable.

"No doubt," said Rinalda, "we live in outrageous times. I can't have you arrested, but I can invite you to retire to one of the palace's quite pleasant waiting rooms, and strongly advise you to stay there until I decide what to do with you." She motioned to the guards. "Now."

The ambassador was led away, spitting impotent curses, along with his companion. Linet tried to peer over the taller woman's shoulder at the document she held. "What's it say?"

"Haven't the slightest, it's written in Thazovi. I had some instruction in it years ago, but I think this calls for a more professional translation."

Once translated, the document proved a disappointment. It spoke of the ambassador's observations at court, opinions, and attempts at bribing minor functionaries about the palace without much success. A search of the ambassador's quarters revealed similar messages, and drafts of messages, relaying plans to influence the chancellor and the king himself if possible in myriad matters favorable to Thazov. Trade routes, marriage alliances, court gossip, relations between Argovan and Pelona, the likelihood of Phynagoras's invasion, and the like.

"But nothing that implies the voivode's in league with Phynagoras himself," Linet said with frustration when reading the translations. "Dammit, I was so sure!"

"When you want something to be true so badly," Rinalda replied, "it can cloud your judgment. A good cryptarch has to recognize those biases and try to set them aside."

They'd gathered again in the chancery rather than the cramped confines of Rinalda's office, Essimis having taken a keen interest in the incident once it became known. Presently he scowled down at the pile of papers. "This kind of low espionage is unavoidable at a royal court. A nuisance, but a necessary one. I honestly wish you hadn't pulled this stunt. It creates embarrassment on both sides."

"But we had to," Eyvind protested, "for all we knew he was the one—"

"Yes, yes. But now we've no choice but to dismiss the ambassador, if only to save face with the voivode. He won't find a warm welcome back home though, having been caught. Just when we most need to be gathering allies!"

"What's a voivode, anyway?" Eyvind asked.

"It's what Thazovi call their princes. Don't ask me why."

"I'm sorry about this, Chancellor," Linet said. "I was so determined, grasping at straws—"

"No," Rinalda insisted, "I'm the cryptarch, the responsibility was mine. Though, perhaps our guests will be a bit more circumspect about accusations in the future?"

"There will be blame enough to go around when I tell the king about this," Essimis said with a tired sigh. "Though I imagine he has more important matters on his mind."

★　　★　　★

Aerrus returned from his secret errand without Thanis, who'd been dispatched back to the Lodge. By this time the palace guards knew them all well enough to let him in without challenge, and he rushed directly to Essimis, interrupting a meeting with the fleet captains before the final departure. He dragged the infuriated chancellor up into a tower broom closet, a room with no windows or furnishings, and there behind a locked door they conversed for some hours. Linet heard all this secondhand, and when she finally tracked him down Aerrus would only say, again in the hand language, to be patient. Essimis went about his duties in a daze, struck as though with some terrible news. From all this Linet deduced that Aerrus had discovered something, but for some reason was keeping it from her. She knew he must have his reasons, but the uncertainty niggled at her brain.

"Pack up," Aerrus said suddenly, some days after his return. Linet had been sitting, as ever, in the chancery chamber reading transcripts of various interrogations. Her cast had finally come off, to her infinite delight, and only the sling was needed now. Her skin had itched terribly beneath the plaster, and now she felt as free as a bird suddenly uncaged.

"Where are we going?" she asked.

Essimis tottered into the room after Aerrus. "That, my dear, is up to you." Eyvind came in behind the chancellor, walking normally for the most part. "Recent events have spurred His Grace to action, and the fleet will be departing ahead of schedule." He spoke the words loudly and clearly, a far cry from the nervous ferret of a man he'd been the last few days.

"To action," Linet repeated, "to fight?"

Essimis let out a great guffaw. "Oh, heavens no! No, the royal court will remove to Ayala tomorrow morning. This is to be a closely held secret, understand, and you'll not speak of it until it's a done thing."

"I was afraid of that. How can you leave us to fend for ourselves like this? The whole country's counting on—"

"That point has been debated more times than can be counted, and the decision is made." Essimis made a grand sweeping gesture with his hand. "Now I have explained more to you than you're due, and you may either accompany His Grace as a friend of the court, little though you deserve the title, or return to that arboreal paradise you hold so dear. For security, the king will sleep in your chamber in the old wing tonight with minimal guard to draw attention, but by sunup will be aboard ship and gone. No others are to know this. You can sleep here. I suggest you make your preparations." Without further comment he turned and left the trio alone.

"I'm going with them," Aerrus said with finality. "We still haven't found our traitor."

Linet glanced at Eyvind, and he nodded once. "We as well. We've been working on an idea. It's not all put together yet, but we're going to need Queen Synophae's help. I think we can use—"

"Fine, fine, later," Aerrus whined with a yawn and a dismissive wave. The interruption was uncharacteristically rude even for him, and after a brief flash of temper Linet realized that something was very wrong. "Right now both of you come help me carry our belongings down to the docks. We can load up and get an early start tomorrow."

Eyvind frowned, confused. "What—"

"All right," Linet said, looking hard at Eyvind and hoping he got the message. "No need to be an ass about it."

No words passed between the three until they stood before the line of ships, the wind and gentle lapping of the water drowning any possibility of eager ears overhearing. Aerrus drew the pair in close, and many things at last became terrifyingly clear.

★   ★   ★

A full blood moon shone its bronze light through the window, casting an unnatural pallor over the room's stone-carved serpents. All was still and quiet but for the slow breathing of the form buried beneath sheets and blankets even in the mild night weather. The elaborate canopied four-poster bed was out of all proportion to the cramped space. A king's bed. A gold circlet lay upon a table beside it. Against the adjacent wall a tattered old tapestry swayed the slightest bit whenever a breeze wafted through the window.

At some point in the night, the scene was disturbed by the door to the room swinging silently open. A dark shape with no recognizable features almost floated across the short distance to the bed and stood over the rise and fall of the linens.

After a long pause, the figure produced something from the many folds of cloth wound tightly about it. A glint of moonlight bounced off the slender blade as it was raised over the sleeping form. Like the moon itself, it hung over the scene, then descended with a swift swish.

Clink.

The blade plunged only a fingernail's width into its target before being halted by hard metal. With a gasp of surprise the assassin raised it up, thrust again wildly. *Clink. Clink-clink.* Mail armor! Dropping the weapon, the assassin dashed out of the room into the hallway beyond, while the tapestry on the wall exploded outward as two new figures emerged from the space behind it to give chase. The bed's occupant moved more slowly, weighed down by the mail hauberk and hampered, now only just a bit, by a healing thigh wound.

Linet and Aerrus tore down the hall after the lithe, wiry would-be killer who looked like a mummy from Marzahn brought back to life thanks to the ash-dark wrappings it was bound in. Just before reaching a twisting stairwell, they both lunged, but their quarry turned at an impossible angle and ducked past them to run in the other direction, slowing Linet in particular with a jab to her healing arm. But just as it passed the doorway to the chamber, Eyvind burst out and tackled the assassin, and they went down in a tangle of limbs. Finally shouting an alarm, Eyvind summoned a host of armored guards seemingly out of nowhere, and soon the entire hallway was crammed with shining steel. The assassin still struggled, squirming and twisting viciously out of one grasp even as another took hold.

Aerrus and Eyvind wrestled the figure to its feet and into the hands of the waiting bravos, whose grips were like iron shackles. Essimis emerged from an adjacent room and charged through the fray to face the assassin, his face a vortex of fury and gnashing teeth. Without a moment's hesitation he ripped the topmost layers of cloth from the prisoner's outfit.

"Rinalda," he growled, falling backward as though physically struck. "They...they said...but I couldn't believe...why?"

The cryptarch's eyes blazed, her mouth twisted in pure contempt, though at whom none could say. "I have nothing to say to you."

"Then say it to me!"

The guards all jumped, turned to the booming voice, then kneeled only part-way, crowded as they were in the hallway. A path between Rinalda and King Osmund formed. The mild, even-tempered monarch from before was gone, replaced at once by two different men sharing a single body: one visibly stung almost to death with pain plain in his eyes, the other raging furious at so deep a treason.

He approached Rinalda slowly, held back a bit by Essimis lest she still produce some hidden weapon. Osmund looked her up and down, perhaps hoping to find some explanation for this betrayal without the pain of words passing between them. "How—" His voice cracked, a most unkingly sound, and he took a breath before beginning again. "How could you do this to me? Why? What evil have I done you that would drive my most trusted officer to...this?"

"Evil," Rinalda spat, poison on her breath, "would be preferable. Evil's what's coming for you. For all of you. There's nothing to stand against it. There's no other choice! I know that even if you fools don't. At least Phynagoras—"

Osmund bounded forward and slapped Rinalda hard across the face, then again, harder. "*How could you do this to me!*" Tears poured from the king's eyes, and a dribble of slobber fell from his lips. He grabbed a bravo's belt dagger and came to within a hair's breadth of plunging it into Rinalda's heart, as she would've done to him. He stopped, snarling, pointed it close to her eye. "I almost wish you had killed me. It would've hurt less." He flung the dagger to the floor. "Captain Eimar, get her out of my sight. I have plans for this one, though I wish to all the gods and saints I didn't have."

One of the bravos, a towering blond man of Cynuvik extraction, hied Rinalda away, and Osmund went somewhere to weep with Essimis following behind, trying and failing to comfort him. Oddly, Linet and Eyvind and Aerrus were quickly forgotten, and they gathered in the loathsome serpent room. Aerrus reached into a small chest in the corner and produced a wine bottle.

"Figured whichever way things went tonight we could use this." He uncorked the bottle and took a swig. Eyvind threw off the mail shirt before snatching the bottle for himself.

"I can't believe it," Linet said, still in shock. "I...trusted her. Admired her. How could she do this?"

"She must've been planning this for years. Putting those sound-bouncing shields in Essimis's offices both here and in 'Nocca, digging pipes to funnel 'em into her own to listen. That's not an impulsive act."

"What else did you find in Lenocca?"

"The cryptarch's office, as here, is right above the chancellor's. I managed to sneak in there and do some digging. Security's not as tight as in the palace. There was a listening hole on the floor, and another of those dish-shaped shields beneath the boards to direct the sound. I suspect we'll find the like here. I found papers with references to numbers of men and supplies. Vague enough to look innocent if you didn't know what to look for, but real big numbers. Dates, past and future. One of those dates was the night of the battle with the Marchmen, the night we were betrayed. My guess, selling us out was just a gesture to get Ordovax firmer on their side. No proof of that, but damn suspicious. I swiped what documents I thought I could get away with, had to have some of it translated."

"Why translated?" Eyvind asked.

"They were in Porontan."

"Rinalda said she was posted in Porontus, years ago," Linet said. "Could that be when Phynagoras got to her? That scares me more than anything, the planning that's gone into this."

"I took all this to Essimis as soon as I got back," Aerrus continued, "and he almost had a heart seizure. Then we planned the trap. The rest you know."

"But still, why did she do it?"

Eyvind shrugged after his third gulp of wine. "Wouldn't you throw your lot in with the side that spends years planning an invasion instead of the one with barely any army?"

"More good with a few whispered words than a strong sword arm. That's what she said. Gods, maybe she actually thought she was sparing everyone a worse fate by plotting with Phynagoras rather than resisting him."

Aerrus sneered. "She was, to put it overly fucking mild, mistaken."

Linet wiped a tear from her cheek, and reached for the bottle.

★   ★   ★

Two days later the good people of Carsolan witnessed something that had not been seen by anyone in a hundred years, and the sight would stick with each one until their dying day. Crucifixion was designed to be the most horrific, cruel method of execution imaginable, a feast of suffering doled out over the course of hours or days, shared liberally among all and sundry as a display of what fate befalls traitors. Thus its value as a deterrent. Or so went the prevailing wisdom.

The evening before Rinalda's crucifixion, a brand-new cross was erected in the plaza before the palace. Stones that had been in place long enough to be worn smooth were rudely uprooted to make a spot for the great beam, and engineers that had been engaged in making improvements to the palace found themselves having to consult dusty old military manuals for the specifications. It wasn't as simple an affair as it looked, it turned out. Fortunately, Rinalda's frame was light, so it was easy to keep within tolerances.

Rinalda herself had said nothing further, and a search of her office offered little of value. Again, handwritten notes could very well have been oblique references to plots and plans and instructions from Phynagoras, but if so they'd been well coded so that none but Rinalda herself might interpret them. No matter – her trial was swift, her sentence final. King Osmund did not attend, having kept himself shut up in his private apartments, where wailing could occasionally be heard at odd hours.

Essimis kept himself sealed behind a mask of courtly stoicism, though up close one could see the pain in his eyes, and shame at having been taken for a fool. The shield and listening pipe from the chancery to the cryptarch's office were ripped out and the voids in the stonework filled with concrete, and orders sent to Lenocca to do the same there.

On the morning of the execution, guards beat a path through onlookers still gawking at the cross erected so hastily in the night. It had been propped upright with a dummy to test it, and was now uprooted and set on the ground again. King Osmund, wearing a blue and silver coronation robe and splendid golden crown instead of his modest circlet, was hemmed in by his bodyguards, leading a train of various important people from the court toward a dais set up before it: Essimis, the wealthier county governors, ambassadors, one or two

Marimines bankers who happened to be present at the time. The three people most instrumental to the apprehension of the day's victim trailed at the end, none of them in any great rush to see the sentence carried out.

"It's like a godsdamned fair day," remarked Aerrus as he looked around at the gathered crowd. Indeed, a couple enterprising folks had already set up stalls to sell breakfast to the masses.

"You don't have to watch if you don't want to," Linet said.

"Yeah, I do. I started this, I need to see it through. I owe it…to them. All of 'em." He blinked and looked away.

Linet glanced at Eyvind. "And you?"

The soldier set his jaw. "I guess I'd better watch. I intend the same for Lord Armino when I get my hands on him, for what he did to the cap'n."

Even after the sentence was passed Rinalda resisted with impressive violence, and had to be drugged into docility just to get her to the site. She now staggered out of the palace held between two strong guards, still wearing the dark outfit she'd been captured in, though her hair had been chopped short so it wouldn't get in the way of the engineers. She was brought before Osmund and his court, and all waited in silence.

The king stood, weakly, and held up a sheet of vellum. He drew a deep breath. "Rin—" He'd tried to bellow so all could hear, but his voice cracked again. He motioned to a richly dressed fellow holding a heavy staff with a gilded trumpet fixed on top, who ascended the dais to stand next to him. Osmund began again in a much softer voice. "Rinalda of Seagate…." The official he'd summoned repeated his words in a great, sonorous baritone that carried across the plaza and almost out to sea. "You have been found guilty of high treason, of consorting with an avowed enemy of the crown, namely the despot Phynagoras of Porontus and Bhasa and of other lands, of plotting the murder of our royal person, King Osmund the Second of Greater Argovan, and acting to carry it out. Your sentence is death by crucifixion. May the gods have mercy upon your soul, for I will not."

The guards dragged Rinalda to the cross and laid her down atop it, though she was so addled they had to exert little effort. They held her as engineers tied her arms and legs down. Finally the moment everyone had either been anticipating or dreading came, when they laid heavy iron construction staples over her hands, one tine just below the wrist joints and the other over the palms. The head engineer, already green in the face at the task she'd been given, glanced once at the king, who gave an almost imperceptible final nod. The engineer in turn nodded to her subordinates, who'd drawn lots for the job, though whether to win it or avoid it only their own hearts knew. They raised heavy building mallets with steel heads, brought them down. Half the crowd looked away already.

Rinalda let out a great cry that even her drugged state could not stifle. After all, it wouldn't do to have the crucifixion victim anesthetized to the point of indifference to her own sentence, otherwise what value the spectacle? Blood began to pool on the ground where she'd been pierced, though one of the mallets had missed its mark and crushed her wrist, thus another blow was needed. When both arms and feet were nailed securely, the whole grisly assembly was hoisted with ropes. Rinalda screamed, and her body quivered when the central beam dropped the three feet into the hole made for it. Blood dripped from the crossbeam like rain, and several ladies in the king's retinue fainted when a sudden gust of sea wind spattered them with some of it.

Osmund stepped forward, legs wobbling, and descended the dais to stand at Rinalda's feet. She looked down at him, and for a moment she seemed almost lucid. Her lips curled in a mockery of a smile. "You...I'll save...a seat. For you." Desperately trying to ignore her, he ran a hand over her blood-soaked flesh, returned to the dais and held it aloft to make the old axiom clear to all: a king always has blood on his hands. "You!" Rinalda yelled, apparently at the crowd entire. "All you...will follow me. Plenty of seats...in the nineteen hells! No 'scape from it. Save...save a seat...Phyn...Phynag...he'll send you all! You'll see!"

While Rinalda continued to scream and laugh and moan nonsense and bleed, Osmund turned to Essimis and said, "It's done. Now to the rest of it." Without another word to the court or crowd, he began making his way back to the palace. Several guards and members of the court excused themselves to vomit, but many others continued staring at the terrible sight, only vaguely aware that the real horror would be in the coming days, as blood loss, dehydration and exposure would extract every possible iota of suffering before allowing Rinalda to escape into the sweet embrace of death. The howls, and that terrible cackling, told the stallkeeps that they'd do no more business today, and they soon packed up and left.

Aerrus stood motionless, frowning up at the result of his oath. He'd gotten his wish: their betrayer was going to become a corpse, very slowly. Still....

"What is it?" Linet asked. "Isn't this what you wanted?"

"I...suppose so. After all this it just seems so...so stupid."

★   ★   ★

The trio stood before Essimis, their mood necessarily sober. The chancellor's sunken eyes showed he hadn't been sleeping, and there were a thousand different reasons for that. He cleared his throat. "I, er, never properly thanked you, each of you, for what you've done. You very likely saved His Grace's life."

"Very likely?" asked Aerrus.

Essimis sighed. "All right, definitely. I can't think of any reward to offer that you'd value, but His Grace has consented to these at least...." He drew three small red leather folios from his desk, handed one to each of them. "Marques of safe conduct, genuine ones this time. Should let you move more easily about. And I've arranged to have your weapons returned to you."

"Thank the Chthonii for small favors," Aerrus remarked. The folios contained letters of passage bearing Osmund's seal, and enameled badges of the same design that could be carried or worn. "Fancy."

"The truth is, there's now no one with any authority to deny you. Without a cryptarch, administering palace security now falls to a slapdash gaggle of guard captains and sergeants with no practical experience in such matters."

"But," Linet said, "the bravos—"

"Are responsible solely for His Grace's personal safety and defense, no one else's."

"Why are you telling us this?" Eyvind asked with a sinking feeling.

"I think you can guess. Until the court is firmly ensconced in the apparatus of Ayala, we are vulnerable. Rinalda's foreign operative, whom you encountered, is nowhere to be found, though not for lack of looking. Now we must discard any plans they knew of and formulate new ones. I suppose you'd prefer to return home now that your traitor's been dealt with, but I'm forced to invite you to stay with us a bit longer. You clearly have heads on your shoulders. Even if," Essimis glanced at Aerrus, "your mouths don't always follow."

Aerrus looked down at the seal in his hands. "I'll not wear his colors," he warned.

"Certainly not, nor should you presume to be worthy! No, this is a decidedly lower profile role."

The three looked at each other, but only briefly. Eyvind said, "I've got nowhere else to go now, so it's not a hard choice for me."

"Nor me," Linet answered. "We've been hatching some schemes that might bear fruit, if you'll help us." She turned to Aerrus.

He bit his lip and wobbled his head as though deeply weighing his options. "Well. Perrim will be furious, so there's a mark in favor."

"Be serious."

"Fine, fine. Maybe we can convince others with more courage than His Fluffy Grace to help us fight Phynagoras."

"You impertinent…." Essimis huffed, but there was no fire in him now, only fatigue.

"Very well then. To Pelona."

Linet and Eyvind nodded agreement and said together, "To Pelona."

★   ★   ★

The last of the twenty-odd ships were loaded, with Antero supervising the stowage of his alchemy lab and crates of Vrril packed tight with straw and sand. The crates were labeled as 'gardening supplies', for if the porters and ship captains had any notion of what they truly carried they'd have refused outright. Finally King Osmund boarded the royal cog flying his blue and silver banner, trimmed in gold thread to shimmer in the breeze. He was joined by his two-year-old son and heir, three brand-new officers of the court, and Chancellor Essimis.

Eyvind regarded his two companions as they walked side by side up the gangplank. He thought he'd known them well enough, but now he wasn't so certain. Their weapons had indeed been returned to them, including those smuggled in the luggage. Lots of weapons. Aerrus and Linet both wore vicious short swords at one hip and a full quiver of bodkin-tipped arrows at the other, dark recurved bows strung across their backs and a host of razor-sharp knives at each belt. Next to those, pouches bulged with phials of...what? Medicines? Poisons? They wore tunics and split-leg chausses of dull green and brown forest colors, all cut to a close fit with no errant bits to catch or grab, hair trimmed and tied to the same effect. Thus arrayed, there was an air of sheer ferocity about them he'd not appreciated before. Was this who they really were?

The trio stowed their meager gear under a canvas tarp on the topdeck near the king's cabin, and when lines were tied off, sails unfurled and anchors weighed, the city slowly began to drift away from them. Eyvind watched Linet on the bow as she untied the sling holding her arm, trying a few careful, stiff movements. Finding no great pain, she held the fabric aloft and let the wind carry it away. Unbound at last, a tiny smile crept across her lips, and in that moment Eyvind felt perhaps he was truly seeing her for the first time.

And as though in mockery of the tall masts and beams, Rinalda's cross stood yet in the harbor plaza. Amid the bustle and pageantry of a royal peregrination, she died unnoticed and unmourned, and when both spectacles passed the citizens of Carsolan remained, wondering to what fate their king had abandoned them.

PART TWO

CHAPTER NINE

Emperor of Kings

If one could ride on the back of some immense mythical bird as it flew east of Argovan, and summon the nerve to look down on occasion, a stark contrast would be observed as the beast soared across the Edra Mountains. Western winds saturated with warm ocean currents kept the peninsula more or less green and verdant even as the land rose to rocky heights, almost until snow capped the peaks. Afterward, as it fell again, one would now see mostly dusty waste, dotted here and there with patches of scrubland. If this mythical bird could continue flying even farther east without rest, it would cross flatter lowlands where enough water pooled to allow a village or two, though in no manner of luxury. Finally, just before reaching a narrow inland sea, enough fertility could be scraped together to support a city.

It hadn't always been that way. In the past, regular flooding had turned the plain to vast green farmland and Sarpoor the greatest city for two hundred parasangs, or almost five hundred miles as they'd say in Argovan. But shifting weather patterns and centuries of careless overfarming had slowly turned the breadbasket of the Bhasan empire to a semi-arid dust bowl, the floods bringing only erosion and death.

A solitary figure covered head to toe in saffron robes walked the mud-brick streets of that city, dipping and weaving through the hot crush of the crowds and ignoring the cries of junk merchants, the outstretched hands of beggars and that hard gaze of aggressive indifference particular to young men without employment or prospect of it. Though that last would soon be of great use, if he had anything to say about it. The robes were defense against the fierce afternoon sun and not, strictly speaking, a disguise, though they did afford a degree of privacy.

From behind the folds of silk, eyes sparkled with ambition, hazel on the outside and burning green fire near the center. The face that bore them could have belonged to a man of any age between twenty and forty, not classically handsome but effective at inspiring trust, and underestimation. Qualities that had allowed him to conquer this very city and more without a drop of blood being spilled. Such victories always seemed sweeter to his taste, though his generals would balk at such a notion. But as he trod the lanes of his prize, he felt not satisfaction but gnawing hunger for more victories, greater prizes. He glanced westward.

Almost as though in mockery of that thought, the air soured as he passed a livestock pen where pigs fed greedily on a corpse. It had been a harsh summer, and harsh choices had to be made. The sight and smell convinced him even further of the rightness of his course. Hurrying on, he came at last to a steep grade, which decades spent on foot and in the saddle gave him calves powerful enough to mount with ease. He turned and looked down on the city laid out before him, all red and amber clay boxes stacked no higher than two stories. From a distance it looked like some titanic child's toy blocks strewn randomly about. The remains of a stone wall from an age past ringed the central part, and where a river once ran though it was now a fetid trickle of sewage. Yet, it was still the greatest city for two hundred parasangs.

He continued on his way to what had once been called a palace, though repeated sackings had degraded it to being simply the least uninhabitable building in Sarpoor. He strode through the gate and across the gravel courtyard toward the keep. Its current inhabitant, a fool named Amza o Uzaraq, who styled himself King of Sarpoor, came out to meet him with a painted-on smile that always made him want to spit.

"Ah, my friend and lord, welcome back! Welcome, welcome. Did you enjoy your—"

The figure charged past into the keep without stopping or even slowing.

"—walk?" Amza's smile faltered only a fraction as he followed after his guest like a puppy desperate for affection.

The living chambers inside the keep were a bad imitation of the cool colors and sophisticated patterns of Pelona: paint instead of polished stone tile, strips of cloth strung along brick walls instead of gracefully rippling silk pavilions. Cloying perfumes wafted by great slave-powered fans mocked what should have been superior cooling air drafts born of ingenious architecture. Still, by the standards of the city below it was luxury, opulence that magnified rather than eased the crushing poverty surrounding it. The man ignored all this, for there was only one luxury that interested him.

In the center of the chamber's floor was a pool, rimmed with green marble and filled with water from the deepest, coolest well in Sarpoor. He took his robes in one practiced hand and with a few twisting flourishes whipped the garments from his body, tossing them away into the shadows of flickering lamps to leave himself naked and without a trace of modesty. For the first time that day a genuine smile spread across his face as he looked down at his treasure lounging in the water. His treasure looked up behind heavy lashes.

"Hello, my lord Phynagoras," the treasure said.

"Hello, Caerdig," Phynagoras answered with a light sweetness. "Are you enjoying the hospitality of our gracious host?"

"You were gone longer than you said you'd be," the boy replied in a voice both demure and petulant. It was a skill forged from long hours of practice and coaching, tailored and tuned precisely to both soothe and excite Phynagoras's psyche. Nearly every eastern potentate kept at least one catamite, but in Caerdig Phynagoras had found a jewel beyond price. Just the cost of the boy's teachers was greater than the value of some of his conquered kingdoms. He was the embodiment of that which such rulers usually only dreamed of: beautiful, perpetually oiled, stormy-eyed, golden-headed but otherwise hairless.

"Oh, I'm so sorry. I got lost."

The boy laughed and splashed water at Phynagoras as he stepped into the pool that could hold three or four people at once. "Liar, you never get lost!" Phynagoras took Caerdig in his arms, and suddenly all the cares and concerns outside the cool ring of marble melted away.

Later, while Caerdig dozed, Amza tiptoed into the chamber as though he thought he somehow wouldn't be noticed if he approached slowly. "Yes, Amzi," Phynagoras sighed, "what do you want now?"

His host winced at the ridiculous nickname Phynagoras insisted on using. It needled the man, but anyone calling himself king of anything had to be kept on a short leash. "I'm sorry to disturb your, er, relaxation, my lord. But I wanted to inform you of the arrival of another guest. My daughter."

"And?"

"W-well, she has been accounted a great beauty, by some, and I was wondering if you would care for an, uh, introduction?" Amza held his hands out wide in heavy implication.

Phynagoras frowned, his good mood suddenly evaporated. "How many times must I go through this farce? I'm going to say this to you once, Amza. Just once. Every petty baron, bey and siridaar of every worthless dunghill from here to Ghresh thinking themself clever has tried to shove me into the cunnies of their whelps in hopes of joining a royal family which *does not exist*. I presently have sixteen – no, make that seventeen wives, all got by treaty from crushed enemies far more impressive than you, and I've plowed not a one. Nor will I."

Amza quivered in frustration. "But, my lord, think of the future! Surely an heir—"

"Everyone out! Not you, Amzi." Phynagoras stepped out of the pool, careful not to slip on the water he sloshed all over the floor. He maintained the lean muscularity of a panther mostly in order to look the part that he was required to play, for surely should not the

Emperor of Kings be the ideal man in form and deed? Now he adopted also the predatory gaze he'd practiced in the mirror so often, intent on putting this idiot in his place. He glowered at the servants, all trained to remain still and silent as the furniture and unseen until needed. "Out! Now!" The sudden thunder inside the cavernous chamber sent slaves scurrying into the darkness. Caerdig opened one curious eye, hearing by the tone that the order was not meant to include him, and went back to dozing.

"Amzi, Amzi. Sit." He indicated a bench of carved granite next to the pool. Amza sat and pretended not to notice the water soaking his clothes as Phynagoras joined him naked and dripping. "Have you ever heard how I first came to power?"

"I...no, my lord. Porontus is farther south that I've ever—"

"I murdered my father. Well, he was also my uncle, and probably other relations besides. Lots of incest in the family, for all the usual political reasons. I poisoned him. Took a good deal of practice to fool his food tasters, too. Went through a lot of test subjects. Eventually though, I got him. Terrible way to die. I've since accustomed myself to regular small doses of every known poison so I don't suffer the same fate. Now, I didn't hate my father. Didn't love him either, but whatever. I killed him because he committed the one sin I cannot forgive. He never lived up to his full potential, never came close. I knew I could accomplish all *this*, and more besides." He waved his arm in a great circle meant to encompass the whole world. "My father probably couldn't have, but he could've at least made a good go of it. I was intelligent and gifted. I knew I was better. He was in my way, so it was a simple calculation. He had to be removed.

"Now here I am, and here we are. How many times in history has Bhasa conquered Porontus, only to lose it again? The last emperor, whose name I hope remains damned in memory, lost it all. One too many miscalculations and his enemies united just long enough to depose him. Did having a whole legion of heirs stop that? No. Now I rule over it all, with the green fields and forests of Barg-o-Bhanii soon to follow. The difference, my dear satrap, is that I do *not* intend to be dispatched and damned in memory, and certainly not by some intelligent, gifted little shadow of myself that might spring from one of those aforementioned cunnies. I conquer, I drink my wine, I fuck my boys, and beyond that the future can take care of its *own godsdamned self*!"

Amza did not mention his daughter again after that.

★　　★　　★

Phynagoras's army was camped less than a parasang south of Sarpoor. Well, a small part of it was. The tip of the spear. And unlike the chaotic jumble of the city, the camp was a striking marriage of geometry and geography. If one was allowed to approach it, the first sight at eye level would not be any camp at all but a steep, arrow-straight slope of earthwork. Pointed stakes protruded from it at irregular intervals, making it impossible to charge in any numbers, with a wooden palisade lining the top. This high earthen wall formed a large square that enclosed the camp, a stadion long on each side with three breaks in it to allow entry, each gated and guarded. The measurements and proportions of the camp were so precise, the building of it reproduced so exactly wherever the army went, that one could feel at home in any country at any point in Phynagoras's nearly fifteen-year-long campaign of expansion.

Phynagoras now rode through the foremost of the gates, where the earthwork had been sliced away on either side to form sharp triangular walls. He rode not a massive charger nor gaited palfrey as one might expect, but a pack mule. Had any regular ruler done so it would've meant scandal, but Phynagoras understood the minds of common folk, and knew that the gesture would only add to his legend. Caerdig rode next to him on a like animal, dressed in a smaller version of Phynagoras's saffron robes. As they passed through the gates and saluting guards and into the confines of the camp, Phynagoras breathed a slight sigh of relief. The camp was rustic and monotonous, but it was home. No matter how many parasangs they marched or how many petty dictators he subdued, the camp always waited to welcome him, as familiar to his soldiers within as their own mothers. This was their privilege, and for it and for him they would move mountains. Marching over them was as nothing by comparison.

He never grew tired of the sights that greeted him each time he entered the camp: hundreds of tents all in rows, thousands of men here and there drilling or toiling at some task or another with occasional specks of color sprinkled among them indicating women. Some whores, some wives picked up along the way, though over time the latter became more numerous. Camp followers with their workshops and smithies, stables, all the things that one would find in a small town. Except this town could be packed up and on the move in a day and, whether moving five parasangs or five thousand, planted right back down again and nothing changed but the scenery. Such was the discipline of a Phynagorean camp.

"Keep your naked painted berserkers," he said, "your whooping cavalry. Give me a marching, building man and I'll hammer him into a fighting machine. So many battles we've preemptively won just by the sheer terror inspired by the very sight of my machine on the horizon, yes?"

"Yes, my lord," Caerdig said dutifully.

Phynagoras smiled for the second time that day. "Sorry, I was woolgathering again. It happens when a man starts to believe his own myth. Have to be careful of that!"

The mules carried them down the camp's primary thoroughfare. He tossed friendly grins and waves of encouragement to the folk who crossed his path and they were returned a thousandfold. They'd come to him from a dozen nations, spoke a dozen tongues, yet he could flog them, endanger their lives, make them march through muddy fields or sleep in scorpion sands and they'd do it all with a smile, so long as he kept their love and loyalty. So long as they believed he'd lead them to some promised better world they'd invented in their minds. That loyalty couldn't be bought with gold or jewels or slaves, but only with loyalty in return. A lesson so many rulers before him had never learned.

They came to the center of this mobile town, the command tent. A small thing for all its import, Phynagoras's personal living chamber. He dismounted the mule with a short hop, and almost before his feet touched earth an attendant came up to take the reins. "Thank you, Vazzem," Phynagoras said with a nod. The young attendant beamed at the recognition and the sound of his name on his lord's lips. Phynagoras lifted Caerdig with almost no effort and set him down, and the attendant took both animals away to stable.

No guards stood watch outside Phynagoras's tent. He'd ordered it so that all could see he trusted his men and shared their dangers, and sent a message about his expectations of safety within the camp. It also cut down on eavesdropping. He brushed aside the colorful hanging cloth that served as a door, and Caerdig ran ahead into the relative darkness of the tent, knowing from habit exactly where to find the bowl of figs that would undoubtedly be kept full. Inside waited two more allies, one newly won, the other his oldest friend. They had either been discussing or arguing over something, which often amounted to the same thing where General Boras was concerned. Beside that bearded mountain of muscle and bone a comparatively slight woman sat, looking for all the world like a coiled serpent ready to spring.

"Cassilda, you've joined us at last! How does my newest general find our little campsite?"

The woman rose from the folding chair and faced him. If Phynagoras had felt any attraction to women, he supposed his cock would be rising, and quickly. Her wild red hair framed an elfin face almost as pretty as Caerdig's, her tightly fitting hide clothing accentuating strong hips and legs. He'd heard legends of these warrior women that claimed they sliced off one of their breasts so as not to interfere with the shooting of the horn-and-sinew bows they used. It was a ridiculous notion that she very prominently debunked. The display had no effect on him but it might on Boras, something he made a mental note to keep an eye on in the future.

"It reeks of shit and ball sweat," Cassilda replied. "You've been squatting here for an entire season, and it shows. And don't call me general."

"Ah, yes, I'm sorry, I forgot. Force of habit. Of course your mounted archers would make an ill fit to our marching hedgerows. The Bhasans say your people are known as Haiads. Is this accurate?"

The woman smirked. "Close enough. In our tongue it is *Hoeorbhadhae*. It means 'man-slayers', but I won't expect you to pronounce it."

"Thank the gods for small favors. As for the camp's aroma, think of it as the aging of an exquisite cheese. An action such as we're planning must be timed perfectly. In fact, thanks to the most recent in the long line of incompetents I must deal with, the schedule is moving up. We march across the mountains very soon, I promise."

"Good. If we remain idle neighbors much longer, I fear my girls may start impregnating some of your men out of sheer boredom. But, what in the nether hells is a *cheese*?" Phynagoras briefly described the process of cheese making, and Cassilda's expression grew increasingly revolted. "Disgusting! I feel as if I may need to vomit. Why did I ever agree to join you barbarians on this fool's quest in the first place?"

"I believe, my wildflower of the steppe, it was something about a Ghreshi zamindar torching your grazelands after you castrated one of his sons. And hordes of plague-ridden rodents suspiciously devouring what little was left shortly thereafter?"

Cassilda flipped her fiery tresses over one shoulder and shrugged. "Oh, that's right. Well, the little bugger deserved it. There's no grazeland here though. If we don't move soon—"

"Five days, my dear. Then we set out and we don't stop until we see the forests of Barg-o-Bhanii, Argovan as the locals call it. As the way is cleared, more will follow. Whole nations, and more than enough land for your horses."

"I still don't understand why so small a force though. How many fighting men do you have gathered here?"

"Five hazaras," Boras answered, his voice deep and rumbling.

"Only five thousand men? Why not go over the mountains with all you can, hit them as hard as possible as fast as possible, like we horse warriors do?"

"Why? Well...."

"Oh, here we go," Boras said, eyes rolling. "I done heard this story a hundred times—"

"But Cassilda hasn't," Phynagoras said. "Don't complain, you come out of it looking far better than I do." He sat across from the woman and poured them fresh cups of the local cherry wine.

"It was my first expedition as king of Porontus. I was sixteen, lean and beautiful as you are, or so I choose to recall. And vain. Oh, I thought I was a little god then! I picked as the first feather in my peacock cap the principality of a distant cousin whose lands lay near Thazov. I mustered every man I could find, and a few women too. Any who could hold a weapon. I put all the pikes and swords I had in their hands and when those ran out, spades and pickaxes. I blundered off to claim my victory. I wanted to hit them as hard as possible as fast as possible.

"We got about halfway there when the food ran out. Then the water started going. We picked the countryside clean and still it wasn't enough. Then the sickness began. I myself caught dysentery, and for the first time in my life considered the very real, terrifying possibility of my own mortality. Hard to believe, coming from a family known chiefly for murder, but whatever. I half expected Boras to lead a mutiny against me."

"Perish the thought, lord!" Boras chuckled, then drained half his cup in one go.

"Well, I wouldn't have blamed you. Of course if you'd failed I'd have had you impaled on a spike through your arsehole and out your mouth."

"Of course." Boras nodded.

"Sick, starving and surrounded by a country that quite understandably hated us, and not even halfway to our goal. After pawning all my gold yet developing a golden *tongue* out of necessity, we limped back home, humiliated. And the hell of it was, I knew I could've beaten my enemy with a fifth of the men I had, if I'd only planned it better. But I had no training in logistics, nor had Boras in those days. I'd raised him straight from the ranks as reward for helping me get the kingship."

"But," Cassilda said, "didn't you have other advisers, officers that knew—"

"Well, we *did*," Boras said with a grimace, "but...."

"In Porontus a sudden change of administration traditionally includes a certain, er, purgative period," Phynagoras explained. "I executed the old generals loyal to my father perhaps a touch too enthusiastically."

"Don't worry," Boras said, "I done studied up on the subject of logistics since then."

"Yet the worst defeat of all came after we returned home in shame. My intended enemy, that distant cousin, heard of my abortive expedition and sent ten cartloads of lemons to me. 'To aid in your recovery after your recent illness', he said. Lemons are for scurvy, not dysentery, but whatever. I swore never to make a mistake like that again. I spent two years doing nothing but studying and drilling along with what men I had left. When I set out again, I repaid my cousin's little joke. With interest."

"Had 'im impaled on a spike through his arsehole and out his mouth!" Boras howled with laughter.

"That is why 'only' five thousand men. It's a long march even before the mountains, and they're enough to my purpose."

"But," said Cassilda with a worried frown, "why not take ships and invade the southern coast? Much though I loathe sea travel, surely—"

"It would be an easier journey, yes. But the welcome would not be so warm. I have a traitor on the other side of those mountains ready to go over to me, and a castle. Better a hard march with a friend at the end of it than the other way round. And as I said, more will come once we take both northern and southern coasts and widen the cracks. And more, and more, until I wet my feet on the marshy shores of the Western Ocean."

Cassilda nodded sharply. "All right, Emperor of Barbarians. Five days." The barest hint of threat wafted through the stale air, then the unspoken understandings that always exist between leaders signaled that the meeting was over. Phynagoras drew back the cloth just in time for Cassilda to stride through into the sunlight as Boras admired her hindquarters.

They remained in silence for a few moments after as Caerdig munched on figs in the corner of the tent and read some book or other. When the crunch of Cassilda's boots on the gravelly ground faded completely, Boras let out a growl of contempt. "Uppity bitch. She dares call *you* barbarian?"

"Everyone's a barbarian to someone, Boras. Don't take it personally."

"I liked that 'general' bit, though. You forgot? I'll eat my boot if you done forgot a thing since we left Porontus."

"You know how I like to needle new faces a bit, see how much they'll swallow."

"Hmph. I don't think that one's *swallowed* anything in her life. So, how was the city?"

"As I expected," Phynagoras replied, "it's a seething, stinking, steaming pile of desperation. It's perfect for us. When we go, many will follow after. Added to those already with us, we'll have Barg-o-Bhanii completely settled with loyal subjects in a year's time. Then on to the next target."

"Which is?"

Phynagoras smiled for the third time. "You'd never believe me if I told you. You won't until it's upon us, so I'll save it as a surprise. But I've already sent the order to put things into action."

"Ha! Don't know whether to be excited or terrified. Anyway, there's a dispatch arrived for you, here. It weren't marked urgent so I didn't bother tracking you down." Boras handed over a folded piece of vellum sealed with blue wax but bearing no stamp.

"Hmm. From one of my many pairs of eyes. More bad news?" He broke the seal and scanned the few short lines, frowning. "No shortage of irritations from that country. First Armino lets a spy escape, forcing us to accelerate the timetable, and now our own asset at the court of their pathetic excuse for a king has been exposed. Apparently she was crucified in dramatic fashion after a failed assassination attempt."

"That's creative," Boras said, finishing off his second cup of wine.

"What a waste. She took years to cultivate! And Osmund has run off to Pelona. Predictable. Let's activate one of our assets there, see if we can still prick him whilst he's running scared."

"I'll get right on it, m'lord."

"That'll be all, then."

Boras bowed deeply and left the tent as Phynagoras swallowed back a mild wave of heartburn. It was more unsettling than he'd let on, this loss of Rinalda, but there was too much to do in the coming days to let it slow things down. He eyed Caerdig as he finished off his figs. "Were you paying attention to any of that?"

The boy put down his book, looked up at him through golden bangs and nodded. "To all of it."

"And what did you think of our new friend Cassilda? Beautiful, isn't she?"

Caerdig frowned. "I don't trust her, and you shouldn't."

Phynagoras let out a guffaw. "No? Whatever could possibly make you say that?"

"She doesn't believe."

"Believe?"

"In you. Anyone who doesn't believe in you betrays you. Then they die."

A slight chill ran down Phynagoras's spine. "My sweet, perhaps you shouldn't pay *quite* so much attention to things."

★   ★   ★

A day before the expedition was to depart, and the scramble to pack up the entire marching camp was at its most fevered, the plans were interrupted by the unlikely sight of Amza o Uzaraq storming up to the main gates and demanding entry. Behind him two of his own guards dragged a despondent-looking fellow clearly belonging to Phynagoras's legion. The soldiers manning the gate detained him until Phynagoras himself could be brought, and he arrived wearing a look of extreme irritation. It was an expression that only deepened when he saw the cause of the interruption.

"Amzi, in case you hadn't noticed I'm more than a little busy at the moment. What do you – Vazzem?"

Amza nodded sharply, and motioned for the captive to be dragged forth and dumped between the two men's feet. "Yes, I see you recognize him. This is good, it will make things easier."

"What is the meaning of this?"

"This *vagh do-tsvegh* was caught last night in the city, stealing from my already meager stores. Wine, olives, cheese. Since you have assured me that surrendering Sarpoor would prevent any pillaging, I have brought him to you." Amza said that last part conspicuously loudly, so that all might hear the cause of the disturbance and remind every ear of his conqueror's promise.

With an apparently genuine look of shock, Phynagoras knelt to look the attendant in the eye. "Vazzem? Is this true?"

The man wept openly, blubbering and dripping slobber and tears into the dusty earth. "Lord, I...."

"Answer me. Is it?"

Vazzem squeezed his eyes shut and nodded weakly. "Y-yes, my lord. I'm...so sorry...."

"But *why*? We were leaving here. I was about to give you the whole world!" Phynagoras was aware of a thousand pairs of eyes on him, and suddenly knew how this must play out. He felt a wave of sadness at it, but the sense of inevitability was stronger still. He was only a player, and the ending was foreordained.

"I..." Vazzem whimpered, "I was just, so envious. We live on hard tack and vinegar, and the city had so much more. It seemed so wrong...."

"Vazzem, I gave my word. Sarpoor yielded to me, and I gave it my protection. Who were you to violate it? You wound me, my friend.

And what of your comrades in arms, who've pledged their very lives to my cause? You wound them too. I loved you like a brother. How could you do this to me?" He said it gently, but clearly and loudly enough that the words would be heard and repeated in the camp and eventually in the city.

"My lord, please. Forgive...."

Phynagoras turned to Boras, who stood a few paces behind him. A look between them born of long comradeship said all that needed to be said. Boras drew a long kindjal dagger and pressed it into Phynagoras's hand. He turned back to Vazzem. Drawing the man shaking to his feet, Phynagoras in turn forced the blade into Vazzem's hand. "Here. If you would harm me, as you've harmed all your brethren, at least do it openly. Here!" Phynagoras threw his head back, exposing his bare throat in a dramatic display. "Strike now, strike true! Don't dishonor me further by doing it behind my back!"

Behind him, Phynagoras heard Cassilda approach, heard her sharp gasp before being silenced by Boras. "What! What is this—?"

Vazzem's hand shook, the sun glinting wildly off the blade as tears fell. Phynagoras gave the man a look of intimate sympathy. "Vazzem, you know what you have to do."

Vazzem looked down at the dagger, back at Phynagoras. In one jagged motion he raised the weapon, and slashed open his own throat. Blood gushed and everyone around gave a shout of shock. Except for Phynagoras himself, and Boras. Vazzem fell forward into Phynagoras's waiting arms, and he embraced the dying man. "I forgive you, brother. I forgive you. Be at peace now."

Vazzem finally collapsed to the ground, a pool of red spreading outward. Phynagoras was covered in blood, and stood before Amza with arms outstretched. "I trust this discharges the quarrel between us."

Amza nodded, quivering. His face was almost green. "Y-yes, lord. Justice has been...satisfied."

Phynagoras called out to the guards gathered all around, though not to any one in particular. "This man's offense has been forgiven.

He is redeemed! Bear him away with honor." Phynagoras turned away without another word and marched to his command tent as soldiers and camp followers alike stared in wonder.

Inside, Caerdig was packing his few belongings for the expedition, and started in wide-eyed shock at seeing Phynagoras in his blood-drenched garments. "It's not mine," Phynagoras said quickly before motioning to a waiting servant. "Dispose of these," he said while undressing. But as the clothes were about to be taken away, he held up a halting hand. "Wait. Vazzem has suffered...an unfortunate accident. Have these placed upon his funeral pyre."

Boras and Cassilda barged into the tent while Phynagoras rummaged through his baggage for new clothes. "What in the nether hells was *that*?" Cassilda demanded.

"Sorry, lord," Boras said apologetically. "I tried to stop her, but—"

"It's all right, Boras. That, my dear, was the meting out of justice in my camp. I can't have thieves, even among conquerors."

"That's not what I mean. How did you make that man take his own life? Only black magic has that kind of power—"

"It is black magic," Phynagoras said, pulling a fresh tunic over his head, "of the worst sort. I'm no mere emperor of barbarians, Cassilda. I'm a *messiah*. Do you know that word?"

"No," she answered. "What does it mean?"

Phynagoras gave an evil grin. "It means I'm wrapped up in a myth greater than myself, as much as my followers are. It's an insidious drug to be sure. No doubt it'll destroy me one day, but while I yet hold the reins I intend to use that myth to my own purposes. And my gods but it's one hells of a drug!"

★　　★　　★

At long last the marching camp, with its tents, shops, animals and wagons, was packed up and made ready to move. A long snake of soldiers, beasts of burden, baggage and followers spilled out of the place with Phynagoras and Boras at its head. Several thousand spectators had come from Sarpoor to observe the sight, and many to join it. Cassilda's mounted women, the Haiads, broke their own camp just next to the square earthwork to take up positions on the forward flanks, giving an even more snake-like impression if our previously mentioned mythical bird were to spy it from far above. Though depilated of its spears, the earthen wall would remain standing for years to come, marking it out as one of those places either blessed or cursed by the advent of the adventurer-despot. Some previous such sites had become shrines to his cult. Others had been left too depopulated to be used for much of anything.

Cassilda sidled up to Phynagoras's mount on her powerful steppe horse, once his guard let her through its protective ring. He was dressed in searing white linen with bands of gold worked through it so that he shone like the sun. She looked with light disdain on the special saddle crafted to hold both him and his catamite just in front of him. "So, in truth a boy leads this grand adventure?"

Phynagoras tossed her a faint grin. "Oh, I never considered that. I like it, makes for a good line of the legend."

"But not on a donkey this time."

"Certainly not, it's almost a hundred and fifty parasangs to the mountains. Sometimes, substance must take precedence over style. Not to worry though, you can see we've picked up more than a few true believers from Sarpoor."

"Yes," said Cassilda, glancing back at the growing train of aimless souls latching on to the expedition like seaweed caught in a shark's tail. "And how many of those will die on the way?"

"Quite a few, I imagine," Phynagoras said casually. "It's mostly desert, and the Edra Mountains are no easy passage. But they've little to live for anyway, and those who survive will consider themselves blessed by the gods, by fortune, and by me. They'll be all the more loyal because of it."

Cassilda laughed involuntarily. "Your mind moves in strange directions, I'll give you that."

"And speaking of loyalty, there's one little something I forgot." Phynagoras reached into a pouch strapped to the saddle, rooted around in it before drawing something small and shiny. A ring. "A silly gesture, but gestures can be quite powerful. I require it of all who serve me, or serve with me. I'll let you decide which you are." He put the ring on his little finger and extended it out toward Cassilda. He held his hand remarkably steady amid the horse's bouncing gait. It was a silver ring with his sigil worked in carnelian intaglio: a rearing stag and a man with the head of a panther facing each other, and a small starburst in between.

Cassilda almost laughed again when she realized what he was demanding. "You seriously want me to—?"

"Yes. Now." Suddenly the friendly, jocular manner was gone from him, and his voice cut sharp as an icicle and carried the promise of imminent death should he be defied. Caerdig turned his head just the tiniest bit toward the woman. He said nothing but his eyes were wrenched as far in her direction as he could manage without making it obvious. Boras, on the other hand, stared at her openly, his hand moving toward the long dagger at his hip.

Without further argument, though the look on her face made it clear she burned to disobey, Cassilda leaned over and touched the ring with her lips. Making it a light, perfunctory gesture was the most rebellion she dared, but no matter. It was done, and all had seen it done. Boras's hand went back to the reins, and Cassilda rode away without another word.

The tension melted away, and Boras grunted. "She didn't like that, not one bit."

Phynagoras shrugged while he put the ring away. "I am profoundly unconcerned with what she likes. She did it, that's what matters. Are you satisfied, my little adviser?"

Caerdig looked up at Phynagoras, unconvinced. "I still don't trust her. She did it too easily."

"Ye gods, you are the most suspicious creature! And I love you for it." Phynagoras kissed the boy on the head as he urged his mount faster. "We're underway now, Boras. Let's make some distance on this flat ground. Send the order back!"

The massive expedition headed by a child increased its pace, obedient to the command all the way from the front to the very rear.

CHAPTER TEN

Something To Get Used To

One aspect of sea travel that most land-bound don't count on is the unending routine. It wasn't uncommon for travelers to go a bit stir-crazy even on short voyages, and the trip from Carsolan to Ayala was anything but short. Eyvind didn't mind as much, still enjoying the experience of not running or fighting for his life nor looking over his shoulder for traitors' knives.

He did suffer from terrible seasickness, which reached its worst just as the fleet began rounding the swampy gulf coast of western Argovan known affectionately as the Bastard Child of Earth and Sea, or just the Bastard. As Linet's arm continued to heal, her mood improved, and she used what open space there was to distract Eyvind from the nausea by teaching him the basics of archery. He'd never have the physique for the heavy warbows some armies used, whose years of training warped the bones of archers, but hers was a finer, precision weapon. His first, fumbling attempts at hitting a target only yards away atop a pitching deck did him little credit, but it did take his mind off the seasickness. And he couldn't deny enjoying the company.

Aerrus and Essimis played game after game of castra, and when Aerrus finally managed to win one he made sure the whole ship knew. King Osmund rarely left his cabin thanks to his own seasickness, but little Prince Pharamund proved very popular with the crew, a kind of good-luck mascot.

On the twenty-ninth day under sail they awoke earlier than usual, the sky under which they'd slept still mostly night-blue but for a furious slash of pink fire along the eastern horizon. It had been a long crossing, weeks of boredom, and every soul watched for some sign of their destination. The rumble of the crew rousing about them carried an undercurrent of expectation they hadn't experienced since they'd set out from Carsolan. That excitement had borne the flavor of a journey's beginning, while this one was of its conclusion. No rest for the weary though, for as soon as they made port the crew's work would only just be begun, so an early rise was the order of the day.

Eyvind yawned, shook away the remnants of sleep still clinging to his skull, wandered forward and leaned against the stempost. Ahead and on either side other ships of the fleet sailed, the men atop each mast exchanging crude jokes over the distances via lantern flicker. He'd already learned the flash signal for 'your mother'.

As dawn began its course and the sky slowly caught fire, a razor-fine line chalked out along the horizon in brilliant white stretching east and west without end. He stood and watched for...how long? Ten minutes, twenty? An hour? There was no one instant when he could say he saw any change in the scene, but by the time he was conscious of Aerrus and Linet standing next to him the line was a definite coast, full of beaches, islets, coves. In the distance loomed the shrouded outline of mountains, and in stark contrast before them the unmistakable lines of a city. Ayala.

"Oh, at last," said Aerrus. "I was beginning to feel gills growing on my neck."

Since Ayala was Ólo's sister city straight across the Bay, Eyvind assumed it would look similar: another place of wormy wood and red brick, of fish and fog. He was terribly mistaken. The searing buildings spread out like a field of white diamonds from one end of the gulf to the other, low and wide and occasionally capped with blue or green domes. Nothing of wood or thatch could be seen, though they were still a mile or so off. The only structures higher than three stories were the harbor lighthouses and the towers of the queen's palace. The palace was covered in some polished opalescent stone that broke the sunlight into a wild rainbow, and dominated the landscape such that the path of the shadow cast by its sharp central spire turned the whole city into an enormous sundial. There were tiny patches of flora around the edges – olive groves, he thought – that quickly gave way to red sands.

As they approached, he became aware of something even more unusual – the smell. Or more precisely, the *lack* of smell. Every port carried the stink of fish, salt and rot that was so omnipresent it overwhelmed even the closer odors of a sailing ship. Every port, it seemed, except Ayala. It smelled *clean*. Aerrus and Linet, for all their sylvan cynicism, seemed to share his sentiment.

The last mile of their voyage saw the sea beneath them change from wine-dark to blue-green, then to brilliant turquoise as sails were struck and oars rowed them into the harbor. The trio stood gawking in open amazement at the colors the water took, most of which they'd never even imagined, let alone seen.

Essimis appeared behind them, smiling thinly at the reactions of his young companions. "Well, what do you think? You only get to see Ayala for the first time once."

"I—" Linet started, then faltered. "I think…after all the dark business behind us, I'd forgotten what hope felt like. Until just now."

The chancellor's smile widened. "My dear, you do have a way with words when you so choose."

The ship moved in slowly to keep the low-sitting cog from striking the seabed, and they had time to take in the city more fully up close. The buildings were common stone and clay, but each one had been painted with some sort of gypsum sand, giving even the most humble structures an ethereal shimmer. In the two-mile-wide harbor, a multitude gathered either to watch the spectacle of the fleet's arrival or to labor in its unloading. Ships and boats of all types crowded the ports, some flying flags of countries so far away their names couldn't be pronounced in either the Argovani or Pelonan tongues. Both of these and other languages could be heard as workers shouted and ran about their business with a vitality that made even Carsolan seem a lethargic, provincial backwater. Beyond them, suntanned citizens crowded markets and warehouses, or just hid from the heat under colorful silken canopies.

The cog slowed to an idle drift just before the dock. It was no different from many of the other vessels of the fleet except for being slightly larger, sitting lower in the water, and the dozen armed men peppering the deck. Just when it seemed as if it would drift into the pier and cause a catastrophic collision, the maneuvering oars thrust into the water and brought the ship to a startling halt. Then the foremost oars on either side whipped upward, pivoting toward the sky. The second pair did the same an instant later, then the third and so on to give the effect of a wooden wave passing stem to stern.

"Spectacle in everything," Aerrus said with a chuckle. "Give 'em that and they'll dash themselves on a forest of pikes for you."

"A bedrock principle of kingship," Essimis confirmed. Lines cast by sailors were caught by their fellows on the pier. A few strong heaves and the whole cog was turned sideways. A wide, reinforced plank flew over the starboard side and was quickly pounded into place with wooden pegs. "Now," Essimis said, hand clasped behind his back like he was a lecturing academic, "as of this moment you are emissaries of His Grace. Please try to at least *act* the part. Come with me."

They were among the first to debark, after a score of bravos and lesser guards who'd traveled with them. The honor guard formed a line out from the gangplank, projecting into the quay and clearing gawking Pelonans from the area. Where spectacle failed to disperse them, pole weapons succeeded, until the area all around the cog was clear. Essimis took up a position at the end of the double line. Eyvind stood to his left, and then finally Linet and Aerrus, once again kitted out in all their sharp and pointies. Wedged in between such wielders of power both politic and lethal, Eyvind felt particularly ineffectual, even with his badge displayed on his chest.

Two final bravos appeared and unrolled a burgundy carpet down the plank before taking their place in the line. All fell deathly still, and even the din of the city beyond seemed to recede until crying seagulls and the flapping of banners were the only sounds. When Eyvind's knees began to ache from standing, Osmund emerged. He walked slowly, as though recently recovered from illness, his head a little bowed under the weight of his crown. He wore some light, silken finery that seemed to be an attempt to imitate Pelonan fashion without much success. Next to him the toddler prince wore a miniature version of the same clothing, turning his head every which way and mesmerized by the strange and new sights, smiling with the unreserved delight of a child, not ill or fearful at all.

As the pair descended the plank, Essimis stepped forward to meet them. Where the plank met the white stone blocks of the quay, he knelt in a grand gesture. "Your Grace."

"Gods, it's hot," Osmund said without ceremony. "I suppose that's something we'll have to get used to."

"No doubt Your Grace will find the palace of Queen Synophae more welcoming," Essimis replied, rising slowly.

"That remains to be seen. Where is the old bat, anyway? Wasn't she supposed to meet us?"

Essimis nodded. "We're a bit ahead of schedule, sir. I can see her train approaching now." He turned and pointed to a line of horses and carriages in the distance, already snaking out from the palace toward the harbor. "If Your Grace wishes to remain aboard ship until then—"

"No! Not a moment longer. Let's get this over with, the heat is already—"

"*Look out!*"

The shout had come from one of the bravos standing next to Osmund.

"What the devil—?" Osmund staggered back in confusion. The man who'd shouted threw himself at the king, and in that instant no one knew whether to stop him or join him. In the next instant he jerked and exhaled sharply as he fell to his knees.

"Your Gra...."

Eyvind didn't need to see the bolt buried in the bodyguard's back to know what had just happened, nor did Aerrus or Linet. They all three burst forward past the honor guard.

"Down!" Aerrus screamed.

"*Essimis, get them down!*" Linet repeated, whipping her bow from her shoulder. The chancellor obeyed, instinctively covering the king and prince with his own body, his old bones afire in painful protest.

A second bolt tore through the air where Osmund had just been standing, and as they all fell together it grazed along Essimis's back. It had been no more than five seconds between shots. This time Eyvind had seen where it had come from. "There!" he cried, pointing up at a window on the third floor of a nearby building, a warehouse of some kind. Through it a shadowy figure could be seen scrambling away into darkness.

Without thinking, Linet nocked an arrow, but when she tried to draw it a lightning bolt of pain seared through her not-quite-healed arm, and she nearly dropped the weapon. "Aaargh!" While bravos swarmed the king and pandemonium gripped the dock, Aerrus took off toward the warehouse, and Eyvind moved to follow. Linet tossed her bow to him. "Go!" He caught it running as he passed.

A narrow stair clung to the outside of the building. After kicking in the third-story door, Aerrus shoved an arrow from his quiver into Eyvind's hand and plunged into the darkness beyond. Eyvind followed, but couldn't see more than a few feet in front of him. A shaft of light shot through the place through the open window, under which lay a discarded crossbow. The room was crammed with boxes, sacks and crates stacked high, cargo from a hundred points of origin bound for a thousand destinations.

Aerrus still had his bow slung from his back but his sword drawn. He held up a staying hand and put a finger to his lips. He pointed to a dull light on the far side of the room – another window shuttered with thin paper, the only other exit. *Still in here*, he mouthed, *somewhere*. Eyvind nodded his understanding.

They strained to hear breathing, see any movement of shadow, something among the labyrinth of goods. Aerrus crept silently forward on the balls of his feet, careful not to reveal his own location to the assassin. He motioned for Eyvind to stay where he was and cover both him and the exits. Eyvind suddenly wished he knew their more precise sign language. Aerrus moved up, disappeared behind crates before reappearing seconds later. Using a weaving pattern, he inspected much of the floor space in little time. Eyvind's eyes darted back and forth between him, the stairs and the window, while his pounding heart threatened to drown out the very sounds he listened for.

Drip.

Eyvind froze. It was a soft sound, just a little tap that barely stood out from the growing commotion outside, but there was no doubt of it. *Ahead, and…a bit to the right?* He scanned for any space in that direction obscured from his view…*there.* Three crates high, and beside it a pallet with tall barrels lashed together. He held his breath to hear again.

Drip.

Sweat hitting the floorboards, and not his own. Eyvind waved to get Aerrus's attention, then pointed to the pile. Aerrus nodded, crouched, and advanced on the spot like a stalking predator.

Less than a yard away, Aerrus stepped on a loose floorboard and it creaked. An instant later he dove out of the way of a bolt slicing through the dark, barely avoiding impalement. Stealth was broken like a thunderclap, and a lithe figure exploded from behind the pallet, tossing away a second crossbow. Eyvind raised Linet's bow and let fly at the dark blur. It wasn't a bad shot but still a clean miss. Their prey took a desperate leap straight at the shuttered window. There was a crash of soft wood and ripping paper followed immediately by a fresh arc of sunlight that blinded them.

Aerrus took up the chase again, pausing only to make sure he wasn't about to fall to his death before diving through the window as well. "Come on!" Eyvind slung the bow over his shoulder and shambled after. The window opened onto the roof of an adjacent building. A vast white maze of them seemed to cover much of Ayala in unbroken paths, another whole city atop the one at ground. Even up here people lounged and market stalls hawked wares. Already yards away, Aerrus tore after their increasingly distant quarry.

They raced through the rooftops of the city, at times leaping from one structure to another across narrow alleyway canyons, occasionally drawing dirty looks from the inhabitants. At some point Eyvind became aware of someone following them from the ground. He risked a glance downward, and out of the corner of his eye saw Linet keeping pace, weaving through all manner of traffic, tracking their progress.

A wider chasm opened up before him, and his clumsy leap came up just short. He slammed against the ledge of the roof ahead, ignoring the agony of the corner's impact on his belly while he grappled for a handhold. But he was exhausted thanks to the many weeks of forced inactivity, and hadn't the strength to pull himself up. As he was about to drop two stories to the hard ground, a pair of hands reached out and grabbed him by the wrists. Aerrus dragged him onto the rooftop. "Thanks," Eyvind breathed.

They stood casting about furiously, but the assassin had disappeared. "Dammit," Aerrus growled, "lost him!" Then, from below they heard a shrill whistle cut through the city's hum. In the heat-shimmering distance Linet pointed and gestured wildly. *That way.* They ran once more.

The assassin had dropped down to the roofs of single-story buildings, and now they followed easily, watching from above. Perhaps thinking himself escaped, the killer slowed, looking about for any sign of pursuit. Eventually he came to a place hemmed in by higher walls, and they knew they had him.

"Stay here," Aerrus said, handing Eyvind another arrow. "I want this one alive, but take the shot if things go bad." Before Eyvind could protest his lack of skill, Aerrus leaped with catlike grace down onto an awning, rolled, and dropped to the lower level of roofs. *How does he do that?* Eyvind wondered. *I'd break my legs if I tried.*

The assassin turned around as he realized his mistake, and they got their first good look at their prey: a slight figure clad in tight, light-gray fabric that could blend into either shadows or sunlight with ease. A matching hood that hid all but the eyes was drenched in perspiration. No weapons that they could see. Not quite identical to Rinalda's outfit, but similar enough that Eyvind wondered just how many assassins Phynagoras would throw at them while risking nothing himself.

Aerrus now had his own bow drawn with an arrow nocked and ready. He crept forward deliberately. When the assassin saw him he froze.

"Give it up! You're cornered! There's nowhere left to run. Now you just—"

The assassin surprised even Aerrus with the jump, latching on to a second-floor windowsill of one of the high walls, then immediately leaping up again to the upper roofs. Aerrus sent an arrow after, but the moving target avoided it. Deciding this qualified as things going bad, Eyvind took his shot, to even less effect. He found himself face to face with the killer. Alone.

Silently they squared off, mere feet from each other, each watching the other for any movement, any threat, any opportunity. The assassin took a step to the right. Eyvind matched it. Half a step forward, half a step back. Time seemed to stretch interminably as Eyvind sweated buckets onto the sun-baked rooftop. The assassin dove at him, and they grappled, clawing, twisting, spinning to try and throw the other down. Closer to the ledge, closer, then....

As Eyvind felt the last of his strength sap away once more, the assassin jerked. Eyes wide, they both looked down to see an arrow lodged in the assassin's groin, shot from an impossible angle. The killer collapsed.

Looking behind him and down, he saw that Aerrus had climbed atop the awning to get some height, then sent his arrow up and *between Eyvind's feet* to strike its target. His head swam at the closeness of the shot, or perhaps it was sunstroke. Now it was Aerrus who seemed the clumsy one in comparison, scrambling back up to join Eyvind where the assassin had almost flown. He tore off the sweaty mask to reveal a thin, wiry fellow with the ruddy features of eastern Bhasa. It wasn't Rinalda's agent, the one they'd seen in Carsolan, but some other.

Aerrus drew his short sword. "Talk," he spat, breathing heavily.

"Talk and you may yet live." Even then the assassin raised his fist in defiance. No, not defiance. They watched in horror as he shoved something into his mouth. A swallow, and a sneering smile. Then they understood.

"Poison!" Eyvind exclaimed. They punched the assassin in the stomach to force him to vomit, but it was no use. Already his face was turning demonic colors, his breathing labored. Yellow foam erupted from his mouth, and the killer was no more, taking whatever secrets he held into whatever hell awaited him.

CHAPTER ELEVEN

What We're Fighting

News of the brazen attack reached Queen Synophae's retinue before she reached the harbor, but rather than turn back to the palace out of caution, it surged forward ever faster. Finally a host of bronze-skinned soldiers in glimmering green and gold armor spilled out across the docks, pole weapons flashing in the sun, and commoners shouting either to make way or in indignation at being shoved aside. The rhythm of the soldiers' hobnailed sandals set the docks to tremble as they formed a ring around King Osmund's ship, double-time.

By the time Linet, Aerrus and Eyvind made it back, the crush was so great that they could barely get within earshot of the ship, and that only thanks to the king's badges they carried. "Let us through!" Aerrus shouted, holding the safe conduct high and hoping the foreigners recognized it. "In the name of King Osmund, let us the hells through!"

From a distance they saw a statuesque, middle-aged woman in fabulous shimmering silks step from a gilded carriage and toward the ship. The queen, no doubt. Instead of a crown of gold, she wore an elaborate headdress decorated with a hundred different colors of peacock feathers and beads of opal, malachite and lapis lazuli. Half a step behind her a tall, craggy-faced Marzahni wearing a finer set of armor kept pace while frowning and grumbling orders. The Pelonan soldiers both formed a protective cocoon around her and parted before her like the waves before a surging galley. They and Osmund's bravos glowered at each other with suspicion.

At last the trio fought their way close enough to get the attention of one of the bravo captains, the big Cynuvik. "What's happened?"

Eyvind demanded, waving his badge about as well to avoid a spear to the face for his trouble. "Is the king...?"

The captain nodded, frowning. "Aye, His Grace lives, and the prince. The king has retired to his cabin, and refuses to come out until Essimis assures him all is safe. The sandcrab queen is with him."

Linet looked about in confusion. "Essimis? Where—?"

The captain pointed with his halberd. The chancellor lay facedown on the dockside, breathing weakly and his skin a sickly pallor. A thin line of red ran across his back. Beside him the bravo who'd intercepted the first shot lay motionless, the bolt still buried in him. "Poisoned. It was just a graze, but who knows how bad it is. The king's doctor is tending to His Grace, but...." He shrugged.

"So Essimis won't be assuring anyone of anything at all," Aerrus growled. "Get that doctor out here now!"

"I don't take no orders from—"

"It's all right, Captain Eimar," came a weak voice. Osmund emerged once more, white-faced, to descend the gangplank, looking about nervously. He was escorted – no, carried more like – by Synophae, the 'sandcrab queen'. Up close they could see she must've been beautiful in her youth, still was in fact. Added to that a calm strength that men would still clamber over each other to die for. She held Osmund tightly by the arm lest he begin to faint, though from a distance it would seem that it was he that escorted her, with her hulking Marzahni still close behind.

Osmund regarded his newest officers once again with something like a mixture of wonder and mild disdain. "My doctor is now free to tend to the chancellor, gods save him. The queen has...apprised me of the situation. Tell me, how many times must I owe you my life?"

Being in the presence of so much royal power at once, Eyvind actually forgot to kneel, though no one noticed. "Your Grace," he said, "we chased the assassin down, had him cornered, but...."

"He took poison," Aerrus finished. "Killed himself rather than be taken. The kind of determination that implies...." He shook his head in wonderment.

"Yes," Osmund nodded, "there'll be time to discuss that. For now we must get the prince, and Essimis, to a safer location."

"To the palace," Queen Synophae said in heavily accented Argovani that lost nothing of her iron will in translation. "This cowardly act here in my city shames me, and I must make amends. If Phynagoras thinks to confuse and divide us, he has this day done the opposite!"

★ ★ ★

"Will he live?"

The doctor could only spread empty hands wide at the question. "Only time will answer that, Your Grace." Essimis lay in semi-consciousness on a cot in the palace's infirmary, a host gathered about him with a thousand different questions unanswered. The doctor poked and prodded the red, swollen wound, hoping it would give him some insight. It didn't, even with the help of his learned Pelonan colleagues. "The wound is consistent with various snake venoms from the east, but also with certain plant-based poisons. It may be a decoction to fell the victim with multiple ailments at once, taking no chances. I've cleaned the wound as well as may be done. If the chancellor's will to live is strong, he may pull through. If not...."

Osmund leaned over the man, a pained expression on his face. "Essimis, my old friend. I feel quite naked without you. Please come back to us." Essimis only mumbled incoherent nothings, whether in response or in some fevered dream none could tell.

"What about this bastard?" Aerrus pointed to the other body adorning the place. The assassin lay cold and stiff, flesh turning all manner of horrid colors at the mouth, the throat, the limbs. One finger had swollen so large and red it looked like a sausage link, squeezed by a ring the killer still wore.

"Ah, yes," said the doctor, clearing his throat to speak more confidently. "Well, this fellow took common fast-acting poisons to evade capture, plus a mix of exotic frog skin toxins, shellfish and algal growths. Quite impressive!"

"And something else," came a voice from the periphery of gathered onlookers. The alchemist Antero stepped forward. His ship with its precious cargo had arrived some hours before Osmund's, and he was already installed in the palace's laboratories. "I, um, had a chance to look at the body as well. The deterioration in the limbs, the heart... I'm not a doctor, nor even a physic, but at the University I heard accounts of substances that had these effects. You said the man jumped incredible distances, heights."

Aerrus nodded. "Aye, I've never seen a mortal man climb like that. That kind of strength, balance, just doesn't exist."

"It can, for a short time. I think the assassin took drugs that gave him just these qualities. But the price is that it wears out the body completely. This man was dead even before you caught him. Even if he had killed His Grace, and had gotten away, the drug would've ended him within hours. However it went, this was a one-way mission."

"Gods," breathed Eyvind, examining the ring and the device adorning it, "who would volunteer for something like that?"

"Someone very committed," Antero said as he pulled a brandy flask from a hip pouch. "Someone with nothing to lose and everything to gain, even in death." He took a casual swig of liquor and waved the flask at the stiff body. "That's what we're fighting, friends."

★   ★   ★

The palace in Ayala was as much a marvel inside as out, a far cry from the comparatively ramshackle one in Carsolan. A circular wall enclosed almost an entire town of its own, with a network of halls, passages, chambers and minarets, all of cool polished granite or marble and decorated with colorful mosaics and stained-glass windows. Above this a forest of domes and towers pierced the sky, dwarfed only by the central keep and spire that thrust up from the earth as though to assail the very gods themselves.

King Osmund and his whole court had been installed in one small corner of the royal wing, and one could be forgiven for losing track of them in that vast labyrinth of stone. After making sure Essimis was as comfortable as possible in the infirmary, Linet, Eyvind and Aerrus were led to their rooms – a private room for each of them, an unheard-of luxury. And the same for each of the courtiers and bravos, though the regular guards were billeted together.

Linet unpacked her baggage slowly, careful not to irritate the arm that stubbornly refused to complete its mending. Her chamber was a small cubicle with a bed of pillows and cushions, and an oil lamp set well away from the light silk hangings adorning the walls. There was no hearth and no need of one in such a warm clime, though a brazier sat by the unshuttered window for use during whatever passed for a Pelonan winter. In the distance she could see a miles-long aqueduct snake down from the Pelossus Mountains to deliver water – running water! – to the city. As 'great' as Greater Argovan thought itself, Linet thought, it still had much to learn from the wider world. *Is there a lesson for me in that too?*

"There you are!" She spun around to see Eyvind in the carved granite doorway, dripping wet and draped in some kind of robe. "This palace is a maze. I'm terrified of getting lost and never found again."

In spite of herself, she laughed at the pink, floral-patterned cloth that covered him. "Found a bathhouse, did you? This truly is a miraculous country."

Eyvind shook his head, sending droplets flying from the wild tangles of his hair. "Not exactly. I don't know what their word for it is, but they got this, well, bowl—"

"Bowl?"

"Aye, a kind of big clay bowl with holes poked in the bottom. You stand under it, and a servant pours hot water in. The water falls down on you, all over you, then drains away to use in gardens and farms and such. Like a hot rain. It's refreshing, better than a bath."

"And you sought me out just to tell about it?"

"Well, I just wanted to make sure I could find you. Both of you, I mean. That Aerrus fella, I wasn't sure about him at first, but after today…he's a good chap."

"I'm sure he'll sleep easy knowing that."

"Gods, that shot of his! Are you that good?"

"Better! When I'm in full form, anyway. You, uh, did well yourself, too. For a peacetime soldier, that is."

Eyvind looked away, uncertain. "Aye. Well, it ain't really peacetime anymore, is it?" He rubbed his thigh. The pain that he had set aside during the chase now came rushing back all at once. "Argh, the doctors are hoarding the opiphine from me, I know it. It's almost healed, but I damn near killed myself just tagging along."

Linet walked closer to Eyvind, feeling a sudden thickening in the air. "Still, what you did today. It was...very brave."

Eyvind cocked his head to one side to hide a tiny grin. "Cap'n Coladdi says – used to say – that being brave is just a matter of acting before you got a chance to be afraid."

Linet fixed his eyes with hers and nodded. "I agree." Unintentionally, the words came out a heavy whisper.

She'd spent her whole life training to anticipate attacks, to counter them. This one took her completely off-guard even though she'd expected it, invited it, even. One moment she was keeping the world and all its wonders and horrors at bay with the snide cocoon of sarcastic wit as she'd always done, and the next, well....

The reluctant, peacetime soldier pressed his sudden attack with zeal, and Linet found herself crying in shocked delight at yielding to it. They both collapsed onto the pillows and cushions, and did not arise again until the next day's sun glinted through the open window.

★   ★   ★

Aerrus sat taking his breakfast in the palace guards' refectory along with Osmund's bravos. As he sipped something hot, Linet stepped over an empty spot on the long bench next to him and sat down, saying nothing.

"You ever try this?" he asked, holding up the steaming cup. "Mint tea. It's good. Oddly cooling, even in – Lin?" He looked at her, squinting, with sudden suspicion. Even beyond their hand language there was often a certain, nearly psychic bond between siblings, and they were very nearly that. It wasn't really a form of communication, but still a vague kind of knowing. That knowing tickled the back of Aerrus's skull now.

"What, what is it?" Linet just looked at him, then down at her hands.

Aerrus sighed. "Oh. Well. I was wondering how long that would... yeah, this complicates things a bit."

"I know, I know," Linet huffed. "So stupid. And dangerous! I don't know how this happened!"

"No? Well, you see, when a man and a very foolish woman—"

"Would you be serious!"

"Why?"

A pause, and they both broke out in rare shared laughter. Aerrus laid a rough hand atop Linet's. "It's all right. I'm happy for you, really. Maybe he'll put you in a bit better mood."

"My mood is perfectly—!"

"Just try not to spill too many of our secrets to your new boyfriend. And remember, we have a job to do here. A lot of lives are depending on us."

"I said I know." Linet reached out and stole Aerrus's mint tea. "Now find me some breakfast, I'm famished!"

★ ★ ★

As scandalous as the attempt on Osmund's life had been, Ayala was to receive a greater shock only days later when another foreign ship laid anchor in the harbor. This one was immense, armed with ballistae every few yards and sharp ramming prows on each end. Four banks of oars guided it brazenly into its berth with chirurgical precision while a gargantuan mainsail, a great black square with gold worked into it, billowed.

The star design made by that gold was enough to drop jaws from one end of the city to the other. It was not an unusual one, but the mere sight of it adorning such a vessel was a tale that the citizens would tell to wide-eyed children and grandchildren for decades to come. It was not any old star, but one of internal loops and bends, all blending and curving into and away from each other from a snaking, circular center to end in eight radiant spokes of short and long lengths. This was the sigil of the Artameran Polytheon.

Stirring as this sight was to the townsfolk, the arrival had quietly been announced beforehand to certain members of Queen Synophae's court, including Osmund. Now, he sent Captain Eimar to gather up his ornery trio and convey them to the audience hall beneath the central spire of the palace. Eyvind, used as he was to taking orders, was the first to be dredged into the captain's net, and followed dutifully behind as they sought out Linet and Aerrus. But he didn't do so without some anxiety.

Ever since their – to his mind, completely spontaneous – romantic collision, Eyvind had gotten the distinct impression that Linet was avoiding him, busying herself with seeing that various members of the court were properly installed in their quarters and checking the palace's security arrangements. He wondered if she'd regretted it, or if he'd not performed well, or if he'd misread her intentions. But he didn't think that. As a good soldier, he'd frequented brothels from Everwest to Wengeddy and the haylofts of bored farmgirls everywhere in between. Linet was different. There was a whiff of something dangerous in the woman, a hint of...what? Despair? Desperation before an assuredly bloody end?

He put all that out of mind, or tried to until Eimar found her as well, two thirds of his charge completed. "Come," the captain said, "His Grace requires your presence, and that of your other friend."

"Why?" Linet asked, not even looking at Eyvind.

Eimar just stared at Linet as if she'd asked why the sun shone or the tides turned. "Right," she said, turning briefly back to the palace steward she'd been conversing with. "That's good enough for now, but I'd like to go over those floor plans again sometime." The steward nodded curtly, and Linet gestured down the long hallway they stood in. "Lead the way."

They found Aerrus in the infirmary, hovering over Essimis, who clung to life yet was still in his daze somewhere between asleep and awake. A worried frown was plastered on Aerrus's face, and he bit his thumb like a child afraid of the dark. He glanced momentarily at the three of them. "He's not getting better," he said, "not as far as I can see."

"At least he's not getting worse," Linet answered. "Sometimes that's as good as a victory where poison's concerned, until time itself heals the wound. Come on, leave him to the doctors. They know better than you what to do."

"Come? Where?"

"The big room," Eyvind said.

CHAPTER TWELVE

Their Inward Face

The 'big room' was their shared euphemism for the audience hall. The palace's central spire reached almost two hundred yards high, and the vast space that dominated the structure's footprint soared up to almost a third of that height. Inside it the marble columns formed their own petrified forest, and the golden light that poured through acres of colored glass windows didn't so much fade into shadows above as dissolve into a mist, as if the chamber had its very own clouds and weather.

At the end of a long procession pressed in on either side by a crowd that dwarfed the court in Carsolan, a raised dais boasted a throne with a polished mirror at the head that seemed to gather up all the room's sunlight and reflect a brilliant halo onto whoever sat on it. Eyvind shielded his eyes as Eimar shooed them past to stand next to King Osmund, a few paces to the throne's right and down one step. To Osmund's left, nearest the throne, stood the enigmatic Marzahni man who'd accompanied the queen to that dockside disaster, now in magnificent robes of green and saffron, yet silent and scowling as ever. The king gave a neutral nod at their arrival, careful not to dislodge his crown.

"Ah, there you are. Keep close to me now. I want you to witness this."

"Witness *what*?" Aerrus demanded. Eimar moved to wallop him for his impertinence before Osmund held up a staying hand.

"It's all right, captain, stand down. To be honest, I'm not exactly sure what's about to happen. But I can tell you it will be significant.

Now, I know you have your damned privileges in your own country, and I know our crown has agreed to them. But when the queen arrives, I strongly suggest you kneel along with everyone else. You've no such freedoms here, and if you don't blend in you could very swiftly find your heads off, with little I could do to stop it."

Aerrus seemed about to argue, but then just sighed and nodded.

"Good. Think of it as an infiltration, if you like. Now, I don't suppose any of you have ever been to Holy Artamera?"

"Why do you ask?" Aerrus asked. "Erm, Your Grace," he added when Eimar tossed an acid snarl his way.

Osmund opened his mouth to answer, then paused as the great wide doors to the hall began the glacial process of swinging open. Light poured into the hall, beams lancing through the stone forest. "Oh, dear. Old Essimis will hate to have missed this. Just watch." In spite of the vast attendance, the entire hall fell quiet.

A large palanquin, covered in black silk, was borne by at least ten porters with shaved heads and clad in undyed linen tunics, who marched slowly into the chamber, their hobnailed steps echoing off the far walls. The whole assembly was barely able to fit through the doors as it trundled toward the still-vacant throne. When it had covered about half the distance, a side door opened, and Queen Synophae stepped through. The entire court, of which Osmund's faction was again only a small portion, sank to its knees in a wave that spread out from the throne like a pool with a stone suddenly tossed in. The queen wore her peacock headdress, walking carefully to keep it upright as she approached her throne. An observer would realize only at the very end of the spectacle that the timing had been perfected so that both palanquin and queen reached their destinations simultaneously. Neither power waited upon the other. Eyvind glanced to his side to perceive yet another wonder: Linet and Aerrus were on their knees. Well, one knee each, which was miraculous enough.

Synophae sat, and the court rose. The porters lowered the palanquin, drew back the silken canopy, and two of the most curious creatures Eyvind had ever laid eyes upon emerged.

At first glance they seemed to have skin darker than any Pelonan or Marzahni or Ghreshi, almost blue. No, not skin, *ink*. Every exposed inch of their flesh was covered in a vast network of tattoos. Writing, maybe. Their eyebrows and cheeks sported a system of piercings through which black cord had been laced, creating a pattern that reminded Eyvind of how the eyes of corpses were sometimes sewn shut before burial. Their necks appeared absurdly long and barely able to support the bizarre headgear one of them wore – a roughly hemispherical cage of interlocked lengths of wicker enveloped the head, held up by some kind of skullcap. The other's head was shaved like the porters', the scalp also inked blue-black. Both had additional piercings stretching from each ear down those hideously long necks, with polished red gems dangling from every stud. They wore the same linen as the porters but instead of simple tunics, it was wrapped tightly about them in wide strips. The strips were stained bright red where it passed over their hearts. Their feet and hands were bare, and their nails very long and painted brilliant blue. They looked so bizarre that Eyvind couldn't determine the sex of either, though the one with the strange wicker helmet might have been female. At some unspoken signal they began walking, in step as one, toward the throne.

Eyvind cast another glance at Aerrus and Linet, and they stood just as rapt and open-mouthed as he, as did the rest of the court. To his left the king seemed similarly entranced, though he managed not to let his jaw hang open quite as much.

Two porters who had escorted these weird beings out of the palanquin stood at the sides of each as they ascended the dais, very slowly. All four came to a stop mere feet from the throne and Synophae herself, all on the same level. Eyvind wondered how well they could see through that crisscross of stitching over their eyes. The porters leaned in front of the creatures, ears in front of mouths. In the case of the wickered one, the porter had to duck his head underneath the rim of the cage. Again as one, the two whispered something, almost imperceptibly.

Eyvind spoke a little Pelonan, mostly in order to better haggle with the merchants who sailed into Òlo after every soldiers' payday. But the words that followed made a dizzying sound to his ears. In perhaps another calculated display of complete equality, both porters – translators as well, it seemed – and Queen Synophae spoke all at once. It sounded formulaic on both sides, something like "Greetings, Queen Synophae of Pelona" and "Welcome, emissaries of most Holy Artamera", but all jumbled together. After that initial exchange, the translators whispered into their masters' ears. It was rumored that they spoke an ancient, lost tongue in Artamera, one so alien and complex none outside could ever learn it. Eyvind wondered if that was what they used now.

The pleasantries became mercifully sequential after that. The 'emissaries', if that was what they truly were, thanked the queen for the welcome and said that their journey had been long and they had things of importance to discuss. Synophae agreed and conferred on them full ambassadorial sovereignty, a necessary formality since no one in living memory had ever received an ambassador from the Holy City.

Though it seemed tedious, especially since every word had to pass through the whisperings of the translators, in reality it was only minutes of shocked gawking before the emissaries thanked Synophae again and took their leave, stepping back into their black palanquin. The black canopy covered them once more, and the porters bore them out of the hall. Once they were gone, Synophae stood and spoke to the whole court in a voice trained to perfect projection.

"In light of the arrival of our esteemed guests, there will be no further court business today. Return tomorrow and your suits will be heard. Adjourn!" Over the rumbles of disappointment from several dozen petitioners and the shuffling of hundreds of feet, Synophae called to Osmund. "My lord king," she said in Argovani, "a word, if you will."

As Osmund and Synophae conversed in hushed tones, Eyvind turned to Linet and Aerrus. "Have…have you ever seen…heard…?"

They both shook their heads. "Not even close," Linet said. "Not even in hearsay or gossip or drunken ramblings."

"But, I mean, they were human...right?"

"I *think* so," Aerrus said, sounding not quite convinced himself.

Captain Eimar broke his silence as he nudged between them. "I heard stories from sailors, of far-off tribes of people who wear tattoos, carry out ritual body mutilations, but nothing like that, and nothing I've seen."

Osmund joined the group once more after concluding his conversation with Synophae. "There is to be a meeting later today. The queen, myself, and the emissaries with their translators. No one else." He eyed Eimar. "*No* one."

"But, Your Grace—"

"You and two others may wait outside the chamber that has been chosen, but that's all."

Eimar frowned and grumbled, but held his peace.

"King Osmund," Linet said with more than a touch of irritation, "I may be just a backwards forest ranger, so forgive my ignorance, but...who *were* those two? Why would simple ambassadors undergo such extreme—"

"Those were not simple ambassadors. Holy Artamera *has* no ambassadors. I'd bet my kingdom no one in this entire great hall's ever seen their like before, and I pray never to again. Those were Priests of the Polytheon."

★　　★　　★

It was during Osmund and Synophae's meeting with the new arrivals that Essimis finally awoke. His poison-induced fever broke at last, and the king's doctor sent for Aerrus, not knowing who else to inform since Osmund had given explicit instructions not to be interrupted. Aerrus, Linet and Eyvind all crowded around the bleary-eyed chancellor lying on his cot, glad for the old man's recovery. "Gave us a godsdamned fright, you crazy old coot," Aerrus said, though his eyes smiled.

Essimis nodded weakly. "I'm so terribly sorry, boy. I shall endeavor to take your feelings into consideration in future assassination attempts.

The doctor tells me you three cornered the killer but couldn't take him alive. What happened, couldn't control your temper as usual?"

"He took poison, killed himself," Aerrus replied, suddenly serious. "Essimis, disturbing things have happened, are happening now. I know you're still recovering, but…."

"Tell me," the chancellor ordered. They told him of the assassin, of Antero's suspicions. Of the incredible ship in the harbor and of its more incredible passengers, and of the conference taking place at that very moment. Essimis listened to all of it, ashen.

"Gods," he whispered, "gods, gods. That is a troubling sign."

"What do you mean?" Linet asked.

Essimis took a deep breath. "The Artameran Polytheon that you know – the temples and priories, the robed brothers and sisters, their charity, their medicines and breweries – these are its outward face, a veneer to make it palatable and welcomed the world over. And it's remarkably successful. Two kingdoms could be at war, with the most savage battles raging all around, and a temple would, in theory, be perfectly safe in the middle of it. Their holy oaths of neutrality and absolute refusal to take part in the world's politics make them so. The true Polytheon never leaves the city-state of Artamera. Never. Only there are the priests and priestesses found, and they lead lives quite different from those of their more secular foreign disciples. And fanatically defended ones – no army to invade Artamera has ever returned. It's suicide. But then, if they're here, themselves, mangled flesh and all…I don't know what it means. But probably nothing good."

They left Essimis to get what rest he could after receiving that news, and as they ascended from the coolness of the partially underground infirmary Eyvind called after Linet. "Hey, wait a bit!" Linet paused, turned, then perhaps considered ignoring him but waited after all. Aerrus thankfully took a hint and continued on his way as though he'd not heard.

Linet sighed. "What is it?"

Eyvind scowled, stung. "*What is it?* Really? Lin, did I do something wrong? Why are you avoiding me? Was I really that bad in bed?"

Linet rolled her eyes dramatically, but it was not a convincing act. "Oh, for...no. You didn't do anything wrong. I'm just very busy—"

"Bollocks," Eyvind spat.

"Look, I got what I needed from you and now I'm done, all right?"

"Try again. I know you better than that by now, much as that might terrify you."

"Oh, gods." She rubbed her eyes, forehead with her hands, then cupped his sparsely bearded cheek. Just like that the rare softness buried deep in the heart of her returned, but brought a nameless fear with it too. "I'm scared, okay? Scared for you, for us. Everyone I dare to care about dies, and things are just going to get worse. You're...a weakness. One I can't afford and can't bear to lose."

Eyvind fell back a step, nonplussed. He wasn't sure what he'd expected, but not that. "Well, you're not a weakness to me. I feel stronger, safer knowing you're by my side. I feel like we could take on the whole world as long as we're together! We might be doing just exactly that. I'm sorry you don't feel the same."

"Eyvind—!"

He turned and walked back down toward the infirmary. Not that he had any business there; he just needed to get away. Burning with embarrassment, he stalked back into the recovery ward where Essimis lay, wide awake and looking at him with some bureaucratic version of sympathy.

"Did you just hear all of that shambles, chancellor?" he asked with irritation.

Essimis shrugged as much as he could. "Sound does carry down here, and I can't exactly excuse myself to be discreet."

"Wonderful."

"Son, I know this sounds ridiculous given my dour speech just now, but don't fret. I've made my career reading people and trying to winkle out their motivations, intentions. Trust me, she'll come round. You, all of you, need each other. I'd never say this in front of Aerrus, his ego needs no puffing, but you three may be the most formidable weapon we have against Phynagoras. Linet knows that, even if she doesn't want to face it right now."

Eyvind gave a short, bitter laugh. "Thanks. I hope you're right."

"Of course, I'm always right! Most of the time, anyway. Now go fetch a sick old man another pillow, will you?"

CHAPTER THIRTEEN

Lunacy!

The secretive meeting went on well into the night, and when Osmund finally emerged from the chamber in an upper level of the palace's spire, he was pale-faced and red-eyed. Captain Eimar greeted him with the news of Essimis's improvement, which seemed to give the king some encouragement. By sunrise the Polytheon priests had returned to their ship and sailed away, perhaps anxious to return to the enclave they so seldom left. So abrupt was their arrival and departure that some in the city would later question whether they'd actually been there at all, or if it were some mass insanity that'd momentarily gripped Ayala.

While Synophae held court to soothe the anxiety of the previous day's jilted petitioners, Eyvind and Aerrus canvassed every courtier, ambassador and foreign dignitary they could corner to at least consider providing aid to Argovan when the time came, assuring all often and loudly that the adventurer-despot would surely not stop at swallowing them, and had appetites that the whole world would not sate. All of this was met with noncommittal platitudes, however.

Aerrus had consented to dress more in the Pelonan style. He felt absurd in the light linen tunic, with no undershirt or chausses hugging his body, but it was undeniably more comfortable. Linet, on the other hand, kept to her woolens, and spent all day in the massive exercise yard behind the palace where Synophae's armies camped and drilled. She'd found a line of archery butts, and slowly, painfully trained her arm back to enough strength to draw her weapon. The ache affected her aim, but the day's effort made improvement, and that brought back some measure of confidence. Still, with every shot she silently cursed Eyvind. *Stupid man*, she thought. *Stupid, sentimental man.*

Thwack! The arrow bit into the cloth-covered haystack twenty yards away. A child's distance, but it was a start. Why couldn't he just take her quim like a good dumb soldier and be satisfied with that? Why did he insist on falling victim to foolish lunacies? Why did she? She'd known it was a mistake the moment he'd leaped on her that night. Or had she dragged him down? She couldn't remember. No matter, she'd yielded to her desires and now things between them could never be mended. *Stupid, stupid!* They'd likely all be dead within one or two seasons, and it was no time to be distracted by... what? *Ridiculous!*

Thwack!

And then for him to cast all that weakness back at her and call it strength...how dare he! He was a stupid, stupid man, she was a stupid girl for falling for it, and that's all there was to it. And perhaps worst of all, Perrim had been right in her accusation. She'd just been too proud to admit it.

Thw— BOOM!

Linet jumped nearly out of her skin at the sound, and half the men drilling on the field almost fell faint. But after a moment's terrified confusion she realized she knew that sound. Someone nearby was messing around with that diabolical stuff, that Vrril.

The Pelonan soldiers on the field stared up at the clear sky in shock, scanning for whatever storm had birthed the thunder. They were looking in the wrong direction. The boom had echoed off the great wall encircling the palace complex to bounce back at them, which meant that it must have come from the small outbuilding between there and the field.

Having had her fill of muscle pain and self-recrimination for the day, Linet walked toward the square building of smooth sandstone and plaster domes. The entrance was blocked by a regular Carsolan palace guard, not one of Osmund's bravos. He moved to bar her entry, then saw the royal badge she presented.

"Stand aside."

"Yes, ma'am. But I wouldn't wanna go in there 'less I had to."

"Why?" she asked. "What's going on?"

"*Alchemy*," the guard whispered, as though speaking too loudly would summon demons themselves. "Deep alchemy. Them P'lonan wizards, they got deep magic, wanna make that horrible shit even worse! Burn all enemies o' the king I say, but keep it well away from me!"

"Uh-huh," Linet said, not sure how to counter such ingrained superstition, and not entirely doubting all of it herself. She nudged past the guard into what looked like a stone warehouse with a workshop along one side. Two figures stood there, pondering a spreading cloud of smoke and blackened stones far larger than the courtyard demonstration in Carsolan. Antero the alchemist was there with another fellow, an older Pelonan wearing green robes.

"Yes," Antero said in response to some previous dialogue, "I think you're right. If we push the distillation another six hours we very well might increase the yield even more. I just wonder if we can store it safely."

The Pelonan man shrugged and said in a thick accent, "*Nistaq?* Wonder, my son, is poor substitute for observation. *Aqta provu!* More experiment!"

"You know, Pharses, we'll have to hold back *some* Vrril to use against the enemy. Experiments are useless if we can't put it into applic— Ah, my pretty woodland nymph! Welcome. I hope we're not making too much racket."

Linet frowned, her skin crawling at the man's intimations. *Nymph* was not a good word to use with her today. "You just made half the queen's army shit itself out there, if that's what you mean. What are you doing? I thought you had this all worked out."

Antero's expression brightened. "You'd think, but no! No, the alchemists of this country are brilliant, and after their initial shock that a nobody like myself could invent it, they say they can make Vrril even more mindlessly destructive. We've already produced a liter of an improved formulation that should wreak absolute havoc with human flesh. Rejoice, the end of the world is at hand!"

"Humph. Can't come soon enough for me," Linet grumbled.

"Oh? Well, welcome to the club! Say, would you like to come drinking with us tonight? Pharses here knows of a bawdy house in the lower city that caters to all—"

"Yech, no! What, you didn't bring your child-whores with you?"

"Sadly no, they weren't mine to bring. Those two were professionals, you know. Richer than some aristocrats. Don't feel bad for 'em. Not that riches will matter much once the ravening hordes spill over the mountains and bring all to ruin."

Linet jerked a stubborn chin at the smoldering wreckage before them. "Don't you believe your Vrril will stop that?"

Antero sighed. "Whatever the commoners think, there's no magic here that I can see. No weapon carries the kind of certainty kings imagine in their heads and then demand. It's powerful, sure. Is it enough, will it be in time? Damned if I know. Damned if I don't. We'll make as much as we can, but using it's the business of those who're not me. Until one end or another comes, I intend to keep my cup full and my balls empty. The rest is noise."

★　★　★

The next day Osmund summoned them to another gathering. The room high up in the palace's spire was reached by an ingenious system of platforms, pulleys and wheels turned by servants heaving at a capstan on the ground. As Linet stepped clumsily off the wobbling contraption, she wondered what they'd do if there was a fire. She rode up with Aerrus, followed by Eyvind with Essimis, sparing them the long, awkward silence of the ascent. She followed the chancellor, still a bit peaked from his ordeal, into a circular, wide-windowed room. The view was breathtaking, literally, as Linet paused before it and gasped. The highest tower in the palace at Carsolan reached less than a third the height, and from here all of Ayala lay spread out like a miniature city, with little ant-like people, animals and vehicles creeping along at an imperceptible pace. The sun glimmered off the sea like a vast mirror while birds flew in circles *below* them.

"Quite a sight, isn't it?" Osmund emerged from a shadowed part of the room where he'd been talking with Synophae. Captain Eimar followed two steps behind.

"It's beautiful!"

Synophae gave both Linet and Osmund a look of confused distaste. "My lord king, are you so…familiar with all your subjects?"

Osmund laughed, a rare thing as far as Linet could recall. "No, my lady. Only those who thwart multiple assassination attempts against the royal person. Oh, don't bother, Essimis," he said as the chancellor began to kneel. "We can dispense with that. I give thanks to the gods that you're back on your feet. Let's keep you there as long as possible. Er, with your permission of course, my lady queen."

"Very well," Synophae said with a sigh, "but we shall not let such lapses of protocol become routine."

"Of course." Osmund cast a significant glance at Aerrus as he rolled his eyes. The queen bade them all sit, and Osmund introduced each of them, referring to Aerrus and Linet only as members of 'a band of irregulars in the service of the Kingsmarch'. Aerrus made an amused face at that but didn't dispute it.

"Interesting," Synophae replied skeptically, "most interesting. Perhaps this is the source of your wild lack of manners. But if His Grace the king trusts you, I have no recourse but to do so as well. And, you have seen but certainly not heard from my chief of staff, General Davenga." She motioned to the Marzahni who seemed to accompany her everywhere. He'd sat silently, and now simply inclined his head a fraction. "His role is to disapprove of things. He does this very well."

Osmund nodded. "Now that we're all acquainted, to the heart of matters. You all must be wondering about what happened yesterday."

Essimis sat up, excited. "Indeed, Your Grace. A deputation from the Polytheon! For the first time in recorded history. What did they have to say?"

"I'm afraid I can't discuss it," said Osmund, sounding truly apologetic.

Essimis blinked. "I'm sorry, my lord?"

"Sorry to disappoint you all, but we, Queen Synophae and myself both, have been sworn to secrecy, and may not speak of what was said unless and until the proper time comes. So don't ask."

"Your Grace...."

"I know, I know. Trust me, my old friend. If all goes well you will never know. But things seldom do. Until then, there's still plenty to discuss, and I'll hear not another word on the matter. Now, as you all know, the despot Phynagoras has suborned one of my border lords, namely Armino of Northmarch. Thanks to brave young Eyvind here, we've learned that Phynagoras will invade through passes in the Edra Mountains and receive a welcome at the fortress Phenidra, using it as a base from which to take all of eastern Argovan, and eventually the entire kingdom and beyond."

"Possibly," Synophae said.

"Probably. And as you also know...I have no standing army."

"But I do," the queen said sharply. "And I am not yet convinced. Phynagoras has made no move against Pelona, and would be fool to do so."

"My lady queen," said Essimis, almost pleading, "he's already made a move in your own harbor. Surely you must see that you would undoubtedly be next? Phynagoras sees the whole world as his rightful dominion. Once he's taken Argovan, he'll have all the farmland he needs to feed even greater armies, build fleets of ships. Then gold from Thazov, mined with millions of new slaves, to pay mercenaries to fight and the Isles Banks to look the other way...."

"With that much power," Linet said, unbidden, "he'd be fool *not* to try for Pelona. Um, my lady queen, I mean." Far over Osmund's shoulder, Captain Eimar winced.

Synophae looked at Linet the way one might inspect live lobsters in the fish market before selecting which one to have for supper. "My dear, how old are you?"

"What? Oh, um, about twenty-four. I think."

Synophae smiled thinly. "Twenty-four. I remember being twenty-four. Well, you see this grand palace about you? This tower which, my scholars assure me, remains the tallest in the world? It required no fewer than fifteen of your lifetimes to construct. Pelona has had peace, more or less, for all that time precisely because we train our armies as though peace does not exist, and we don't get involved in the squabbles of others. Before I risk those long years of peace, my kingdom's wealth and the lives of my loyal soldiers on a foreign battlefield, I will need more than…what is the word? Conjecture."

Osmund sat back in his chair, defeated. But Linet sat up straighter, emboldened by the apparent invitation for debate. "We're only involved in this mess because a traitor sold us out to the Marchmen. A local nuisance, a skirmish. But that's how Phynagoras works. He finds a little crack to sneak in to, then widens it bit by bit. Divides allies, distracts, subverts. If there was a way to plug one of those cracks now, we might stand a chance."

"What do you mean?"

Linet glanced at Eyvind. They'd not spoken since yesterday, but now he took up the cause with confidence. "My lady queen, I heard Phynagoras's plans with my own ears, from the lips of his emissary and the traitor Armino. I only survived to escape thanks to Linet, and we left the mercenaries sent to fetch me back lying dead on the road. Armino suspects we know of his intentions, but he doesn't know for sure. I believe the invasion will still come through the fortress Phenidra, by way of the passes through the Edra Mountains. But I think he'll move more quickly, perhaps this year. We've been discussing the possibility of taking a small, fast company across the Bay. If we can march on Phenidra and take it before Phynagoras comes, we can block him. You can't bring siege engines through those mountains. It won't stop him completely, but he'll have no base of operations."

Synophae raised an eyebrow. "A small, fast company? Forgive me, Osmund, but I have studied your fortifications – for academic purposes only, I assure you! – and Phenidra could hold off an army without siege engines for a season. How would you take it?"

"Good question," Osmund replied, looking at Eyvind with a quizzical expression. "I've not been a party to these grand stratagems. How, indeed?"

Eyvind swallowed. "Forgive me, Your Grace, it was just some ideas. We thought we'd have more time, but…."

"But we don't. What's your idea?"

"You see, I've been a soldier there for years, was born nearby. I know the land, the lay of it, all around. There are two main ways to approach – from the west, like the garrison march up from Vin Gannoni…and from the east. From the mountains."

"Yes, of course, as Phynagoras intends," Synophae said with impatience. "How does that help?"

"There are also paths into the mountains from the north coast, out of sight of Phenidra entirely. Now, Armino doesn't know what Phynagoras's horde will look like, and he's certainly never laid eyes on the man in person. None of us have seen more than a handful of Bhasans in our lives. If we can cut south from the coast, then turn and approach Phenidra from the east, arrayed in, well, in disguise—"

"You want to dress my soldiers up like a troupe of prissy, perfumed Bhasans and pretend to be the invader himself?"

"—Armino might be fooled and open the gates to us on his own! Those are peacetime soldiers, like me. Once we're inside they'll have no stomach for fighting. We could take Phenidra in one stroke."

Synophae let out something part-way between a derisive laugh and a gasp of disbelief. "This is…*tllaljuna!* Lunacy! Even trusting to Osmund's black magic spirit is more sensible. I cannot believe you would bring—"

A small sound interrupted the queen. Small, but so unusual and so rare that she was compelled to silence in a heartbeat. It was something between a sigh and a grunt, with perhaps a hint of a cough thrown in. And it was not the sound itself but the source of it that stopped Synophae's rant cold. She turned toward that source, incredulous.

For the first time they could recall, the general spoke. He spoke to the queen in Pelonan, too low and too fast for Eyvind to understand, or even Essimis, who was nearly fluent. Synophae replied in kind, and this back and forth continued for some moments. Finally the queen said, "It seems we live in days of wonder indeed. General Davenga wishes to speak."

Davenga stood, towering over even Eimar. His robes of state did not suit him nearly so well as his armor. He nodded at Osmund. "I give all respect to my queen's honored guest, Argovan King. To these others: you are fools, and your manners are very bad. But you may be right." His voice was deep but sonorous and oddly melodic. "Marzahn has not had such long peace. I fought most of my life to bring unity and strength to my country. Now I lead the armies of Pelona because I know a strong ally is as important as bravery in battle. I will not give up what I fought so long for, not to some...." He frowned, looked at Synophae. "*Mugghru?*"

"Upstart."

"Some upstart from the east. I calculate this foolish plan at no better chance than one in fifty of success. Yet. I have seen this liquid lightning, this black magic for myself. If we can disrupt the invasion for time enough to make more of it, my life is a small wager to lay for that chance. If it please my queen, I will lead this, as you say, small, fast host myself. It is no idle boast to say that should increase the chance to one in twenty." Davenga sat.

"One in twenty," said Aerrus. "Things are looking up."

"How much of a small force are you thinking, general?" Osmund asked.

"To move quickly, and unnoticed? One hundred, no more."

"Enough to appear as an honor guard anyway, when we approach the gates," Eyvind said.

"But," said Synophae, "how do you know what to do, what to say? Will you pretend to be Phynagoras himself? You may be bowshot before you even come near the gates."

Eyvind smiled. "My lady queen, you have the bloated body of an assassin down in your infirmary—"

"Not anymore. When you die in this country we don't keep you waiting around long. The smell, you see."

"His possessions, then?"

"Under lock and key."

"Good. He bore a certain ring. Much like one I saw once before, when Armino was compelled to kneel and kiss its device. He won't soon forget that. Phynagoras would send a representative ahead of him first, to humble Armino once more I think. If we bear that ring, I believe the lie will hold."

"Incredible. Very well. If my lord general, who has earned his quiet retirement at my side, wishes instead to throw his life away on this wager, I shall not stop him."

Osmund looked suspiciously from Eyvind to Linet and back again. "You two, you came up with this?"

"Erm..." Eyvind stammered, "mostly, Your Grace? Yes."

"Intriguing. Quite a pair."

Awkward was too mild a word for the pause that followed that. "Um, thank you, my lord. Ahem. The only problem is when we should set out. We'd need to know when Armino expects Phynagoras to arrive, and do so ourselves just before. I didn't hear them discuss timing...."

Osmund shook his head. "Not a problem. You should set out right away, for we've had new intelligence just this morning. That's another reason we summoned you all here. The timing has indeed been advanced, and Phynagoras is on the move. *Now*."

CHAPTER FOURTEEN

Once More Unto the Beach

While the expedition was being assembled, Aerrus and Linet found little to do themselves, so they spent more and more time at the archery butts on the exercise ground. It was only now that they were soon to depart that Linet had acceded to the climate and doffed her tunic. Wearing only shift and chausses rolled down to the knees, she'd have been considered scandalously close to naked in Argovan, but here no one took notice. She had nursed her shooting arm almost back to full strength, and now stood shoulder to shoulder with Aerrus at the forty-yard mark, their arrows grouped even closer at the center of the target before them. One shot impacted into the cloth-wrapped hay bale with a dull *thwopp*, just outside the red circle painted in the center.

"Gyah," Aerrus whined. And in mimicry of Osmund's voice, "T'was but a sudden crosswind, my lady queen!"

"Whatever you've got to tell yourself, my lord king," Linet replied with a grin as she took her time lining up her own shot.

"Yeah, yeah. So. Seems His Fluffy Grace went for part one of your grand plan. You intend to tell him about part two, or leave that as a surprise?"

Linet drew and held for only a fraction of a second to aim, trusting more to instinct than eye as she'd been taught. Now only the slightest twinge of pain tickled her arm before the arrow took flight, hitting the target just a little low of center. *Almost there*, she thought. *Almost.* "It's our plan, now. We'll need all the help we can get once we're back on home soil."

Aerrus shook his head. "I still don't know. Raising the commons, at a moment's notice...."

"They'll rise. They'll have to, there's no one else. Besides, we've done it before."

"I think you might be reading a bit much into the archives, Lin. Surely there's more than a little exaggeration in there. Peasant rebellions have a habit of ending badly for the peasants. It's a losing strategy."

"We don't have to win," Linet insisted, "just hold out until that damned Vrril comes to save us."

"How long will that take? Antero says it's a drop-by-drop process. Could be ten, fifteen weeks before then. Even if we do last that long, you think the mob will be happy to put their pitchforks down again, just go back to how it was before? The crown's spent years clawing power away from the nobility."

Linet sent another shot arcing out across the field. *Thwopp*. Dead center. "Not our problem. Osmund ran away, so he's got no say in it."

Aerrus nodded. "Aye to that, we've enough problems of our own. Ugh. Speaking of which...."

Eyvind jogged up to the pair, walking right across the field and earning annoyed glances from other soldiers also at practice as he interrupted their shots. He carried a strung Pelonan bow, heavier and rougher than their own but of sturdy manufacture. A quiver was slung over his shoulder.

"Hey," he said casually, setting down the quiver and squinting at the distant target.

"Really?" said Linet with skepticism.

"What? I could use some practice too, you know."

Aerrus seemed about to say something, then reconsidered. Eyvind clumsily nocked an arrow, closed one eye, and yanked on the string like a sailor hauling a forestay. Two arm-shaking seconds later, the arrow tore off on some wild course to bury itself in the ground halfway to the target and ten yards to the left. "Hmm." Though wearing a bracer, he still rubbed his arm where the string had whacked against it. "Well, I guess there's some room for improvement. It was so much easier on the ship...."

"Lighter bow, closer range," Linet said with exasperation. "Totally different animal."

"Oh. Look I, uh, I'm sorry for stomping off on you the other day. I guess I just didn't think of things from your side, you know? Your fellows, all killed like that…enough to make anyone nervous about getting close ever again."

Aerrus fidgeted nervously. "I'm gonna go get some water. This damn dry heat…."

"You stay put," Linet snapped, stabbing a finger at him before turning back to Eyvind. "I'm sorry too, I guess. Call it a panic reaction, whatever. I just think it's best we set all that aside for now, for all our sakes."

Eyvind nodded. "You're probably right."

"Which means, you should probably stop staring at my rear. Like you're doing right now."

"Oh. Sorry. It is such a nice one…."

"*When* we get back," Linet continued, ignoring Aerrus's snickering, "even if this crazy scheme works it won't be enough to just hide out in Phenidra. When Phynagoras comes, whether he has a fortress or no, he'll bring fire and death to the whole Carsa Valley before moving west."

"I know. Osbren might just stay shut up behind his walls, and the other Marcher lords, assuming they don't go over to Phynagoras entirely. But without an army, what can we do but wait?"

Linet looked briefly at Aerrus, who shrugged and nodded. "Our written histories," she began, speaking carefully thanks to a lifetime spent learning to keep secrets, "tell of how the Heron Kings first got started. Some of it's hard to believe—"

"There's an understatement," Aerrus muttered.

"—but a lot of it was just regular people, common folk sick and tired of being victims of a war they had no part in. So a few dozen banded together, took to the forests and started hitting back in ways that favored them. Sneak attacks, traps, hit and run, outright terrorism. Some of it was brilliant, most was just brutal."

"Thrilling story," Eyvind said as he stubbornly readied himself for another shot. "But what does that have to do with— Oh." He lowered the heavy bow and looked pale-faced at Linet. "Oh! You don't mean—"

"I do. And not just us this time. Back then it was against scattered companies of conscripts just as scared as they were. What we're facing is a beast, well, as different as the bow you're holding is to the Vrril we're trusting to save us. You'll have to stay at Phenidra and hold it against Phynagoras, but we mean to launch a popular insurgency, fight him on not remotely fair terms."

"His retaliations will be terrible," Eyvind said, incredulous.

"The alternative is worse."

"Has…has the king given his consent to this?"

Aerrus shook his head. "Nope. And we don't intend to ask. He doesn't like it he can come back and fight himself. But we all know he won't do that."

★　　★　　★

The plan was put into action with frightening speed. When two monarchs at once both decreed a thing, it was as good as done. Davenga assembled his hundred, bade farewell to his family and appointed his successor should he fall. A ship was made ready to convey the small force across the Bay of Pelona. This was no fleet weighed down with cargo and a royal court, so it was rigged for speed and stripped of banners or sails with any identifying device. Within a week all was made ready, the ship packed with provisions and weapons and bunks stacked three high. It was all done at night to avoid any spying eyes.

The night before they were to depart, King Osmund and Essimis summoned Eyvind alone to the royal apartments. An hour later, shaking, Eyvind accompanied the loading of one more crate of cargo, insistent that it be conveyed extremely carefully and tied down for stowage. An hour after that he considered going to look for Linet. And an hour after *that*, in a mood of dour resignation he joined Antero in the lower city, seeking out any brothel that employed slight, athletic women around twenty-four years of age with dark hair and bright eyes.

★   ★   ★

The following evening, a section of Ayala's harbor was cleared of all traffic as a hundred Pelonan soldiers, all carrying their own shields and sets of new armor, filed into the ship while Davenga inspected them, nodding approval to each in turn. Two other figures clad in dark, hooded coats stood by, trying to look unimportant and utterly failing thanks to the mixture of guards foreign and domestic gathered closely about them.

"I don't see why their armor can't just be loaded with the other cargo," said one, his voice muffled by the hood wrapped across his face.

The other, more shapely figure shook her head. "This foolish plan will not remain secret, but fewer dockworkers will keep it a little longer. Besides, every soldier must be a self-sufficient unit. If they cannot carry whatever they might need, they will be of no use. You really should have raised your own army long ago, Osmund. Then we might not have even been in this situation."

"I know, I know! But it's different in Argovan. Memory of the old nobility is still strong, and demanding men flock to a distant king's banner rather then their own lord...besides, standing armies are so *expensive*."

"Expensive! You cry to me of expense *now*?"

The argument was cut off by the approach of Essimis, with Linet, Aerrus and Eyvind behind him. The three had changed back fully into their woolens in expectation of the journey into the mountains, once again bristling with weapons. Eyvind had even gotten a bow of his own somewhere, though lighter than the one he'd fumbled with in the exercise yard.

"All is ready, Your Grace," Essimis said. "They've only to depart."

"Thank you, my friend." Osmund turned to the trio. "I know what you must think of me, of a king who abandons his kingdom. So

I won't send you away with any commands. What you're doing is the height of either bravery or stupidity. Either way, you have my thanks."

Eyvind bowed his head. "The honor is to serve, Your Grace."

"I've sent word to my brother, Osbren, and the other border lords to hold their castles and defend their lands as best they can, but if they can aid you, to do so. Whether they obey is…yet to be seen."

Synophae drew back her hood, discarding the ridiculous attempt at disguise. "My alchemists say they can begin making the Vrril in earnest soon. When they judge we have enough, it will follow you."

"The loss of Rinalda is a wound that still stings," Osmund said to Linet, "but Essimis tells me the security arrangements you've put in place for us here have calmed his fears. That means you've calmed mine as well. Thank you."

"You're very welcome."

Osmund at last turned to Aerrus. He paused, perhaps trying to think of something to say. "I know you're not doing this for me. I also know you must have plans of your own that you're not telling. Very well. But I do care for my people, whatever you believe. For their sakes I'll say only, may the gods light your path." Aerrus just nodded once, but at least he did it without a sarcastic sneer.

Synophae said something to Davenga in Marzahni dialect, and he snapped a fist to his heart in salute and farewell. With nothing further to be said, the four ascended the gangplank. As the ship's crew drew in cables and weighed anchor, the two rulers stood watching in silence. When the ship finally began to sidle away from the dock, Osmund said quietly, "I wonder, do you think this plan really has any chance?"

"No," said Synophae. "But you've left us no other choice." She turned back toward the palace.

★   ★   ★

It was only a five-day trip to Ólo, through calm and well-traveled waters. But that was not their destination. Halfway across the bay, the ship adjusted course eastward, toward a point Eyvind had indicated on a nautical chart. Charts of such accuracy and detail were a new science, and the captain grumbled at letting him mark all over the precious document. "The queen will buy you a new one," Davenga said as they hovered over the chart in the privacy of the cabin. "Is there anything there, at this landing of yours?"

"Just a fishing village," Eyvind replied. "You won't find it on any map, but it's there. And a trickle of a river that flows out of the mountains. We'll follow that up until we hit the pass that leads to Phenidra. I hope your men have brought warm clothes."

"They have, and strength to endure, in any event. Do not worry about my men, just about your little plot."

Eyvind pulled out the ring taken off the assassin. Phynagoras's ring. "Aye...."

The captain must've recognized the device, for his eyes widened. "Is that...?"

"None of your business," Davenga said sharply. "We're about the queen's work! You just get this boat to where it must go. And tell *no one*."

Eyvind had little trouble avoiding Linet, small though the ship was. A kind of mutual understanding had settled between them, and if their brief affair was not ended, it was at least put down into the root cellar for the winter. His romp at the brothel – several in fact, as Antero somehow had gained access to King Osmund's substantial line of credit – had been predictably unsatisfying, and did little to clear his head of her. But the cargo they now carried made the whole situation more real, more dire, and he felt little motivation to do anything but get on with the business of getting himself killed. He busied himself with a renewed attention to archery practice, with his bow of more reasonable weight this time, though he refused to tell anyone exactly why. At the very least, this time he was too distracted to suffer seasickness.

*   *   *

The next morning one of the crew called land a-ho with the enthusiasm of one who'd earn a silver penny for being the first to sight it, and through the fog the promised fishing village slowly took form. A few wide-eyed locals stared at them from the shore, and as the ship drew near it became clear there was no dock large enough to berth them. Deckhands prepared the ship's two longboats for landing, with Davenga, Eyvind, Aerrus and Linet all in the first to go ashore. Eyvind barely managed to suppress a laugh when the boat hit water and began rocking from side to side, startling the grizzled general into grasping at the wales to steady himself.

"Egh," Davenga grumbled, "man was not meant to live on water!"

The boat was rowed aground, the gravelly beach announcing itself with hollow scrapes against the hull as they lurched to a halt. Eyvind wasted no time in hopping out and approaching the villagers, who still stood transfixed by the sight. "Hail and g'morning!"

Two of them, a man and woman with fishing nets dangling from their fingers but now forgotten, looked once at each other, then at Davenga. "What..." the man stuttered nervously, "what is this? Are we bein' invaded?"

Eyvind held up his hands in what he hoped was a calming gesture. "No! Well, yes. I mean, you are being invaded. We are. But this isn't it. We're sent from King Osmund. Um...." He fumbled for the royal badge in his belt purse as proof, not even sure they'd recognize it.

"Ozzie?" The woman screwed up her face in a sneer. "I heard he done hightailed it to sandcrab country, scared off by some boy-lover from east'rd. Rot 'im! Lucky for us we got good old Lord Armino to keep things in order here!" Some of the other villagers gathered nodded in affirmation.

"Aye," Eyvind said, "about that...."

"What?"

"Never mind. These soldiers are allies from Pelona, here to help. You've nothing to fear, unless there are fish-thieves among 'em."

"Hummph," another villager said, "like as not. You get blown off course? Why land here and not Ólo?"

"Well, that might take some explaining, but I'm afraid we don't have time."

"Smells rotten to me, and I don't trust foreigners."

"I'm from Edrastead!"

"Aha! Goat-shagging mountain folk I trust even less—"

"Enough of this," said Davenga as he stepped in front of Eyvind, totally eclipsing him. "Your king has commanded our expedition, and my queen. You will assist us in unloading our ship's provisions, and speak of our presence to no one!"

Eyvind hastily stepped to the side to reveal himself once more. "And we'll pay you well for it."

Davenga frowned. "We will?"

Argument and haggling continued in this vein for some minutes, while Aerrus and Linet stood back with arms folded and eyes rolling. "If this is how things get done in the knee-bent world," Aerrus said, "I want no part of it."

"Phynagoras'll have the whole kingdom conquered by the time they sort this out," Linet replied.

In the end, a price was agreed upon to rent out some fishing boats to help quickly unload men and cargo, with only a couple of villagers recruited to aid the task. Eyvind took special care with one crate in particular, never leaving it alone even for a moment. When the hundred and their provisions were finally ashore, sixteen silvers changed hands, plus another two to keep the villagers quiet about the whole affair for five days and then spread the word of the invasion far and wide thereafter. The villagers immediately fell to arguing amongst themselves over how to divide the profit.

"This country is insane," Davenga said, shaking his head in wonder. "How you avoided being attacked thus far is a mystery to me."

"Just lucky I guess." Eyvind pointed southward, where a small river meandered to the sea between lines of rocky hills that rose into the mountains. "There's our path. How soon can we be underway?"

"Soon," Davenga replied, seeing the soldiers already breaking open the crates to dole out weapons, supplies and food among them. "Within two hours we'll be gone from here, and carry all we need. Tell those greedy fishermen they may keep the empty crates."

CHAPTER FIFTEEN

Heron Kings of the Hill

Davenga shivered as a fresh breeze froze his spine.

"As I said," Eyvind began.

"Yes, yes. And as *I* said, we are strong to endure. Still, I did not expect it to be *this* cold. How can men live in such a place?"

They were three days into the mountains, following the increasingly frozen river that became a creek, then only a brook. The pass that led to Phenidra was in sight, and they'd reach it by nightfall. This fact did little to stop Davenga's shivering, or his hundred soldiers. The canyon almost seemed to funnel the chill wind into their faces as they scrambled over rocks and shards of ice.

Eyvind grinned, happy to be able to gloat a little for once over the tough-as-nails general. "Well, you're supposed to be impersonating Phynagoras. You think he would complain like that?"

"I know nothing of him," Davenga replied with his customary frown. "But to wish to conquer this land he must not have much sense."

The soldiers snaking back into the rear either wore or carried their gear, with only five or six horses brought from Pelona. Eyvind looked back nervously as the crate he'd shepherded so far wobbled atop the back of the largest mount. It was tied down tightly, but still.

Linet and Aerrus came up behind them, seeming to have no trouble negotiating the rocks or the cold. "How much farther to Phenidra once we reach the pass?" Linet asked.

"Only another day or so," Eyvind answered. "By tomorrow we should be all the way up the hill." He took out the ring emblazoned with Phynagoras's sigil. "I was thinking you should pose as ambassador.

To make the introductions. I'll have to keep my face hidden, obviously. Armino won't forget his lost prisoner."

"Me? I don't think I look very Bhasan."

Eyvind grinned again. "Have you looked in a glass lately? Pelona's given you a tan."

"It has?"

Aerrus nodded in agreement. "He's right, you know. Freckles, too."

"Faint ones, just under your eyes. Very cute."

Linet wrinkled her nose in exasperation. "You two are impossible." She dropped back, pretending to inspect some piece of baggage or another.

"I do not understand," said Davenga. "Is this woman your lover, or no?"

"Well," Eyvind looked at Aerrus, who only shrugged uselessly, "not at the moment. Not with...all this."

"Ah, that I understand. Many years ago, my wife refused to marry me until I had finished with my wars. I once thought she wished to marry only a soldier who brought victory. Now I know that was not it at all."

The next morning the wind grew even colder, harder. All around them snow-capped peaks towered, some painted orange as the sun rose, others still cloaked in shadow. The pass was little more than a low point among the sharp crags, yet still climbed up as it led westward toward their destination. It was here the plan was put fully into effect. The soldiers carried shields of wood covered with plain hide that now became an explosion of color and shape when containers of paint were opened to disguise their Pelonan origin. Each man was left to let his imagination run wild, decorating his shield with whatever design he liked. Davenga himself painted several spare shields with the image of a man all blackened and aflame yet sporting a mad grin as he burned.

"Xolthoc," he pronounced with pride, "demon ruler of the Cloud Kingdom of Uxtaphrath, of Marzahni legend. A hero to child Davenga."

"Must've been some childhood," Aerrus remarked while helping to pass out the flowing robes the foremost of them would be wearing.

"You have, as they say in your tongue, no idea. And I am to impersonate the conqueror himself? Surely they aren't so ignorant as to mistake Marzahni for Porontan?"

"They are," Eyvind confirmed. He held one end of a long pole that was in the process of being fashioned into a makeshift palanquin on which Davenga would be carried. "Armino himself, probably not, but then his suspicions shouldn't keep him from opening the gates to us, not at this late stage. He fears Phynagoras, I saw that in his face as he was made to kiss his ring."

"So I will ride this thing like an invalid?"

"Arrive in style, of course. They certainly won't know Bhasan customs about such things."

"And I his ambassador," said Linet while she wriggled into a blue robe. "Never thought myself particularly diplomatic."

"If you don't want to, I could always make a go of it," Aerrus said with a grin.

"No!" Linet, Eyvind and Davenga all shouted at once.

Thus costumed, the host continued up the pass while the painted shields dried. Frightful figures of roaring bears, winged serpents, skulls, demons, including Davenga's burned man, all marched up toward Phenidra. Above them a few standards painted with the stag and panther-man sigil snapped in the wind. Eyvind found himself walking next to Linet, who stared straight ahead yet struggled to keep pace in the awkward robe. "You nervous?" he asked.

She shook her head. "No. Not nervous. I'm completely terrified. Somehow I never really expected this to happen. Now I can't stop thinking of the thousand things that'll probably go wrong." She laid a hand on the back of the packhorse next to her, her bow and short sword hidden there under a blanket. "When I first mentioned taking Phenidra from Armino, Perrim and Lom mocked me for it. I was angry then. Now...maybe they were right." She tried a smile, but it was unconvincing. "Must just fill you with confidence, doesn't it?"

Eyvind shrugged. "I don't know. It's good at least to know you're as human as the rest of us, doubts and mistakes and all."

"Oh, I've made some truly epic mistakes in my time, don't you worry. I just hope this isn't the last of them." Then, in an exaggerated attempt at a foreign accent, she said, haltingly, "My...my Lord and master Phynagoras bids you...dammit. He sends his greetings and asks you to grant him the hospitality...ah, no...."

"No," Eyvind said, "not asks. He doesn't ask. Say...say he extends his hand in offer of peace to his newest satrap, and invites Armino to welcome him."

★   ★   ★

"...and invites the Lord Armino to welcome him!"

Linet's words echoed off the chilled rocks and the wall before them. They stood silent and still as statues, each of a hundred pairs of eyes looking up at the men lining the battlements. Four unlucky soldiers bore Davenga as he sat on the palanquin, trying to look bored and imperious at the same time, while Linet stood forward with the ring extended toward the gathered forms and spoke the rehearsed words. Eyvind sat mounted just behind, ready to whisper advice should it be needed, his face covered by a heavy helm. He wouldn't have recognized any familiar faces from such a distance, but even then he could see the men on the walls were not regular soldiers. *More mercenaries*, he thought with disgust as two dozen crossbows were pointed just away from their general direction. *Armino's grown even more paranoid.*

A new form appeared, and the noon light glinting off his bald head left no doubt as to his identity. Frowning, Armino squinted at Linet. "You...you're not the same emissary as before. My...my lord Phynagoras? Is that you?"

"Who else?" Linet answered with a haughtiness she almost certainly did not feel. "We have come, as agreed, ahead of schedule thanks to your bumbling incompetence. My colleague has briefed me on all particulars. The greater part of our expedition awaits mere miles back. Our road has been long and cold, and you will now welcome my Lord Phynagoras and his small honor guard."

Davenga sighed heavily and said nothing, but tossed a look of annoyance up at Armino as he lounged on the platform.

"But...." Armino shook his head, then made a gesture toward somewhere out of sight. "Yes, yes very well. Um, please tell my lord to come round to the gate, where he is most welcome. Hail, m'lord!"

Without giving answer they marched around the fortress's perimeter to the western wall, where a gate and portcullis began a slow process of opening. Linet was first through, followed by Eyvind, then Aerrus and Davenga on his palanquin. The twenty forward-most soldiers formed a protective flank on either side of them as they entered the courtyard, the keep just ahead of them.

Eyvind looked around and still saw no one he knew. It seemed almost all the garrison had been replaced with mercenaries. As Armino descended into the yard to welcome them, Eyvind instinctively turned his head away, even though the helm concealed his identity. Then, something caught the corner of his eye. He looked upward, and over the gate, strung from the inner wall, was a body. Though the flesh had decomposed over the course of a season, the cold had preserved enough to leave no doubt in his mind – it was Captain Coladdi, strung up as a gruesome example.

Despite the horrors he'd witnessed since fleeing Phenidra, this one filled Eyvind with dread and nausea, and he was suddenly dizzy. He doubled over, almost falling from the horse, but caught himself just in time. But the helm, which didn't fit him very well to begin with, fell off completely, leaving his face exposed to the world.

And of course, it was at just this point that Armino arrived, went down on one knee before Davenga and said, "My Lord, we welcome you to this humble hold, and to Argovan, where we are sure your reign will – wait. Who...you?" He stared in open shock at Eyvind. "You!"

Of all the things that could've gone wrong, this was one that none of them had remotely considered, and they stood motionless, each glancing at the other. The spell was broken when realization spread across Armino's furious face. "A trick. Impostors! All to me! Kill them!" Suddenly a host of crossbows were aimed directly at them.

"Ranks, form square!" Davenga bellowed, leaping from the palanquin. Before his feet were on the ground he grabbed the platform out of the hands of its bearers and held it facing forward. A fraction of a second later bolts tore into it, some punching clean though. All around men screamed and scrambled to obey the order. A wall of painted shields went up around them, with a stubble of sharp spears projecting out from it. Eyvind wrenched his horse around to fight his way behind the line of Pelonan soldiers. But a bolt took the animal in the rump, and he went tumbling. As the horse ran off somewhere in terror and taking his bow and sword with it, Eyvind scrambled through greaved shins to the protection of the shield wall. Linet and Aerrus already had their weapons out, costumes thrown off, and were sending arrows out to answer the hail from the mercenary crossbows.

"Square, advance!" At the general's command the line of shields began inching forward, further into the courtyard. A second line of men formed up behind the front, holding their shields over the heads of their fellows as shots rained from the battlements. Behind, the disordered remainder of soldiers rushed in through the still-open gate.

Linet and Aerrus picked off one enemy after another along the wall, while on the ground the Pelonans pushed their human machine inexorably forward. Ballistae were mounted along the battlements but faced outward and couldn't easily be turned around. Armino stared in shock at the sight for only a few moments before turning tail and running toward the keep. Eyvind watched this and was filled with a sudden red fury. Growling, he reached to the side and drew Aerrus's sword from his scabbard.

"Hey!" Aerrus shouted between shots. "Eh, be my guest."

Eyvind charged back through the shield wall, dodging a bolt to pick up a small shield someone had dropped. He ran across the yard, bashing one mercenary in his way and getting bashed in turn by another. An ax thundered against the shield, its bearded brute of an owner spitting curses at him. The mercenary hooked his ax around the rim, trying to rip it away.

Eyvind fought to keep hold of the shield, snarling back at his enemy. Just when his grip began to weaken, he felt a gentle wind breeze by his ear, and suddenly the mercenary was off of him and writhing on the ground, an arrow having suddenly sprouted from his neck. Eyvind spared only the space of an eyeblink to look back and see Linet already nocking for another shot. *Barely an inch from my head!* he thought vaguely as he took up his course again, crashing against the keep door. Locked. Of course. Without a second thought he went around the side of the structure, up the stair that led to the storage loft, where all this nightmare had started. He kicked the door in and ran over to the hole that opened onto Armino's private chamber. But how to get to him?

He looked around for something to pry the floorboards away. There were practice swords, but...then, in the light of the open door, he saw that big stone statue in the corner. The ugly bust of a fellow with faintly Marchman features, and heavy enough.

Eyvind went behind the statue, which was sat atop a wooden frame for transport. He wedged himself between it and the wall and heaved. The thing toppled over, right onto the hole in the floor. There was a loud crash, and Eyvind had to leap out of the way to avoid falling into the widening chasm made by shattering old wood. There was an agonized cry from below, and looking down he saw one of Armino's mercenary bodyguards pinned under the fallen debris.

He leaped down the short distance to the top of the statue, then again to the ground. He raised his shield just in time to block a blow from a second bodyguard, then slashed at the man's unarmored legs. He went down, whimpering. Eyvind turned and found himself face to face with Armino.

"You!" Armino snarled. "I should've killed you when I had the chance, you spying shitespittle!"

"Aye, you're probably right. Now you're going to die a traitor." Eyvind raised his sword.

"You idiot! You think it matters what we do here now? There's no stopping Phynagoras! That fool of a king saw to that. I had no choice!"

"And no choice but to string up the cap'n like a common criminal?"

Armino sneered. "Aw, does your heart bleed for the precious old man? Well, you can join him!" Armino plucked up the sword and shield of one of the fallen bodyguards and charged. But Eyvind's long hours in the yard drilling with Coladdi served him in good stead, and he at last fell into his wards without having to remember them. Blow after blow fell, but Eyvind deflected each.

In the saga songs, the heroes always endure painfully, absurdly long duels, with blades clanging on and on for hours. But in real life, a battle with sharp swords does not last. Thus it was with some surprise that barely fifteen seconds after theirs began, Eyvind bound Armino's sword up between his own crossguard and buckler, then bashed him with the boss to send him tumbling backward. Before Armino had even hit the ground Eyvind pressed the attack and plunged the blade into the Marcher lord's black heart.

Armino lay motionless for a few seconds, examining the odd sight of his own impalement with curiosity. "Oh," he mumbled, "that's... you...you idiot." And then he died.

Eyvind unlocked the chamber, then the keep itself. Fighting fatigue, he dragged Armino's body to the entrance and flung the doors open to reveal the battle grinding on. A few Pelonans and more than a few mercenaries lay in the yard, and over them men still fought.

"*Hold!*" he shouted at the top of his lungs. "*Hold!* It's over!" Slowly, too slowly, faces from both sides turned toward him, toward the corpse still wearing the black sable signifying his title. "Don't... don't die for a dead traitor."

The fighting gradually broke off, the sides each pulling back to their respective lines. The remaining mercenaries looked with horror on their dead employer, then at Phenidra's open gate.

"Shite," one of them spat. "Contract's canceled, lads!" He ran right past the line of Pelonans and out of the fortress, and the rest followed suit. And just like that, it was over. A few of the regular garrison still present stood fidgeting nervously after throwing down their weapons, not sure what to do. A great victory cry went up among the Pelonan company, and Eyvind was almost knocked over when Linet ran to embrace him.

"Oh," she said, fighting back tears, "I was wrong. I was so wrong!"

"Well best call a scribe to take down this rare moment in history! Um, wrong about what, exactly?"

"When I saw you tear off after Armino like that, I was filled with...."

"Disgust at my monumental stupidity?"

"I knew then that somehow, we'd already won. It was all over but the dyin'. I was wrong, you aren't a weakness. You're a strength. *My* strength."

Eyvind smiled. "Oh, was that all it took to bring you round? Can't help but notice you only seem to want me after I've done something really dangerous."

Davenga came up to him, still wearing his ridiculous and now blood-spattered robe, yet every inch the victorious general. "Phenidra is ours. It seems my calculation of our chances was a bit...conservative." The slightest hint of a grin cracked on Davenga's face, like a sliver of sunlight breaking through a storm cloud.

"I'm sorry," Eyvind said, shaking his head, "I gave us away from the start!"

"No matter, we would've had to drop the disguise eventually. The surprise was still ours, and it could not have ended a better way." Davenga swept a hand over the remaining garrison and the wounded. "What shall we do with these?"

Eyvind turned his gaze on a pair kneeling with hands bound. "I was a slogger here for years, and I don't know you two."

"We're new," one of them said nervously. "Everyone still here is."

"Figures. Where's the rest of the garrison?"

"Sent away, to Vin, or Edrastead for some reason."

"And what reason do you suppose?" He raised his voice so all could hear. "Armino was a traitor, wanted only mercs and you greenhorns here when Phynagoras arrived, as we pretended to be!" He pulled out the royal badge given to him by Essimis. "We're here at the behest of King Osmund, and we've retaken Phenidra in his name. You men, you can stay and defend it with us, or go. But when Phynagoras comes for true, I think you'll want to be on this side of the walls."

The pair looked at each other for only a second before nodding. "We'll stay!"

"Good. Now," he pointed up at the sorry sight of Coladdi still hanging from the walls, "as your first duty, you cut that man down and give him a decent burial." He then kicked the lifeless head of Armino at his feet. "And string *this* piece of shite up in his place."

★　　★　　★

With those dark tasks behind them, a strange peace fell over Phenidra. The place looked different to Eyvind somehow, and not just because of the bodies that'd littered the yard and had only just been cleared away. So much blood and pain, and now it was like it had never been. The unease hit him as soon as he'd handed Aerrus his sword back, still dripping with Armino's blood. Aerrus had just wiped it clean and returned it to his scabbard, obscenely casual. No, he was certainly no longer a peacetime soldier, and Phenidra was no longer an uncomfortable though familiar home, but a true military asset that bodies would fall to possess. Would it all happen again when Phynagoras arrived? He felt suddenly swept up in the rush of events he had no control over.

He'd walked the barracks, stables and chambers of the keep with Davenga to make certain no more mercs lay hiding in wait to knife them in the night. There were none, but the store of food and mounts and supplies that had been laid in in anticipation of Phynagoras's arrival was a welcome surprise. The small infirmary was well-stocked, allowing them to tend to their wounded. The last place they'd inspected was the lord's bedchamber, where the man he'd sworn to serve under and then killed had slept. A chill went down his spine upon entering the room with its plain but comfortable bed, bureau, locking chest and writing desk.

"I suppose you'll be taking this for yourself," Eyvind said haltingly. "You're the ranking officer here after all, by far."

The general shook his head. "No, I will bed down with my men in the barracks. In this foreign land they should have a familiar face among them, even one as ugly as mine. You take it – you did vanquish the former owner. That is the way of things."

"I—" he started, then faltered. He could think of no route to make argument.

Davenga must have sensed his discomfort, and laid a heavy hand on Eyvind's shoulder. "It it not always about what you want, boy. The few others of your fellows who served here need leadership now, a new face to look to. And mine is too strange. You are the lord now. Perhaps even…invite young Linet to join you, for the danger is past for now." Davenga let out a strange, rhythmic sound, and Eyvind was a few seconds realizing that it was the general's approximation of a belly laugh.

As it turned out he didn't need to invite her. She somehow found her way to the bedchamber on her own as Eyvind was preparing to retire, though perhaps others had had a hand in directing her.

"Nice," she said, looking around the room, in a tone that made it very clear that she didn't find anything nice about it. "Bit of a severe bastard, was old Armino."

"Well, it's no cave hacked out of the earth, for certain," he replied, instantly happier at her presence. "But it serves. Our little Lodge above ground, you might say."

"I wouldn't say," she said with a sudden sharp frown. "It was entirely too easy to get in here. Your security's absolute shit. The lord should be executed, if I had anything to say about it!"

Eyvind stared at her, agape. "I, uh…."

Linet broke into a quivering paroxym of laughter. "Oh Eyvind, I'm just teasing you."

"Oh. Who are you, and what've you done with the dour huntress I used to know?"

"Just relieved to be alive, I guess."

Eyvind scowled. "Everyone seems cheerful all of a sudden, and I can't see why. I slaughtered my own sworn lord today. Whatever else he'd done, that's a hard thing. Not sure I could've done it without seeing…without the cap'n…."

"You're right. I guess I never thought of that, I was so wrapped up in my own fears. Maybe that makes us even." She stalked closer to him, curled her lithe fingers about his waist and smiled. "This room, it's all ours?"

"Uh," he stammered, tensing.

Linet moved away, red-faced. "I'm sorry, I shouldn't have—"

"No! It's all right, I was just surprised—"

"Seems we're destined never to be of the same mind. I understand. I'll go if you don't want to."

"It's not that! I do. I do, I just feel like I shouldn't, you know? Like, it shouldn't be so easy."

Linet shrugged. "We're blood bags. Prick us a bit and we leak. It's easy to forget with all the planning and scheming and high politics. Those mercs shot you and smashed up my arm. I can't exactly feel sorry for them."

"No. But we sure beat 'em today, didn't we?"

Linet smiled. "We did. Thanks to your stupid courage."

"And your crazed wits. Oh, toss it. Come here."

It wasn't a furious collision this time. It felt more like a long goodbye, one he didn't want but couldn't bear to refuse. Later, as Linet lay half-asleep in his arms, she said, "I can't stay, you know."

"I know. Though I was hoping my expert skills at bedsport would convince you."

Linet trembled a bit with laughter. "Almost. *Almost.* But I can't, we need to prepare. Spread the word far and wide. It's our only chance. We'll be together again, if I have anything to say about it."

"If. Armino, he died without issue. Tired old bloodline, they say. If we do by some miracle survive this, Phenidra's going to need a new lord. Do you dare think…?"

"Osmund would be a fool to hand it over to anyone else. Course, he *is* a bit of a fool, so who knows? If he doesn't, I'll come back here and take it again!"

Eyvind laughed at that. "Good to know. But what I was getting at is, well, every lord needs a lady by his side. Maybe, I mean if—"

"That's one more big *if*," she said hastily. "We'll talk about it, my mountaintop lord, when *if* becomes *then*."

★   ★   ★

When the next sun rose over Phenidra, the new garrison took up their duties almost as if nothing had changed. Sentries, Pelonan and Argovani both, walked the walls side by side, staring, straining their eyes eastward for what must inevitably come. Soldiers from Vin Gannoni and Edrastead were recalled slowly, gradually and only after being made aware of what had transpired and their intentions well understood. Some refused to believe it and refused to return. But in truth many had already suspected Armino's scheme without having the courage to act on it. With those most trustworthy reinstalled at the fortress, the place was at last accounted reasonably secure.

"Which means it's time for us to go," Aerrus said to Eyvind as he packed one of the horses in the yard. "I know that's not what you want to hear, but that was the plan."

Eyvind nodded. "I know, I know. This insurgency of yours. You think it has any chance without high walls to shield you?"

"The other border lords have walls enough, and what help do you imagine they'll be? Honestly, none of this ever really had much chance, but here we are."

"In that case, there's something I've been keeping from you that I think might help."

Aerrus raised a curious eyebrow.

Wood creaked and groaned as Eyvind heaved with the prybar in the far corner of a garrison stable. The top came off with a sudden crack to reveal, perhaps anticlimactically, a mass of hard-packed hay.

Aerrus and Linet looked closer. "Is there anything in there?"

Eyvind tore out handfuls of the hay, tossing it behind him. "I didn't trust anyone else to open it. Not safely. I was told to tell no one until it was time but...ah, here."

The hay finally cleared away, the crate revealed row after row of phials. Small, delicate phials, each containing a tiny amount of liquid. There were more than twenty altogether, and Linet and Aerrus both backed away with alarmed expressions.

"Is," Linet said weakly, "is that—?"

"Aye, Vrril. Fresh from the blasted alchemists. Portioned out into just the right amounts to rip people into red stains."

Aerrus's mouth hung open. "You mean to say you been carryin' this stuff with us the whole time?"

"The king gave it to me just before we left Ayala. I wanted so badly to use it against Armino, but I was given strict orders. Against Phynagoras only. Way I see it, we'll both be fighting him in our own ways, so I want you to take some."

"How much?"

"Much as you dare. Antero assures me, for whatever his assurances are worth, that this batch is less temperamental. You needn't fear so long as you keep it and its vapors away from flame."

"But," Linet said nervously, "we don't know how to use this kind of weapon."

Eyvind laughed. "I've had to learn more than my fair share of new ways over the last season. Seems fitting you should expand your horizons too, and something tells me you lot have the imagination to put it to good use. Or terrible use, however you want to think of it. I'm just a man in a castle, and the days when such relics decide battles and wars and the course of history are coming to an end. I feel that in my bones. You're the future, much as you are the past."

Linet couldn't help herself from reaching into the crate and pulling out one of the phials. The liquid once again seemed to shimmer with its own, tantalizingly evil light.

She embraced Eyvind once more but said little, for it had already been said. Davenga wished her and Aerrus both good luck and glorious deaths, and they rode two strong horses out Phenidra's gate under the putrefying corpse of Armino. Six phials of Vrril rode at their belts, and as they began the journey down to the valley the sense of terror at holding so much destructive power against vital organs eased little.

CHAPTER SIXTEEN

Shameful, Really

"You two are insane! Or drunk. Probably both. Shameful, really."
Linet and Aerrus stood in Vin Gannoni's council hall and endured the
scathing words of its mayor, a cantankerous old woman who would've
given even Essimis heartburn to deal with. She sat behind a heavy
Qassorian oak desk piled high with tablets and scrolls, weighed down
by an equally heavy frown and gilded chain of office around her neck. A
few town councilors and mercers frowned with her at the interruption
of their routine affairs. The dissolution of the nobility had led to the
rise of a certain type of civil service class, and the bureaucratic mindset
seemed to be the hot air that rose to the top of it most quickly.

"Surely we would've heard of this supposed invasion from official
sources. And yet you claim you've not only taken over Phenidra but
killed Lord Armino? Ha! Not even the old Chthonii of myth could
bring that boar down. Lies! I should have you in irons for wasting
my time...."

"If you'll just listen," Linet said again, her patience beginning to
fray. "King Osmund sent out no word of his...uh, departure so as not
to let Phynagoras know how much we knew. Now that Armino's
treachery is exposed, the invaders are coming earlier than planned, and
there was no time to send 'official sources'! You see here—" She held
up her royal badge yet again, and Aerrus did so as well.

"Yes, yes. Those could be fake, how would I know? King ain't
been here himself in years. Shameful, really." She pointed a broad
gavel down at the pair. "We here still remember Bergovny of old,
and how his 'Vani line took over, then took away our noble lords

so they can't rebel, leaving folk like little old me to run things. So let us run 'em, and kindly bugger off!" The councilors nodded in silent agreement.

"Phynagoras. Is. Coming!" Aerrus fought not to scream through gritted teeth. "What about that don't you understand? And not just to rule. He'll swipe you all aside to make room for his worshipers then move on to take the whole world. We're offering you a chance to hold him back."

"Fantasy," the mayor said, waving her hands dismissively. "Pure fantasy, and badly written at that. On the unlikely chance that them badges are genuine, I'll give you two one more chance to get out of our hair before having you arrested for disturbing the peace. You are dismissed!"

"Disturbing...." Linet shook her head in disbelief. These people were so inured to the idleness of peace their minds couldn't comprehend the danger.

Aerrus looked around at the growing crowd, gathered to witness the spectacle in a town where little of interest occurred. Gawkers spilled out the door behind them and into the street to watch and listen. Some were garrison soldiers who had already heard some of the news but were yet to take action. He turned, walked out of the hall and into the town square to address them directly. "You, all of you, listen up! When those armies come down from the mountains, you'll have little time. Either run, flee west for all the good it'll do you. Or, if you suddenly grow a mind to fight, look south for leadership. We...." He looked questioningly at Linet. She nodded, her jaw set and clenched as she felt the sky turn a bit faster in that moment.

"Whether you've heard our name or not, you know us. You've heard the stories. Rangers or demons of the forest, the vengeance of the Marchwood, the fury of the few who stood for the many in the wars of long ago, whatever. We never went away, we never lived in peace though we fought for it. We'll do so again if you'll join. When Phynagoras comes, rise up with us."

"The Marchwood Massacre?" Incredulous voices came from among the crowd. "That was *you*? And you think you can win this thing?"

"No," Linet answered, "we can't win. They have every advantage. But we don't have to win, we just have to not lose until Osmund's return. And he *will* return."

The mayor had had enough, and at her order bailiffs stalked towards them with halberds and chains at the ready. "Think we've outstayed our welcome," Aerrus said, and they quickly unhitched their mounts and began the long journey south.

"Maybe we should've given a demonstration of the Vrril," Linet said when they were away.

"Nah," Aerrus answered, "it'd only be wasted on them. Did I really just do what I think I did?"

"Gave away our secret to the whole world? You did. To Vin Gannoni, anyway. But it was the right thing to do. To win this war the Heron Kings are going to have to leave the nest and fly. Can't stay hidden anymore in caves. Or castles."

"You're worried about Eyvind. He's got a good head on him, for a soldier. He'll be all right."

"You don't know that, don't say it!" She blushed at her sudden temper.

"Okay, sorry! But we have to believe it anyway, don't we?"

"Yeah."

Aerrus nudged his horse a bit faster. "Come on. Couple days to the Carsa headwaters. Then Nostrada, Wengeddy. We'll have better luck there. I hope."

★   ★   ★

They stopped at every town and village along the way to spread the word and raise recruits. All through the Northmarch and Midmarch both, the result was depressingly similar: a roughly equal number of people either didn't believe them or began packing up to flee west. You could count on one hand those who pledged themselves to the fight, and then only thanks to their royal badges, which were only occasionally recognized. Aerrus had fallen to making some dubious promises about rewards, offices and even new patents of nobility when the invader was defeated. Linet was tempted to gather all volunteers at the Lodge itself to organize them, but some vestige of caution held her back. They said only to look for leadership near where the river road branched off toward Thoriglyn. They made a brief detour to the Polytheon priory, where Linet and Eyvind had once taken refuge, only to find the place deserted. "Don't know if it's a good sign, or bad," Aerrus remarked.

Wengeddy proved a slight improvement, at least. The prosperous town was run by a *de facto* business cartel holding several exclusive patents to the crown, thus their badges proved a bit more convincing. Having interrupted an important meeting about taxes or something, Aerrus and Linet made their case before another committee of mercers, jewelers and other merchants clad in rich dark fur-lined woolens. It seemed the truth of Phynagoras's invasion had finally begun to leak out, and when warned of the danger, more than one wealthy aristocrat left the assembly hall in the middle of town to make hasty departure plans. But not all.

"But you must understand," said one plump fellow who seemed to be in charge of the proceedings, hand held out wide as though in supplication to the rangers, "we are men of business, not warriors. Why, we pay taxes precisely so that this kind of thing doesn't happen!"

I doubt you actually pay them, Linet thought but didn't say. "Sir, I'm sure that's true. But it doesn't change the fact that he's coming and the king is not here. Just us."

"Well, this is *most* irregular," said a similarly dressed woman already gathering up her courtly belongings. "I have contracts! Concerns! You cannot expect us to just up and leave, or less to play at rustic rebels—"

"Madam," Aerrus said with a sigh, rubbing his temples, "at this point we don't expect much of anything from you. We're just telling you what's about to happen, and what can be done about it. I suggest you spread the word."

They left the hall just as dejected as they had in Vin. Linet noted a man leaning up against the doorway to the building and eyeing them intently. "Hey," she called out. "You. Yeah, you! Don't I know you?" The man ducked down an alley, and they followed.

"Not so loud," he grumbled when they caught up to him. He was an average-looking fellow of seemingly middling means, but wore a nervous frown. "Who knows who else is listening."

"Who is this?" Aerrus asked.

"One of Bolen's contacts, from the intelligence network we were trying to set up," said Linet.

"Humph," snorted the man, arms crossed. "Contact? Pretty word for trappin' me in your debt. Was all that cack you just told the committee true?"

"'Fraid so," said Aerrus. "Don't suppose you might have better luck convincing everyone?"

The man shrugged. "Still got some o' the right ears on my side. I might...."

Linet scowled. "If?"

"If you account my debt paid, and I never have to lay eyes on you noggin-fracted folks again."

"You'll get your wish if Phynagoras gets his hands on you, though not in the way you'd want. Fine. Get these people to evacuate and you're a free man."

He nodded. "Deal."

"You could join us you know," Aerrus ventured, "help us fight."

"No thanks, I done my part. I'm for 'Nocca, fast as I can make it."

The man was as good as his word. By the time they left Wengeddy all the aristocrats had begun packing up their wealth and belongings and servants, ready to abandon the city just as Osmund had abandoned the kingdom. Since rich tongues wagged the loudest, the news quickly permeated to the general population, and just before the town of about four thousand souls disappeared out of sight the beginnings of a mass exodus could be spotted. Aerrus gave a bitter laugh. "Looks like we been going about this all wrong. We should've been threatening the pockets of the rich to get things done, not appealing to common sense they don't seem to have."

"What a pathetic showing," Linet remarked, "that I'd account a panicked retreat a *good* result."

"Not so good for the folk who have nowhere to go."

★   ★   ★

Even that partial success was not to be repeated, however. "Useless!" Aerrus complained for the thousandth time as they finally rode into the familiar territory of the Marchwood. "So used to peace they don't even consider the possibility. I blame Osmund, going without any army worthy of the name for so long."

"An army that doesn't exist can't be turned against you, I guess," Linet answered. "And no rebellious nobility. I guess it makes sense so long as there's no external threat."

"Which has worked out just beautifully, hasn't it? Eh...." He cast a sidelong glance at Linet. "What do you think Perrim and Lom will have to say about all this?"

"I don't know. But in a way it doesn't matter. The thing's done."

They turned off the road onto a path a few miles north of the Lodge, taking a winding route partly out of the habit of leaving no trail when not in a hurry, but maybe also out of a subconscious desire to delay the inevitable confrontation. When they were before the rockface, with its hidden entrance and waterfall splashing in the distance, Aerrus looked up at it and sighed. "It seems smaller now, somehow. Doesn't it?"

Linet nodded. "It does. In fact—"

She never finished her thought as Thanis and Haskell jumped out of some hidden sentry post, bows raised only long enough for them to recognize the pair.

"Gods' tits," Haskell grumbled, his goatee rippling. "Where in the nineteen hells have *you two* been?"

"All over the world, it seems like," Linet answered. "I trust Thanis delivered our message?"

Thanis nodded. "I did. You could hear Perrim screaming in every cell of the Lodge."

"I hope she's calmed down by now," said Aerrus.

"You'd better go check in. Just—" Thanis broke off suddenly, looked at Haskell.

"What?" Aerrus pressed.

"Nothing," Haskell said. "Just get in there."

*　　*　　*

"I don't even know what to say."

They stood before Perrim in the low light, feeling the annoyance radiating off the woman even if they couldn't quite see her face. Lom sat at the end of the table, observing but silent. Linet fidgeted nervously.

"Perrim, I—"

"Be quiet!"

They stared each other down for several more seconds, looks of hurt and anger going both ways.

Finally Aerrus cleared his throat. "Look, we don't have time to stand here playing at statues while Phyn—"

"I said be quiet!"

"I know," Aerrus said, more than a little defiant, "and I understand you're mad, but we don't have the luxury of caring right now. Rules are about to go out the window, washed away with that waterfall outside along with a lot of blood. I know we didn't have permission to go to Pelona, but a chance was in our grasp and I wasn't going to let it slip away!"

Perrim shot a hard finger at Aerrus. "I almost expected something like this from you. You're a weapon I know how to use. Gods help me, I wish all of us had a tenth of your brashness...though only a tenth. But *you*." She turned to Linet. "I expected better. This was something to do with that man, wasn't it? That soldier. I should've known."

Linet thrust her chin forward, as she often did when indignant. "Will you let us make our report or not?"

"Oh, fine, gods damn you both! Make it."

They told her all of it. Carsolan and the king, Rinalda, the Vrril, Pelona, the Polytheon, Phenidra and back again. When it was done Perrim sat for a long time, in thought or disbelief they couldn't know. Finally she said, "You had no right to set us on this path, not on your own. But you've done so, and no turning back now. It seems one cannot stop the course of the sun. Leave me, I must think on these things."

Lomuel stood, approached them holding a lamp. As the light danced more brightly across Perrim's face, Linet nearly gasped. She looked even older than she had the last time Linet had endured her lecturing. Much older, and tired. Something was wrong. Linet glanced at Lom, who only gave her a stern look.

"Now," he said to them both, "out with you. You are, after all, far behind on your duties and chores." He shuffled them out of the council room, but instead of closing the door to shut them out, he joined the pair in the stone corridor. "Come with me," he said quietly.

"Lom," Aerrus said, trailing a half-step behind the man, "what was that? What is going on here?"

He led them into the archive study, where Linet had pilfered the incriminating documents before sneaking away with Lom's tacit approval. After scanning the hallway for any eavesdroppers, he said, "Listen carefully. Perrim is…not well."

A cold wave washed down Linet's spine to pool in her stomach. "What do you mean, 'not well'? She looks on the edge of death." She immediately regretted the words, and the pained look on Lom's face.

"You may not be wrong. Myrtho says it's the wasting sickness. Live long enough and everyone gets it eventually. She may have a year, or five years, or just weeks. No telling how fast the disease will spread."

Despite her recent hard words, tears now welled up in Linet's eyes, and even Aerrus looked away. "Isn't…isn't there anything that can be done?"

Lom nodded. "As always in such cases, make her concluding days as peaceful as we can. But it seems that may not be possible now. For what it's worth, I agree with you. This invasion will dash us on its rocks whether we fight it or no. I didn't speak in your favor earlier because, well...."

"Because it doesn't matter," Aerrus finished. "Because you're really the one running things now, isn't that right?"

"I help as I can, more and more. I'm determined that what she doesn't know will not harm her. Everyone else more or less knows this."

"Does she?"

"It's a hard life we lead. She knows that to reach her age, or mine, is a privilege, one I hope you both share. And she understands this is the way of things, even if she can't say it outright."

Linet wiped away her tears. "As always, Lom, you make a bitter pill go down easier. And what do you think about what's to come? About those ways?"

Lom curled his lip. "Insurgency, terrorism? I think it's like picking up a sword by the sharp end to strike. You're just as like to cut yourself as your enemy. But if what you say about the king's dangerous gamble is true, it's the only path left to us. Nothing you could've done differently would change that. You've both done very well. Perrim will come to see that too."

Aerrus gave a soft grunt. "Even if she can't say it outright?"

"Precisely."

★　　★　　★

"I don't understand," said Drissa. "You expect us to...to go *out there*? To lead the commons in a war? That's insane!"

Linet took another patient breath, prepared to explain it all again from the beginning. Being trained in one way one's whole life could make comprehending the opposite a momentous feat. "No, not exactly a war. We can't fight them on those terms; that *would* be insane. What we must do is hurt them bit by bit, make them pay for every pace of earth, every life they take. Hit Phynagoras's forces where it's easiest for us, then run like hells. Assassinate his captains, set traps, poison his supplies. Immobilize him until Osmund returns. Make him jump at shadows in the night but never engage straight on…. It's all right there in the archives. This is how we used to work."

The Lodge had come abuzz with their return and as word of the plan spread. Normally only half of their number would be inhabiting the place at any given time, but now it was crowded to bursting as everyone was being called in to hear it. But not everyone liked what they heard.

"Ancient, desperate days," said Vander, his temper showing on his cheeks with a color to match his hair. "We're not like that anymore; we're trained to track bandits, not hunt genocidal armies!"

Aerrus stood to address the circle of twenty or so gathered outside the Lodge. "No, we'd be even better at it now! Think about it – everyone here's a crack shot with a bow and at least fair with a blade. We have hand language, spies, codes, disguises…. We're trained better than any slogging soldier. We can move without sound, without leaving tracks. And all for what? Babysitting the forest, swatting at bandits, joining the occasional skirmish? That didn't work out so well for us last time, did it? This is what we're made for, we just need the backbone to do it."

"What about the Marcher lords?" The question came from Thanis, grown more confident than when Aerrus had last left his young protégée. "Isn't this *their* job?"

"It should be," Linet conceded. "But things aren't as they once were. I learned a lot when I was at the palace, searching out our betrayer. A lot about politics. The long peace has made them complacent, same as it has us. They can handle a few raids or Marchmen, but not this, not without a real army backing them up. Osbren might help, but Valendri? Trastavere? They'll just stay shut up in their fortresses and wait things out, see who wins and try to cut a deal afterward. We'll send messages to them all, begging for aid. Don't expect much."

"But you're talking about giving up our secrecy," argued Vander, "the advantage we've had since forever. No one even knows we exist. If we lose that, what are we left with? We're just rangers with good aim."

Linet and Aerrus looked at each other, the question and answer all contained in the same glance each way.

"There's something else we have, too," said Linet. "But I only want to have to show it once, so we'd better gather everyone together."

The next day all Heron Kings who weren't away on extended assignments assembled in a field between the Carsa River and the road that followed it. The field had been hit by blight a few years before; nothing grew there and no one had any interest in it. There Linet and Aerrus reproduced the demonstration that had first shaken them to their souls in the courtyard of the palace at Carsolan.

"You sure you want to use one?" Aerrus asked, standing well away from Linet with a burning branch in hand. "We don't have many."

Linet nodded, poised to cast a precious phial at a rubble pile in the midst of the field. "The others need to see, to know what hope we have. They'd never believe it otherwise, as we wouldn't have."

When the Vrril exploded, nearly a hundred bodies all shrank back in terror, many knocked from their feet as much from surprise as by the wave of expanding air.

When it was over, the field lay blackened and smoking. Little fires all around smoldered. The sky was filled with flocks of terrified birds flying every which way, and no doubt many earthbound folk would have liked to join them in their flight. After an appropriately long period of appreciation, Linet turned to the pale-faced crowd.

"This is what we have. Like the founder Alessia wrote, when your enemy's too strong you don't fight them, you murder them. I don't think she ever imagined a weapon like this. But this is what we'll do it with."

"B-but, why *us*?" Drissa's voice quavered with lingering shock.

"Because," Aerrus said, "there's no one else."

PART THREE

CHAPTER SEVENTEEN

Our Definition of Military

"One, two, three, heave!" Another corpse tumbled over the edge of the narrow path and into the surrounding fog. The sudden avalanche just hours before had buried almost a thousand camp followers and, more importantly, a good amount of the baggage train under a falling wave of snow and rock. Though the pass they trod through was well below the snow line, a late summer breeze from the west had dislodged a good chunk of it from above, and the rear of Phynagoras's combined army and migrant horde had been hit. Now Phynagoras himself worked alongside his men to dig out what could be retrieved, every sathav, a hundred-man unit, given its own quota to recover. But they kept running into bodies.

"Fortunately," he grunted as he hauled a crate of something up out of a snowbank, "few of the fighting men were struck, only some stragglers."

"Aye," Boras said with a nod, pulling up a much larger box with his bear-like arms. "Plus some of Cassilda's horse bitches. She won't be happy about that."

"Her mood must have a bottom somewhere. No matter, we're almost there. Two more days and our journey will finally have begun!"

"I fail to see, my lord, how you manage to maintain such good cheer in the face of this catastrophe," Boras said. His heaving breath sent jets swirling to the air, turned to gold by the noonday sun. He, like most of the laboring men, had doffed the warm furs they'd worn since ascending into the mountains to do the work of digging, but they'd need them again soon, and the supplies still hidden under half a parasang's stretch of snow.

"Simple, Boras. You see—"

"M'lord!" A young Bhasan captain approached them with a perfunctory salute, the medallion about his neck the only mark of rank visible over the winter clothing. "I, uh, heard some of the camp followers talking and, well, I thought I should report what I heard." The captain looked away nervously. "That is...."

Boras frowned at the interruption. "Well, out with it, man! Can't you see we've work to do?"

Phynagoras held up a hand to silence him. "Must be of some import to bring it direct to me, now. What is it?"

"Well, there's some talk from the more, er, influential among 'em about turning back. Saying the expedition's cursed, and this is proof of it."

Phynagoras considered silently for a moment, his face unreadable. Finally he said, "What is your name, captain?"

The man gulped nervously. "Erm, Musa, my lord."

"Musa, you will provide Boras with the names of these *influential* followers, and then think no more on it. And you will give it out that...."

*   *   *

"That there's to be no more talk of turning back!" That night at an impromptu rally Phynagoras repeated the orders he'd given the captain. The narrowness of the pass made it difficult to gather the remaining thousands of followers together, but he'd packed them in as closely as could be managed and strained his voice to make it carry. "We've suffered a terrible loss to be sure, and I weep for those souls taken to the gods too early. But think on it – our way back is blocked now, there's nowhere to go but forward! It's a message from those very gods that our road is true. And you who've survived it, you live because you are the chosen! You who will follow me to a new world, a better world. And it's yours. The whole world is yours! Come with me and get some of it!"

A wild cheer went up among the thousands, and spread outward as the words were repeated. Phynagoras hopped down from the pile of retrieved crates he'd stood upon and walked back to his tent, Boras in tow. "Brilliant speech, as usual," Boras said.

Phynagoras snorted. "Pull your tongue out of my arsehole, Boras, it was standard stuff."

"I especially love how you always refer to 'the gods' without specifyin' *which* gods you mean. Works for that whole motley lot."

"Hmm. And the names Captain Musa gave you?"

"Oh, won't see them no more."

"Good. If any dare to ask, let it be known that they were buried in the avalanche."

"But," said Boras, rubbing his beard as he often did when confused, "they were seen after, obviously. They couldn't have been—"

"My dear Boras, how is it after all these years that you can still surprise me? Anyone can tell a believable lie and have it believed. To tell a lie that everyone knows is a lie yet still compel them to *act* as if they believed it such that it might as well be truth? That's true power."

Boras regarded Phynagoras with a look that could've been fear, concern or utter devotion. Then he smiled. "And you can still surprise me, lord, even after all these years. I assume any who *don't* act as if they believe it will also have been buried in the avalanche?"

"Of course. How much supply did we recover, all in all?"

"About half. The rest is too deep to get at."

"And any chance of resupply is cut off as well until the snow decides to melt. Very well, that'll have to do. As I said, we're almost there. But I am looking forward to a warm welcome from my groveling Barghii satrap."

They arrived at the tent, one of only a few hastily erected when they were forced to make camp after the avalanche, with the rest of the men having to curl up on the frigid ground. It was a small, sparse thing, with only a small brazier to provide warmth. Caerdig was curled up in a bear fur next to it, half asleep.

"Aye, lord," Boras continued. "But it's a small castle, I've heard, won't hold even a tenth of our men."

"You've seen the same maps I have," Phynagoras answered, pouring the general a generous cup of wine. "There, that's the last that wasn't lost, so savor it. There's a town a few days beyond. After this it'll be a trivial walk to get there. You'll continue on and take whatever is needed or wanted for our men and followers, but Phenidra will be my base of power at first."

Boras nodded. "With pleasure."

"Such an ugly name. Phenidra. I think I'll change it to... Caerdigion." He stroked the boy's golden hair with a smile. "Would you like that?"

"Mmm," Caerdig mumbled.

"Then it's settled. Now, we just have to get there."

★   ★   ★

The next day they were on the move again. It was, of necessity, a slow start, for to stop such a roiling mass of humanity in its tracks was a tedious thing, even when a natural disaster was the cause of it, and getting it to go again even more so. But at last the great snake resumed its ever-westward course, Phynagoras at the head. Boras was somewhere along the line, seeing to some detail or other, but Cassilda had once again taken up a place riding next to Phynagoras after sulking for some time following her public submission.

"There you are! I was afraid you'd been taken by that horrendous avalanche. Do you know, I had to teach these Bhasans that word? Very little snow in the country, as you can imagine—"

"Afraid, or hopeful?" The woman sneered without looking him in the face.

He chose to let the interruption pass. This time. "Why, what could you possibly mean by that? My dear, I absolutely adore you!"

"Sure. I lost twenty women and horses in that white hell, barbarian. Each one a sister to me."

"As I said, there will be casualties, and more to come. You must see the bigger picture – their sacrifice will win vast lands for those who survived. Please try to focus on the positives. The first leg of our journey is nearly finished. Oh, I am looking forward to a bath! I hope they have baths in Barg-o-Bhanii."

"Humph," Cassilda exhaled. "Funny that cleanliness would mean so much to someone who plumbs boys' holes with his prick."

Phynagoras fought down the sudden surge of rage, knowing full well that this was a game of who could rattle the other the most. It was a common route of attack, of course, and easily deflected. "Oh, I've no interest in buggery. Most unsanitary!" He allowed himself to enjoy the look of confusion on Cassilda's pretty, punchable face.

"But, I thought...."

"Of course you did. But if you're that interested in my sexual habits, I'll tell you that when I feel the need, my dear Caerdig's thighs, well-oiled, function beautifully for the purpose. He's been trained to hold his legs together so tightly it's far more pleasing than any girl's cunny." Caerdig, sat as ever in the custom saddle in front of Phynagoras, let out a little grin of pride that surely unsettled Cassilda even more.

"Well...how would you know?" Cassilda asked. "Have you ever even—?"

"I have, long ago. But that is a tale that I will *not* be sharing with you."

Having apparently lost the battle of words, Cassilda let her horse fall back as Phynagoras chuckled. When she was out of earshot Caerdig said, "Why do you put up with her?"

"Because she brings a disposable cavalry that I don't have to worry about feeding. Perfect for a first strike, I think."

"I wish you'd let Boras tame her."

"So bloody-minded! I'd rather give her to you. We've never

discussed it, but...." Phynagoras licked his lips, the unfamiliar feeling of awkward nervousness entirely unsettling him. "I'm painfully aware that you're coming to the age when you'll probably want to take your own pleasures. And it seems most boys tend to prefer the feminine variety."

Caerdig didn't look up at him, but Phynagoras felt the lad tense. "I...don't know what to say to that."

Of course he didn't. Caerdig had been raised – groomed, really, just like his nations of victims – to exhibit no outward notion but for his lord's whims. How long until pretense for survival became reality within such an assaulted mind? Phynagoras was vaguely aware of these unsavory facts but had long ago learned to dismiss them. "Don't say anything," he answered finally, "just understand. We're about to move into an entirely new country, and there'll be even more after. Much of all that I'll give to you, like I told that rabble behind me. But for you it's absolutely true. Anything, any*one* in the world you want, it's yours."

"If I ever want Cassilda it'll be to throw her off a cliff."

"If that's what you desire. But you'll have to wait until I'm done with her first."

★   ★   ★

After all the build-up, their first sight of Phenidra proved something of a disappointment. It *was* small, blocky and boring. Of course it was not intended as a palace, yet the place barely stood out among the mountains from which its walls had been quarried. As Phynagoras drew nearer, a sense of unease settled in his gut. It looked deserted, with no sight of sentries, or laborers, or horse drilling or patrolling outside the walls. All was still and quiet but for the screeching winds.

Boras ordered the hazaras to form up into marching ranks, and when they fell into common step the stamping of their boots set the mountains to rumbling. There could be no mistaking their arrival. Still not a sight or sound emanated from the fortress.

"What do you think?" Phynagoras asked Boras.

"No clue. Maybe they evacuated to make room for us. Maybe it's just the one lord now. But then, where is he? I don't like it."

"Let's get closer, have a better look."

The army came to within half a stadion of the walls, and Phynagoras sent his ambassador to try to get their attention. She walked up to the wall and began calling out in Argovani.

Meanwhile Cassilda once again graced them with her presence, scowling. "What's going on?"

"Seems nobody's home," Boras said. "Suggest you send someone 'round the other side, see if the gate's open."

Phynagoras nodded. "Good idea. Cassilda, see to that."

She scowled some more at being ordered like a common soldier, but didn't disobey. One of her Haiads tore off southward around the perimeter, then reappeared a minute later, reporting that the gate was closed.

Boras spat a clod of phlegm onto the ground. "Dammit! We been betrayed already?"

"Possibly. But why, why now? I want inside that place. One way or another. You know what to do."

"Aye, m'lo— Look!"

Something tumbled over the top of the wall, then dropped to the ground with a thud. It was a body. The ambassador stopped her shouting and regarded it with terror. She looked back at Phynagoras.

"It...it's him! That's Armino! We are deceived—!"

A sharp crack echoed off the wall and across the mountainside, and at almost the same instant the ambassador was staked to the ground, impaled through the midsection by a large ballista bolt. She looked in wide-eyed confusion at her lord as blood soaked through her blue robes, then fell dead.

Phynagoras stared in a rare moment of shock at the solitary figure that now graced the wall. The true commander, no doubt. He seemed so young. They locked eyes, and a moment of understanding seemed to pass between them. Phynagoras nodded. *So, this is to be the way.*

A tidal wave of arrows and crossbow quarrels immediately followed, shot by men suddenly appearing from behind merlons, from watchtowers, from nowhere at all.

"Shields!" Boras howled. "Raise shields! Now!" Some of the soldiers managed to obey, but many were caught flat-footed, their shields still stored inside hide covers for travel. Screams rang out as men and horses were peppered with missiles.

"Fall back! Back!" Phynagoras waved his arms wildly to signal the retreat, and did not see the bolt flying directly at them until Caerdig let out a shrill scream. At the last possible moment Boras, not carrying a shield himself, wrenched a nearby mounted soldier from his horse and shoved him into the path of the bolt.

"Huargh!"

"We should withdraw," said Boras, tossing the body away.

"Only to just out of range. I still want that fortress!"

When the army had fallen back to a safe distance and Caerdig had been sternly instructed to stay at the very back of it, Phynagoras called a hasty war council of his top officers. "It seems," he said to the twenty or so captains, Boras and Cassilda, "that Phenidra is under new management. That idiot Armino couldn't keep his secret, so it's likely their king took preemptive action. Uncharacteristic of him from what I've heard, but whatever. There were Pelonans up on those walls, and if they've gotten involved I won't risk bringing reinforcements from a north coast that could be completely blockaded. We've no siege weapons, obviously, no ladders nor wood to make them. So here's what we're going to do...."

Later the front ten-man squads, the dathavi, of each hazara advanced toward the fortress again, at a much more deliberate pace in a tight formation and fully covered by shields formed into a shell, front back and above. Arrows and bolts rained down on them, turning the giant tortoise into more of a porcupine but doing little damage as they marched right over the bodies already littering the stony plain. Occasionally a ballista bolt would tear a hole right through the mass, only for it to be plugged immediately by more men from within. They came right up to the wall, but it seemed there was little else they could do without ladders.

Then, to the apparent consternation of those atop the battlements, some of the men comprising the porcupine began to pile atop each other. One line hopped up onto the upturned shields of those from another. Then a third line, shorter than the first, alighted on top of those, using shoulders and shield rims as foot- and handholds. Then yet another atop those, in a human pyramid, each protected by shields and growing narrower with each level so that the weight of each man was distributed among those below. A second company of soldiers began to approach the fortress, and it would be these who climbed the finished structure for the assault.

"I know they done practiced this many times," said Boras as he watched, "but I never actually believed it'd work in a real battle."

"Where did you get them, anyway?" asked Cassilda, entranced by the spectacle.

"Acrobats, all," Phynagoras answered. "Every city of any size has circus performers. When I conquer a new one I draft all the acrobats into the army. You never know when you'll have to scale a wall, or a cliffside, a gorge, whatever, but not have the equipment for it."

"Amazing."

"Not the best fighters, of course, but they stack up well. And now...there they go."

They watched as the second company endured the same volleys and blocked most of them in the same manner. But it was a lighter rain, as the shots were now divided between both groups of targets. Defenders crowded corner towers that protruded out from the fortress wall to take oblique shots at the pyramid pressed hard against the stones, now realizing its purpose.

"Cassilda," Phynagoras said calmly, "now, if you please."

The woman gave a signal to someone, and all at once a hundred mounted archers rode in a wide arc toward Phenidra. Their horn and sinew bows were powerful enough to send arrows up at the defenders while staying mostly out of range of any return shots. Loosing while their horses were at full gallop, they presented no stationary target, and few were hit before circling back to a safe distance.

"Marvelous," Phynagoras said, "what a feat! I might have to train up a few units of my own."

"Humph," Cassilda snorted. "Takes a lifetime of training to do that, barbarian. And I doubt your men's brains can handle so many tasks at once."

"Then I'll have to rely on you for the time being. Send another wave!"

A second unit of Haiads made a like circuit, taking pressure off the assault and picking off a number of defenders in the process. By now the assault group had reached the wall to climb the human siege engine. The acrobats groaned under the added weight of men and armor, but the structure held as the first troops reached the top. The man to win the honor of first reaching a hand over one of Phenidra's merlons had it cut off for his reward, and he tumbled from the pyramid, clutching a bloody stump the whole way. The second fared little better, actually stepping up into the crenelations before a spear thrust sent him falling backward. But there were many more scrambling to take his place.

"Won't be long now," Phynagoras said. "Boras, start sending one hazara round to the front to storm the gates once we manage to open it from inside. Cassilda, you protect their flanks – wait, what are they doing now?" He pointed at the little flashes of light gathering on the tops of the corner towers.

Boras squinted, then laughed. "Fire arrows? They must be getting desperate. Those won't do shit against our armor. Hells, even the shields are proofed. Eh, almost disappointing how easy this'll be."

Phynagoras frowned. "They must know there's no point in that. If they were going to pour flaming oil on us they'd have done so already. I have a bad feeling about...."

He watched as more of his soldiers stormed the wall, slowly fighting their way onto the battlements. Meanwhile, the towers swarmed with figures tending to some odd task he couldn't quite make out. They were indeed fiddling with arrows, tying something to the heads of each. Phynagoras bit his lip nervously. Fire arrows were finicky things, and rather obsolete. They'd do little damage and be a waste against a properly disciplined force. And yet....

One man stood out atop the tower with such an arrow and bow. The young commander he'd seen before, Phynagoras thought. He stood apart from a few others, and lined up along a shallow angle to take aim at the pyramid.

"Cassilda," Phynagoras said, "send one of your women to take down that fellow, right there."

"Why? One man isn't—"

"Just do it!"

The man nocked his arrow. It was a strange one: there was something small attached to the shaft, just behind the bodkin-tipped head, and the flaming bit just behind that. He aimed high and pulled only to a half draw. The arrow sailed in a gentle smoking arc, with too little force or speed to fully snuff the flame. It descended right onto the midpoint of the pyramid. One climbing soldier had even seen it coming, and swung his shield to knock the minor nuisance away—

BOOM!

Time stopped, or so it seemed. The fighting, the screaming, the shooting and clamor of battle were all swallowed up with the horrendous emerald flash of light and thunderous sound. Phynagoras stared in wordless, thoughtless awe, spine chilled solid and testicles shriveled up halfway to his stomach. When the smoke cleared, where the top of his human pyramid had been was now a dripping, writhing mass of bone, blood and viscera. The upper wall of Phenidra was suddenly painted bright red, and bits of men in a million pieces littered the remains of the pyramid and the ground below.

Then the screaming began again.

Men howled in agony, howled in fury, howled in joy if they were among the defenders. There was a flurry of activity atop the towers, and at once more figures appeared to take up the fight using... whatever it was that had just been used. Power of the gods or of devils, it made no matter. Phynagoras sat paralyzed, gripped with a sudden terror that he'd not felt since he was sixteen and dying from dysentery. "N...no...no..." he mumbled.

"Gods fuck me," Boras whispered. "Gods...fuck us all with a red-hot poker, what in the hells was *that*?!"

More of the demonic arrows were raised, and Phynagoras and Boras watched in helpless horror as two were sent out again.

BOOM-BOOM!

The human pyramid was totally obliterated as flesh flew in every direction. A scene that would sicken the hardiest butcher lay before them, with more than three hundred men churned into slop, some pieces squirming and screaming, most not. The blood was so thick that a hazy pink mist of it clogged the heated air. The wall had taken some damage, but the thick blocks mostly held. A few lucky surviving souls ran or crawled away from the carnage, dodging falling debris of loosened stone or troops being soundly pushed back over the battlements. The assault had, to put it mildly, failed.

"M'lord," Boras said shakily. Phynagoras still sat motionless, glassy-eyed and sallow-skinned. "M'lord!" Boras reached out and slapped Phynagoras across the face. He jumped in his saddle, shocked back to his senses.

"Y-yes. Yes, Boras. We...we must—"

"We must get out of here! Now! We ain't equipped to fight no fucking magic, lord. Figure it out later!"

"Yes. Please give the...you, you know what to do."

"Yes, lord. Captains, form up! Prepare to withdraw, now!"

"Nooooo!"

The cry had come from somewhere in the front ranks. Boras looked toward it, and saw a hundred or so hands pointing up at one of the other fortress towers. A ballista was mounted there, and a team had manned it when the assault began, launching heavy bolts at the shield tortoises. Now it was being readied for another shot, but this time fitted out with another one of the horrific devices that had chewed the assault to shreds. There was a sharp crack, and to all eyes it seemed the bolt flew in slow motion, straight at them.

Boras didn't wait for the inevitable result, grabbing Phynagoras's horse and wrenching both it and his own away from where they stood. "Go! Get away!"

The ballista bolt had been shot for distance rather than accuracy, and thus struck at some point at its farthest possible range, right where Phynagoras and Boras had just been. The bolt itself thudded harmlessly into the rocky dirt, but a split second later sheer inertia drove the vessel attached to it and the burning oilcloth about the shaft into the ground. From that ground sprang pure hell.

Phynagoras didn't hear the thunderous boom this time. In fact everything went eerily quiet except for a distant ring. He did register a bright green light, heat, and pain. A searing wind, like the air itself was afire, slammed into him, knocking him from his horse. His head hit hard gravel; he tasted blood in his mouth. He didn't quite know how long he lay there, but eventually felt himself being dragged to his feet. Boras, face riddled with bruises and cuts, yelled something at him, but the ringing was drowning it out.

"W-what…?"

"…said, come on! The bastards have more of those damned lightning bolts, were waitin' 'til we got close. We gotta go now!"

Phynagoras looked all around him in a daze. More distant explosions rang out, but less and less distant as his hearing returned. Men scattered in terror, with no way to know where the next would hit. Some just sat on the ground and wept, maddened by the experience.

"Cassilda!" Even Boras's booming voice struggled to overcome the din of general panic. "Cassilda, where are you!"

"Here!" The woman was still in shock herself, shaking atop her mount. "But I'm not staying! I didn't agree to fight demons!"

"You send someone to shoot down those ballista men. You're the only ones who can get close enough."

"Fuck that," she spat, then pulled the rein to turn away.

"Do it," Phynagoras ordered weakly, his senses still hazy. "Do it or we're all dead."

Cassilda sneered at them both. "Pssh. Emperor of Kings, my sharp-toothed twat!" She rode away as the retreat became a rout.

The army broke into three or four groups and moved in a generally westward direction, staying well away from Phenidra. Boras managed to assemble enough of their own archer units to put regular shots up at the ballista, keeping them off balance until the bulk of the army could get out of range. They still lost men to the vicious weapons.

The camp followers were still mostly ignorant of the situation, but knew something horrific had happened. The migrants followed bits of the army as best they could, though some were caught flat-footed and became lost. The defenders launched a few more explosive bolts at them, but before long any targets were too far off. As Phynagoras rode wherever Boras led him, he heard a cry of victory erupt from the fortress. He felt the right side of his face grow more painful with the receding shock, and when he touched his cheek the burned and mangled flesh made him gasp. The very first foot he'd set in Barg-o-Bhanii had resulted in disaster, and the shame of the defeat burned him far worse than the lightning weapon. It was an injury he swore to repay. With interest.

$$\star \quad \star \quad \star$$

Eyvind gazed down on the incredible carnage below, suddenly shivering in his ill-fitting plate armor. "I can't believe we're still alive."

At his side Davenga shrugged. "I have seen far worse battles."

"I don't mean because of the battle. It was a harder fight against Armino. I mean *that.*" He waved across the field of gore before them. "How can it be we could do that and take so little injury ourselves? It seems wrong."

"Maybe my skill with your tongue is not what I thought it was. I would think that preferable to the alternative. Phenidra remains ours and Phynagoras has been cast away."

"Aye, cast free into Argovan to do as he wishes while we stay locked up here like the other Marcher lords. What've we really accomplished?"

"He is without a stronghold," Davenga said insistently, "exposed! It will go hard for him when your king returns."

"And harder for the people caught in the middle."

"That is the calculation you chose to make. Much will now depend on your ranger friends."

"And just what do you calculate their chances at?"

Davenga shook his head. "I cannot say. I am a military man, and their ways are not at all military. But they may be our only chance."

Eyvind held up one of the unused Vrril arrows they'd improvised. They'd tied the phial to the shaft, gently so as not to shatter the fragile glass. Behind it, a blackened stretch of wood showed where the flaming cloth had been. It was their terrified uncertainty about just how close the flame could get without igniting it that had delayed them from shooting until Phynagoras's weird tower of tumblers was built and his men about to spill over the wall. A wall still dripping with blood kept from freezing by the rising heat of the bodies and parts of bodies piled below. *That horrible explosion of flesh, the mangled corpses, the moans....*

Eyvind wrinkled his nose at the smell wafting upward. "I think, general," he said, slowly turning the small but devastating weapon in his fingers, "we may soon have to reconsider our definition of 'military'."

Davenga glanced at it also. "Yes. But not, thank the gods, before I retire."

CHAPTER EIGHTEEN

The Kraken

They'd ridden downhill, toward the town that Boras had intended to take after settling in Phenidra. Most of the army had been reassembled, and though their physical losses were light at fewer than four hundred men, a large portion of those remaining had been terrified into near uselessness. When night fell they stopped at some point on the gentle slope, the valley still almost a day ahead of them.

The doctor finished bandaging Phynagoras's face and left the tent to see to other wounded. All around were the sounds of defeat – crying, cursing, sentries shouting watch words at dathavi detailed to forage for water. Phynagoras sat silently as Caerdig knelt before him, rubbing unguent into his myriad cuts and scrapes.

"Is it bad?" Phynagoras asked, turning his head to display the burn more fully.

Caerdig shrugged. "It's not that bad. It'll heal, like the doc said. But you'll have a scar, probably."

"I won't make a very pretty messiah then, will I?" He laughed bitterly. "Maybe I should prop you up in my place. Oh, my dear, I'm so sorry. We should be enjoying a hot bath right now, not freezing our balls off on this mountainside. I see that I've underestimated our enemies, been lazy. It's been too easy, these past few years. I relied on reputation to fight my battles. Now they have this, this *thing* that cares nothing for reputation as it burns and tears you into pig feed. That's all over now. I see that I'll have to do this the hard way. I just hope I can keep you safe while I do."

"It's just a setback," Caerdig said with certainty. "You'll win in the end. You have to."

Phynagoras managed a brief smile, but it lasted only a moment as Boras's voice echoed outside the tent. "Lord, m'lord! Come out if you like, we've found her."

"Ah, excellent. Come with me, I think you'll enjoy this."

The hillside was dotted with hundreds of small campfires, and thousands of soldiers and followers crowded around them. But the largest had a space cleared next to it a short walk from Phynagoras's tent. That space was now occupied by Boras and two soldiers who held Cassilda tightly between them.

"Found 'er and her cavalry skulking around the camp followers, trying to bum food from anyone she could. One of 'em sold her out."

Phynagoras nodded. "Make sure whoever that was is rewarded for such loyalty. And, could you please fetch me a pair of tongs?" He walked up to the woman, frowning and spitting curses but unable to move beyond that. "My dear, so nice to see you! I thought you'd left our little fellowship." A day ago his tone would've been light and smug, but now it was just bitter.

Cassilda snarled in the soldiers' grip. "You look like shit. Not so divine you can stand black magic, are you?"

"No, it seems not. I was foolish, and my beauty's been marred in punishment. Fitting. But what about yours? You swore faith to me, in sight of gods and my men and your women. Yet at the most critical moment, you disobeyed me."

"I had to. It was suicide! There's no way—"

"*You. Disobeyed. Me.*" He said each word like a hammer blow, loudly enough that all around could hear it, yet not yelling. He took out his signet ring and held it before her, the polished carnelian glittering in the flames. "You remember this? I made you bow your head and kiss it to show your oath to me. Yet you've spat on that oath. Whatever shall I do with you now?"

The sneer disappeared from Cassilda's face, yet seemingly resolved not to show fear, she answered, "I suppose something involving a spike through several of my orifices?"

Phynagoras nodded. "Normally you'd be exactly right. But luckily for you, I'm not in a position to turn away any assets, even one as traitorous as you. I'll give you a choice. You can leave now, take what you can on your own in this foreign land and die horribly if I ever see you again. Of course, I would keep your Haiads to use as I see fit. Or, you may renew your vow and return to my service, following a necessary…chastisement."

Cassilda's mouth hung open. "Chastisement?"

"Yes. Sweet Caerdig once pleaded with me to give you to Boras, but you wouldn't survive that and I've no need of another corpse. I suppose a simple beating at my hands, in view of all, would suffice. Now please, it's been a long day and I'm very tired, so tell me. Which do you choose?"

Her mouth trembled, her teeth clenched so tightly Phynagoras could almost hear the grinding. Cassilda regarded Phynagoras with the deepest loathing, made deeper by the look of utter disinterest he returned to her. She looked left, right, out into the surrounding dark and maybe weighing her chances. Breathing heavily, she spat on the ground. "You godsfucked kraken," she growled. "I'll stay."

"Of course you will. You are many things, but not a fool."

Phynagoras had her stripped naked, and he himself down to his breechcloth to avoid soiling his clothes. The soldiers formed a tight circle around them, with only the bonfire breaking the wall. Phynagoras drew close to her, close enough to smell her hatred, her fear. He leaned in to whisper in her ear. "I was hoping you'd make the right choice." Then he drew back a bit and slapped her square across the face. She went down disappointingly easy, so Boras had to lift her up again to receive her beating. Phynagoras drove his fists into her stomach, her sides, her breasts, doing just enough damage to hurt and to leave bruises, but not enough to make her useless. She moaned at each blow, each new place on her body he found to wound. It was so satisfying, he thought, hitting female flesh. He thought it must be the feedback each hit gave, the feeling underneath the fists that told one exactly how much hurt had been inflicted. Not at all like punching at some knotted mass of muscle that might as well have been a side of beef.

He grabbed her from Boras and threw her to the ground. Sitting astride her, he slammed his fists into her pretty, punchable face once, twice. Blood flew up from her mouth and nose. She fell almost into unconsciousness. Almost.

He stood and, looking down on her, was amused to see his cock fully erect. "Huh. Maybe I was wrong all along, lads. Maybe I do like women after all!" The circle of soldiers laughed. He called for the tongs and used them to put his signet ring into the bonfire. When he judged it hot enough, he went to hover over Cassilda's whimpering form.

"Here's a kiss of faith you won't soon forget." He pressed the searing hot sigil into her forehead. Skin sizzled as she screamed, and the stench of burnt meat filled the air. From the edge of the circle, Caerdig grinned in the firelight.

That night Phynagoras's sister came to him. Of course, of all nights it would be this, after one defeat, the memory of another. Maybe it was the sight of naked, broken Cassilda beneath him that had summoned up the too-familiar dream.

He vaguely remembered loving Eulalia, in a way. But it had been so long ago it was hard to grasp.... *Lots of incest in the family, you know*, he said to Amza o Uzaraq as they sat, watching his fourteen-year-old self couple with her. Their parents had approved, since after all they were to be wed to keep the royal line pure and under control, sharing the throne of Porontus as was custom.

I don't like sharing, Eulalia said as young Phynagoras rolled off her. He took up a wine cup from somewhere and sipped, then offered it to her. She drank deep.

He then spat out the wine, which he hadn't swallowed. *Neither do I.* Eulalia sat up, suddenly gasping, clawing at her throat and struggling to breathe. Poison. Her eyes rolled back, and her skin turned blue, then purple. No different from the fate she had planned for him. She shivered once more, then stilled. A tear ran down Phynagoras's cheek, youth and man both as they watched. From that moment on female flesh would signify only betrayal and decay to him. *Father is next. But not right away.*

You forgot something, Eulalia said. Her body was now white, and his sigil burned into her forehead. Yet she spoke. This part of the dream was new. *In your haste, you forgot.*

What? adult Phynagoras asked, his young self gone off to claim his throne. *What did I forget?*

Assets, and orders. It was not his dead sister who now spoke but Caerdig, who appeared where Amza had been. *So hard to keep them straight. A surprise, but maybe for you too.*

What? What does that mean? Explain, I command it!

You command nothing.

★   ★   ★

Phynagoras and his army descended on Vin Gannoni like piranhas. The hardship of the journey, the hunger and danger and betrayal, and most of all the defeat at the hands of black magic would all be unleashed on the town without mercy. Even at half a parasang off, Phynagoras could see little antlike dots scurrying westward, toward the broad plains beyond and the distant Sellinac range. *Let them run*, he thought. *We'll get them eventually.*

He'd struggled not to let his fury get the better of him, or his fear after waking from the terrible dream in a cold sweat. Whether a message from the gods whose supposed existence he ignored or his own tangled mind, something had tried to warn him. But of what? What had he forgotten? *No matter now. Now there's other business at hand.*

"Now remember, Boras," he said as they rode at the head of their re-formed forces, "it's no longer to be like our previous conquests. We're not here to rule but to supplant, and capitulation no longer serves my purpose. Keep as many as needed for labor, but only as many as you can control. Wipe out the rest."

Boras smiled, clearly feeling no similar need to restrain his ire. "Well fucking understood, m'lord. I shall take great pleasure in following that command."

"Don't luxuriate overly long though, I want to exterminate then move south. Repeat over and over again as quickly as is practical as well as link up with those upland savages we bought so cheaply. The sooner we can get a secure supply line the better, and I won't send ships within striking distance of Pelona. Right, best get started then. Cassilda."

The woman nudged her mount closer. She sported a patchwork of purple and yellow bruises across her face, her arms and exposed thighs. Phynagoras's sigil had swollen into a red welt on her forehead. Since her chastisement her eyes bore a sublime deadness, and no trace of further defiance.

"...yes, lord."

"Send half your cavalry round the other side of the town to cut off retreat. And set a few to circle the perimeter to deal with any problems, and the other half on our flanks as we go in." She nodded, then rode off to relay the orders.

"Such a feeling of accomplishment with her," Phynagoras said, "and one sorely needed, the molding of a person from wild individual into a useful instrument. Craft married with artistry, to my mind. Now I'll want an orderly harvest of the town's supplies, not some chaotic sacking. When the army has all it can use, our followers may pick over what's left."

"I'll tell the quartermaster." Boras motioned to Captain Musa, waiting eagerly nearby. "Second Hazara from the north. Third Hazara from the east. Third's to wait until Second is in place, then advance together. Clear and hold. Go now." The captain made a hasty salute and ran to obey.

"Second Hazara," Phynagoras said casually. "Didn't they take the greatest injury from our abortive visit to Phenidra?"

"They did," Boras confirmed. "Figured they'd be the most motivated to return the favor."

Vin Gannoni had no walls of note, except for low stone fencing more to discourage adventurous sheep than an attacking force. The columns crept toward the routes into town with the wild mounted women riding on the wings, and when both were of a distance, rushed inward. The screams followed soon after. With the troops under orders to preserve as much as possible, little fires appeared here and there but did not spread much. The Haiads swarmed the fleeing townsfolk, and soon the western plain was dotted with little unmoving forms, and only a lucky few still streamed away at an apparent snail's pace. Every once in a while, the clang of metal echoed up, signifying some token resistance, but the few remaining soldiers, either still loyal to Armino or not believing the news of his demise, didn't even slow the process. It was over in less than an hour.

Phynagoras strode through the streets of the town, which had been trampled to mud by the marching and in places a purplish gray color where the blood had mixed in. Many of the wood and plaster buildings had taken some damage, yet most remained serviceable. Yet every single door or wall had been marked in chalk with a crude symbol that proclaimed, 'clear: no enemies within'. And of course, the current definition of 'enemy' in Phynagoras's army was very, very liberal.

Bodies already filled the streets, piled along the sides so as not to block the way while Fourth Hazara dutifully carried off every sack of grain, animal and tool that could be found. A line of blank-eyed natives had been tied together and yoked into assisting the effort, the lucky survivors. A scream rang out in the distance as Phynagoras approached the taphouse near the center of town that Boras had chosen as his makeshift headquarters.

As he stepped into the place, a warmth enveloped him. A fire still burned at a hearth, and even some manner of local pottage simmered in a cauldron. "Cozy," he remarked. He turned to a soldier counting casks of beer stacked along the wall. "Where's the general?"

The soldier pointed toward a far doorway. "In there, m'lord. He's, uh, a bit busy."

Phynagoras laughed. "I know, I know. He always is after." Peering through, he decided to wait politely, knowing how cranky Boras could get when interrupted. He had a young girl bent over a table, who cried and moaned pathetically while he raped her from behind. As he fucked faster, Boras took up a knife laid nearby. When he climaxed he took the girl's hair in one fist, yanked back, and dragged the blade across her throat. Her eyes went wide in wordless horror. As he spilled his seed into her, her blood sprayed out.

"Ah! Ah, that's the stuff...." Breathing heavily, he let go of the nearly dead body, and it flopped to the floor like a fish.

"How I enjoy watching you work," Phynagoras said.

Boras gave an amused grunt while he redid his breechcloth. "If I knew I had an audience, lord, I'd have drawn the performance out longer."

"No need. As I said, we mustn't dawdle. There's no telling how much of that monstrous lightning these savages still have."

"Still, I've found another amusement for you. That big building nearby? I think that's the town assembly hall."

"And?"

"Just go in. I think you're going to like it."

Phynagoras climbed the three steps to the platform that elevated the hall off the ground, pausing to scrape the gray-purple mud from his lambskin boots. Two soldiers standing guard pulled the double doors open for him as he stepped through, not entirely sure what he'd find, though the stench of viscera hung heavy.

The chamber was simple and rectangular with audience galleries on either side and a raised oaken desk in front. Bodies lay flung all over like forgotten rag dolls, some draped lazily over the gallery barricades or against the desk, all hacked or punctured by sword and spear. Phynagoras laughed when he spotted the solitary figure reigning over this high court of death.

A small, elderly woman sat in the center of the desk, cradling a gavel and fumbling with a shiny chain about her shoulders. Her hair was a mess, eyes wide and staring at nothing, blood splashed on her dark woolen robes. At last she seemed to notice Phynagoras's presence, looked down on him with a squint and banged her gavel on the desk.

"You!" she snapped in a heavy northern accent that strained Phynagoras's understanding of the Barghii language. "You there, young man, do you have an appointment? So many rude folk keep barging in here these days without an appointment. Shameful, really."

She was in shock, he realized. Probably didn't even understand what'd happened. One of the guards cleared his throat.

"She, erm, must've been hiding in here when we first came through, m'lord. Later we heard her mumbling about appointments. General Boras, he thought—"

"Yes, yes, I'm sure he did," Phynagoras said amusedly. "He does have a fine appreciation for the ridiculous. Who are you, old woman?"

She sneered down at him. "'Old woman'? Why, you impertinent whippersnapper, I'm the mayor! Who else?" She grabbed her chain, thrust it forward for emphasis. "Now, *if* you have an appointment, we can come to order. What business with the town council?"

Phynagoras nearly choked on his own spit for laughing. "Business? Why I'm here to take over the place!"

"Take over? Well, I haven't heard anything about that. I'll have to speak to Lord Armino...."

"Then I shall speed you to him presently." He turned and left the insane old bat to bang her gavel. Stepping outside, he let out a chuckling sigh and wiped away a tear. "Oh...oh, that's funny. I needed that."

"What should we do with her, lord?"

"What? Oh, bar the doors and burn the place down."

After the doors and windows had been nailed shut, the thatch roof was set alight. The fire took nearly an hour to spread, and inside the mad mayor continued pounding the gavel and mumbling "shameful, really", until the words turned to shrill, blood-curdling screams. But those did not last long.

The thousand or so captured citizens of Vin Gannoni of least use for slavery were given over to Second Hazara to do with as they liked. By sundown the field west of town had been turned into a strange kind of forest, with folk of every age and station impaled on tall pikes while still alive. The job was not, Phynagoras noted, the professional artistry of the level practiced in Porontus that would keep the impaled alive and in agony for days. Thus only a few hundred were able to sing their anguished moans across the grassy plain that now provided the Haiads' mounts with very good grazeland indeed.

While the camp followers had their turn at scavenging the remains of the town, Boras took Second and Fourth Hazaras and began the long march south. Phynagoras watched half his army disappear over the horizon, with orders to locate the Marchman Ordovax, thoroughly sanitize any other local population they encountered, and secure a southern port. Given the circumstances, things were going as smoothly as possible. And yet, he couldn't shake that unsettling dream, and the nagging feeling that he'd forgotten something important.

★   ★   ★

Aerrus sat in the armory, surrounded by hundreds of bows and thousands of arrows and adding more to the mix. Their long journeys, their daring adventures had been a whirlwind that left the mind mercifully unable to process the unlikeliness of surviving it all, so the mundane chore of fletching was actually a welcome respite. But it was interrupted when Drissa and Linet poked their heads in.

"Ah, Goldenrod and Rookling," Aerrus said with a smirk, "you come to help me with this tedious task?" Both women scowled when he teased them with their childhood nicknames. The two were as unlike in manner as in hair color, but Linet always took hers with less grace, insisting her hair was just very dark brown, not black. Little difference as it made in the gloom of the Lodge.

"Keep it up," she said, "and you can stay in here for a week straight. Not like we won't need the arrows."

"You have another option for me?"

"Maybe," Drissa replied. "You two've been spreading the word about us, haven't you?"

Aerrus nodded. "Didn't have much choice. Not that it seemed to matter much, not many even believed what we were saying."

"Well, someone did. Lom's been sending out extended patrols all up and down the river road. Young Sorweth says a fellow's parked himself at the crossroad, camped in the ruins of the old fort. Has himself an old bow and a pointy stick that might've been a spear once."

Aerrus perked up at that. "Really?"

Linet nodded. "Vander went to talk to him in the guise of a fellow traveler. Seems he heard strange talk about people who can stand up to the invasion, wants to wait for them and others."

Aerrus stood up quickly, tossed the unfinished arrow away. "Gods' tits, there's one at least!" It was a small victory, but a victory. "Should... should we go see him?"

"Don't bring anyone to the Lodge just yet. We'll find somewhere out of the way to hide him and any others who show up."

"Seems you got your insurgency," Drissa said. "I just hope you know what to do with it."

★   ★   ★

Aerrus approached the man slowly, openly so as not to spook him. They saw each other from far enough off, and the fellow had the sense to know Aerrus was no common traveler. He'd been reclining against rotten planks that had once been part of a forgotten fort but now stood up, holding on to the shaft of a worn pike, his silhouette stark against the white overcast sky.

The man was about thirty-five, with well-built shoulder and calf muscles, short-cropped hair and beard. He wore a bright blue tunic and plum chausses, and a dagged hood rolled into a cap atop his head in the current fashion. A farmer, but a prosperous one.

At about six paces' distance Aerrus stopped, and the pair regarded each other. Finally Aerrus said, "What's your name?"

"Leofric," the man answered without hesitation. His fingers tightened on the shaft he held, but Aerrus made no movement in response.

"What are you doing here, Leofric?"

"Two weeks ago my world was a different place. Work was hard and harvest was poor, but when ain't that so? I heard invaders might be coming, but when ain't that so too? I didn't worry. Then my...." He took another hard breath. "My wife and...and son went away to market, to unload two piglets. I never saw them again. That...that *bastard*!" He looked away, ashamed of tears that hadn't yet fallen but threatened to.

"Phynagoras," Aerrus said with a nod.

"No, his thricedamned general! Killing everything that moves while he cuts south. I heard the news of it from them clever or lucky enough to run away early. I heard that Vin was...gone. Just gone. Everyone. The fortunate ones right away, the rest spitted on pikes."

"Gods," Aerrus breathed, "we were hoping it was just rumor."

"And no King Ozzie, no Lady Val to oppose 'em. Then I heard about other things. About sorts that might want to.... I been waiting here four days, watching all the dead-eyed fools pass by without slowing. Something tells me you might be who I'm looking for. My life's over now. I just want to end it by taking as many of them with me as possible. Mayhap you can help with that."

"I'm so sorry," Aerrus said. "Though I know that doesn't mean much. But nothing is over, you hear me? Not while you can still draw breath, still draw that bowstring. You're right, I am who you're looking for, one among many. But I'll tell you right now, we can't use noggin-fracted madmen with death wishes. We need folk with enough fire yet in their guts to fight hard and run and live to fight on. Is that you?"

Leofric nodded. "For a while, anyway."

"That'll have to do. Welcome to the war." Aerrus stepped forward and clasped arms with the man.

To Leofric's left, completely out of sight, Linet lowered her bow and stepped forth. "Aye, welcome."

Leofric jerked his head to the side. "Can you teach me to sneak up on 'em like that?"

"We can."

"Then I'm glad to join ya."

*　　*　　*

Haskell spat hard onto the ground, mostly for effect as he sneered at the pathetic gaggle set before him. "Is this it?"

"More will come," Linet said, already feeling her patience with him beginning to fray. "Trenca village is overrun, and Nostrada too, by now."

"I don't need more, I need *better*. Any you lot know how to use bows? Other weapons?"

There were around thirty of them, men and women both escaped from all points north along the Carsa valley. Some had livestock with them, some had children. After the massacre of Vin Gannoni, word spread quickly, and geography left the refugees few options. Some fled into the Sellinac Mountains to the west, others south toward Lenocca or Thoriglyn. But those places were already swollen to bursting. Hostile Marchman tribes, the towering Edra Mountains and apathetic border lords made eastward an impalatable choice. So those who'd heard whispered rumors of someone to lead them at the crossroads now assembled nervously, not sure what they'd find. Of this first group, a few stepped forward.

"I, uh…" a craggy-faced man said, seemingly about to admit some high crime. "I been poach— Er, *hunting* the Midmarch woods my whole life. I can use a bow."

"Uh-huh," said Haskell. He eyeballed another man near the back of the group, clutching a crossbow. "You. Where'd you get that?"

The man started, looked to his left and right as though hoping someone else had been the one addressed. "Me? I took it off a dead mercenary."

"A dead mercenary. Lots of those just lyin' around, are there?" Haskell bit his lip. "Fine. Hope you know where to get bolts for it. Anyone else?"

One woman stepped forward, holding up, oddly enough, an old sword. "I was in the militia."

Linet frowned. "What militia? I never knew of one."

"It was back when that whoreson Gray Posca was raiding and pillaging the valley. We got the king's say-so to form up and take care of him ourselves, and we did that well enough."

"Gray Pos…that was fifteen years ago!" Actually, the Heron Kings had done most of the work, as Linet barely remembered, but no point in debating that now.

The woman shrugged. "Still kept m'sword." She held it up higher, as though that would make whatever point she thought she had clearer.

Haskell stomped forward, tore the thing out of her grip and tossed it onto the ground. "Anyone else carrying the like?"

Two others slowly held up even older, rustier blades, expressions like guilty puppies on their faces. Haskell ordered them to throw those down as well.

"Listen, this ain't no militia, and sure ain't no army! Sword distance is where you die. We only carry the shortish kind, if that. You fuckin' *shoot* these bastards from afar, or walk them into traps, or spit 'em on spears or pikes. And if you have to get close, get close enough to use this." He whipped out a belt knife and dashed forward three yards in half an eyeblink, taking hold of the militia woman and pressing the edge to her carotid artery while twisting her arm behind her back.

"Ow!" she yelped.

Haskell let go. "Sorry. But that's how we – how *you* deal with 'em. We'll teach you as much of that as we can, but in turn you obey our orders without question or hesitation. Am I well fucking understood?"

The crowd nodded in wide-eyed astonishment, momentarily more afraid of Haskell than Phynagoras. Linet had to admit, he did have his moments.

"Good. Now who wants to learn first?"

Two days later, a scouting party brought news to the Lodge that Boras, Phynagoras's general, had taken up residence in Wengeddy, and anyone fool enough to remain within its walls was strung from them by the neck, facing outward so all could see the truth of the change in administration.

CHAPTER NINETEEN
Enough of a Hassle

"This is all? This is all there are?" Eyvind gave Davenga a look of alarm, and it was answered with one of confusion.

"Would you prefer there were more? Where would you put them?"

It was hard to argue that point. Phenidra was not a large place, and it was already crammed with soldiers both Pelonan and Argovani, as well as refugees of Phynagoras's exterminations. As Boras began his march south, the remaining forces continued flushing out any pockets of population to make room for Phynagoras's followers, avoiding only Phenidra. From their vantage point on the battlement, there was barely a patch of courtyard visible, it was so choked with souls, and now the few to escape Edrastead were adding to it. Too few.

"I don't know. It's my home village, or it was. I recognize a few faces, though none of my kin."

"Ah," said Davenga with a sad nod, "I did not know this. I grieve with you." The general made a kind of consoling gesture, touching his forehead then spreading his fingers outward. "Yet, the question remains what is to be done. We cannot accept any more, kin or no."

The villagers loitered just within the gate that had been hastily raised to admit them then lowered again. Eyvind finally spotted Aunt Tess among them, and in between racking sobs she told of a company of mounted archer women descending on Edrastead and killing indiscriminately. Those lucky enough to get away did so only thanks to the attackers' lack of discipline and the uneven terrain, which they seemed unfamiliar with. The survivors had picked their way through mountain brush all the way to Phenidra, so Eyvind wouldn't refuse them, even though their food stores were rapidly dwindling.

What would Linet do? he asked himself, more and more. He thought he'd take inspiration from the rangers, somehow be able to come up with some clever plan just from having been around them. Or maybe it was just an excuse to think of her without having to admit it. This was no forest after all; they couldn't take potshots at their foes from behind trees.

"No," he muttered to himself, "no, we can't. No forest…and no grassy plain either."

Davenga frowned his epic frown. "What?"

"How many of those cavalry attacked the village? All that we saw before?"

"From what I could gather from the villagers, less than a hundred. Looking for plunder, maybe, though what they expected to find up here I do not know."

"Hmm." Eyvind glanced toward the stable in the courtyard. "No shortage of horses, that's for sure."

Davenga gave a hard grunt. "You want to attack them? With what men? You have horses but no riders. Regular soldiers would not fare well against those she-devils."

"Aye, but there's two things we have that they don't. These horses were born and bred here in the mountains. They can handle the terrain. And, we have the Vrril."

"And you think that will be enough to drive them off? They could just return in greater force."

Eyvind grinned. "General, you're still thinking militarily. We don't have to defeat them all, just make the place too much of a hassle to be worth it. Like you said, there's little plunder there. They'll look for easier pickings down in the valley."

"And then what?"

"I don't know. But it would give us some breathing room. I've got to do *something*."

Davenga nodded again, more confidently this time. "Very well, I'll ready my saddle."

"No. It's my home, I'll go."

★   ★   ★

Just as the sun was dipping over the Sellinacs and laying a blanket of twilight over the mountainside, Eyvind led a host of forty mounted soldiers out of Phenidra. Mounted soldiers maybe, but not proper trained cavalry, and they rode poorly even though they were the self-proclaimed best riders from all present within the walls. Even a few volunteers from Edrastead were keen to retake their village and exact some payback. The horses were, on the other hand, surefooted and glad to be free of the cramped stables. The company skirted rocky hillocks and gravel paths to approach Edrastead in as much secrecy as was possible, and the memory of Eyvind's first desperate flight to and from there came flooding back. *I won't be running away this time*, he vowed. He hoped.

Edrastead was an unremarkable little settlement laid out in a jagged line leading from a slate mine and surrounded by a few modest patches of farmland. Gardens, really. But except for those the land rose and fell with each step, like drunken waves of stone. Knowing from lifelong experience which parts of the village were visible from where, Eyvind led them almost to the main path that served as a street without being noticed by the small horde of women riding, walking or just lounging amid the central stretch of buildings. They seemed to be gathered mostly in the small taphouse, draining away the village's cider stores while laughing and jeering as the stiff and horse-trampled bodies of slaughtered villagers clogged the way. Enough light remained for Eyvind to snarl at that sight.

"Those bitches! So drunk and smug they didn't even post any lookouts. Good." He waved the four riders he'd appointed as captains close to him. "I say we ride right into town at a walk and kill as many as we can without raising the alarm. When that's blown, draw them out with noise to make us sound like more than we are, and when they gather to come at us hit 'em with the Vrril. Yeah?" They nodded grimly.

Tess, whose husband now lay dead not fifty paces away, held up one of the precious, terrible phials. "Just try and fucking stop me," she said through gritted teeth.

"Wait 'til they get close to us, get as many as you can. Okay, send the order down."

When all in the raiding party were ready, they crept around slopes and boulders, converging on the buildings in the gloom, the stomping of hooves blending with those of the enemy. It was almost too easy. Eyvind rode up behind one mounted woman riding slowly down the gravelly thoroughfare, raised a spear, and with shocking ease drove it straight through her back. She jerked, tried to scream but her pierced lung wouldn't allow it. She exhaled sharply and fell from the saddle.

All along the line of the village the same absurd scene played out, the silent attack begun but not even known. Eventually screams did ring out, and then shouts in some foreign tongue. Then there was panic and pandemonium.

"Now!" Eyvind ordered. "Now! Make some noise!" He kicked his horse into a trot to charge another warrior woman across the way. She raised a bow to shoot him down but he threw the spear at her. A lance is no throwing weapon and did little damage, but it knocked the bow off balance long enough for Eyvind to barrel into her and swipe a borrowed sword before him. His horse shied away at the last second, though he managed to slice several of her fingers off, and she howled in the dark. More screams, not just of surprise but of agony, from both sides of the fight. Some of the villagers shouted an old mining song as they rode, hoping to frighten their enemy into thinking an entire army was attacking.

At last the greater part of the women managed to stagger out of the taphouse and mount up to make a counterattack. Eyvind gave a loud, shrill whistle, and his raiding party gathered to him at the crest of a slope at the far end of the village. Glad to be given a single target, the women grouped together to advance on them. Already arrows were flying, mostly missing in the dark but not all. One lodged in the gaps in Eyvind's armor, penetrating just deep enough to be an annoyance, but no more. A savage command was given, and the women charged.

"Now!" Eyvind said, waving to Tess. She rode out in front holding a burning makeshift torch, the Vrril phial tied just below the flames. She gathered up all her strength, drew back an arm, and flung the device. Just as she did an arrow lanced out and grazed her in the armpit, and she fell with a hiss of pain.

But it was too late. The Vrril torch sailed down the slope to land right in front of the advancing warrior women.

BOOM!

Horse and human flesh were once again thrown everywhere in tattered masses, the night briefly made into a sickly greenish day. Cries and neighs of anguish. The villagers and soldiers who'd not been present at Phynagoras's attack on Phenidra stared in shock, while Eyvind wasted no time in gathering up Tess onto his horse. "Don't wait around! Back to Phenidra!"

The host turned and fled. *Running again after all*, Eyvind thought, but this time it was no defeat. The warrior women not dead, maimed or in shock attempted to give chase but neither they nor their animals were accustomed to the uneven ground, and they were soon lost in the night. The few to follow their quarry all the way back to Phenidra were driven off by arrow shot.

"Make a hole!" Davenga shouted into the courtyard when Eyvind's party clamored through the gate, almost knocking soldiers and refugees out of the way. When it was shut again Eyvind wrenched his horse around. "Is everyone here? Did we lose anyone?"

The count came up five short: two Pelonans, two Northmarch soldiers and one villager, with six more wounded. "Too many," Eyvind growled as the wounded were carried through the crushing throng toward the infirmary.

★　　★　　★

"I'm amazed any of you came back at all," said Davenga the next morning when they rode out again to Edrastead in the light of day. Though they found a stomach-turning orgy of mangled flesh and burned houses, there were no enemies left alive. "You were right. But was it worth it?"

"I think so. I doubt they'll come back here in much of a hurry, and we'll have the good sense to post watchtowers in case they do. We have somewhere to put the refugees, and maybe most important, we showed that we can hurt 'em."

What Eyvind couldn't know was that the village, little though the victory had been, also marked the first patch of ground that had ever been retaken from Phynagoras, Emperor of Kings.

★   ★   ★

Downhill was a rustic hamlet even smaller than Edrastead. As its name implied, it lay halfway down the mountainside, nestled in the uppermost crop of pines on a slope about a day's ride south of Phenidra. Of course, it could just as accurately have been called Uphill, but few from the valley ever visited it. It had once been a Marchman place, but the interminable tide of civilization had diffused the tribesmen either into Argovani society or even further into the mountains. It now boasted a lumber mill and trading post. Or it had.

After Eyvind and his raiders liberated Edrastead and erected a hasty watchtower in case Phynagoras decided it indeed *was* worth the hassle, the place remained in need of provisions and rebuilding, so Eyvind took an emboldened forage party out to refill kegs with fresh water running down out of the mountains. They came slowly upon Downhill, not sure what they'd find. Seeing no enemy activity but hearing the hum of human habitation from afar, the party rode into the wooded vale that traced the path of the stream, hopeful of finding one place at least to escape destruction.

With a smile, his first in many days, Eyvind sidled up to the nearest building of the hamlet, hand raised in greeting to any who might see.

"Ho! Are any goodfolk about?" He purposely exaggerated his upland accent to seem less threatening, for who knew what horrors they'd been through?

Two figures came out of the thatch hut to face him, then froze.

"What the fuck—?"

Bhasans. A man and woman. Ruddy, hair black and arrow-straight, no doubt of it. Invaders. Eyvind's smile melted into a furious scowl.

The pair turned and fled back into the hut, shouting something unintelligible. Eyvind looked out across the hamlet, now spotting more foreigners scattering to find somewhere to hide.

"Bastards," growled Tess. "They done turned out the whole village and took up residence 'emselfs! Or else killed everyone. What should we do?"

"Round 'em up," Eyvind said without hesitation, "all of them. I want some answers!"

It took mere minutes, the settlement was so small. There seemed to be no weapons among them more dangerous than eating knives, and the forage party went from house to house, driving every person at spear point into the clearing at the middle of the hamlet. They whined and pleaded in their own languages, and not just Bhasan. As far as Eyvind could tell there were Porontans, Thazovi, Ghreshi, and some from nations he couldn't name at all.

At last every invader was corralled within a ring of horses, their riders stabbing inward with little inclination to mercy. Eyvind fought through the barrier atop his own mount, frowning. "All right, you bloody trespassing fucks, any of you speak a civil tongue?" He glanced across the tens of faces, many holding frightened children, most ill-nourished, all uncomprehending.

Finally, a woman holding a toddler raised her hand. "I speak some of you Barghii," she said in a thick accent. "Why are you here?"

"Why are *we* here?!" Eyvind raged. "Why are *you*? What'd you do to the rightful folk of this place? Answer quick, cause my patience is exactly fucking zero right now and more than one of this lot's thirsty for payback and not too particular who pays it."

"We do nothing! We follow the emperor here, he say the lord of this land welcome us, say there is land for us all."

Eyvind gave a bitter laugh. "That lord was a traitor, and he had no right to give it away to anyone."

The woman shook her head, terrified and frustrated. "We know nothing of this. We find this place, all people gone. We do not know where. So we stay. What harm?"

Eyvind jammed his weapon into the ground and jumped down from his horse quickly enough to send a stab of pain through the remains of his old wound. He ignored it as he stomped forward to grab the woman by the shoulders. "Harm? *Harm!* Your precious emperor's butchering whole cities to make room for you savages to worship him! You are *not* welcome here!"

The woman began to quake with fury as much as fear, to weep, as did the child she held. "What can we do? *What can we do?* In Bhasa there is nothing! No green land, no water, no farm, no food, no job, only sand and death. You have everything!"

"Tell that to my husband, you mud-skinned bitch." Tess nudged her horse forward, raising her spear a bit.

The woman had grown almost hysterical. "I follow the emperor for my child. We are not army, we kill no one, just look for better life. Any life! Not there, not here, not anywhere! Just kill us and make done!"

"Good enough for me," Tess sneered, raising her spear even more. A terrified moan rippled through the crowd.

Eyvind held up a staying hand, though it galled him to do it. "Wait. We kill this lot another will just come along to replace 'em, and who knows how tough they'll be? No shortage there." His other hand wavered near the dagger at his belt, drawn to it oh so seductively. He looked again across the faces. Strange-looking, certainly. Scared, ragged, so much like the refugees that still crowded Phenidra. "Shite," he sighed. *What would Linet do?* "Shite! Fuck it, I won't let these wretches turn me into a little Phynagoras m'self."

"You're gonna let 'em go?" Tess asked, angry.

Ignoring her, Eyvind inched closer to the woman who spoke for them. "You know where we come from?"

She nodded. "That fortress. With the evil magic fire. We see the battle."

"That's right. And we have a lot more of it," he lied, "and not with ten years and ten times the men could your precious savior take it. He's far, we're near. And I don't think he cares much for you at all. So how badly do you really want another life?"

Tess looked at Eyvind in shocked disbelief. "You...you're not going to let them bloody *stay*?"

Eyvind pointed toward the abandoned sawmill perched along the stream. "You know what that's for?"

"To cut the trees."

"We need timber for rebuilding the village your army attacked, firewood, watchtowers. And warm pelts for the winter. And fresh water and cider. You will provide whatever we need, and in return I'll conveniently forget to spit you all on pikes, as I'm told your emperor did for the citizens of Vin Gannoni. If the people you displaced ever come back, you'll deal with them on your own. And there's your *better life*. Agree to it. Now!"

Barely an hour later the forage party rode back to Edrastead, making a slow going of it only because they had six carts of timber in tow, some of it cut previously, some there and then. As Eyvind's temper cooled, he mused, "How easily people jump from one savior to another."

"Aye," said Tess, refusing to look him in the eye. "You're a right proper lord now, seems. Just remember not everyone's quite so keen to forget the past."

CHAPTER TWENTY

A River Bleeds Through It

"This isn't going to work," Thanis said as he fidgeted, hunched uncomfortably on his ankles at the edge of the cliff near the bridge. A chill autumn wind blew up out of the forty-yard-deep gorge to smack him in the face.

"It *will* work," Aerrus answered. "Just be patient."

"Patience has nothing to do with it. We could wait here 'til winter freezes the bridge in place and it wouldn't come down. We should just attack them straight on and—"

"Pipe down. They're getting close." Linet stood with folded arms, eyeing their handiwork with almost as much skepticism as Thanis. Their target was one of Boras's foraging expeditions, about fifty soldiers with some migrants along to help. The aristocrats of Wengeddy had absconded with what food stores they could carry, and to everyone's surprise had the good sense to destroy what was left in order to deny it to the enemy. Boras's expeditions had come this way before, ranging ever further afield from the occupied town as they picked the lands west of the Kingsmarch clean. Undermining the bridge over the Carsa would stop them for a while, at least. *Assuming this works*, she thought nervously.

"Okay, nothing to do now but wait," said Aerrus just above a whisper, shrinking back into the concealing hollow carved by a small stream that trickled into the river far below. "You checked those struts again like I asked?"

Thanis rolled his eyes. "I checked 'em, for the ninetieth time! I just hope that engineer who came up with the idea knew what she was about. She was a bridge *builder* before all this, not a wrecker."

"Then we've invented a new profession." The flow of refugees away from Phynagoras's genocidal depredations had tossed all manner of folk their way. Most were of little practical use, but in this case one had been instrumental in teaching them how to weaken the structure so it failed at exactly the right time. They'd had to cut almost but not completely through the supporting struts, cut from the bottom so the sabotage wouldn't be noticed and so the wood would break in the right direction. Hopefully.

"Some profession," spat Thanis. "Won't be able to cross the river until spring. Not that there's anyone left to cross it. None we want alive, anyway."

Linet cast a worried glance at the lad as she rubbed the arms of her bow to keep it limber and her aim true. *That's a bit dark for him*, she thought. But it was dark business, and she feared it would make brutes of them all before long.

The foragers approached, looking as hungry and bedraggled as the refugees they drove before them or slaughtered. Thanis counted at a whisper. "Looks like...five horses, three wagons. Will they be heavy enough?"

"They will," Linet answered with all the confidence of a market-fair grifter. "Just remember to pull the chain when their front crosses the two-thirds point and not before."

"And pull *hard*," Aerrus added.

The party came at last to the bridge, across from where they hid. Close enough to see their faces. They heard the hollow *clop-clop* of hooves on the wood. Thanis visibly shivered, and Linet felt a pang of sympathy for what must be going through his mind. For many of them none of this had been real until now, just an exercise in thought. But it was too late to call off now.

The foragers crossed the halfway point, the beams groaning in mild protest, as bridges did. Linet, Thanis and Aerrus all gripped the end of the chain that ran from the underside of the bridge and snaked along the cliff under concealing brush. The wind died down completely and all was quiet but for the footsteps and low rumble of the wagons. The whole world, it seemed, held its breath in anticipation.

Two-thirds. Linet nodded and as one they pulled. The chain snapped up taut from out of the ground.

Nothing happened.

One narrow beam under the near end of the bridge snapped back and fell away, but that was all. Thanis drew a sharp gasp. "We're dead," he whispered. The mounted officers leading the party halted, looked from the end of the bridge to the struts, to the chain, and followed it straight to them. Realizing what had happened, what had *almost* happened, they waved and yelled in their unintelligible foreign speech, probably ordering the others to get back to the other side.

But the wagons and the foragers on foot, carried on by momentum, couldn't be halted quite so easily and trundled forward toward the officers. This resulted in concentrating the greatest weight directly in the center of the bridge. The beams' groans grew louder. The company only had time to begin a mad dash to one side or the other when the supports finally gave way with loud snaps.

It seemed to happen in painfully slow motion, not all at once with a dramatic crash as they'd imagined it. Smaller bits of splintered wood glided gracefully down to the river. Then the planks followed, first tilting over as one piece to spill men and horses over the side. Then finally the center shattered and two sections fell away to either side, still hanging by bits of rope.

Their victims seemed suspended in midair for a flash, then the illusion was broken and they plunged screaming into the Carsa. Some bounced off the gorge wall, flopping like fish and not at all gracefully. The terrified neighs of the horses died away, muffled by the roar of the rushing current below. A few distant bodies thrashed and scrambled, but most just drifted away with the rest of the debris.

Thanis turned away from the carnage, eyes red and tear-streaked, and let out a low moan. Aerrus patted him gently on the shoulder. "I'm sorry, lad. Hard work killin' men, and don't ever let anyone tell you different."

Thanis sniffled once, shook his head. "Naw, fuck 'em, they earned it. It's just...I never wanted to hurt the horses."

A few survivors yet clung to the dangling remains of the bridge, trying to climb back up. Aerrus raised his bow and sent an arrow arcing across the gorge to bury itself in the back of one poorly armored figure. He jerked and dropped into the gorge as well. Linet likewise sent another after that. Only one managed to reach ground and escape.

"Damn," said Aerrus, "secret's out now. Not that it was much of one before." He clapped Thanis on the back, more forcefully this time. "I thought we'd had it there for a second, but looks like we got lucky. Congratulations, how does it feel to be terrorists?"

"Let's go home," Linet said, not feeling lucky at all.

* * *

The terrain west of the Carsa River rose lazily toward the distant Sellinac Mountains over many miles. They were an old, low range, and the land was in no haste to climb their peaks. The foothills thus made up a vast expanse where only a few scant farming communities dotted the country between Wengeddy and Lenocca. There were nooks and crannies aplenty where a fugitive, or a forest ranger or an insurgent, could hide in relative safety, where armies couldn't move with any speed. Nestled among those rolling mounds lay an old, decrepit place that had been both a fort and a castle in older days.

Dunsmere still had most of three walls and a crumbling tower that was more likely to collapse on its occupants rather than defend them from attack. But in recent days it was surrounded by growth, and hard to find even from a short distance, and that was its advantage now. The place was well-known to the Heron Kings, and they'd funneled their growing band of volunteers there to train and hide while planning raids on Boras's forces.

Linet stepped lightly through the stone portal that had once held gates, suddenly nervous about walking under the ancient stones. Inside, the fallen fourth wall was being poorly substituted with a wooden fence crammed with brush and thornbushes and wooden pikes, and a dozen or so people gathered scattered stone blocks to pile in one corner. At one end Vander shouted commands to a group shooting at makeshift archery butts and mostly missing, while at the other Kanessa demonstrated throwing off an attacker while wielding a knife, a gaggle of others watching intently. The stink of a newly dug latrine pit hung sourly over the whole yard.

Seeing Linet, Kanessa dismissed her little class and jogged over to her. "They're still coming, more volunteers than we ever expected! Dunsmere might not be enough to hold everyone."

"How about feeding them?"

"Most of the peasants brought as much of their harvest along as they could as they fled, livestock too." Kanessa pointed toward the gateway, where Haskell urged on a line of newcomers, each carrying a sack on their backs. A few dropped their loads halfway across the yard, exhausted.

"Oh, not done yet, kitties," shouted Haskell, enjoying himself far too much. "You stack those in the tower cellar, then it's an hour of shooting practice. Hop to it!"

"That plus what we can forage," Kanessa continued. "It'll be a lean winter but we'll manage. We've ordered them to send their children along to 'Nocca or elsewhere. Too dangerous."

Linet nodded. "Good. It's funny, long as I can remember this place has been used as a hideout for bandits. We've cleared more than our share out ourselves. Now here we are."

"Not just us," Kanessa said with the barest tinge of worry. She cocked her head toward a white tent set up against a wall. The tent was in far better condition and of better material than the few others that were being set up in place of the fallen stones as they were gathered. A man with an ankle wrapped in bandages limped out, grimacing.

"Who—?" Linet didn't need to finish her question when the injured man was followed by another wearing a long robe. It was Prior Eribert, from the Polytheon house that'd tended to her and Eyvind while fleeing Armino's mercenaries. It seemed so long ago now, though it'd been less than a season. *Too short a season, even so.*

She stomped over to the tent as the prior whispered some command or other to one of the brothers who accompanied him. "What are you doing here?" she asked without preamble.

"I beg your pardon, young lady, who do you – oh. It...it's you! I should've known you'd have something to do with this. Where is Lord Osbren amid this catastrophe? Whole towns are being wiped out!"

"Osbren? I, um...." She suddenly remembered her false documents, the ones that hadn't quite convinced at the palace. She fished through her pouch for the badge Osmund had given her. "I'm working for the king now, I guess."

"You *guess*?" Eribert frowned so hard it was a wonder it didn't break his jaw. "Are you involved with this, this uprising?"

Linet struggled not to laugh at that and give too much away unnecessarily. "I, erm...yes. Yes, I am."

"Humph! No surprise. Well, if that's all that's left to us, I suppose we're in the right place. Our skills at physic seem to be of some use, after all. And certainly the people will need the comforting sermons of the Polytheon in these dark days."

"But doesn't leaving the priory violate your neutrality? Even to practice physic, this *is* still a kind of war camp."

The prior seemed about to say something, drew a breath to answer, then stopped. His mouth hung open then, perhaps he reconsidered. His face shifted entirely into what he probably thought was an enigmatic smile. "Well. I suppose that's a matter open to some interpretation."

A cold twinge ran down Linet's spine. "No, no, it's really not. I'm not a very, er, observant temple-goer, but even I know that—"

"Perhaps," Kanessa said, having sneaked up behind with her usual complete silence and making Linet jump, "we shouldn't look too closely at the provenance of this particular gift, ken'ee?"

Linet dragged Kanessa away from the tent, where they could whisper in privacy. "Kay, I have a bad feeling about this. Something... very strange happened in Pelona. I didn't tell anyone but Perrim and Lom about it but...."

"What?"

"It might be nothing. Just keep an eye on those robers, okay?"

"I keep eyes on everything," Kanessa said.

★   ★   ★

The land just south and west of Wengeddy was pockmarked with hills and marshes, wooded paths, and even a few caves. It was the perfect place to keep a watch on the town without being seen in return, and Linet now crouched inside one of those caves. It was dark and wet and the complete opposite of a built-up place like the Lodge. They were planning their first attacks with the Vrril they'd gotten from Eyvind, and everyone was on edge around the stuff.

"So what do you do," Haskell asked, holding the phial well away from the fire built at the back of the cave, "just light it then run real fast?"

Linet shook her head. "You saw the demonstration. Nobody can run that fast. We'll have to find some way to fire it from a distance. Unless you want to be a martyr."

"No thanks." He turned the vessel around in his fingers, watching the flames reflect off the faceted glass surface. "I wonder how many you could take out with one of these."

"Enough," Linet said grimly, "though more than that's the fear it'll inspire. It's an enemy no soldier can fight and kill. Swords and shields won't stop it. Not even water will put it out once it gets going, according to the alchemist who invented it."

"Huh. Well, I hope Kay gets back soon, I'm keen to know the cocksuckers are sorted out so we can – gyah!"

"Watch out!"

Haskell tripped over some unseen root or stone on the floor of the cave, and he went tumbling. The Vrril fell from his hand into the dirt. "Shit!" It was unbroken, but the cool weather had stiffened the wax-sealed stopper. It had come open, spilling about half the phial onto the ground, and now a foul-smelling stain spread outward. The air rippled above it. He plucked the vessel up in two fingers and replaced the stopper. "Argh, sorry about—"

"Get out!"

"What?"

"The fumes, the fire'll light them too! We have to get out of here!" Linet grabbed Haskell's tunic and dragged him a few paces toward the exit before breaking into a full run. "Come on!"

Haskell followed with a continued string of curses, and no sooner had he emerged into the overcast daylight than they almost collided with Kanessa, back from her reconnoiter.

"Oh!" she yelped. "Sorry, two of their scouts spotted me and they're on my tail. We can handle 'em—"

"No time," Linet huffed, "come, get down!"

"Say wha—"

"Now!" Linet jumped down a short ravine and hunched in a muddy pool at the bottom, out of sight. Haskell and Kanessa followed, pressing themselves against the earth. Above, heavy footfalls, crunching leaves and foreign conversation grew louder. The three of them held absolutely still while listening to what sounded like arguing. Apparently thinking that their quarry had taken refuge inside the cave, the two scouts charged in, spears raised. Their shouts grew more muffled, angrier. Linet and Haskell exchanged a look, while Kay just looked confused.

Pop-WHOOSH!

It was like an extended roll of thunder from far off in the middle of a windstorm. A puff of hot air billowed from the mouth of the cave, followed by maddening screams. The two scouts burst forth, burning from head to toe and thrashing about. One tried to roll around on the ground to extinguish the flames, but it did little except ignite the dead foliage. The screams were so horrible Haskell climbed up from his hiding spot, bog water dripping from his ankles, and drew a long knife to go end their misery, if only to not have to listen to it.

When it was over, Linet and Kanessa looked down on the two cooked scouts with ashen faces.

"I…" said Haskell, his hand shaking as he wiped off his blade, "I see what you mean about inspirin' fear."

They decided not to launch any attacks that day. What they did do was tie the charred corpses to crossbeams made from fallen timbers, and prop them up against trees at the edge of Wengeddy, in full view of anyone atop the walls. "Waste not, want not," Haskell said grimly.

★   ★   ★

The autumn fogs had turned the roads to mush, and the incessant trampling of the advance column did so even more. Hiding eyes had seen it ride out from Wengeddy and south along the river's rougher western bank. Slow-going and little more than a footpath in places, but without the bridge across, it was their only choice. *Boras is getting desperate*, Linet thought, though the idea filled her with dread rather than satisfaction. She pressed herself further down into the mud as the column approached, its outrider patrols jerking their heads every which way for any sign of what they now feared. *Let them look. They won't see us until it's too late.*

"Are we ready?" she asked.

Next to her, Vander nodded. "Ready as ever. I've got to admit I'm anxious to see it in action. Though I don't think anyone ever expected it to be used like this."

"That's the idea. I just hope it's not too wet."

"We'll find out soon enough."

That was too true. The fall carpet had turned brown early, leaving the forest washed out and dead but without the cover of the snows to come. Cold rains had saturated the land, and it was still to be seen if their plan would be a waste of the half-phial of Vrril. Linet had refused to risk another full one without need after what had happened at the cave. Besides, to detonate one all at once in the midst of the marching, riding company of invaders would be devastating, yes. But what they intended now could have even greater effect. If it worked….

"Okay," Vander whispered as the grunting of men and animals and the *slop-slop* of splashing hooves echoed closer, "no point in delaying now. Give the word whenever you're ready."

Linet set her jaw. "Ready? No such thing. But then nobody ever asked us. Do it."

Vander turned back into the gray wood, where Drissa would be watching unseen, a tiny burning wick at the ready. He gave a sharp hand signal, then said, "You might want to cover your—"

BOOM!

It was much smaller than the explosion of a full phial, only a drop's worth. But it was frightening enough. A bright flash appeared, then evaporated.

BOOM!

Another, ignited by the fireball of the first, just a pace away.

BOOM, B-BOOM!

More, one after the other in irregular succession, each one a bit closer to the road where the advance column rode. The whole company jumped at the first explosion, perhaps well-traumatized by the experience at Phenidra. But when the second came, closer, then the third, fourth, fifth, each drawing ever nearer to them out of the forest like some stalking firedrake, it caused utter panic.

Shouts of terror answered each succeeding charge, and by the time the Vrril droplets had passed Linet and Vander's hiding place and reached the road itself, the mass of flesh and iron broke and ran. It was here where the cleverness of the plan revealed itself. The road sloped sharply downward as it ran south, and almost the entire expedition naturally broke in that direction as it scattered, hemmed in on either side by brush and rocky outcroppings. Only a few retreated back northward toward Wengeddy. Faster and faster downhill they ran, ran without looking or thinking about where they headed.

At the bottom of the slope the road leveled out, and that was exactly where a team of volunteers under Haskell's harsh supervision had flooded the ground. The column charged blindly into the new-made bog and were brought to a crashing halt. As men and horses struggled in the muck, a host of thirty starved and furious commoners emerged from cover and poured a hail of arrows down onto them. Those who weren't shot down had their mounts shot out from underneath and died drowning or crushed. Whoever survived *that* was met with charging peasants, hacking and slashing with spears and knives and, despite Haskell's warning, one or two swords. Though outnumbered five to one, the commoners nearly wiped out the column of soldiers as Linet, Vander, Drissa and Haskell stood and watched, almost like proud parents as their children demonstrated their new skills.

"We should probably have them collect the arrows again when they're done," Drissa said absently. "We'll need each one."

As the blood drained down toward the river, Haskell looked northward with a frown. "A few still got away. But just a few."

"Perfect," Linet said.

*   *   *

With the bridge near Wengeddy demolished, the nearest river crossing was between the villages of Firleaf and Plisten. After depositing their new insurgents at Dunsmere, Linet and Vander continued southward to that bridge, then turned back north on the eastern side of the river. The volunteers were straining the Heron Kings' supply of riding horses, so being in no great rush, they rode donkeys instead. Some peasant stragglers, whom the years had taught to distrust rumor and still did so even now, scurried westward. Some drove wagons or carts piled with their meager possessions or food stores; many went on foot. A few gave Linet and Vander approving nods or wordless glances of encouragement as they passed.

"They've always known, haven't they?" Vander asked with a shake of his head. It was a rhetorical question, Linet knew. Of course they have.

"I just wonder if we'll still be here when they come back. Or if they'll come back."

As they came to within five miles of the Lodge, Vander suggested taking a longer, winding path back home, a trail whose head was near. "Lots of bodies still on the move, lots of eyes, and we can't be sure whose."

"Agreed." They edged their donkeys off the road and up the slight incline. It was an old hunter's trail that branched off at a certain hidden point. They followed it for a few miles, and when they came to the fork, Linet noticed Vander was no longer beside her. She looked back to see him halted, head turned in the direction of the main path. "Van?"

"You smell that?"

"What?"

Vander wrinkled his nose. "Shit and smoke." He urged his mount further along the hunter's trail.

"Um," Linet said, "that might not be a good idea. There's only two of us."

"I just wanna take a look."

The shit and smoke grew stronger. It could just be a campsite. Or not. One little detail that the heroic sagas gently leave out is that it's more than common for people to void their bowels when they die by violence. When the two came upon a small hunting cabin, there was little doubt left which was the case.

The hut had been burned to the ground, and before it, laid in a perfect triangle, were the mutilated corpses of what had probably been a family. A man, a woman, and a boy about twelve. A bundle of kindling still smoldered in the space between them.

Vander bent forward and fell from his donkey. Fortunately the animal was small so it wasn't a long fall, and he recovered in time to avoid getting bile on him when it jumped from his stomach. "Oh, gods...."

"Marchmen," Linet said angrily. "A sacrifice to their ancestors."

"Earning their petty kingdom. Shitstains! They're bolder now. This is what happens when the Marcher lords hide in their castles, and we're stretched too thin to do anything about it."

A small sound meeped out of a stand of trees. It was no sound made by any forest critter Linet knew of, and she turned toward it sharply while drawing her short sword. "You hear that?"

"Yeah." Vander unslung his bow and was halfway to nocking an arrow, then stopped. He squinted, scanned with furrowed brow. "Wait a second." He lowered his weapon and motioned for Linet to do the same. He crept forward.

"What are you—?"

"Shh. It's okay. We won't hurt you. Do you want to come out of there? Let us help."

Linet was a moment understanding, then cursed herself. A small child, a girl perhaps seven years old, emerged skittishly from cover, cheeks dirty and eyes red and swollen. "Are you all right, dear? Where are your—?" She remembered the grisly scene at her feet. "Oh, no. She must've hid when the killing started."

Vander took a spare kerchief from his pouch and wet it from a waterskin. He made a poor job of wiping down the girl's cheeks while she continued to sob. "M-mummy...."

With no one left to care for her, they took the child back to the Lodge. This time neither Lomuel nor Perrim made any complaint about the intruder. This was precisely how the Heron Kings maintained their numbers after all, but for once Linet desperately wished it was not.

CHAPTER TWENTY-ONE

Lily Pits

"I hate these things," Linet said, wiping away a splash of mud from her chin and plunging her shovel into the earth once more to finish the task.

Aerrus bent to place the first spike at the bottom of the rectangular hole. One down, nineteen to go. "Lily pits? Why? Anything that pokes them without us being nearby is a plus, I'd think."

"You ever range south toward Seagate?"

"No," he answered, "don't think so. Why?"

"Last squabble 'tween Osbren and Trastavere, must be…eight years ago, ten? You remember."

"I remember we stayed well out of it."

"Some of Trastavere's paid thugs made pretty liberal use of the pits. Hundreds. Worked well at first, but then Osbren's men figured how to spot 'em, even dug some of their own. So it ended up that most of the people caught by them were just peasants."

Aerrus grunted. "Why am I not surprised?"

"When the fighting ended they just forgot about the traps, left 'em where they lay without a second thought. So every once in a while someone falls in. Usually some kid too young to remember the war they were dug for. Some pits are so overgrown you could walk over one a hundred times and be fine. Then if the ground gets soft or too much weight's on it…down you go."

"How'd you get to be such an expert?" He placed another spike, pressed it firmly into the hard dirt.

"We found one once, out on a long patrol. We smelled it first, that's the only reason we found it. Perrim made us all look. I didn't want to, but...."

"What did you see?"

Linet took a long, slow breath at the memory. "Two, well, not quite skeletons, not yet. But not whole bodies anymore either. One was...very small. Run clean through with spikes."

"Gods, I don't envy you that sight."

"Perrim said it was a reminder of just how much the lords value our lives. I volunteered to spend the rest of the summer finding and destroying as many of those damned pits as possible. Now here we are, digging our own."

"Well, this one'll be sprung soon enough," Aerrus said, glancing at the smattering of buildings not far off. "And we won't be forgetting where we put it."

Dwelfal had become a ghost village, like almost every place along the river until Lenocca. Dead or fled, Boras and Phynagoras's march south had cut a swath of depopulation broken only by pockets of roving Marchmen and bands of looters. *No one I'd mind falling into one of these*, Linet thought.

Aerrus finished placing the upward-pointing spikes at the bottom of the two-yard-deep hole and crawled out. Then they laid a mesh of branches and twigs atop the pit thick enough to be covered with leaves. The road leading into Dwelfal looked much as it had before the trap was set. "Looks good," Aerrus said. "If I didn't know better I'd walk right into it."

A familiar cadence of footsteps tramping through the leaves grew louder behind him. "Ah," he said without turning around, "just in time to avoid helping us build this contraption, Thanis. Very clever."

"I aim to please. Kanessa says they're coming, be here in minutes." Others of their number also melted out of the trees, picked for their marksmanship.

"You send the volunteers home?"

Thanis nodded. "If by home you mean that old ruin of a castle, aye."

"Might be a ruin," Linet said, "but it's the safest place for them right now, outside of the Lodge. And they acquitted themselves well enough last time we hit. I wish you could've seen it. Those peasants tore into them like hyenas on a rabbit. Maybe we underestimated them."

"Maybe," Aerrus admitted. "But this Boras whoreson isn't stupid. He sends out fewer and fewer companies, and better armed. This might be one of our last chances for an easy hit."

"Then let's make it count."

It was a simple tactic, as the best ones usually are. They'd wait for them to walk onto the lily pit at the edge of the village, then attack from both sides in the confusion. The trap wouldn't kill many of them, but the point was to make them terrified of where others like it *might* be hidden. Some of the insurgents had volunteered to help dig the pit but the ambush itself would be close quarters, too dangerous for any but expert archers. The harsh arithmetic meant that using the ever-more-precious Vrril on such a small group wasn't an option.

Getting smarter, Linet thought as she spied the approaching party from a distance, crouching in a ditch just off the road. Boras's men all wore armor when they went out now. That meant tougher targets – faces, legs, joints, anything that wasn't protected. The insurgents would only get a few shots off, then disappear again.

There was only one two-story building in Dwelfal. It was a messenger relay house built with the king's coin for royal dispatches up and down the highway. It had a small stable downstairs and a bunk room upstairs that stayed warm and dry all year round, which meant it was off-limits to locals. Now it stood as a silent sentinel at the entrance to the village. The landmark had been chosen as a rallying point where everyone could check in before scattering into the forest.

'Everyone' included painfully young fledglings, brought up somewhat before their time. Linet knew their names but was forced to admit she didn't know them as well as she should have. Far to her right knelt a teenager named Kordd, whom she suspected of harboring a secret forbidden crush on her. It was his first mission. Across the way waited Laurigan and Marton. To her left, Thanis. All lifelong Heron Kings, though by comparison she and Aerrus were grizzled veterans. There was a rustling from behind, and she turned to see Kanessa approach. She said nothing, only nodded and leaped up into the crook of a tree, bow at the ready. Seven of them, plus a pit, against about three dozen of them. Not bad odds, really.

Their targets came fully into view, and were visibly less confident even compared to the last lot they'd hit, moving slowly and with more caution. And more steel helms. They half-marched, half-walked casually but all bunched up close together, as if they were already surrounded by enemies. In addition to the weaponry of their home countries they now carried crossbows and poleaxes looted from Wengeddy. Linet switched to short, shallow breaths to keep the chill from giving them away, and stilled her body's instinctive movements in order to hear better. The next sound she heard did not come from the enemy, though. It came from the village.

Thwack. It sounded like a window shutter. Linet snapped her gaze toward the village, scanning for some indication of what had made it. It was on the top floor of the relay house, slapping against its frame. *Just the wind whipping it open*, she thought. But that wasn't right. There *was* no wind. She looked more closely at the window, squinting. *Oh, no. Not again....*

There was a small child standing at the window. A toddler who must have unlatched it by accident. What was a child doing here? Everyone was supposed to be gone. A second later a pair of hands appeared and yanked the child out of sight and pulled the shutter firmly closed again. *It's another damned family!* Right where they were leading the enemy.

There was nothing to be done. No one else was at an angle to see what Linet had seen, and the enemy was too close for her to call it off now. The only choice was to stick to the plan and hope the idiot villagers kept quiet.

The company came upon them as she hid in wait, and when they passed by Linet almost gagged at the stench of unwashed bodies. Or was it fear? The front line stepped onto the pit. It held. The next also, and it still held. *Just a little more....*

The next set foot on the trap, and all at once it collapsed. They sank straight downward in what might have been a comical sight under other circumstances, twelve men all suddenly reaching upward to claw at a distant sky for lack of anything else to reach for. They all shouted in surprise as one, then again in agony. The armor protected some of them, but the spikes were made purposely narrow, and many eventually found flesh. The cries shocked the remainder of the company into stunned silence long enough for seven bows to rise from cover and seven arrows to fly into their ranks. They dropped to hands and knees and ducked behind shields, trying to cover vulnerable parts as a second flurry hit them.

With the element of surprise spent, that was all there was time for. Kanessa dropped from her perch, and Laurigan, Marton and Kordd burst from their positions to follow Kanessa to the rallying point. Linet and Aerrus each shot one more time to cover the others' retreat then followed, not stopping to count their kills.

"We have a problem," Linet breathed as they ran. "Villagers, hid up there." She pointed at the top of the relay house. "Saw 'em just before."

"*What?* Too late now!"

Some of the remaining soldiers chased them into Dwelfal, navigating around the pit that still held their comrades. A crossbow bolt tore through Thanis's tunic, ripping open a hole and slashing his side, just missing his ribs. Kordd and Laurigan appeared out of the corner of Linet's eye as she passed the building and they loosed another shot each, giving their pursuers pause. *Keep them away from the house*, Linet thought frantically. "Scatter! Scatter now! Don't wait!"

Everyone moved off in different directions to find cover that would let them diffuse back into the woods. But Kordd fell victim to temptation, lingering to shoot one last arrow at the enemy. It glanced off a helm, doing no damage. But it did get the owner's attention, who rushed Kordd with a spear and a hateful roar. Kordd sidestepped the attack with ease then dove for cover, sending the man barreling into, and through, the door to the relay house. The crash was immediately followed by a series of startled screams from above. The rest of the soldiers looked at the building and, perhaps sensing the easier target, stormed the house.

Linet had paused her flight just long enough to look back, then watched in horror, knowing she was helpless to do anything about it. The soldiers poured in through the smashed doorway, so thirsty for vengeance for the attacks they'd suffered of late they almost fought with each other to be first in. A few seconds later the screaming started anew. *Oh gods, what have we done?*

Kordd tore out from whatever hiding spot he'd momentarily found, and before Linet could stop him, he rushed after the soldiers with a mad growl.

"No! Kordd, wait!" Linet rose to go after him, but was immediately jerked backward, held by the scruff of her woolen hood.

"Stop. It's too late," Aerrus said bitterly. He pulled her toward the cover of the forest. "We have to get out of here. I'm sorry."

"But—"

"There's too many of 'em! He's already dead. They all are."

★   ★   ★

"Dammit! Godsfucking*dammit!*" Linet kicked the rock wall of the Lodge's entrance hall, again and again, the darkness barely concealing her wine-red face.

Aerrus gingerly pulled her away, careful not to upset her even further. "Stop that, you'll just break your toe. There was nothing you could do—"

"Yes, there was. I should have checked, made sure no one was still in the village. That's basic, especially after what happened at the hunter's rest. I fucked it up and now who knows how many people are dead!" She flung her bow to the floor, and it was kept from snapping only by the old rug that'd lain there for thirty years. "I...I think I might've made a terrible mistake." Her voice quavered.

The others filed past, not sure how to respond to Linet's

uncharacteristic display of emotion. Thanis clutched at his side while making straight for the infirmary. Kanessa stopped, put a hard hand on her shoulder. "You're right, you should have checked. Next time, you will. When you set us on this path you must've known no one would come out of this with clean hands. There's no rulebook for this kind of thing, we're learning as we g—"

"There is!" Linet protested. "The archives—"

"Half-remembered half-truths from a bygone time," Aerrus said. "It's time to throw that book away. Listen, I grieve for those folk too. But if we give up now it'll all be for nothing. We will get better. And pardon fuckin' me for saying it, but this ain't just your fight. You don't get to martyr yourself—"

The argument was interrupted by a small sound echoing from one of the passages. The hearth cast a frightfully familiar shadow, though it approached now with a frightfully unfamiliar frailness. Perrim entered the hall with the aid of a cane but the same sour scowl she always wore when she knew bad news was coming. "What is all this racket?"

Linet took a heard breath. "Kordd is dead. And several other commonfolk besides. And it's my fault."

Perrim winced, lowered her head. Aerrus seemed about to add something when Perrim at last said, "That is sad news indeed. And... what of the enemy?"

"What? The enemy is...I don't know. Killed a dozen at least. They'll fear lily pits now forever more. But—"

"Then their mobility is further restricted while ours is expanded, and it was a successful raid. We've gotten too used to safety, to sacrificing nothing. Trusting to our precious archery and spies and stealth and the superstition of the gullible. Soft. We'll have to grow out of that." With apparently nothing more to say, Perrim turned and hobbled back toward her cell.

Haskell and Vander had come out of the opposite passage, headed out on a scheduled patrol. "She's right in that," said Haskell. "I've had enough of these piddly-shit little ambushes. Just pinpricks that teach 'em how to do better next time."

Linet sneered at him. "Oh? And what exactly did you have in mind?"

Haskell just shrugged. Then Aerrus said haltingly, "I...um. I had an idea. It's a crazy one, but if it works it'd sure strike a blow. And no risk to anyone else. I'd need a little help, though."

"I don't think we should take any more crazy risks for a while." Linet stomped off down the corridor to find someplace to be alone without waiting for a reply.

Aerrus raised an eyebrow. "Is that an opinion or an order?"

CHAPTER TWENTY-TWO

Bad Meat

"It's funny," Linet said, "how casual I am with it now. It used to terrify me. Or maybe now it's just I don't much care anymore." She rotated the phial in her hand, watching the liquid catch the afternoon sunlight. The glass alone was expensive. The Vrril inside...there was no way to measure its value.

"Don't be dour," said Drissa, "and melodramatic doesn't become you either. What happened in Dwelfal was as much the villagers' own fault as anyone's."

They sat outside a stable in a little out-of-the-way orchard hamlet about a mile from the Lodge. It was effectively owned by the Heron Kings, a staging area for horses and supplies hidden right out in the open in the hills. They'd been using it as a place to try out creative new traps and devices using Vrril, most too complicated to be practical.

"Fault, fault," Linet sighed. "I never heard a child's dead body ask whose fault it was that it got so cold. I was so confident in our oh-so-impressive skills I never considered what could go wrong. Haskell was right about one thing, though. We need to step things up. Bands of Marchmen have been slinking down out of the mountains into Wengeddy. Too few at a time and moving too fast for us to engage. We need to start using this more." She held up the phial again, and Drissa drew back instinctively.

Linet nodded. "Exactly my point. We need to stop being afraid of this, of the future, otherwise we're useless. Can't stop the course of the sun, Perrim said." The autumn chill had put a sheen of moisture on everything, and the phial suddenly slipped out of Linet's grasp, tipping over onto the worn wooden table they sat at. A tiny trickle of the substance splashed out. Once again, the wax around the stopper had cracked. "Watch out!" Both women stood up quickly, backing away from the drop.

"Maybe don't get too comfy with it just yet," said Drissa as Linet carefully righted the phial, keeping well away from any errant liquid.

"Gods, I can't do anything right! I'm as clumsy as Haskell." Linet shook with frustration. "There aren't any flames around, are there?"

"No. Again, dramatic. It's the colder weather, making the wax brittle. You need rest." Drissa set a hand on a quaking shoulder. "You're no good to anyone exhausted."

"I can't sleep. I just keep seeing Dwelfal over and over again." *And Eyvind*, she didn't add, *dead and strung from a castle wall.*

"Myrtho can help with that. You're punishing yourself. Aerrus was right, we don't need a martyr, painted up on some temple wall to inspire future generations. We need you here and now. Perrim is, well—"

"Perrim," Linet snapped, "is our leader, until she isn't. I don't want to hear anything more about that."

Drissa made a mocking parody of a salute. "Yes sir, general sir."

While they were arguing, a starling flitted onto the table and began to drink up the puddle of spilled Vrril. It stopped almost immediately when it realized the foul stuff was most definitely not water, but even that small amount was enough to send the little thing into violent spasms. The two women now looked on in horror as its wings beat faster and faster, until it flapped itself over the side of the table to land on the ground. It jerked once more, then stilled permanently.

"Gods," Drissa whispered, "it's just all kind of terrible. You didn't get any on you, did you?"

Linet looked at her fingers, was relieved to find them dry. "No. But…let's go home. I've had enough experimentation today."

Time for bed, time for sleep,
Time for darkness warm and deep.
Think not on today but of horrors to come,
A dream to others, a nightmare for some.

The stupid rhyme from Linet's childhood intruded on her fitful rest as faces danced before her, appearing only in the flash of green explosions all around. Each shouted accusations before bursting into flames. Bolen, Ellandi, even Perrim, dead and arranged into a ritual triangle. *Arrogance! Ambition! Foolishness! Disobedience!* She was a child playing with adult tools, playing with magics she didn't remotely comprehend. A toddler at a window. The shutter closed, and when it bounced back open the child was replaced with the charred face of a Bhasan soldier. *We're coming for you.* She tried to run, but she fell down a pit, and at the bottom a Marchman waited with an evil smile.

"Aeiow!" Linet awoke with a nonsensical cry, her limbs jerking violently and shaking the creaky wooden cot she slept on.

A dark shape rose in the almost total black of the dormitory. "You okay?"

Linet fought to slow her breathing. "Fine," she wheezed. At the moment she couldn't place the voice.

"Liar."

"Just a bad dream," she insisted. She'd taken Myrtho's sleeping draught after all, and this was the result. Knowing she'd not attempt that again anytime soon, she threw off both the blanket and the grogginess, navigated around the other mostly unoccupied cots in the chamber and through the stone corridors beyond. Having lived in the Lodge all her life, she knew the ways even in complete darkness. She passed the nursery where the few fledglings enjoyed the untroubled sleep of the young, then came to the cistern that drew fresh water from the springs and splashed her face, relishing the shock of the cold.

"Can't sleep?"

Linet turned toward the voice. It grew weaker each time she heard it, thus each time it made her more afraid. "Perrim. No, I…can't."

"Ah. Walk with me, will you?"

Linet followed a step behind, and she found herself in Perrim's private little sleeping cell. She lit a taper from a flint and steel wheel sparker set into the wall. "I know that look," Perrim said when the flame flickered in Linet's eyes. "I recognize it from both sides."

Linet shook her head. "How did you do it? How *do* you do it?"

"Do you remember Votris?"

"Huh?" Thrown off by the abrupt change of subject, she stammered, "I-I…think so, a little." She smiled in spite of herself at the half-memory. "I remember a big old man with a gruff voice who used to come to the nursery and let me ride on his back while he crawled on all fours like an ox."

Perrim nodded. "Votris had a way with children. I never did. He knew leadership too. I asked him the same thing, long ago."

"What did he say?"

"He said the answer is something that can be learned, but not taught. It was right before he retired, when he put my name forward to replace him. I think I was the only one surprised. And shocked when I won the vote. I expected Lom.

"Not long after, a sheaf of us were tracking some highwaymen. They'd made off from Plisten with stolen tax money and a pile of bodies left behind. We caught up with them…." Perrim waved dismissively. "You know the routine. We were about to move in to finish them off. Oh, I was limber back then, and a good shot, though not quite as good as you. But Lom took hold of me, held me back. He said, 'No, you will lead all of us soon. Your place is here,' and he pointed at the ground. I was so furious, I nearly hit him."

"That'd be something to see," said Linet. "You thought he was jealous. 'Cause you were voted leader and not him."

"Yes, I did think that. Foolish of me. But he was right. Leadership often means sending others where you may only look. Part of that is the cold hard fact that the leader is less dispensable. But something we don't often speak of is that a single human heart simply cannot take in all that must be done alone. Our founders learned this the hard way. Those broken souls would never be allowed into our family today, that's certain. You must learn to send others once in a while."

"But...I'm not leader—"

"You are. Of this mad battle of yours, and maybe of all of us soon."

"Perrim, I—"

"Very soon. Take my advice or don't. But I can tell you for sure which one of us will be getting more sleep tonight."

In the morning Linet found Aerrus. "Whatever you were planning, we've got a whole castle full of help at Dunsmere. Do what you need to do."

★   ★   ★

The peasant insurgents proved useful in unexpected ways. Enough of them knew their home stomping grounds that they could sneak about the forests and marshes and high-grassed fields without being spotted, and thus made excellent spies and scouts. So on the increasingly rare occasions when Boras was forced by hunger to send forage parties beyond the protection of Wengeddy's walls, the fact of it was known at Dunsmere within hours.

One such party was now returning to Wengeddy, pitifully light in the larder. The waning autumn had sent geese far north and burrowing game into hibernation. So when Leofric, dressed in drab, concealing colors, loosed a captured fawn onto the road just as the straggling end of the party passed by, two enterprising soldiers wasted no time in peeling off from the party and giving chase deep into the forest.

When they and the fawn had left the others well out of earshot, they passed by an overturned tree trunk, large and hollow enough to hide a man. An arrow flew out after them, taking one in the back and piercing the worn cloth armor. As he yelped and fell to the ground, the author of the shot burst forth and tackled the second soldier, drawing a sharp knife across his throat.

But instead of the customary gush of warm blood, there was only a cold *shwwwwwink!* sound. This one was better equipped it seemed, with a steel gorget. The men grappled, and the soldier got the better of his attacker, turning the knife around against him and slowly, slowly driving the tip of the blade down toward an eyeball.

When it was a hair's breadth from popping Aerrus's eye into jelly, there was a shout and a crash, and the soldier flew backward. Dazed and with his helmet knocked clean off, the soldier tried to crawl away, but got only a few yards before Leofric fell on him with a hatchet, cleaving his skull into three or four pieces. Then he cleaved some more, and more.

Aerrus sat up, breathing heavily and watching the carnage. "I think you got him," he said at last.

Leofric turned back to him with a blood- and brain-spattered smile. "Just wanted to be sure." He offered a hand and pulled Aerrus to his feet.

"Thanks. Didn't I tell you to stay put?"

Leofric shrugged. "Did you? Must've missed that part. Not that I'm complaining, but what was the point of all this? Only two low sloggers won't make much difference."

"I wasn't going to tell you until the last second, in case you wanted to back out. It's…a bit gruesome."

"Take a good hard look at me right now, and tell me that again," said Leofric with a sneer.

They spent the next hour stripping the bodies of armor. Though it smelled like they'd already been dead for a week, Leofric pointed out.

"You're right," Aerrus agreed. "I think they sleep in it now. Never take it off, thanks to our attacks. That can't be comfortable, and anything that makes them uncomfortable is good for us. But things are going to smell a lot worse in a bit."

The next task proved significantly darker. They cut the bodies up into small bits, drained the blood off, then stowed the flesh in two large sacks. The worst part was the intestines, and Leofric had had to pause to vomit more than once. "I can't believe I'm doing this," he mumbled, green-faced.

"You told me you wanted to drag these pigs down to the nineteen hells with you," Aerrus said. "Well, this is a step on that road. Now to let it ripen for a time, then get it inside."

"Inside? Where?"

"How well do you know Wengeddy? You've been there often?"

Leofric nodded. "Sure. Biggest market fair of the season is held there. Well, excepting this year I guess."

"And you know the layout? The streets?"

"Aye. What's—"

"And you know where the well is?"

Leofric paused a moment, bemused. Then the understanding that crawled over his head like a spider enveloping a fly reflected in his eyes. He glanced at the sacks, and it seemed he was about to puke again. "You...you mean you want to...into the well?"

"Yeah. We're going to market anyway, but fair's the last thing it's going to be."

"Gods! But how will we get in there?"

Aerrus pointed at the now-vacant armor. "That's how. They're hungry, and I aim to feed the bastards to themselves."

★   ★   ★

The corpses of the enemies they'd killed so far were all long dragged off by wild animals, thus they had to spend a week letting their latest victims putrefy at Dunsmere. When enough people began to complain about the smell, Aerrus and Leofric packed it back up and set off for Wengeddy. The foraging parties were just the right combination of starving, paranoid and angry so that one in particular didn't even notice two extra members tagging along at the end. They marched back into town at sunset, their helmets obscuring Aerrus and Leofric's faces enough that none recognized them as locals. Suddenly they found themselves smack in the belly of the beast they'd been fighting for weeks.

Wengeddy's great town gate and portcullis had stood open, even at night, for so many peaceful years that to see its rusty hinges wrenched shut behind them was a strange sight. Within, the straight cobblestone streets and tasteful homes and guildhouses dominated by the high-spired assembly hall where Aerrus and Linet had made their case to the committee had all been ransacked for anything that could be eaten or used for firewood. Heaps of refuse and debris littered the road. The forage column merely wended its way around these obstacles as it made its way to what had been butchers' quarter to deposit what little they'd obtained. There was a stench of the unbathed permeating the whole town, held in by the walls like a gigantic bowl of diseased meat. Appropriate, considering their current mission. The occupied town retained little of the discipline that Phynagoras had become so famous for. Here, men milled about arguing or gambling, or running ambush drills among the streets clearly inspired by the recent insurgent attacks. One thing neither Aerrus nor Leofric saw many doing was eating. There was one small victory.

Just before the column reached the yard outside the slaughterhouse, Aerrus leaped to the side down an alley, yanking Leofric along. He hid his sack under a pile of ashes that looked like it'd been there for days. "Now, show me where the well is, and tonight we'll go." He then fumbled at a belt pouch and pulled out some bleached knucklebones. "Then we'll play at bones and try not to be noticed until morning."

The two went through the motions of gambling until it was fully dark and the bulk of the soldiers fast asleep wherever in the town they were billeted. Sentries were posted only along the walls, staring bleary-eyed out into the dark, thus Aerrus and Leofric moved about freely. The well lay in the middle of a courtyard, with little cover all around. There was one soldier nominally guarding it, sitting on the stone ledge around it with his cheek propped up by one fist and a poleaxe rested across his lap. His helmet lay on the ledge next to him while he scratched and picked at his greasy black hair and ten-day stubble.

Aerrus strode out in the full moonlight as casually as you please, still clad in his stolen armor, and nodded at the guard while reaching for the bucket attached by rope to the turncrank. The guard reached toward Aerrus's arm to stop him, shook his head and said something in his own language. Aerrus then began spouting bits and pieces of the sounds he'd caught while in the process of killing the men who'd spoken them. It was gibberish in any language, but it had the desired effect of confusing the guard long enough for Leofric to sneak up on him from behind. He swung a long length of ash that had so far escaped hearth or cookfire, cracking into the guard's temple and sending him reeling. Aerrus followed him to the ground with his knife and held a hand to his mouth while stabbing up through his jaw and into the brain. He held the position tightly for many long, exposed seconds until the jerking stopped, then motioned for Leofric.

"Come on," he whispered, sure someone must've seen or heard, "help me hide the body." They buried it under the same pile of ash that had hidden the sacks, then returned to the well.

"Now," Aerrus said, "at last." He opened one sack and tossed a hand into the well. It was deep enough that the splash was muffled. Aerrus nodded. "Good. Now for the rest, quickly. We'll tie the bags up tight and toss 'em in whole. Don't want any bits and pieces discovered until they're good and sick. Drink deep, my friends."

When that task was done, they sat shivering in a dark corner of the town until morning, when they once again joined another forage party to give it the slip and head home.

That was the plan, anyway. Having left their weapons forgotten somewhere in the night, they were the only two in the column unarmed. This must have gotten someone's attention, for just as they were about to pass through the gates once again, a sharp voice rang out just behind them.

"*Maqaat!*" Aerrus and Leofric both jumped and spun around. An angry-looking soldier, somewhat above the lowest rank of slogger by his meager armor decorations, sneered in their faces. A sergeant? *"Zhim ki khesta? Aslaq ishma qishasht? Danda zhama ninqu eshet!"* A few other soldiers near the end of the forage party's line glanced back, then forward again quickly to continue on their way, apparently not interested in getting involved in whatever was transpiring. The sergeant held a hand out toward Aerrus's poorly fitting outfit, then smacked his shoulder with a derisive snarl. *"Piasaq!"*

"Um..." muttered Leofric, "okay, what do we do?"

The sergeant gave Leofric a confused frown, then reached out and wrenched his helmet from his head. *"Zhim ki...Barghii!"* His eyes widened, and he took a step back while reaching for a dagger at his hip.

"Run," said Aerrus calmly.

"Huh?"

"I said..." Aerrus kneed the sergeant hard in the groin, where the armor coverage was mediocre at best, "...run!"

While the sergeant staggered, the two took off toward the thickest grouping of houses. Incomprehensible shouts echoed from behind, and suddenly a hundred pairs of eyes were on them. They sprinted down another alleyway that turned slightly at the far end. They emerged to face the town's wall in front of them. To the right a small company of soldiers closed on their position. They ran left.

"Up there!" yelled Leofric, pointing at the stone stair that climbed to the wall's defenses.

"Don't...they have guards up there?" Aerrus huffed.

"Not as many...as down here!"

A walkway ran almost the entire length of the wall, and soldiers were indeed stationed every few yards. They surprised the first one and barreled right into him, knocking him down into the mud below. But the second was ready with a poleaxe, and now began to charge them. They turned back the other way, making it only two steps before spotting another coming from the other direction.

"Um...." Aerrus looked out over the wall, bending down to get a look along the exterior. "Oh, well, that's...."

"What?" Leofric followed his gaze, and his face turned green. "Oh, no."

"It's the only way. Come on!"

Aerrus hoisted himself over the wall, and climbed down using the only hold there was: the still-decaying corpse of someone unfortunate enough to have been caught by Boras's advance. The body was mercifully unrecognizable, left exposed to the elements and held out of reach of scavenging animals where it was lashed wide-armed to the stone with ropes looped through rain gutter holes. Aerrus held his breath and clawed into the soft mass of mostly goo, just enough to slow his descent until he hit ground. Leofric scrambled after just as the soldiers converged on them, falling a good third of the way as the corpse fell apart entirely. Amid a rain of filth and bone, the two tore away from the wall and into the forest, two or three thrown spears just missing them.

The contaminated water wasn't noticed until almost a week later, letting the foul brew steep even further. By the time the odd taste was noticed enough to cause concern, a hundred soldiers were sick. When the well began bringing up errant chunks of human, the revulsion and disbelief spread much more quickly. Boras raged, but that was all he could do.

CHAPTER TWENTY-THREE

What Victory Looks Like

On the night of Aerrus and Leofric's gruesome escapade, Linet walked along the perimeter of Dunsmere. It was only supposed to be a cursory inspection of the forward sentries they'd set, but then she'd come across one of their guards dead asleep. It was the woman who'd claimed to have been with the militia years ago. Linet had been about to smack her awake with curses, then relented and left her to slumber, taking up the route herself. A sleepless night watch might be second nature to Linet, but these were raw volunteers. Peasants who, until losing their homes, had learned to rise with the sun and toil until it set. *Better a night patrol than more dreams*, she thought as she crept quietly through the woods surrounding the castle.

Near the spot farthest from the front gateway, she paused. A movement? She held her breath and froze to spy the scene before her in its native stillness. Definitely movement, and not the jerky skitterings of a small creature. Steps. Human steps, crunching leaves.

When the source of all this moved farther away, she waited a bit longer then followed at a distance. It was a single person, wearing a cloak and thus moving slowly through the brush, away from Dunsmere, due northeast. Whoever it was stopped at a clearing, the moonlight shining down onto the circle of high grass. They leaned against a tree, seemingly waiting. *What is going on here?* Linet wondered. *Nothing good*. She crouched, moved laterally to try to get closer, then bumped into something soft. Some*one*.

Before she could react, a hand reached out to cover her mouth. A strong arm spun her around while whispering, "*Shh!*" In the moonlight she could make out a shiny head and a goatee. *Haskell.*

"Who is it?" she asked in the lightest breaths she could form into words.

"One of our recruits," Haskell replied in the same manner. "The one with the crossbow. Dead merc, my ass! Live one, more like. Meeting up with the enemy to sell us out for a few silvers."

"How do you know?"

"I spied 'im sneaking out of the castle, same as you. Guessed he might be coming here and went ahead." He held up a bag of lightly clinking metal. "I met his sweetheart date first."

Linet reached for her skinning knife, furious. "I'll pay him steel instead of silver." But before she could go after the traitor, Haskell held her fast.

"No. It's my responsibility, I'll do it. No need to risk the brains o' the outfit for this."

She was about to protest, but in that moment she imagined a shadow of Lomuel holding her also, and she remembered Perrim's words. Fighting against all instinct, she nodded. Haskell disappeared into the darkness of the woods, and Linet went back to the castle alone.

★   ★   ★

When hunger, sickness and superstition at long last forced Boras to abandon Wengeddy and resume marching southward, the volunteers gathered at Dunsmere until the army was safely past, though their nerves trembled. It was only then that Linet learned the particulars of Aerrus's plan. "I still can't believe you'd do something so incredibly reckless," she said, shaking her head.

"Really? Have we not met? I told you we were going to foul their water supplies."

"I didn't think you were gonna walk right into town!"

"Details," said Aerrus dismissively. "It worked. Half of 'em are too sick to fight."

"Which leaves a lot more still able. And they're still coming."

"Which is about to turn into going," Aerrus said. "Let's just hope they don't change their minds and decide to march on 'Nocca."

"They won't, it's too hard a target alone. They need a beachhead in the south to bring reinforcements."

Aerrus grinned. "Maybe it was you shoulda been playing castra with Essimis."

Before Linet could come up with some rejoinder, Haskell came running up between them with a sheaf of a dozen painfully young fledglings in tow, all breathing heavily. "Problem," he huffed.

"Always is," said Aerrus. "What is it?"

"They're coming."

"We know," Linet replied, "but they should be continuing south soon enough—"

"No, no," said Haskell, "they're coming here. Now."

"*What?*" Linet and Aerrus both exclaimed at once.

"We were keeping an eye on 'em, watching for any deserters we could mop up easy. They were marching south like you said, then as soon as they were about even with the castle they just…stopped. Halted all of a sudden, turned sharp as a corner to the right and began marching into the trees, over hills. Making straight for here. Good odds they know where we are. I didn't want to make a panic by spreadin' the word, but—"

"Right, right," Linet said, head swimming. "I guess we couldn't keep it a secret forever but, how did they find…?"

Haskell sneered. "Our little sellout. That might not've been his first outing."

Aerrus frowned, rubbed his increasingly scraggly beard. "But over that terrain it'll take them half an hour to get here. They must know we could be gone by then. Unless—"

"Unless they intend to hold us here," Linet growled. She looked up toward the remaining stretches of walls, where pitifully few of their number stood sentry. But the surrounding foliage made that a tough duty. "Laurigan!" she called out. "Do you see anything out there? Anyone?"

The girl looked down at them. "No, nothing. I think—"

Thwack! Laurigan's eyes doubled in size and she let out a hard, involuntary breath as a cruel, barbed arrowhead exploded from her chest. Pause. Silence. Shock. The body fell from the wall to land on the hard-packed ground below. The spine shattered, a brief fountain of blood sputtered upward. Silence again.

"*Attack!*" a voice shouted from the wall. Now a hail of arrows came from somewhere out there. The sentries dove behind crumbled excuses for merlons for cover. Most made it. Not all. More screams.

"Attack!" Aerrus shouted, echoing the alarm. "Defenders, get to your post! Go!"

Linet stood immobile, still half in shock, staring at Laurigan's unmoving form while chaos erupted all around. The shining black obsidian arrowhead protruding from her lung left no doubt about the source of this new horror. "Marchmen," Linet said bitterly.

"Yeah," Haskell said, snarling, his teeth bared like a rabid wolf. "That's how they got so close. Sneaky fucks." He reached out and slapped Linet across the cheek. Not hard, just hard enough to snap her out of whatever fugue had taken her. "Hey! We got one chance to stop a massacre here."

"What? R-right. The, the corner!" The northeast corner of wall was the most vulnerable, mostly fallen and crammed with wood and brush for a barrier. They'd surely attack there in force.

Haskell nodded. "We'll cover the gate." He turned to his sheaf and about a hundred terrified insurgents, some wearing bits of stolen enemy armor but most not for fear of being taken for one and shot in the night. "Come on, we'll hold them bastards at the front door!"

Aerrus grabbed Haskell before he could depart. "Wait." He opened one of the little hard leather pouches at his belt, pulled out a small glass phial. The dry hay it was wrapped in for cushioning floated to the ground. "If it comes to it...."

"Right." Haskell took the phial then tore off toward the gate.

The northeast corner had planks laid both vertically and horizontally, with rubble pressed in between and sharp thornbushes piled against the exterior. Almost as soon as Aerrus and Linet arrived, hard pounding could be heard from the outside, and already sections of it had begun to wear away. It was never intended as a true defense, and it served as none now.

"*Hoo-hoo-hwah! Hoo-ha-kow! Kaaah!*" The chant sent chills down every spine, no doubt as it was intended to do, as sentries, now desperate defenders, shot arrow after arrow, darting out from cover when they dared, shot down onto some as-yet-unseen foe. But each shot was answered with ten in return.

Linet strung her bow for the first time since Dwelfal. But all thoughts of that disaster were banished, replaced with the image of Laurigan's broken and twisted body, once so lively and now never so again. Aerrus did the same. Already the brothers from the priory were dragging wounded into what was left of the tower keep. From a crumbling balcony above, Kanessa sent shots down over the wall with frightening accuracy.

When the whites of eyes appeared through the failing barrier, Linet let arrows fly. One well-aimed shot went right through one of those eyes, and its owner fell back howling. Dark forms crawled from the shadows of the dying day and leaped upon the pile of debris, and at last they saw their enemies for true.

The Marchmen of old had often adorned themselves with the body parts of animals, believing it would endow them with the beast's powers. Ram's horns on the head, stag's fleet feet lashed onto their own, and the like. A chieftain could appear as nothing even remotely human with enough decoration. These days they usually did little more than paint their bodies with woad or madder and run thick lime paste through their hair, but it made them no less terrifying. It was said they consumed plants that let them feel no pain or fear in battle, and the berserker now atop the wall seemed a likely candidate. With wild eyes, red and blue face and white-streaked, arrow-straight hair, it mattered not whether he was a warrior or a Chthonus of myth. The insurgents defending the northeast corner now shrank back in fear, spears and bows faltering while the wild man roared with a mad, joyous rage.

Linet fought through her own fear by latching on to the only thing she had left – fury. Snarling, she raised her weapon and sent a shaft straight into his forehead. The warrior registered only a brief moment of surprise – how could this happen, for was he not the hero of the story, after all? – before falling back and out of sight. That gave the defenders some heart, and now spears thrust out through the gaps in the defense, occasionally tasting flesh.

Out of the corner of her eye, Linet spotted Leofric descending from the wall and running toward a pile of weapons and supplies just behind them. "Need more arrows," he breathed, scared but at least not terrified.

"Good man," said Aerrus, "don't be shy about using 'em now. You get a look at how many are out there?"

Leofric shrugged. "Hundred maybe? No more." He climbed back up the ladder to the wall, a bundle of arrows under one arm.

"You were right," Aerrus said to Linet, "they're just pinning us down 'til the others arrive to finish us off."

"We need to get out of here," she said.

There was a loud *crrrack!* behind them. They turned to see the rudimentary gate that'd been built at the southern entrance snapped in the middle, and shuddering from continued strikes from the outside. Shouts from without came soon after, any odd word or syllable they could make out was no Marchman dialect, but Bhasan. Very angry Bhasan.

"They're here," Aerrus said with finality.

"Oh gods," moaned one of the insurgents, a wiry young fellow more suited to a clerk's office than a terrorist camp. "Oh gods, what've we done? We're all dead! Fuckin' dead!"

"Shut up," snapped Linet as a Marchman arrow whizzed by her. "Get stuck in on that wall and fight!"

"No use," he continued, now fully out of his mind with fear. "Nowhere to run! The game's up! Oh shit oh shit oh shit—"

Aerrus ran over to the man and, without a moment's hesitation, socked him square across the jaw. He fell, dazed, against a stone section of wall. Aerrus laid him down as gently as was practical, which wasn't very gently at all in truth. "Just what we need," he grunted, "panic plague."

Linet turned to the remaining insurgents, feigning confidence she didn't feel. "You! All of you, keep fighting! We ain't done yet." She pulled out a phial of Vrril at her own belt, held it aloft. "You might've heard of this stuff. Well, now you'll get to see it rip those bastards out there to shreds, but only if you can bring 'em all close enough. So make 'em want to drink your blood and eat your hearts, or whatever savage shit they do. Bring them to me!"

The words made little sense, but they didn't really need to in that moment. It rallied them well enough, and after a cheer of comradeship they took up the fight again, shooting and thrusting and taunting the Marchmen just yards away, ignoring the failing defense at the front gate.

Two female warriors climbed over the barrier and into the yard. One managed to open a defender's belly with a broad axe swing before being spitted on two spears, the other following soon after. Aerrus dropped his bow to tangle with a burly man who was reaching for his short sword. Aerrus gave it to him by ramming the pommel into his teeth then bashing his skull. Another thought to set the barrier on fire, but most of it was newly cut wood, and only a short stretch of it was lit before Linet, temporarily out of arrows, drew her own blade and sliced the top of the warrior's scalp away. But sword distance is where you die, so she jumped back from the wall just in time to avoid a return blow from some new opponent.

Linet looked across the gap, and among the wild attackers saw an island of calm. He was older than most, with hair similarly limed but also worked into intricate patterns and spikes. His beard was forked and painted red, and he was missing one eye. He sat astride a horse that did not shy away from the din of battle or the nascent flames kissing the wooden barrier. Even from across that distance his long, bronze leaf-shaped sword had almost taken her. They locked eyes, and she knew that this must be the chieftain. Ordovax. He smiled at her, looked her body up and down with an air of blatant sexual evaluation. He must've judged her favorably, for he nodded in apparent appreciation before lifting a heavy spear and heaving it at her.

So transfixed by the sight was Linet that she would've been transfixed by the spear as well, had not Aerrus knocked it aside with his sword, now blunted and bent near the tip. Someone shot an arrow at the chieftain, but he raised a hide shield and casually absorbed the shot before turning his mount and trotting away, his curiosity seemingly satisfied.

The front gate collapsed at last, and the insurgents who had been told in no uncertain terms that they were definitely *not* a militia or an army were suddenly forced to fight that way. A few who'd gotten shields from somewhere hid behind them while thrusting spears forward. They clogged the gateway, fighting as wildly as the Marchmen, but even this small detachment of soldiers of Phynagoras had the numbers and the training, and slowly pushed their way inward, killing as they went. The defenders on the wall continued shooting as quickly as they could, but it was a losing fight.

Linet heard Haskell scream himself hoarse behind them, something like, "Sell it, dear! Take 'em with you!" She risked a look back, and among the other fighting forms saw him running toward the smashed gate, a torch in one hand and something else in the other. He disappeared into a storm of slashing, flashing blades.

BOOM!

The explosion knocked them all back, and a split second later sent rent body parts raining down on them. The shock wave knocked several stone blocks from the tower. But the front gate…the front gate was gone, and the gateway was gone. Flaming piles of flesh and fallen stone blocked the entrance, and perversely it was the soldiers' own superior numbers that now hampered them. Those attackers who'd been outside the blast now couldn't get past and inside the castle grounds, at least not right away. Haskell had indeed sold his life dearly to delay the attack in a way only he would consider.

"No!" Aerrus moaned. "Aw, you crazy bastard! Only one way out now."

Linet drew her Vrril phial once more. "I know." She held it high. "Back! Everyone, get the hells back! We're ending this here and now. Get out of here and don't stop for fire or fear."

Aerrus glanced nervously toward the tower. "What about the wounded?"

Linet shook her head, tears welling up anew. "I don't know! I don't know anything else to do. I'm sorry."

Aerrus nodded. "All right. Do it."

When everyone had drawn back to the far side of the tower, Linet stood as far away as she dared, then tossed the Vrril phial into the dying embers of the barrier. It landed in a clod of hay and sticks, and she ran in the opposite direction without waiting for what came next. For one terrified moment she thought she'd missed. Then the flames began to tickle that section of hay, the phial began to heat up, and then....

BOOM!

The Marchmen had no sense of discipline like Phynagoras's adoring legion, for they were warriors, not soldiers. They had been clamoring against the barrier, straining between their craving for blood and glory and their agreement to stay in place and prevent the insurgents' escape. So crowded and tight were they packed that the Vrril tore through more than half their number in one blow. The barrier itself was mostly obliterated, leaving no stones to block the way. Except for the abattoir of human viscera, the way was now clear. The explosion hadn't even fazed Linet, not anymore.

"That's it," Aerrus yelled, "get out! Now! Don't group close together and don't stop! We'll find each other later!"

The two hundred or so surviving insurgents and Heron Kings charged the opening, which was ringed with fire and stench and smoking bits of meat. They paid none of it any mind as they scrambled and slipped over the slick waste, scrambling into the failing light of the forest.

Aerrus and Linet instinctively ran single-file in a leapfrog pattern, one holding an arrow at full-draw and covering the other, who surged ahead twenty yards, then switching. Despite their instructions, people

266 • ERIC LEWIS

were still in shock and unwilling to go off alone. Most clung together, and stumbled through the wooded hills in search of others. And large groups in the forest do not move quickly or silently. So when Aerrus and Linet finally stopped running to catch their breaths, they found nearly all of the survivors around them, gathered at the end of a gully that opened onto a field with rocky outcroppings to one side.

"This...isn't a good idea," Linet said between breaths. "If...there are more out here—"

"There are. That wasn't even a quarter of the men I saw in Wengeddy. Even if they're partly sick, they're— Oh. No...."

"What?"

Aerrus pointed into the trees. A line of horses emerged slowly, followed by soldiers marching in tight formation as much as was possible. In the middle of the line the largest of them rode ahead. He wore a heavy helmet, but took it off for a moment to better survey the scene, revealing a bushy black beard and a mean, ferocious glare. An equally imposing figure rode next to him – Ordovax, the chieftain Linet had hoped had been blown to pieces. There was nowhere to run now.

An odd calm washed over her. Her hand found Aerrus's, and they clasped tightly. "We gave 'em a good fight, didn't we?"

"We did. The best anyone could. It just...wasn't quite enough."

"It might still be. It might still be enough. But I guess we'll never know. I'm sorry."

"Don't be sorry. You were amazing." Aerrus smiled one last time. "I guess I did pretty good too. If there's another side I suppose I'll see you on it."

"Yep. Go down swingin'?"

"You know it."

The line of horses advanced at a walk to block the only easy way out of the gully, with the foot soldiers a few steps behind. All bore spears, a forest of them all pointed straight ahead. Aerrus turned left and right so any still with a will to fight could hear. "Anyone with arrows left might as well use them now."

Next to him, Leofric nocked one of his last few. "Thanks for giving me this chance."

"Wish I could've given you better."

Leofric shook his head. "Nah, it was more'n I hoped for. Gods'll light my path now. Or they won't."

The line charged. Aerrus gave the signal with a wave of his bent sword, and against a sky lit by a dozen brilliant colors of approaching sunset their final volley of arrows flew. A few, too few, brought cries that were cut short by the tramping of replacements marching forward. Then a crash.

All along the line Heron Kings and insurgents fought and screamed and killed and died. Some dodged the spears only to be cut down by swords or trampled under hooves. Others managed to jump atop the mounts and wrench their enemies into the mud to be trampled in turn. Some ran, some tried to climb the rocks. Some, most really, remembered Haskell's lesson and closed the distance to fall to knife work.

Resigned to death, Linet fought with a kind of grace, like it was a dance instead of a battle. She dipped, spun, slashed, shot, ran, shot again. She knew she'd taken punctures and blunt blows but felt none of them. Over the course of minutes, or maybe it was an hour, she fought her way to where Ordovax and the other leader – Boras, no doubt – sat and hacked away with long swords, just behind the tattered remains of the front line.

At some point during all this she thought she heard a distant cry ring out louder, though the blood pounding in her ears muffled so much. She looked left and right for more enemies to kill, and was surprised to find the paces of ground around her oddly vacant. Then she was struck from the side by something heavy, knocking her to the dirt. A horse. It leaped over her and tore off sideways. Then another form, a soldier, followed. Running. Where?

She sat up, more in a daze from the battle fever than the strike. She looked around and saw a mass of men and beasts running…northward? It was dusk now, and hard to tell. She stood, turned about once more, slashed at a soldier who was about to run into her. But his padded armor protected him, and he continued on his way. She turned again and saw the two commanders, Boras and Ordovax, seemingly arguing. Ordovax spat something unintelligible and wrenched his horse around to follow the others. From the south, new forms were appearing. More soldiers, but not Bhasan and certainly not Marchmen.

Boras pointed his mount northward as well, perhaps considering following Ordovax and the bulk of his own army. Then he rested his eyes on Linet, and she on him. Without making any conscious choice to do it, Linet charged the big man and jumped up onto his horse to grapple with him from behind. *No, you're not getting away*, she thought in a red haze. *Not this time.*

Boras howled curses at her in whatever tongue he spoke, his armor and muscular bulk keeping him from reaching back to grasp her. Though the helmet was strapped tight, she grabbed a length of his black beard, yanking wildly. From the edge of her vision she saw someone – Aerrus, still alive somehow? – raise a bow. She extended an elbow forward to present a target and he reached up for it, exposing an unprotected section under his arm.

Aerrus's shot was true, and the arrow bit deep into his armpit. He jerked, almost falling from the horse that now bucked and stamped. Using the heartbeat's breadth of time, Linet drew her last slender knife and wrenched it up under his helmet and across his throat. Blood sprayed out. Boras's bulk began to wobble in the saddle, and Linet could've sworn she heard him laugh out loud, softly but surely, and utter some final thought that no one would ever decipher. Then he fell into the mud, his neck snapped at an ugly angle.

Linet toppled from the mount as well with a bit more control, though not much. She fell to her knees, then recovered and ran into Aerrus's arms. "How," she said between relieved sobs. "How?"

Aerrus released her and pointed toward the newcomers. "There." The host carried torches aplenty, every man of them in fact, appearing in the twilight to be many more than they were in truth. A new horseman rode up to them, slowly, then dismounted. He wore polished armor that glimmered even in the almost-dark, the finest manufacture. Behind him a herald bore a banner very similar to the king's, except that it was a castle atop a mountain instead of a bridge, and twinkling stars above. He stood before them a moment, then lifted the visor of a bascinet trimmed with fine black sable. Linet knew that face. Or almost did.

"Uh-huh," he said simply, looking around at the carnage, the bodies clogging the gully and the path out of it. "Looks about right." He turned around and called out to someone. "Get a physic out here! Get all of 'em, now!"

Aerrus wiped sweat from his brow. "Lord Osbren, I presume?"

The man nodded. "You presume right. And since you make no effort or attempt to kneel, I can guess who you are." The volunteer insurgents, realizing in whose presence they stood, now indeed did sink to one knee, a lifetime of conditioning still not overridden by the nightmare they'd just endured.

Linet realized now why he seemed familiar: though she'd never seen his face, he looked like a younger, harder version of Osmund. A warrior king in some other life, rather than the clerk king they had now. "Took your time getting here," she said, the thought coming out of her mouth before better judgment could stop it.

Osbren gave a hard guffaw. "You want me to go home? I can, you know. I can ride right back up into the mountains and let my idiot brother clean up this mess he's made."

"Please don't do that," said Aerrus, exhausted even of sarcasm now. "Please...." He faltered, fatigued almost to death.

"Aw," Osbren said with a swipe of his hand, "I don't mean that, obviously. Though you did leave me with little to do today but scare off the leftovers. I got your message, by the way. Can't say I approve of your little band, but we done worked together well enough in the past against the damned dirty Marchmen. Ozzie told me about what happened last season, that ambush, that traitor Rinalda. Figured you've earned a helping hand now."

"Earned a helping...?"

Osbren shrugged his massive pauldroned shoulders. "Bad choice of words. Anyway, you ain't the only ones with scouts. When I heard those Bhasan shitspittles had left Wengeddy, I marched north to meet 'em. Then when they turned toward old Dunsmere I figured they knew something I didn't."

"Dunsmere," Aerrus said, "our wounded—"

"They're fine," Osbren said with another wave. "Bhasans broke off the attack chasing after you. Old weasel Ordovax lost half his warriors, the rest scampered off north at first sight of us, not to mention sundown."

"They retreated? A Marchman chieftain *retreated*?"

"Ha! Marchmen don't retreat, not ever. But that don't rule out a 'strategic withdrawal' in light of the enemy's dishonorable tactics. Namely your black magic lightning, or whatever it is. But victory's a victory however it comes, that's what I say."

Linet looked at the massacre around them, then down at Leofric's corpse with hands still clenched around an enemy's dead throat and a grim smile on his face. She curled her lip in distaste. "Is this what victory looks like?"

Osbren nodded gravely. "Sometimes, young miss, I'm afraid it is."

★   ★   ★

Linet lay on the ground among the remaining bodies, stripped to the waist and trying not to shiver as a priory brother stitched up a spear slash along her side. "Are you sure there's no opiphine?" she asked again, wishing to all the gods Myrtho was here. The battle fever had passed, and now every wound screamed for attention.

"Not anymore," the young novice replied, again. "What we had was all used up for the worst hurt. Sorry. I'm almost finished."

"Right. Well, just make sure you keep those eyes on my bloody bits."

"Yes, ma'am."

Other brothers as well as Osbren's physics flitted across the gully, seeing to the casualties. They'd worked throughout the night and still it continued. Linet had drifted in and out of consciousness. At some point someone handed her a waterskin and she drank greedily until it was yanked away. She'd expected to be visited in nightmares by the bloated corpses of Haskell and Laurigan, accusing her of…something. But sheer exhaustion had blessed her with oblivion before waking to a pale dawn and the brother attempting to take her shirt off. She might've instinctively drawn a knife on him had she been able, but her limbs were too stiff and painful to move much at all. And she'd run out of knives. So she just lay there like a helpless infant while her flesh was knitted back together.

Aerrus and Lord Osbren appeared above her. Two more unlike warriors one couldn't imagine, yet both gave her the same pained look. "How bad is it?"

"Pretty godsdamned bad," said Aerrus. "Looks like a little more than half our volunteers survived. For us, well you know about Laurigan and Haskell. We also lost Sorweth, and Vesh. I don't know if you knew them too well."

"I knew them. Not as well as I should have, but I knew them. What a butcher's bill."

"I know from personal experience it don't soothe much," said Osbren, "but it was worth it. That Porontan pederast just lost a chunk of his fighting men, his top general, and the chance for a southern port anytime soon. No true army could've done better. We gave chase and cut down a few more, but they ran like the devils were on 'em. Ordovax too."

"Will you go north to finish the job?"

Osbren shook his head. "It's not like the old days. I've got less than a thousand men, all told, barely enough to guard the Kingsmarch from small-time raiders. We wouldn't have a prayer in open battle against Phynagoras. Now, if I had a thousand of *you* lot…."

"Keep dreaming," Aerrus said. "Any chance this'll convince the other Marcher lords to join the fight?"

"Not likely. Valendri's a snake and Trastavere's a coward, though

I'll deny ever saying so. Half my men are borrowed on loan from them already, and they'll give no more."

Osbren excused himself to some other urgent task, then Aerrus cleared his throat. "I sent word back home to bring help, what can be spared. I thought…well, I thought we might as well bring the survivors into the Lodge. There's no secret to be kept now."

Linet figured she should've been alarmed by that news, but found herself as much numb in mind as pained in body. "Are you sure?"

"No. But Dunsmere's blasted even more to hell than it was, and there's still Marchmen out there."

They were interrupted by a horse neighing as it entered the gully, perhaps spooked by the gruesome sights and smells still littering the ground. The youth astride it strained to control the beast as it lumbered up to them.

"Thanis!" Aerrus exclaimed. "What're you doing here? I just sent—"

"M-Myrtho sent me," he said, his voice shaking.

Linet looked up, surprised. "Myrtho? Well, why didn't he come himself?"

"We didn't know about this. I…I came…." He grimaced in apparent anguish, his eyes red.

"What?" Aerrus demanded. "What's happened?"

"It's Perrim. She's dead."

CHAPTER TWENTY-FOUR

Nothing But the Song

Eyvind peered down the slope between the trees, squinting to make it all out. "How many are they?" he asked.

"Count comes to thirty," Davenga replied next to him, his naturally booming voice requiring great effort to keep low as they pressed themselves against the earth. "All on foot."

"Thirty foot to our mounted forty. Tempting. What do you think?"

"I think they are ready, and I am hungry."

Over the last hard weeks Eyvind's forage party had morphed into true raiders, scurrying down from Phenidra to prick small groups of Phynagoras's soldiers and followers when they ranged further and further afield for food and supplies. The Argovani and Pelonans had learned to work as a group, even learning bits of each other's languages to speed communication as they harried the enemy. But they'd never attacked so many of them at once, or so rich a target. The supply-train wagons below them trundled lazily northward, following Phynagoras toward Ólo and piled high with all manner of loot they'd no doubt seized from some unfortunate farm or settlement before burning it to the ground. Thus Eyvind found no shortage of reasons to attack it. As the convoy passed by, Tess came and lay down on the ground to the other side of him, whispering, "Everyone's ready. Just give the order."

Eyvind's stomach rumbled. Even with the emptying of Phenidra, the nascent repopulation of Edrastead and the supplies from Downhill, resources remained tight. He nodded. "The order's given. No Vrril this time, so we'll have to do it the old-fashioned way." The devastating substance was indeed beginning to run low as well, and he dare not let that fact out nor waste what they still had.

"Best way to do it," replied Davenga, who'd also grown noticeably thinner of late, such that as he rose to crawl back to his horse he moved carefully so as not to set his loosened armor clanking.

The line of low hills on either side of the road made it an ideal spot for an ambush, and it'd be the last such before the broad, flat coastal plains ahead. The host quietly nudged horses forward into the gaps between trees in a staggered line above the road, some yards ahead of the train's path. Estimating the timing of their descent from recent experience, Eyvind gave a silent hand signal and the raiders readied spears and lances and charged down the slope. There was no shouting or mad war cries or whatever else a fool might imagine, for this was work, not adventure, and by the time Phynagoras's soldiers noticed the attack it was too late. A cry *did* go up from the supply train, one of alarm mere moments before the line of horses exploded out of the trees and slammed into them. Spears skewered soldiers clad only in cloth or mail and sent those with plate tumbling. A few mounted enemy officers shouted orders and tried to defend with drawn swords, but they were outnumbered and scattered. Several wagons were overturned, spilling food and precious warm clothing onto the road.

Suddenly a sharp whistle pierced the din of battle, given by some officer or other. And all at once, as though it were predetermined, the surviving soldiers abandoned their prize and retreated. Or rather, they continued on their route at a breakneck run.

"After them!" screamed Eyvind, his spear already dripping with the blood of three enemy soldiers. "Leave none to tell of us!" He kicked his horse into full gallop. With himself and Davenga at the head, the raiding party tore after the soldiers, riding some down as they ran while others disappeared around the last low hills through which the road wound. A terrible feeling put Eyvind's neck hairs on end, disturbing the calm he'd come to feel even in a fight. *Something's wrong*, he thought. He glanced over at Davenga, who just frowned his usual frown. They turned a corner and emerged from the last hill.

No.

There, arrayed across the road lying in wait, calm as a snake in the grass, stood a line of the mounted warrior women. *A trap!*

They loosed a hail of arrows straight at them, even as the fleeing foot soldiers retreated behind their line of horses. Eyvind instinctively turned away, feeling the breeze of one arrow as it whizzed by, the tooth-rattling clang of another when it bounced off his simple skullcap helmet. Cries of anguish rang out all around him. Horses screamed. Bodies fell. The women charged, yipping wildly. Out of the corner of his eye Eyvind saw Davenga throw his lance, strong and straight, spitting one of them in the saddle.

"Back!" Eyvind shouted, wrenching his horse around. "Get back! Scatter!" He made a wide circular motion with his spear, hoping there were even enough of his party left alive to make too many targets to follow. Wishing to the gods that he had just a droplet of Vrril now, he stood in his saddle, twisted himself around as much as he could, and hurled his spear back at the nearest attacker. Only a glancing blow, but it sent her stumbling sideways, knocking yet another off stride.

To his left and right they peeled off the road, into trees or around hillocks or onto open plain. Some made it; others didn't. Ironically, their pursuers' tight riding formation was hampered by the wreckage of the supply train they'd attacked, still lying in the open on the road. Another volley of arrows sliced forward, hitting fewer targets of the spread-out host. Where individuals were caught it came down to simple hand-to-hand brutality.

Eyvind pushed his mount as hard as he could and still hold on. He rode without direction or purpose besides getting away, across grassland and brush. When his heart and breath stopped thundering in his ears he realized he no longer heard the shrill cries of the warrior women on his tail. Slowing the exhausted horse to a walk, he turned and found himself alone in a field of flax, left unharvested amid Phynagoras's genocide. Far off, the distant sounds of battle faded. He dropped from the saddle and pressed himself into the tall grass, though hiding would do little good if they spotted the horse.

He crawled through the field, popping his head up just enough to get his bearings and move vaguely southeast, toward a little wood where they'd gathered before launching the abortive raid. The maples blazed purple and orange in their full autumn color, making them an easy place to spot. To his chagrin the horse followed after, though thankfully at enough of a distance that he might make a run for it if they found him. As he was pushing his way across a muddy furrow, a hand reached out from somewhere and took a strong hold. They'd caught him after all! He struggled.

"Gyahh, let go of me, you witches—"

"*Hushhh!*" came a loud, hoarse whisper. The hand dragged him forward into the next row, and Eyvind nearly pissed himself with relief to see Davenga at the end of it. "It is us." Next to him Tess hugged the ground.

"Thank the gods," Eyvind said. "Are there any others?"

"A few," said Tess, "precious few. Come on. Quietly!"

They inched toward the maple wood, and eventually Eyvind noticed that Davenga was breathing in labored wheezes and clutching at his side. "Are...are you hit?"

"Yes," he replied. "Be quiet."

Once under the cover of trees, they rose, covered in dirt, and picked their way through the brush to a cleared patch of ground where several others of their party had retreated. Some wounded, some not likely to leave the place ever again.

"They were waiting for us," Eyvind said, only stating the obvious out of a need to say something. "I should've known it, it looked too easy! It's all my fault."

"Not all," Tess answered. "Our scouts didn't see the ambush either. They must've been hiding the whole time. They ain't stupid, not anymore."

"Ah...." Davenga sank to his knees, still clutching his side as blood flowed freely from beneath his Pelonan armor.

"General! Help me get this off him!" Eyvind held the big Marzahni still as they peeled off the bits of mail and plate to reveal a broken-off shaft protruding from a gap where two pieces came together.

"A lucky…shot," Davenga grunted. "Too bad I was never…a man to gamble. Please give apologies to my wife, to the queen…."

"We have to get this out of him," Eyvind said shakily.

"We had a physic along," Tess said, "but…." She looked at the gaggle of faces around them. "I don't think he made it. We don't have anything to get it out with."

"Dammit!"

"It is…" Davenga mumbled weakly, "…all right, my friend. Today my sword sang, and I still hear nothing but the song. That is as it should be with me."

"It's not all fucking right! Just, just hold on—"

"No," he wheezed, bleeding, "I have held on…long enough. Let me go. This is a good death, done good service. Now…finish it." Davenga forced a grim smile. He coughed up a great spurt of blood, and then his face went ashen, and still.

Eyvind squeezed his eyes shut, as though that could shut out the truth of what was before him. "No. Godsdammit, no…."

The Pelonans gathered around Davenga, their faces stony. They each made the grieving gesture, fingers to forehead then spread wide while emitting a low, keening sound. Eyvind knelt over the body in surprise at the grief he felt for his unlikely friend, for the old general who'd died defending a country not his own.

Over the next hour a few more of the party trickled in, bringing their total surviving number to twenty. At one point one of the mounted women came close to the wood, riding through the tall grass with a fierce expression and glancing every which way, bow at the ready. They'd hunkered down in silence and waited for the searcher to give up. She'd come within thirty yards of them, but it seemed the enclosed space of the wood held no appeal for the steppe-born huntress. She rode off again.

When wounds were dressed as well as might be done in such rude surroundings and the dead mourned as briefly as decency would allow, they gathered to plan their escape. "We can't go out there," whispered Tess, even though no enemies were in sight. "They'll see us right away."

In the hazy distance Eyvind spied the long rise of land toward the mountains. Toward Phenidra. "There's a gorge not far from here, leading up into the foothills. We'll keep to it and out of sight until sundown. By then we should be able to return to the road."

"Should be," Tess replied skeptically.

The Pelonans insisted on bringing Davenga's body back with them, and eventually home, where he could be given a proper memorial. It seemed their custom of quick disposal did not apply to everyone equally, and they tied him securely to the back of one of the stronger horses they'd salvaged from the rout. Some had to ride double to get everyone on horseback, but Eyvind would not allow anyone to be left behind for lack of a mount. They crept out the far end of the wood to the nearby gorge, splashing in the stream that bisected it, which sent necks wagging to look about for any enemy that might've heard. But the two scouts they sent out reported that they were nowhere to be seen, apparently ridden back to Ólo. *They were nowhere to be seen before this catastrophe*, Eyvind thought. A seed of frustration began to grow into fury in his stomach, and he hoped they reached Phenidra before it took too strong a root.

His hope was not to be borne out. In the late afternoon the remnants of the raiding party entered a plateau within the gorge where a small lake had formed, and with it a settlement too small even to be called a village. The thatch houses and stables had several years of wear to them, so it was no new venture. Around them were garden patches, some apple trees, an animal pen. But it wasn't these mundane sights that shook the party to its core.

It was the bodies. What was left of them. Eyvind had heard of what happened in Vin Gannoni but not seen it firsthand. Now he couldn't but guess what terrible spectacle could be worse than this. Over two dozen people – men, women, children, young and old, all included it seemed – were skewered through on spears, poles, anything long with a sharp end that could be set upright in the ground. Some still hung high, dried and rotted tightly to their instruments of impalement, others dropped to the ground in barely recognizable flesh piles as the shafts seemed to spring forth from them out of the ground. The stench was unbearable. One of the Pelonans muttered something but Eyvind didn't know the exact words.

They rode through this garden of horrors open-mouthed, shocked even after the bloody defeat they'd suffered. To know academically what Phynagoras was doing was one thing, and that bad enough. But to see it up close.... Tess rode next to him, eyes wide. She looked at him, seemed about to say something, but nothing came out. Then some new sound drew her attention, and his.

They weren't alone. Eyvind felt a sick inevitability even before he saw the group of five or six come out of their appropriated houses to investigate the racket. More of Phynagoras' followers, from Bhasa or Porontus or who gave a fuck where. The muffled voices coming from the buildings revealed that there were more within.

They stood before the raiding party, stone-faced, defiant. Eyvind wondered how they could stand the sickening smell of decomposing corpses. He reached absently for the sword strapped to his horse. "No... prisoners." Tess nodded. The Pelonans who rode double dismounted and drew their own weapons. Those still riding raised what spears they still had and charged.

It was the complete opposite of Downhill. It was no fight but a massacre of vengeance, one long deferred. When all those out in the open had been cut down, the Pelonans went house to house, killing anyone they found. It didn't take long, really, for Phynagoras's followers had no weapons and put up no resistance. Eyvind did it all in a daze, as though it were a dream. Some hurled foreign epithets before being dispatched, others wailed in terror pleading for mercy, but it made no difference to him. As far as he knew no children fell to his blade, but he couldn't be sure of that.

After it was done, the warm, sour acid salt of blood had somewhat covered up the stench of rot, though not completely. No one said anything, for what could possibly be said? The few animals they found they leashed to horses to take back to Phenidra.

When the red fever left him, Eyvind wondered whether this was what Davenga had meant by 'finishing it'. But he did not wonder very long. They rode in peace and silence the rest of the way to Phenidra, and when they were once again safely behind its walls, a lone messenger who'd risked capture to accomplish his task handed him a tattered note.

Eyvind scanned it once, twice, three times before dropping it absently onto the ground. "Huh," he grunted with an apathy that would've shocked him a season ago.

CHAPTER TWENTY-FIVE

Allies Like These

Phynagoras leaned against the railing atop the lighthouse, cursing under his breath as he scanned Ólo's harbor for signs of a ship, any ship. It was eerie, such a vast swath of docks lining the shore, all completely deserted. Not one ship, skiff or even rowboat remained. *My reputation precedes me*, he thought.

Next to him, Caerdig visibly stiffened as though sensing his master's discomfort, which of course he did. The boy had wanted to climb the lighthouse stair to see the entire harbor as well, but he understood the implication of the sight. "They're all gone."

"They are indeed, my sweet," Phynagoras said. "Fled west, north, anywhere. Or burned." He nodded toward the still-smoldering ruin of a pair of old cogs that'd been set alight in their berths rather than be allowed to fall into his hands, seaworthy or not. "Disappointing. That fool Armino continues to trouble me even in death. I could've used those ships, now they no doubt aid the Pelonans in blocking my relief from Bhasa. I truly didn't think that brown cunny of a queen would get involved so quickly. Damn the gods!" The city itself had likewise been mostly abandoned, and the foolhardy few who hadn't escaped had all been put to work supporting his army and the settlers who still trickled through the mountain passes. None had any skill in shipbuilding, though.

A warm wind blew in across the bay, pressing Caerdig's loose linen shirt against his body and outlining his form. Phynagoras ran a hand down the boy's back, leaned in to smell the salt sea air in his hair. "Mmm. Come, there's nothing more to see here."

"Yes, lord."

As they began to descend the stair again, Phynagoras spied the unmistakable sight of Cassilda's Haiads riding single file down Ólo's narrow streets toward his command post, which had previously been a Marimines Bank lending house.

He arrived at the building's opulent entry parlor to find Cassilda and a few of her lieutenants with her. The bruises of the beating she'd received had mostly faded, but there were still a few traces of disfigurement, and none more obvious than the complete absence of any hint of defiance in her eyes. Or hint of much at all, really.

He smiled. "Welcome back, my dear! What news? Have you taken care of our little gadflies?"

Cassilda's mouth twitched just a bit as she knelt briefly. "We set a trap for them."

"Ah!" Phynagoras held up a finger. "We set a trap for them...?"

"We set a trap for them, my lord. We killed about half of their number."

"I hear a 'but' in there."

"But," she continued, "their leaders escaped, ran away. My lord."

"And remain free to lead still others. So the answer to my question is no. You haven't taken care of them. Though you had every advantage. How? You didn't perhaps...let them get away, did you? Make some secret little alliance against me? Did they work some new magic of persuasion upon you?"

Cassilda's mouth twitched again, more strongly. "Not upon us, oh king. They killed two score of my sisters with their damnable weapon." Her voice remained even, calm. Apathetic. Almost too much so.

"Really. Cassilda, step forward. Now." Without hesitation she obeyed, moving to the center of the parlor before the tufted chair Phynagoras lounged on. "On your knees, and stay there." This time Cassilda hesitated only a moment, jaw clenched. Yet she did obey.

Phynagoras looked down at Caerdig on the little stool next to him. Without a word, he jerked his chin toward the woman. Caerdig grinned, hopped up, went over to Cassilda, and sent a surprisingly powerful slap across her cheek, the crack echoing in the stone chamber. There were audible gasps from Cassilda's lieutenants, quickly stifled. The red outline of the boy's hand welled up on her face beneath nascent tears.

"You'd better not be lying to me," Phynagoras said, a rare strain of unhinged fury rippling through his words. "Or your previous punishment will seem but a pleasant memory. Now get out of my sight before I let my sweet Caerdig have his way with you."

When they were gone from the hall, Caerdig seemed about to ask a question when a captain rushed in. "M'lord!"

Phynagoras gave himself a few seconds to let his temper return to some kind of equilibrium. He took a deep breath and counted to five, then, "Yes, what is it?"

"Scouts report an army approaching, less than a day off. It...appears to be, erm, a portion of the hazaras General Boras took south."

"A *portion?*" He felt his temper flare again already. "Where's Boras? Why didn't he send a messenger ahead?"

"Lord, General Boras seems...not to be among them."

"*What?*"

"There does appear to be one of those, whatever one calls them, lord, tribesmen, at the head, along with very few officers. Details should arrive within moments, but I wanted to—"

"Well, I want those details! Boras should've been on the southern coast by now!" Phynagoras shot out of his chair. "Make my horse ready. I'm going to meet this 'portion' myself and get some answers."

He rode hard through the day and night, with his captains and attendants barely able to keep pace, constantly calling out into the darkness for him to wait, but he would not. *Fools*, he thought. *No one around me understands how worlds are won. Or how much danger we're in now.* What had happened?

Just as the sun rose over the mountains, Phynagoras came upon the remains of Second and Fourth Hazaras, though he would never have recognized them as such. They shambled up the road in no measure of order, with bits and pieces of armor either worn or not as each man chose and weapons dragging along the ground. Most appeared tired, desperate and sick. Among them, in no order either but at least in better health, rode a host of fierce-looking warriors adorned with paints and animal parts. His Marchman allies, no doubt. The sight filled Phynagoras with fury. He'd suffered one or two defeats in battle before, that was inevitable even for a messiah, but this sorry display called itself *his* army? How dare they!

He rode straight for the head of the mob, and as luck would have it as he did a shaft of light broke over the jagged horizon to paint a wild halo about his head. The nearest of his men noticed him in this state and, dropping whatever they happened to be carrying, ran over to kneel at his horse's feet.

"Oh, lord! Lord, save us! Thank the gods – thank *you*! You're here!"

The pathetic display only enraged him the more, and he leaped from his mount, grabbed the nearest kneeling man, and struck him hard across the face. "Shut up! You're a disgrace, all of you! How could you band of wretches ever think to call yourselves my soldiers? Have I taught you nothing over these many hard years? You have exactly five seconds to explain yourselves before I have the lot of you crucified! Where's Boras?"

An officer rode forward, slowly. It was Musa, the captain from the Second, but he barely resembled the man Phynagoras had seen last, he was so gaunt and red-eyed. "Lord," he said grimly, "it was...it was terrible. Nothing at all like you s— Like we thought it'd be, easy pickings and the like. The locals down south, they're insane! They attacked us again and again, day and night. Always a few at a time, ambushes and raids. Nothing like what we trained to fight."

Phynagoras frowned. He caught himself doing that more and more these days. "Impossible, Osmund has no standing army, and had no time to raise one. Foreign mercenaries then?"

Musa shook his head. "No army, lord. Partisans, terrorists."

"You're telling me civilians – *peasants* did this? How?"

"I don't know! They had that terrible magic, but that's not all. They set traps, used the land against us. Somehow they passed into our ranks and fouled our water by putting...oh, lord, just the sight of it was enough to sicken most of us. Some think, well, maybe they are not all completely human."

Phynagoras put a palm to his forehead. "Answer my question, Captain. Where. Is. Boras?"

"I didn't see him after we, erm, that is, after—"

"After you broke and fled," Phynagoras finished.

"We almost had them, my lord! We had to leave the town we held, there was no clean water. We had them cornered, were about to finish them off. Then one of their border satraps attacked, out of nowhere. Took us by surprise. We were in no condition for a battle, and it seemed they had us outnumbered, but I'm not sure...."

Disgusted, Phynagoras spat in Musa's face, though the man barely registered it, so distraught was he to have failed his messiah. "Useless, all of you! I'm assuming Boras is dead, and good riddance. I should never have promoted him just for his loyalty to me. Gratitude is a disease of dogs! All right, I've heard enough. You're general now, little though you deserve it. Go into the town, and get yourselves back into military *fucking order*!"

"Yes, lord. What about...?" Musa pointed out the Marchman leader Ordovax, astride a shaggy mountain horse and watching this exchange with what might have been amusement. His one-eyed expression was hard to read with all the paint.

"I'll deal with them. Now go." Musa made a pathetic mimic of a salute and continued leading the line northward, while Phynagoras forced his way through the stream of slovenly worshipers until he sat two horse strides away from the chieftain.

He regarded the man only for a few moments, for he recognized the type easily. He cleared his throat. "Can you understand me?" he asked. Phynagoras spoke some of the Cynuvik tongue, and according to his scholars the tribesman's dialect seemed a close enough cousin that he'd been able to learn some of it.

Ordovax gave a curt nod. "Understand. My family fights for you king, my family retakes Ar'Vaddfa of my ancestors. Deal."

"Deal, indeed. But it seems retaking your…Ar'Vaddfa is going to be harder than I first thought."

Ordovax shook his head, setting his limed hair and antler headdress to wobble. He pointed a finger at Phynagoras, shaking it as though he were a university philosopher correcting a student. "Hard is part of the deal. My family will fight any man or beast and no complaint. Now I learn the enemy wields the powers of Chthonii. Many of my family burned in their fire. To fight demons is not part of the deal! You king act without courtesy to keep this learning from of me."

Phynagoras bristled, but fought it down. When strange leaders met, great allowances had to be made after all. "I apologize. I did not know about this new weapon. I promise I kept nothing from you. I do not believe they have much of it, or they would have wiped us out. But we have no choice now. We must win or die together. Will you still fight with me?" The chieftain's dialect was not exactly the same as Cynuvik, and Phynagoras couldn't be sure he'd been entirely understood. The man squinted at him for a long time, certainly suspicious and possibly considering murder. But at last he gave another sharp nod.

"So you say, you king. No choice." He turned and kicked his horse forward, leading his warriors north to join the rest of Phynagoras's forces.

With allies like these… he thought.

Phynagoras gave the fleeing soldiers two weeks to lick their wounds and return to some kind of health. He then dissolved Second and Fourth Hazaras and distributed the men among the other three to dissuade any further lapses of discipline. Ólo became a veritable garrison town as the army took over large swaths, with the few remaining natives and most migrant settlers pressed into supporting it. One morning he emerged from the town's one functioning bath with Caerdig by his side to find a breathless scout kneeling at his feet, water dripping onto him from Phynagoras's body.

"Good gods, man, what is it?"

The scout remained on his knees, head down even as he held up a slip of paper. "A-a report, my lord." The man's hands shook.

Must be bad news, he thought, snatching the note. After reading it he crumpled it into an angry little ball and tossed it down, charcoal from the pencil marks smudging his wet hands. "Summon General Musa and Ordovax, and ready the hazaras for forced march."

★   ★   ★

"Back? We're going back already? D-down *there*?" Musa visibly blushed when Phynagoras turned a hard gaze on him for that impertinence.

"Without ships this port is of no use to me, *General* Musa. We must get south, and that idiot Boras failed in the job. I'm going to have to do this personally. So yes, we're going back down *there*." He turned to Ordovax, who sat in the bank parlor with muscular arms crossed and his maddening frown. "I still have three overstrength hazaras, cavalry, and your warriors. With all these we can take the port they call Seagate without fear of blockade and bring reinforcements from Bhasa and Porontus. And I will not stop until this is accomplished."

Phynagoras had engaged a Cynuvik scholar from among his followers with a proper understanding of the savage's language, and he waited while his words were translated. After a long silence Ordovax said something too quickly and sharply for him to grasp entirely on his own, and the woman doing the translating gave him a worried look.

"Well," he said, "what does he say?"

"Ah," the woman replied nervously, "he asks whether you are offering him a plan…or giving him an order, my lord."

Phynagoras stood from his chair and looked Ordovax in the eye. "I am simply stating facts." He walked out of the parlor without waiting to be translated or answered.

PART FOUR

CHAPTER TWENTY-SIX

A Turning of the World

A chill wind blew through the trees, but Linet didn't feel it. She refused to feel anything. Perrim's cairn lay before them, surreal, unreal. *She can't be in there*, Linet thought. *Impossible! She has too much will, pure bile to be so still under there.* As a leader she'd been afforded the privilege of the little stone tomb rather than being interred under the roots of a tree. *Some privilege. No use to her now.* They buried her in a sunny glen about half a mile uphill from the Lodge, a place Lomuel claimed she'd loved to visit when she was young. They'd had to take his word on that, since Perrim hadn't left the Lodge in a long time. She'd been buried just before they'd returned from Dunsmere, and Linet didn't know whether to be angry or relieved about that. So she refused to feel anything.

Aerrus and Kanessa stood next to her, silent and brooding in their own dour thoughts. Kanessa leaned on a crutch Myrtho had fashioned for her. A Bhasan soldier had breached Dunsmere's old keep and knocked her down a winding stair after taking one of her arrows in the face. The young woman who'd loved to run and climb would do neither ever again.

"What do we do now?" Aerrus asked, breaking the silence so the others didn't have to.

"We killed Phynagoras's top general," Linet answered, saying what they all already knew. "He won't stand for that. He'll be back, with a lot more soldiers than before."

"So we keep on fighting," Kanessa said. "Until we can't."

Aerrus sighed. "How did I know you were gonna say that? Until we're all under the dirt, then. Though I don't think there'll be anyone left to bury us. Except Bhasans, and somehow I doubt they'll take such precious care over our mortal remains."

Kanessa joined in a brief, bitter laugh at that. "Maybe they'll eat us, like the Marchmen used to do."

"Pity for whoever gets Lom then. From previous experience I'd say these folks are more than common prone to indigestion from sour meat."

"Stop it, both of you," Linet snapped.

"It's either laugh or scream," said Aerrus. "I've done my share of screaming." Aerrus turned and began the trek back down the slope. "And I've said my goodbyes. Come on, at least they can't hurt Perrim now."

The entrance to the Lodge was once the most closely guarded secret in the Kingsmarch, perhaps even all of Greater Argovan. In less gentle times the unfortunate wanderer who'd strayed a bit too close would simply disappear, never to be seen again. Now there was no secret to be kept, and the area around the rock formation was astir with activity that would've shocked the previous generation of Heron Kings. The priory brothers, always seeming to put themselves at the center of action, had set up their tent not far from it and were helping Myrtho tend to the remaining wounded who were still trickling in, or just those with nowhere else to go who had heard of the mythical place. Upon spotting the trio, the prior limped over to them, a red-brown bandage over his forehead concealing a troubled brow.

He nodded at Kanessa. "Miss, I ain't always been a robed brother. I seen some o' the world, but...by the Sundered God of Man, I've never seen anyone fight as you did back at Dunsmere! You saved more lives than you know defending our wounded. Thank you."

Kanessa shrugged, yet somehow managed to blush despite her dark complexion. "Don't thank me, it's what I know how to do. Or," she said, smacking the side of her crutch, "I used to."

"What you folk have here," he continued, scanning the rockface and the barely visible opening, "it's nothing short of amazing! To have been here all this time, unseen...."

"Local superstition does a lot of the work for us," Linet said. "But speaking of unseen things...."

Eribert held up a hand. "I know what you suspect. But as I am obedient to my oaths, I may not speak on it until a certain time." Kanessa frowned in confusion, but Linet and Aerrus exchanged a knowing glance.

"Until then, then," Aerrus said.

"I do bring a message from Lord Osbren's scouts. The Marchmen have joined Phynagoras, and they're all moving back south. And this time I doubt he'll stop to tarry in towns."

While Kanessa sat outside the Lodge to rest her ruined limb, Aerrus and Linet went inside to find Lomuel. A lamp flickered as he sat hunched over some papers, Thanis and Drissa across from him.

Lom looked up and nodded. "That's all for now. But be sure to post extra guards on the northern approach, and check our salt cod stores. For some reason the river's been a bit foul lately, and the fish haven't fared as well." The two made their 'yes, Loms' and shuffled out of the room. Linet and Aerrus took their place.

"Have you visited Perrim, then?" The old man sounded even older, and for the briefest of moments Linet was terrified that the malady that'd felled Perrim was somehow catching. But no, he was only fatigued to his bones.

"Just now," she said as gently as she could manage, which at the moment was not very gently at all. "It...it's a good spot."

Lom spread his hands dismissively. "Any spot's as good as any other in the end."

Aerrus cleared his throat. "Lom, Phynagoras is coming down himself, now. After the mountain passes I don't think they fear winter snows. We have Osbren's help, but I think also—"

"Yes, yes," Lom said with a heavy breath. "Listen. We must have a new leader, soon."

Linet and Aerrus exchanged another glance, this one not at all comprehending. "But...you're our leader, Lom, obviously."

He shook his head. "I'm too old, tired. This is your war, and win or lose it will be a time of great change. I'm not suited to it. There must be an election."

"*Election!*" They both nearly shouted it at once. Linet couldn't believe what she was hearing. "Lom, we don't exactly have time for that right now. We're scattered all over watching for enemies, and babysitting a couple hundred scared refugees. *You* are our leader now, whether you want it or not!"

"How so? Have you obeyed me even once? Both of you, you've done as you think best, despite the advice of myself, despite Perrim's orders. She's gone now, and I refuse to be a stool to be stood upon when one of you needs a veneer of authority to justify...whatever it is you're doing out there."

Aerrus stood sharply. "Lom, we have no choice in what we're doing out there. It's that or extinction."

Lom shrugged. "You may be right, I don't know. Which is precisely the point."

"I'm not listening to this," Linet said, out of patience. "The moment Phynagoras is dead we'll have all the elections you want. I'm not going to worry about the quality of our diet when we're bleeding to death. Just keep the Lodge running, okay?" Linet rose and stalked out of the room.

"Yes, ma'am," Lomuel said.

"Listen," said Aerrus, "don't take it personal-like. She – we've been through a lot. I think losing Perrim broke something inside her. All of us, really, but...you're right of course. We'll have an election. As soon as we can get enough of us together."

"Ahh," Lom answered with a nod, "which I'm sure will be whenever you two so choose. Leave me now, please. I need a nap."

★   ★   ★

Another week passed, and the weather grew colder. Strange new faces passed in and out of the Lodge, making everyone nervous. But there was no one to complain to since Lomuel rarely left his cell, occasionally visiting the council room or the archives to take comfort in poring over some bit of forgotten lore. The refugees drilled, patrolled, scouted, and actually contributed much to the upkeep of the Lodge. *A regular old town we're becoming,* Linet thought more than once. Which of course negated its value as a secret base, but that couldn't be helped with Dunsmere almost completely destroyed and now well-known to the enemy.

One day she found herself imitating Lom's habit and reading over Alessia's diaries, hoping to discover some new stratagem that might save them. But the antique language made it slow-going, and she jumped nearly out of her skin when Drissa barged in suddenly. "Lin!"

"Gyah!" Startled, Linet jumped halfway off the wobbly stool she was perched upon. "Godsdammit, Driss, don't do that!"

"Sorry. But you'd better get outside. You're needed."

A cold chill ran down her spine. "What, what is it?"

"Riders," Drissa answered with a scowl. "From the north. Very close."

Linet grabbed her bow, full arrow quiver and blade that she kept close to hand at all times now, even within the Lodge. "Have they found us already?"

She ran up the corridor, through the entrance hall and scrambled out the rocky portal whose concealment now served no purpose. She burst into the afternoon forest, icy breath painting an orange sunset halo about her.

Those milling around outside seemed unalarmed, but then Aerrus ran up the increasingly visible path leading away from the Lodge to meet her. "We spotted 'em a mile off, but it looked like they were just passing through. Then they turned uphill, headed straight here, armed, armored and mounted. Come on."

"How many?" Linet asked as they ran, fearing the answer.

"About...ten or fifteen."

Linet stopped cold in her tracks, sure she hadn't heard right. "Fif— What? That's all?" Aerrus nodded, his mouth twitching slightly. "But that's...wait, who are they? Bhasans? Marchmen?"

Aerrus only shrugged and turned away. "You're needed, in any case. Come on."

She followed, more confused than ever. They came at last to a clearing somewhat below the altitude of the Lodge where, as Aerrus had said, about a dozen riders were hemmed in by a ring of scouts, Heron Kings or refugees, none could really distinguish anymore. Bows were notched and ready, but not trained on the mounted interlopers. *What is going on?* Linet wondered.

Aerrus waved an arm at the group, then toward himself, and one of the riders, indeed an armored brute covered in padding and bits of plate and mail scoured from a dozen apparent sources, approached alone. A heavy helmet concealed his face. Coming to a stop ten paces from them, he dismounted with practiced ease, planting a spear butt-end into the ground and using it as leverage. He stepped forward slowly, and Linet instinctively put a hand to her sword.

He stopped, pulled at a strap on the rusty helmet, and lifted it off. Linet almost fell to her knees. "Oh...."

It was Eyvind. Barely a season separated, yet he looked so different: more bearded, more scars on his face, and much more care in his tired eyes, yet undoubtedly him. Dropping his helmet, he ran forward to catch Linet before she fell, wearing a smile that somehow now seemed alien on him. "Whoa there!"

Linet ran a hand over his hair, his beard, his cheeks. "Oh..." she said again, something between a laugh and a moan of disbelief. "You, you're here. You came here!"

"Aye, and you're sharp as ever. Not quite as stealthy a crew as last time 'round. You've fallen on hard times!"

"Much, much has changed. With you too, I see."

"Aye, that's no small truth."

Linet turned to Aerrus. "And you! This was your idea!"

He held out his hands in supplication. "Guilty as charged. Figured you could use a nice surprise for once."

Eyvind ran a callused finger over the fresh lines that adorned the few bits of Linet's exposed flesh, no doubt wondering how many more lay beneath. "Truly love, how've you fared?"

Suddenly it seemed as if a stone had lodged in Linet's throat. An entire autumn's worth of fear and grief welled up all at once along with hot tears. She could only look him in the eyes for a moment before burying her face in Eyvind's mailed shoulder, his strong but whipcord-thin arms bound tightly around her.

"Ah, there then, lass."

"It's been hard," Aerrus said gravely, "but we're still here, mostly. Though I don't think you made the journey down here for a friendly visit."

"No," Eyvind answered, still holding Linet tight. "Two pieces of news. We rode as fast as we could, to stay ahead of Phynagoras. He's coming."

"We heard that might be the case," Aerrus said with a nod.

"And someone else, too."

★   ★   ★

"Osmund? He's really coming back?" Of course that was the plan, but it had been so long she'd almost given up hope and kept fighting only out of sheer stubbornness. Linet was glad to be back inside the Lodge so no one would see her eyes reddened from crying, though the firelight dancing in the entrance hall's hearth didn't entirely hide them.

"He is," said Eyvind. "Seems only now that the valley's been depopulated does he feel some lingering sense of obligation to retake it." His lip twisted with a new contempt that would've been alien to the kneeling soldier of a season before. "Just as well, we're almost out of Vrril."

"So are we," Aerrus said, "and what we have won't hold back the men Phynagoras is bringing, if reports are accurate."

"They aren't accurate, whatever they are. More of his followers come over the mountains every day, wandering in groups too small for us to stop or even keep count of. Not even the snows stop 'em. They're no proper legions, but if they decide to fight anyway, it might be too late. You lot ain't the only ones that can inspire commoners to kill, turns out." Eyvind lowered his head, which suddenly looked weighed down with a century of cares. The middle-aged woman who'd accompanied him inside laid a hand on his shoulder from behind but said nothing.

"What about Osmund?" Linet asked, not daring to feel hopeful. "What strength is he bringing besides Vrril?"

"No idea, the message was brief in case of capture. It mentioned 'northern friends, and others', so perhaps Pelona will finally join the fight for true, levies from Marzahn."

"Well, you might as well join the party," said Aerrus. "Everyone else has. The Lodge is a secret no more. Let's just hope Phynagoras doesn't find it as quickly as they found Dunsmere. Your, er, retinue looks like they could use some rest."

"That's a true thing. About killed our mounts getting here before the bastard. Aunt Tess, will you see to...?" The woman nodded, then left through the portal.

"Who are they?" Linet asked when she was gone.

"Locals, mostly. From near Edrastead, I mean, defending their homes. Some Pelonans. Took a page from your book, harryin' the enemy as we can in a less-than-military manner while the rest held Phenidra."

"I bet General Davenga's just thrilled about that," Aerrus said with a grunt.

"Davenga...we lost Davenga. I did. An ambush. It was my fault and we...." His head dropped again, quivering. "Lin, I've done things. Such things as...."

Linet rose from her chair to take his head in her hands. "Shh, it's all right."

"Damn," said Aerrus, incredulous, "that big old bastard seemed eternal as a mountain. There's a loss. One more to add to the pile."

"I'm so sorry," said Linet. "But we've gained an ally, too. Lord Osbren finally decided to come down out of the mountains to help. I don't think that'll be enough though."

"It's more help than we ever got in the north," Eyvind said with a sniffle. "Even so—"

He was cut off by Thanis tromping into the hall from outside, wide-eyed and out of breath. "Hey! You better come see this. You won't believe it!"

"What is it now?" asked Aerrus with a renewed frown.

"People, lots of 'em. Coming up the road from southway. Armed! With…farming stuff, mostly."

Linet looked hard at Aerrus. "Is this another of your pranks?"

"Not this time, no. Where are they headed? Here?"

Thanis shook his head. "Keepin' on north, straight toward Phynagoras."

"What? That's crazy!" Thanis just shrugged.

Eschewing the rest that his entourage now enjoyed in and around the Lodge, Eyvind joined Aerrus and Linet to ride down and investigate, and as they sat perched on an earthen bank lining the river road, indeed a host of commoners streamed northward, wearing no armor but a motley mass of brightly hued civilian costumes that seared the eye compared to their own dun-colored fall camouflage. Men and women both, some old and some painfully young, some carrying farming tools, some true weapons and even some with just sharpened stakes. It was ten times the number of insurgents they'd been able to recruit. More. If there was a leader they were far ahead already, as the line of people ran unbroken into the distance.

"What…what is this?"

"This," came a gruff voice from behind the trio, "is a turning of the world. For good or ill is yet to be seen."

They all twisted around in their saddles. It was Prior Eribert, leading a mule. The elderly brother had become such a fixture outside the Lodge, he and his younger monks tending to the wounded and sick alongside Myrtho, that few noticed him anymore. But now he stood taller, prouder, as though infused with new purpose.

"Hey, how'd you sneak up on us like that?" Aerrus demanded.

"As I said, I didn't always wear the robes of the Polytheon. But I do now, and it seems I can finally tell you what I was charged to keep secret until this day." He reached into the folds of his cassock and produced a thin, shiny rod. No, not a rod, a roll of foil. Gold foil. He unrolled and held it out. There was something written on its surface. "Erm, to whom exactly do I give this now?"

298 • ERIC LEWIS

CHAPTER TWENTY-SEVEN

You Forgot

Almost as soon as they left the coast with its warm currents, the air began to chill. Phynagoras wrapped a woolen cloak tighter around himself and Caerdig as they rode, once again at the head of his army, the vast baggage train snaking behind them. But now Boras was no more, and the poor substitute Musa now rode beside them while the broken and humiliated Cassilda as usual sulked somewhere behind.

"The names and faces always change," Phynagoras muttered absently after a week, "yet I remain the only true constant. It's always begun and ended with me. I forgot that. I shouldn't have forgotten. I won't, ever again." Caerdig looked up at him worriedly, and Phynagoras attempted a reassuring smile. "Oh, and of course you, my sweet. Pay no attention to me while I brood."

The boy didn't seem mollified by the platitude. "Yes, lord. But...."

"Yes?"

"Are we...losing?"

"Certainly not! We do *not* lose. This quest is simply going to take a bit longer than I imagined, that's all. Not now that I've taken proper control of things." He tossed a glance backward. Every single handful of food, every piece of warm clothing, every potable fluid had been stripped from Ólo and the surrounding counties, the city burned and the captive slaves executed. There was now nothing of value behind them, and everything ahead. He had ordered forced night marches three days out of five, and proper fortifications built at the end of the other two once they'd reached the territory of Boras's defeat, 'Kingsmarch' as the locals called it. Averaging a blistering seven parasangs per day, they hadn't bothered to stop or slow to root out any remaining population. He felt the thicker forestlands pushing in on them, the trees hanging over them and threatening to drop sylvan horrors from their red and brown branches. And if he felt it, his army would be feeling it tenfold. But their feelings were irrelevant.

"Musa," Phynagoras called, and the newly made general sidled closer. "Send two scouts ahead to find us a place to set up for the night."

Musa hesitated just a second, then nodded. "Yes, my lord." He rode off to carry out the order.

"Didn't you send out scouts this morning?" Caerdig asked.

"I did. They haven't returned."

"You think something happened to them?"

Phynagoras gnawed his lip. "Something had better. I've had their names taken down, and if I find that they've deserted I'll use their skins to make my banners. A year ago I couldn't have even imagined the possibility. But this place…." At that moment another new face chose to make itself present, and Phynagoras braced for what would surely be another fight. *It never ends.* "Good afternoon, Ordovax."

The chieftain scowled even harder than usual as he took Musa's place at Phynagoras's side. "Good? How good?"

"No, I was simply wishing *you* a good…ah, never mind. What can I do for you?"

"My warriors tire. They cannot fight well so. You push too hard! We must stop."

"And we will, just as soon as a suitable site can be found."

Ordovax made a sound that, had it come from any of Phynagoras's soldiers or followers, would've earned a lingering crucifixion. "You know nothing! All Ar'Vaddhfa here is like *this*." He waved his tattooed arm all around him, indicating the thick growth through which the road sliced. "No place for your walls of dirt."

Phynagoras gripped his mount's reins tightly, conscious of how much more effort it took to maintain his temper in recent days. "Then we will have to march through until we *find* a place."

"Our enemy is evil. They have no soul, no ancestors. They could attack at night."

Now both confused and angry, Phynagoras shook his head. "What fucking of it? If they attack at night we'll fight them at night, and destroy them at night."

"We will not."

"*What?*" Phynagoras drew rein, causing a sudden backup behind him. His eyes blazed fire at the Marchman, and only now did he notice a host of his warriors surrounding them. Surrounding him. He was suddenly aware that this one wouldn't be cowed or shamed into obedience as Cassilda was. "You want to repeat that?"

Ordovax gave him a look, as far as he could tell, of pure disbelief. "You are mad, as the other evil ones are. You have no soul, no ancestor—"

"What the *fuck* do my godsdamned ancestors have to do with anything?"

Ordovax sighed, rolled his eyes as though explaining a simple concept to an idiot child. "If you die in battle, you go to your ancestors, to Ar'Vaddfa of the spirit life. This is the wish of all with souls. But if you die at night, you do not find the way and wander forever. All know this. And so we will not fight at night. Until sundown, but not after."

"Is *that* why you fled, why you abandoned Boras…? Why, you cowardly—"

In a flash Ordovax drew his sword, the bronze blade flashing yellow. His warriors did likewise, raising spears or axes mostly. "Apology!"

The army was now fully stopped at its head, the rear pooling up behind, and all watched the exchange in some measure of shock. No one had ever directly challenged the Emperor of Kings or threatened him in person. No one living, anyway.

Phynagoras ignored them. "Apology? I'm not interested in your apologies, you half-wit, one-eyed savage—"

"I don't think he's *offering* an apology, lord," Caerdig said in a meek, quavering voice, his eyes stretched wide.

"What? Oh. *Oh.*" As a native Cynuvik before being taken in some battle or other and eventually gifted to Phynagoras, of course Caerdig could understand the exchange. *Careful, careful*, Phynagoras thought as he fought to reassert control. A miscalculation here could result in disaster. He forced a derisive laugh. "Some allies these are. The fools have just signed their own death warrants. Regard them no longer!" He kicked his horse forward once again, leaving Ordovax and his warriors seething.

The second set of scouts failed to return, and it was well after sundown when a patch of ground just big enough was finally located. Though exhausted, the army set to building its earthwork fortification without complaint. The Marchmen watched with a mixture of contempt and envy, recalling their oral histories of the vast network of Tels that had once dotted the entire peninsula, and were now mostly no more.

That night Phynagoras had the dream again. It began exactly the same, but this time it was Ordovax rather than Amza, then replaced by Caerdig. And both he and dead Eulalia taunted him in unison that he'd forgotten something. *You never forget*, they said, *but this time you did.*

What? Tell me what I forgot! Tell me!

"Tell me, tell me I beg you!"

"...tell you what, lord! Please!"

Phynagoras was suddenly wrapped in cold sweat and darkness. He'd awakened from the dream in his command tent with hands around Caerdig's throat and shaking. "Tell...what...tell...oh, gods." Phynagoras released the boy, then immediately drew him into a tight embrace. "Oh, I'm sorry. I'm so sorry. It's a bad dream I've been having."

"Am I in your bad dream?"

"Yes, but you're the only good thing about it."

There was a shuffling of feet from outside the tent, then the sound of cloth swishing back. A night patrol guard appeared with a taper and a worried expression. "Something wrong, m'lord?"

Phynagoras waved the man away. "Nothing, nothing. Be off now."

In the morning they continued south, following the river. They came to a demolished bridge, and in the distance beyond that, the outlines of a town. "Is that it?" Phynagoras asked.

"Yes, my lord," said Musa, shuddering just at the sight of it. "That's where we billeted, where those...those terrorists poisoned us. Please don't tell me we're going back there, lord. Mark me, that place is cursed!"

Phynagoras made a disgusted sound. "I guess we can't, if even a tenth of my army is as superstitious as you. I suppose it's partly my own fault, weaving all that nonsense around myself about signs and portents from the gods."

"Nonsense, lord?"

"Let's keep on."

It had been his goal to establish a southern port before the first snowfall. But now that would not be, as that evening a flake settled on his nose while he gazed southward. "I'm running out of time," he whispered to no one in particular.

"Lord?"

"I sent an order, Musa. Just before setting out on this glorious expedition. But the timing is crucial, and the year grows long."

"We've fought in the winter before, lord."

"I'm afraid this is about more than just the logistics of a battle, Musa. This is much, much more delicate. Damn." Phynagoras kicked his horse faster. "Come on, no stopping tonight. Forced march!"

The march was hard on the soldiers, but harder still on the migrant followers who had attached themselves to the army, and now numbered as many. The next day saw more than the usual amount of grumbling, but Phynagoras would not relent, nor allow more than one scout to be sent out at a time. Whether they were deserting or being ambushed, it could not be allowed to slow his pace. *Osmund is coming, that frail fool,* Phynagoras thought, *no doubt with more of his devil's fire. We must get south!* Then the full extent of his plan would become clear, and too far along for any to stop.

His brooding was interrupted when that one scout returned on a spent and lathered horse kicked into breakneck speed, and a crossbow bolt piercing the light armor on his back. The scout was able to say something to the nearest captain before collapsing from his mount. Dead or wounded, Phynagoras cared not, and he wrenched his horse over to where the scout lay. "What," he demanded, "what is it?"

"He says there's an army, lord," the captain replied, "at the crossroad up ahead!"

"What? How many?"

"About a thousand, lord. They haven't taken any high ground, seem to be guarding the way east."

Phynagoras relaxed just a bit. "Humph, must be one of their border satraps. Not enough to threaten us, but I don't want them nipping at my heels. We'll stamp them out, then continue south. Musa, battle order!"

Phynagoras picked Caerdig up off his front saddle and handed the boy to a captain charged with protecting him in the very middle of the column, the safest place. "Worry not, my dear, this won't take long."

"I know, I know," Caerdig replied.

The hills all around left no room to maneuver, so the army formed an armored line stretching backward. At the order they bunched up as tightly as possible, with shields interlocking and spears pointing outward. The followers were squeezed out the rear, reduced to watching in anticipation.

As they approached the crossroad the enemy came into view. Their armor was in better condition, all new plate, but shining only due to lack of use, and indeed their numbers were far fewer than Phynagoras commanded. "Is that who sent you scurrying back north to me in terror, Musa?"

The new general gulped. "Well, my lord, er, I mean…at the time they seemed more, and we were—"

"Yes, yes, laid low by a little food poisoning," Phynagoras sneered. "A far more fearsome foe. Watch, and learn. Fifth Hazara, wheel left! Don't let them get on our flank." As the order filtered down and the front sathavi began the process of twisting to face the foe, Phynagoras called for Cassilda to attend him. "We've hills protecting our left. You get your women to our right and keep them from poking through. Go!" She said nothing, only nodded and rode off.

The crossroad was packed with troops and cavalry, and even the portion of the army that had pivoted to face the enemy was more than equal their number. From just behind the front ranks, Musa shook his head. "They don't stand a chance. It's suicide! Why do they hold?"

"Never discount the stupidifying effect of pride, Musa," Phynagoras said. "See that blue standard flying there in front? That's Osmund's little brother. Perhaps he sees a chance to move up in the world, eh? More fool him." Atop the surrounding hills a hundred or so archers and crossbowmen stood, readying their aim. But the shield formation would protect from that well enough, and losses from them would be few. It really was a foolish choice this satrap had made.

When Cassilda's cavalry was in position, Phynagoras held up a hand. "Fifth Hazara, prepare to advance at a walk! Inner sathavi, ready shields for cover!" A thousand shields rose higher in front of their wielders, ready to be converted into overhead protection for the man in front of him. The front three ranks thrust long spears forward through the gaps between them, rocking with the thunderous marching step that echoed off the hills. "Fifth, take care and, aaaaadv—"

"Lord, look!" Musa shouted over the clamor of the advance, pointing far to the right, southward.

Having never been interrupted before while giving a battle order, Phynagoras jerked his head toward Musa, ready to cut his throat for his impertinence. Then he looked past and saw what had inspired it. "Hold, hold!" He made a wide slashing gesture across his own neck, signaling a halt to the maneuver that was already underway. To the south a new force had appeared. Bigger than the one they faced.

"Shit," Phynagoras spat, his aura of messianic calm now completely evaporated. "Who the hells are they? Why didn't we see them coming?"

Musa said nothing, rather than remind him that he'd ordered no new scouts be sent out. Instead he turned in his saddle back toward the rest of the army. "Third Hazara, advance! Quickly!" The order went down, and Third and Fifth clashed and jostled around each other in the tight formation. It was chaos, and Phynagoras felt a nagging sense of fear that hadn't struck him since that terrible day in front of Phenidra. But when the new enemy came closer, he squinted at the sight in confusion. They were in no kind of order either, shambling northward in all manner of dress, carrying all manner of...pitchforks? Mattocks? Phynagoras was then gripped by another emotion as he laughed out loud.

"Musa, look closely. That's no army, it's a rabble! Peasants! Is *that* what defeated you?"

Musa looked, then shook his head. "No, lord, not these. That lot have no discipline, no leaders I can see. The others were... different."

"No matter. Let the Third make its way through, by the time those dirtfuckers get close we'll be ready for them."

"Yes, lord. So, we shall fight on two flanks at once?"

"Won't be much of a fight either way. Make ready!"

"Yes, lord."

As he was about to order the Fifth to advance once more, a small figure detached from the enemy army and began walking toward them. Phynagoras laughed again. "What's this now?"

"Seems to be a deputation, lord," said Musa.

"They want to surrender? I'm not inclined to take prisoners this day. But let's see how this farce goes."

The figure took five long minutes to cross the distance between the two armies, and it soon became clear from the gray habit flapping in the chill wind that the ambassador was in fact a temple sister of the Polytheon.

"Polytheon? They're neutral. Isn't that cheating?" Musa asked.

"It is," answered Phynagoras, lip twisted in distaste. "But I can cheat too. Hold ready."

The sister walked with a kind of serene calm that irked Phynagoras already. She strode past the front ranks to stand directly in front of him. She wore a thin smile that unsettled him even further. *Are these people insane?* he wondered. *Or are they resigned to death and have no fear?* Perhaps she'd been drugged.

He took care to show none of this unease, and glowered down at the sister. "Well? Are you all prepared to die?"

The sister nodded. "Quite prepared, thank you." Though Phynagoras had spoken in Barghii, she'd replied in perfect Bhasan, meaning most of his army would also understand. Some game was being played here.

"But we wonder," she continued, loudly enough for her voice to carry, "whether you might wish one more chance to withdraw, and save yourself the inconvenience of complete destruction."

Phynagoras let out a loud, exaggerated guffaw, and many of his men joined in it. "You…you are mad, all of you! It's you who will be destroyed. You think you have me surrounded with that gaggle of farmers yonder? My men have been fighting for me over desert and mountain for fifteen years. We'll crush them and you both without breaking a sweat."

The sister nodded, casually. "Very possible, very possible. But we have allies. And what's begun today will not end today. It will end, Emperor of Nothing, with you not only defeated but damned in memory. Wiped from all mention in history. A fate worse than death or the nineteen hells for one like you, I think."

"Why you cheeky cunny! How dare – wait, what do you mean, *we*? Who do you speak for?"

She smiled again. "Make your next choice carefully, my lord."

A fit of anger gripped Phynagoras, and he reached for the hilt of the sword strapped to his saddle. He hadn't drawn it in almost ten years, but it was always kept oiled and sharp. In one fluid motion he raised it and brought the long cavalry blade down in a great arc to slice clean through the sister's head. The angle was wrong to sever it completely, so it bisected her from temple to jaw in a diagonal line. Even as blood and bone and brain erupted before him, that infuriating smile remained, taunting him until the body fell limp.

Cries of anger and woe erupted from both camps of enemies at the sight.

"There's your answer, bitch! Is it to your liking?" He screamed it, nearly unhinged, making even some of the horses nicker and twitch. "I tire of this! Fifth, go kill those—"

"Lord," Musa said again, pointing south. Yet *another* individual was approaching alone, this time from the rabble army. Mounted, and bearing a bow.

"Ye gods, they think to kill me one at a time by apoplexy!" But this time the figure did not come close, stopped partway in between. It was no peasant. It was difficult to make out details from a distance, but the figure appeared to be completely covered in strange markings, tattoos. A bow was raised, a single arrow nocked.

"What is this?" Phynagoras asked. Musa only shook his head. The arrow shot out in a wide arc. At its zenith it caught the sunlight and glinted brightly. For a panicked moment Phynagoras imagined it was another of those damned black magic weapons, but no, there was no fire.

The arrow landed in the ground bare paces from Phynagoras. An expert shot. Beyond expert. The archer turned around and rode back into the mass of commoners still holding position on the road. Looking at the arrow, he could see a section of the shaft shining. No, something wrapped *around* the shaft. "Bring that to me," he ordered no one in particular. Seconds later it was in his hand. A sense of foreboding and disaster shot through him when he took hold of it.

Gold foil enveloped the end of the shaft. He unwound it carefully, and on the reverse was a message, written in some kind of ink that adhered to the metal. It was written in Porontan, his mother tongue, using the old high dialect familiar only to the royal houses and dated today, the sixty-eighth day of autumn in the year 5614 of the Sundering, as the Polytheon reckoned it.

*   *   *

Phynagoras of Porontus,
You are exposed.
Your own orders and your own agents have betrayed you.
You have plotted to invade and conquer the Holy City Itself.
You have no life.
You have no death.
You have no past.
You have no future.
You are erased from time and memory.
You carry no mote of the Sundered God within you.
You will not stand before the gods above nor the demons below,
For The Polytheon of Holy Artamera declares war against you.
You no longer exist.

The message fell from Phynagoras's shaking grasp. He went completely white and nearly fell from his horse, caught only by Musa.

"Lord! What ails you? Witchcraft!"

"I...I...have to get...out of here," Phynagoras mumbled. "Have... to go. Now. M-Musa, please get me...oh...." He doubled over and vomited in the space between their two mounts.

Musa called for the doctor, but in the continued shuffling of the army to face both enemies, he couldn't be found. Phynagoras leaned forward, gripping his horse's mane to stay upright. He looked ahead, and where before only that motley host of peasants stood, now banners arose. All black, and when they unfurled fully, shining out in bright gold thread, the star of the Polytheon. And to their left, the same banners now joined the blue and silver of the Argovani crown. It was now the enemy who began advancing at a walk, spears pointed straight at them. They were surrounded.

"This...this cannot be," Musa said, dumbfounded. "How can this be? They cannot take sides, it's against the rules!"

"I...forgot," Phynagoras whined, now seeming more of a frightened child than grim warlord. "Somehow they found out...I forgot something. What...." At once it all hit him. "*Rinalda.* I lost her, and all under her, yet I sent my orders through...gods, I am betrayed. This is all my fault! We have to get out of here."

"Lord, but for some flags they're no stronger now than they were a moment ago," said Musa. "Today at least we can still win—"

Phynagoras wasn't listening. "Cassilda. Cassilda! You must clear a hole for me. Punch through them, clear me a path, quick!"

Cassilda had returned from her cavalry when the Fifth's assault was halted, watching the drama play out and only partly understanding the foreign words flying all around. Now, even though the brand from Phynagoras's sigil ring remained upon her forehead, a new twinge of resistance appeared in her eyes. "Punch through? Ourselves? There must be two thousand out there! We'd be cut to pieces."

"I order you! I command you! Do it or I'll rip you apart with my bare hands!" Phynagoras snarled at her, even reached out with one hand to make a weak snatch at her. She backed her horse away, perhaps considering another defiance like at Phenidra. Musa must've sensed it, for he raised his spear toward her.

"Do it, woman. The lord has commanded, and I will enforce, if necessary." Cassilda made a vicious snarl of her own, but rode off to obey, again. "All captains, all hazaras! The lord has commanded we are to disengage the enemy here and press south. Stop for nothing, for no one. Fifth Hazara, make ready for rearguard defense!"

The satrap's army closed, and at only fifty yards' distance their horses charged. Lances met the Fifth Hazara's shield wall, then an instant later Lord Osbren's heavy and armored chargers slammed into it, shattering the front ranks. The ones behind held firm, and so the men of the Fifth caught in the middle were ground to sausage. Horses screamed where spears found their flesh, and when lances broke swords came out. The chaotic melee lasted only minutes, however, as Osbren's cavalry wheeled about and withdrew, making way for a wave of infantry to take up the battle. The tight space diminished the numerical superiority of Phynagoras's hazaras, and as the enemy advanced the battered Fifth retreated, fighting all the way.

Southward, Cassilda's Haiads tore through the peasant army,

shooting and trampling a path through the throng. The mob hacked and slashed at the mounted women, inexpertly but with that blind energy particular to religious zeal. Through this human tunnel Phynagoras's army marched double-time, the migrant followers stumbling after them. No, they didn't march; they simply ran, terrified less by the enemies around them than their messiah's apparent breakdown. There was mass slaughter on both sides.

By the time the Fifth Hazara pressed its way through the remains of the army of faithful, almost two thousand bodies lay strewn upon the road. And for the first time in recorded history, the banner of Holy Artamera fluttered in the breeze above them.

CHAPTER TWENTY-EIGHT

Aim to Murder

"I knew it!"

"You did not," said Aerrus, snatching the golden sheaf from Linet to read for himself.

"Well, I suspected."

"W-wait," Eyvind stammered, "start over from the beginning. What exactly has happened?"

"As you well know," the prior said with a sigh as they rode back up to the Lodge, "the Polytheon does not get involved in politics or war. Neutrality is our greatest weapon. Our second greatest is the vast defenses protecting Artamera. A city-state is much more easily held than a whole kingdom, after all. No one has ever attempted to attack or invade the Holy City. But it seemed Phynagoras wasn't content with the kingdoms of the world; he thought to supplant the gods themselves. When he was done with Argovan, his next target was not Pelona, or Thazov. It was the Polytheon itself, from the land and the sea at once after securing the southern Argovani coast. Can you imagine, the supreme arrogance!"

"But how did you know that's what he was planning?"

"From what I'm told, he sent the order to his home armies in Porontus before setting out over the mountains. Very secretly, of course, using only his most trusted assets. Except one of them was exposed. A traitor, at King Osmund's royal court, if you can believe it."

Linet drew a sharp breath. "Wha— You mean Rinalda!"

The prior shrugged. "If that was her name. You knew of her?"

"We were the ones that exposed her!"

"Is that so? Incredible. Well, it seems one of her agents in Porontus became terrified when he received the news, assumed he would be next, and turned the invasion orders and everything the traitor had learned over to the high temple there, begging for his life. Including, I'm told, a fantastical report of some tremendous new weapon, hardly to be believed."

"That man at the palace," said Linet, shaking her head. "Her agent. Who could've known?"

"Some investigation using the Polytheon's considerable resources confirmed the plot, though it had been kept well-hidden. The historic decision to join the fight against Phynagoras came only recently, and we were ordered to prepare for it. That's why we joined you at Dunsmere, to help as we could without revealing the truth until the official declaration was made. It seems that has now happened."

"This must've been what Osmund was sworn not to tell us about in Pelona. 'Unless and until the proper time'."

"By now Lord Osbren will have also been advised, and will likely engage the enemy along with the army of the faithful."

"Army of the faithful," Aerrus echoed. "Why does that notion make me nervous?"

"No idea. It was to be raised, I understand, from among the congregations in Carsolan and Lenocca, which must be bursting with refugees by now. The people of Argovan have benefited much from the generosity of the Polytheon. It's only natural that in this one extraordinary instance they heed the call to defend it, is it not?"

"Uh-huh. Except one extraordinary instance has a nasty habit of becoming more than one and not so extraordinary."

Eribert frowned. "Why are you complaining? This is the salvation you hoped for, no?"

"Saved from one foreign power only to be—"

"We're not complaining," Linet said, shooting a sharp *shut up!* look at Aerrus, "it's just a lot to take in. But what's our role to be in all this?"

"Why, whatever you decide it is," the prior answered before

nudging his beast faster. "I have only my own instructions to follow, and wounded to tend, so let's pick up the pace, shall we?"

★   ★   ★

By any logical measure, the rearguard action had been a success. Osbren's forces had been held back, and after the initial clash the retreat south was protected. Phynagoras's army had cut through the peasant army like a scythe and kept superior numbers. Cassilda's Haiads had been half wiped out, but nobody cared about them. Still, there was an air of despondence permeating the ranks.

Phynagoras's breakdown had shaken the myth he'd woven about himself, and the faith of his followers. A moment of panic before Phenidra was understandable, with the revelation of that terrible magic. But what was the excuse now? The Polytheon was strong, yes, perhaps the strongest enemy in the world, but untested in living memory. For all their ritual and mutilated priests they were still just men. Maybe it was the foiling of Phynagoras's self-styled genius that'd undone him. Whatever the reason, the mood had changed, and it fell to Musa to deal with it. So he'd had Phynagoras's catamite brought to soothe his nerves and the Emperor of Kings had been left to himself. Now in effective control of the entire army, Musa called a halt to allow it some much-needed rest. Their enemies appeared content to lick their own wounds, so with no signs of immediate pursuit they camped for a day along the highway with minimal earthwork defenses.

As news of Phynagoras's incredible plot to invade Artamera and this 'army of faithful' spread throughout the Lodge, more and more of the insurgents spoke of leaving to join it. And since the Heron Kings had no authority or ability to prevent it, their numbers began to thin somewhat. But during the course of Phynagoras's mad dash south, confusion led two such deserters to run smack into a Marchman patrol.

Phynagoras's previous dismissal of Ordovax and his friendship had left the savages in an undefined position, and though they'd helped punch through the civilian legion blocking their way, Ordovax neither took nor gave any special orders, waiting to see what happened next.

The two young men's captors were half a heartbeat from disemboweling them for idle entertainment when one enterprising warrior thought to drag them before the chieftain, perhaps with some thought of gaining favor. The pair were kicked in the knees from behind, forcing them to bow in Ordovax's presence while he stood with arms crossed, glaring down at them. Mere paces away, Phynagoras sat just outside his tent cradling Caerdig and watching absently, only part-way back to his senses, his doctor believed.

Finally Ordovax nodded, then spoke in heavily accented Barghii. "You, sheep-men, fight me before. With the black magic. Evil, cowards. At the castle we destroyed. So! Where now? Where the others be?"

One of the two men, the younger and shaking with terror, rasped at his fellow, "I told you this was a dumb idea! We shoulda stayed hid up at—"

"Shut up!" the other answered, more defiant. "Don't you tell this swamp rat nothing." This one glared right back up into Ordovax's eye. "Fuck off, savage! We gots nothing to say to you godless animals."

Rather than respond in anger, Ordovax nodded gravely. He looked from one man to the other, then back again twice. He sighed, then knelt down eye to eye with the younger. "What be your name, please?"

"Huh?" He looked to his fellow, surprised.

"Don't tell 'im anything. Don't answer!"

"*Look* at me," Ordovax ordered sharply. "*What be your name?*"

"T...Torald, of Nostrada," he whimpered. "Oh gods, please...."

"Tor-ald," Ordovax pronounced, almost gentle. "Please watch carefully. No panic, no stupid. Understand?" Torald nodded.

Ordovax calmly drew his bronze blade and with an expert swipe, opened the other man's throat. It was a cut of chirurgical precision, at just the right distance and angle to make blood spray everywhere, covering Ordovax, Torald and the ground all around. The man instinctively put a hand to his neck in a useless attempt to halt the gushing torrent. "Glrrrrg...?"

"Oh, shit!" Torald hissed as strong hands from behind kept him from fleeing. He turned almost white as he watched his comrade slowly die. When the body collapsed into a purple-gray pool of mud and blood, Ordovax turned, face red-spattered, back to Torald.

"Now," he said with the same terrible gentleness, "where the others?"

"I...I can't, I can't!"

Ordovax poked the body with his blade. "You see this? You watch careful?"

"Yeah, but—"

"I give one chance to be use to me. Not two. One. So? Where?"

Eyes screwed shut but tears flowing nonetheless, Torald moaned. "They...they're up...up in a cave. A whole maze of caves, a castle under the ground."

Ordovax put a friendly hand on Torald's shoulder. "Good, very good. Right choice. Now, where?"

"About half a day north of Firleaf."

"Close by!"

"Just off the road where it pulls away from the river, half a mile straight uphill and below a waterfall."

Ordovax looked up to those of his warriors assembled nearby and switched to their own language. "You think you can find them based on that?"

The one who'd taken the prisoners nodded with a grin. "That'll do. We'll find it, father-lord, have no doubt."

"Then do so."

"Please," Torald pleaded, "please, promise me you'll—"

Ordovax gutted Torald without another word, leaving him to die slowly on the ground next to his friend whose advice he should've heeded.

It really is too bad they won't fight at night, Phynagoras thought as he sat and watched all this.

Out of the corner of his eye he spotted another figure. It might have been Cassilda, and she might have been grasping for some weapon at her waist, perhaps watching the scene as well and pondering her own options. But he cared little about her at this point, and regarded her not at all.

*   *   *

Linet and Drissa finished hitching the last sacks of barley to the pack mule, and when all was secure, prepared for the tedious trek back to the Lodge. The task of providing for so many with winter arriving meant that no one was above the most menial of tasks, not even Prior Eribert's animal, which he had donated to the cause.

Though almost everyone from the surrounding villages had fled, the Heron Kings operated a few small, out-of-the-way farming plots themselves to grow what they couldn't buy. Too small and unprofitable to attract notice, but sufficient to supplement their regular numbers. But those numbers were not so regular now, and some of those who'd retired into the world to work the plots had stayed to finish the harvest.

"That's it," said a middle-aged fellow with a slight limp. He wiped sweat from his brow while his breath swirled in the cold. "You've picked us clean, you thieving bandits!"

Drissa smiled. "Thanks, Creighton. If we survive the winter we'll rob enough from whoever ends up running things to make you a rich man."

"No need for that," he said with a grin. "Just an extra share of the next batch of old Tillia's icewine will do just fine."

"Tillia fled to Lenocca," Linet said. "Didn't want to risk it, I guess."

"Ah," Creighton replied, his grin fading. "Well, that was probably the smart thing. Guess I would've done the like if I could move any faster 'n a caterpillar." He smacked the side of his bad leg.

"They're coming this way, in a hurry, probably just pass right on by. But stay hidden anyway, okay?"

"Yes, ma'am!" He gave Linet a mock salute, which she did not like at all.

They drove the train of four mules laden with grain up into the hills, along a path now so worn that a half-wit stable boy could follow it right to the Lodge. "Our secret's out," said Drissa, glancing down at the path. "I suppose there won't be any need for farms like Creighton's or Tillia's now."

"That's assuming we survive until spring," Linet said, more dourly than she intended. "I had thought of taking everyone to join Osbren, but I don't know how much use our kind would be to a proper fighting army."

"We've done our part," said Drissa, unusually insistent. "Hells, we've done more! How many have we buried? Or got blown up into bits too small to bury? I never liked Haskell much, but he deserved better."

"No one gets what they deserve in life, except by accident."

Drissa gave Linet a bemused look. "Says who?"

Linet shook her head. "Just something Rinalda said once."

"The traitor? There's a good one to quote. I say we hole up and wait for Osmund. Never thought that sentence would pass my lips, but—"

"What's that?"

"What?"

Shouting. Angry and scared, and bashing sounds. Battle? "It…it's coming from—"

"The Lodge!"

Leaving the mules behind, Linet and Drissa sprinted along the path sideways and uphill, the distance suddenly too far, desperately far away. The ugly noise of fighting grew louder, and the frenzied shouts now included words, but in a savage, unintelligible tongue…*Marchmen!* They both thought it at once but spared no precious breaths to speak it. They just ran faster.

Linet had continued to refuse any official leadership role, giving no real orders. But one thing she stubbornly made everyone promise was never to go anywhere alone or unarmed. Thus, though the two women were tasked with obtaining grain, they still bore bows and arrows and blades. Linet spared a thought of thanks to whatever gods existed that she had done so, unslinging the weapon that had become more a part of her body than ever before, drawing an arrow from her belt quiver and nocking while on the run. Drissa did the same, though less expertly. But when they leaped over the last little ridge crossing their path and the Lodge burst into view, Linet almost dropped her bow in shock. "Oh, no...."

The Marchmen had attacked in force, and the insurgents had been taken completely by surprise. A shield wall advanced on the ragged band of defenders around the Lodge's perimeter, hacking and stabbing, while just behind stood a hulking brute, watching with a one-eyed smile. Ordovax.

Without thinking, Linet loosed an arrow at the chieftain, but a shield-bearer next to him blocked it easily. Drissa shot also, taking one attacker in the side and leaving many more to go. They tried to flank the Marchman shield wall, to shoot at them from the side and make enough distraction for the defenders to counterattack. But they were only two, and it was like pinpricks to an armadillo.

Aerrus and Vander charged out from the cave entrance, dragging a half dozen quivers with them, and shooting like madmen. They made hits so precise they sailed through the gaps in the shields to send individual warriors sprawling, trampled under the feet of their fellows as the wall advanced.

Finally Linet and Drissa's shots had drawn enough attention that Ordovax motioned at the two of them, and three of his warriors peeled off to charge the pair. "Scatter!" Linet said, and they moved away from each other among the rocks and trees so as not to make a common target. Drissa left Linet's field of sight as tunnel vision took over, and suddenly a big, muscled and blue-painted Marchman was the entire world before her. She shot him in the chest only to see him replaced with another, this one a woman but immensely bigger than she. Linet reached for another arrow, only to grasp air and empty leather. She was out of arrows already.

She drew her sword barely in time to block a spear thrust, and the head came off with a sharp *crrrack!* The woman heaved the shaft at her anyway, the cloven stick biting into her chest and sending her to the ground. Her enemy was instantly on top of her, throwing punches from above. They grappled on the ground, Linet trying to headbutt her while mostly failing to block the powerful blows. Stars exploded all around as Linet took a hard left hook, and she fell helpless. The warrior atop her drew a long, shining obsidian knife, raised it to slice her throat. Linet raised a weak hand in a last act of defiance, and the knife sliced clean through two of her fingers. It was a curious sight, seeing something that had been part of her since birth flying off into the air, blood streaming behind like market-fair banners. She might have screamed, she couldn't tell over the thunderous pounding in her ears. The woman who was killing her snarled, sneered, raised the knife again, and this time there'd be no blocking it. But it never fell, as the woman sprouted an arrowhead from her chest. She looked down in apparent annoyance, said something in her own language, then crumpled atop Linet.

Just before losing consciousness Linet saw the last defenders around the Lodge break and flee, and saw Ordovax turn away from the fighting and stride casually downhill, a satisfied sneer on his ugy face.

★　　★　　★

Linet awoke to incredible pain, and the acid bitterness of dried blood in her mouth. And something else....

She spat out blue. The warrior woman who'd died on top of her had fought bare-chested, and one of her tits, painted with wild designs, had jammed up against Linet's face, almost smothering her. The stench of fire and unwashed Marchmen invaded her nostrils, and she would've gagged had not the sudden jolt of pain made her moan.

"Aaaargh!" She grabbed at the stumps of her lost fingers, still bleeding freely. "Oh, gods!" She wept as much at the loss of her ability ever to shoot a bow again as at the pain. The sound drew the attention of someone who knelt at her side.

"Here! She's alive, here!" *Thanis?* Tears blurred her vision.

"Wh...wha...?"

"Don't, just hold still. Physic! Get over here now!" The body was slowly dragged off of her. Still clutching her mangled hand, she blinked away enough tears to see around her, though perhaps that was a mistake.

It was bodies all over. Dead and dying, friend and enemy alike. Fires smoldered here and there, clogging the air with smoke. There was a pile of flesh at the entrance to the Lodge, some torn to pieces. *Vrril*, she thought in a daze. *Someone used Vrril.* But had it saved them or destroyed them?

The prior, sporting a fresh spear wound on his shoulder, was suddenly at her side, wrapping moss and bandages around her stumps, and she cried out anew.

"There, there dear," he said. "Try to keep still, hold this up. Don't let it get in the dirt."

"What...what happened?"

"We lost is what happened. Which probably saved our lives, those that were saved. When the defense broke, the Marchman chieftain left. Guess he made his point. Some of the others pushed into the Lodge, but only a few. Someone must've hurled that horrid substance at them, blew a bunch to the nineteen hells. The rest ran off."

Eribert helped Linet sit up, and she saw the corpse lying before her. It was Lomuel. "No...."

"He went down fighting, the old fool," the prior said as he poured his last drops of opiphine onto her wounds before binding the muscle and veins tightly. "I'd told him to stay inside in this weather, but...." He shook his head.

"He saved my stupid life," Linet said weeping, noting the arrow that pierced her attacker matched the few left in Lom's quiver. She looked further afield, picked out Vander by his shock of red hair, lying lifeless. The little girl they'd found at the massacre at the hunter's cabin was thrashing a dead Marchman with a stick. She saw Myrtho kneeling over another body covered in blackened burns, shaking his head sadly as Aerrus and Kanessa stared down at them. It was Drissa. Linet fought to her feet, fought through the pain. "No...."

"Stop it, you'll reopen—"

Linet ignored the prior's warnings and shambled over to them. She must have looked like death itself from the look Aerrus gave her. "Lin! Lin, I'm...so sorry...."

"Don't you say that. Don't you dare say that! Myrtho can—"

"I can't," Myrtho spat, furious at the fact. "There's *nothing* I can do." He closed Drissa's eyes. Her entire body was charred, clothing fused to flesh.

Linet pounded the ground with her left hand. "Dammit!" She fought to regain control, shaking violently. "What...what about the Lodge?"

"It's burned pretty bad," Aerrus said. "When the line broke they barged in to loot the place, pillage, whatever. We chased 'em in, and they didn't get very far. But the hall's a loss, archives burned, dormitory's mostly fine. That Vrril fire, it just tore through the place. Drissa threw the phial at one of them bastards, one with a torch. It was the only thing left to do. She was just...too close. It was the last we had. I'm almost glad to be rid of the stuff."

"That's it, then," Linet whimpered, "the end of the Heron Kings. Gods, what have I d—" She collapsed in fatigue and grief.

An hour later Eyvind arrived, returned from a trip to confer with Lord Osbren and decide what to do. The attack, the fact that he'd not been there, and Linet's wounds all drove him into a fury. "No more," he growled through clenched teeth as he knelt by the pallet Linet lay upon. "I've had enough of these pricks. Fuck King Osmund, fuck Osbren, and fuck the fucking Polytheon! I'm done waiting for everyone else to end this." He stood.

"What are you going to do?" Aerrus asked as he inexpertly

changed Linet's bandages while Myrtho, the prior and any others who were able tended the other wounded.

"Those bastards ran south and they're still running. Osbren won't attack head-on alone. That mob army served its purpose but it's too disorganized. Osmund's too far away. So I'm going to go kill 'em myself." He reached into a pouch at his waist and drew another glass phial, undoing Aerrus's previous declaration. "I got one more, and I'm using it."

"Don't be a fool," Linet said weakly, "you can't fight them by yourself."

"I don't aim to fight. I aim to murder."

"That's original," Aerrus replied. "Wait a day, at least."

"Why?"

"Maybe the Heron Kings ain't quite done for yet. I'm—" Aerrus glanced at Linet, and she nodded. "*We're* coming with you."

Myrtho tried to forbid it, perhaps made fanatical about safeguarding the lives left in his care now that he'd lost so many. "Absolutely not!" he huffed in between tending to cries for help that continued well after the attack. One of his precious spectacles had gotten cracked during the battle, lending his left eye a vicious serpentine aspect. "We need you here in case those monsters come back...Lin's missing fingers! And you—"

Aerrus took a rough handful of Myrtho's bloody tunic and dragged him around a bend in the rockface. "Look," he growled, more angrily than he'd intended, "they're not coming back. They went south with Phynagoras. As for us...your infirmary's in shambles. You can barely keep the lot of us from bleeding out as it is." Aerrus dropped his voice to just above a whisper. "What are the chances those fingers *don't* get infected?" Myrtho's mouth hung open, desperate to make some reply. But none came. "Let us go. It's likely this'll be a one-way trip for all of us. Let us do what good we still can while we can."

"You're not really asking my permission, are you?"

"No."

"Go then. Kill those demons for me. For all of us."

⋆   ⋆   ⋆

Osbren's men and the Polytheon's 'army of the faithful' followed Phynagoras at a slower pace, not eager to repeat their last clash. Tess had gone to beg for aid for the survivors at the Lodge, while Eyvind, Aerrus and Linet with hand bound up tight pursued at a closer distance, the ravenous horde picking over the farms along the way that had managed to get their harvest in but not take it with them when they fled. Plisten and Firleaf were sacked but not destroyed as hundreds of Phynagoras's followers peeled off to take up residence. Eyvind burned to ride in with his companions and slaughter them, but he now had only the two friends he'd started this journey with, and they were in no shape to deal out death and retribution. So each night they made a cold camp at a distance, huddled around a weak fire while Linet stared at her hand, and the empty spaces where her fingers had been.

It had looked like Phynagoras's army would follow the Carsa down to Lenocca, which would've been another bloodbath on both sides. But instead they kept course south, taking the newly built road skirting the southern highlands toward Seagate. The ports there were to be his prize, then, and the ability to bring ships from Porontus and Bhasa, and no Pelonans to prevent it.

Meanwhile, far to the north, King Osmund at last set foot in the country he'd abandoned when his royal cog drifted into port at Ólo. He descended the gangplank, and at his right hand and a step behind stood Chancellor Essimis. At his left, the alchemist Antero, charged with supervising the massed stores of Vrril in the holds of the ships that followed, and the strange devices crafted to use it. Whatever Osmund had expected upon landing – crowds cheering his return, hailing their liberator, or a glorious sea battle with his new weapon to dislodge the invader – it was a good bet the last thing he imagined was the dead silence of a deserted and burned city, devoid of ships or souls be they friend or foe. He was greeted only by the stench of briny wet ash, and forests of spikes on the perimeter of the city with the subjects he'd failed to protect impaled upon them.

CHAPTER TWENTY-NINE
No Greater Gift

Musa had been forced to abandon Phynagoras's previous order of no more scouts. It was just too perilous along this foreign coast with its jagged chalky cliffs, winding roads and the increasingly heavy fog that shrouded the country all around. But there seemed little danger of terrorists here. Little danger of anyone at all, for the only sounds to echo out of the muffled mist about them were the bleats of abandoned farm animals, quickly tracked down and slaughtered to feed the army. He'd called another halt to get their bearings, and as night settled, the ground proved unsuitable for building earthwork defenses, so they'd made do with sentries peering uselessly into the whiteness.

Phynagoras sat in his tent by his little brazier, kissing and cradling Caerdig as he usually did now, saying nothing beyond mumbling the occasional perfunctory assent to some order of the day. The captain making his report directed all his attention to Musa, who had taken the liberty of placing guards outside the tent and who sat in the place not so long ago occupied by Boras. Dead old Boras. *They all die*, Phynagoras thought again. *The faces change, and only I remain.*

"My opinion, sir, it's too dangerous," the captain said. "The fog makes it impossible to go any further without detailed scout reports. The coastline's like a maddened snake, and in this fog…."

Musa nodded. "Agreed. We'll stay here a day or so to be sure, then press on to the port." Musa glanced once at Phynagoras. "Erm, with your permission of course, my lord."

"As you see fit, dear Musa," Phynagoras said softly.

"That'll be all then."

The captain saluted, then left the tent.

Musa turned to Phynagoras with a worried look. "My lord...."

"Yes?"

"Forgive me if I'm out of turn, but...it might be nice to let the men see you. You know, to give them some encouragement. The whole east of this country will be ours soon, one more push and we'll have room to bring reinforcements for taking the rest. Might help to lift spirits."

"Ah. Except now, because I forgot my own orders, we're fighting every Polytheon temple and priory in the world. It would be false hope. Cruel thing to do."

"When did any of that ever stop the Emperor of Kings?" Musa tried a thin smile, utterly unconvincing.

Phynagoras sighed. "Very well." He set Caerdig on the cushion next to him. "Best stay here, my sweet. Chilly night out there."

"I won't mind," Caerdig said, "I'm Cynuvik-born, you forget." Instantly regretting his choice of words, the boy turned away, red-faced. "But I'll stay, if that's what you want."

Musa led Phynagoras from one dathav to the next as they gathered around campfires to gnaw on whatever rations they'd gathered. Each man shot to his feet upon realizing who was in their presence, and over the roar of the waves crashing below them Phynagoras gave some rambling gaggle of encouraging words he'd memorized long ago. "Be sure, friends, though things seem dark now, it is only so that our final victory will shine all the brighter. Shine down through history for all time, such that our name, yours and mine entwined together, will never be forgotten."

They shouted their praise as they'd done before, hailed him as their savior and lord. But there was something vital gone out of the whole affair, as if it were just a routine they played out because it was all they had now. He did not visit the Marchmen, nor the migrant followers who encircled the camps. Nor the Haiads who'd been devastated by the last battle.

As he was making these rounds, a captain came running up to them, out of breath. "General Musa! My lord! There's trouble!"

"What? What trouble?" demanded Musa.

"I don't know exactly, some commotion at the lord's tent. We heard shouting, and horses in the night!"

The blood suddenly returned to Phynagoras's face, some sign of life and deadly fury. "My tent? Caerdig!" Without waiting for Musa or his bodyguards, Phynagoras threw off the fur cloak he had pulled around him and tore off through the camp, back the way they'd come. Somewhere, far off in the invisible dark, wild screams could just barely be heard over the coastal winds. He ignored them.

Two guards lay in bloody heaps outside the tent. Phynagoras ripped back the cloth covering the entry. Caerdig lay in a pool of his own blood, squirming and groaning in agony from a knife wound in his belly. A doctor knelt next to him, working to stop the bleeding, but it was a losing race. Phynagoras collapsed at the boy's side, his breath taken away in an instant. "Gods! No! What...argh, oh no!" He wrapped the boy's head in his arms, whimpering. "Save him," he ordered the doctor. "Save him or I'll kill you!"

"I'm trying!" the doctor answered, wiping sweat from his brow.

"Who...who did this?!"

Caerdig's eyes focused on him in the dim light. "C...Cass...."

"Cassilda," Phynagoras snarled, from deep in his throat. "Traitorous bitch! I should've ripped her open from the inside!"

"No..." Caerdig said weakly, a thin smile spreading across his lips. "She came to find...kill you. But I sent her...took care of her for you. You'll see."

"What?"

"No one...can beat you...us...my lord." The boy's eyes fluttered, then closed.

Phynagoras wailed in fury for the rest of the night.

★   ★   ★

Musa ordered an all-out search for Cassilda, and the search went on all night and into the next day. At last, when the fog lifted, two pieces of news were brought to him. In the still-bloody command tent, Phynagoras clutched Caerdig's stiffening corpse. The doctor, probably fearing for his life, was nowhere to be seen. Musa continued to take reports there if only to maintain the illusion that Phynagoras was still in control and to prevent panic. Now another captain brought the two pieces of news at once.

"We found them, sir. They're dead."

"Dead? How?"

"Rode right off a cliff! They were riding eastward, likely not bothering to look where they were going in the fog and just…." He shrugged. "We found the bodies of Cassilda, her Haiads and their horses all dashed on the rocks below, half washed out to sea."

Musa frowned. "But why? Where were they going?"

"That's the second thing." The captain motioned to another soldier, who dragged one of the women by a rope around her neck, hands bound, and shoved her at Musa's feet. She was battered and bloody, any useful information beaten out of her. "We found one that managed to avoid the cliff but got lost in the night. Found 'er hiding in a tree stump. Says they were after, er, the lord. Heard tell he was in a town up ahead and were riding hard to catch him alone, assassinate him and ally with Ordovax instead. They must've come here to do the deed, but when they found he wasn't here rode off. But there is no town, nothing ahead but winding cliffs. Don't know who could've told 'em that." The captain turned to Phynagoras, who sat ashen-faced. "I'm very sorry, m'lord. Caerdig meant a lot to us sloggers too."

Then, a most disturbing sound erupted from the broken man. Laughter. Soft, quiet, and evil. Phynagoras chuckled, stroking Caerdig's golden rings of hair. "Oh, my dear boy. Oh you are too clever. Always listening, always. You said you took care of her for me, and you did. Bless you." He laid the boy's body down, then went over to the captured woman. The last vestige of Cassilda's final betrayal. He fell on her, pounding with fists, kicking, ripping with teeth. Such was his wrath that no one present dared interfere, even when the screams chilled their bones. Eventually the woman was a dead mass of flesh, all squishes and squelches, as Phynagoras pummeled the red waste on the floor of his tent.

Finally he stood, dripping viscera and eyes blazing, teeth bared. Musa could only look on in horror, and then Phynagoras said, "This... was exactly what I needed. Cassilda murdered Caerdig out of simple spite, but he gave his life to avenge me, to remind me what I am. No one has ever given me a greater gift. I'll name every city in the world after him, as soon as I conquer it. We've tarried here long enough. We march!"

He ordered a tomb hastily built for Caerdig precisely where he'd been killed. He vowed that when he finished subduing Barg-o-Bhanii he'd build a great mausoleum on the spot, and his capital around it. Then he rode his horse, the special saddle carrying only him now, to the cliff to gaze on Caerdig's revenge. Indeed the waves had done a number on the ruin, yet still the mass of woman and horse parts lay splayed out below them, a drop of more than half a stadion. Phynagoras imagined he could just make out a stretch of Cassilda's hair among it, though maybe it was just muscle. He smiled at the gruesome display, and swore a silent oath to Caerdig that, whatever heaven or hell he now inhabited, Phynagoras would soon send many, many more in Cassilda's wake to serve him there.

★   ★   ★

Argovan had four major port cities. The capital, Carsolan, faced south and west, Everwest north and west, Ólo north and east. Facing south and east was Seagate, a town that had grown in importance over the years, but thanks to the historic hostility of Bhasa and the more recent Phynagorean threat, trade out of there was still a bit of a risky business and thus boasted encircling defensive walls. Adding to this were the coastal cliffs, which divided Seagate into a lower harbor district and the upper city. It was this upper area that was now walled off like a besieged fortress, which in fact it was, leaving the harbor open to whoever wished to pay a visit. Phynagoras knew all this, and knew that it was the port that mattered. The port that would welcome his invasion fleet once and for all, with any fool enough to take refuge in the upper city cut off and starved into submission.

"It'll probably be deserted, like the last one," he said to Musa as they rode, much like his old self again, though perhaps less assured now. "We haven't the advantage of surprise anymore. But this close to home it won't matter. Whether we find one lone ship to commandeer or have to send a fast courier by land, we can get word to Porontus and Bhasa both to begin coming over in force. Which is what I should've done to begin with! I was too precious, too clever for my own good, sought the easier path and paid the price for it. I won't make that mistake again."

"Yes, lord," Musa answered. He'd not been privy to the war plans until replacing Boras, and didn't have a head for grand strategies, Phynagoras could see it in his eyes. No matter, all he needed to do was obey. "But...what about their king? He's coming. And with that... that *stuff*—"

Phynagoras nodded. "Yes. But slowly. I have fifty thousand men ready to counter him, ready to bring just as soon as I can support them. We've picked this country clean and still we're hungry, and this chalky land is useless. We must have a port!"

The scrubgrass coast remained jagged and twisting, and the path the army followed had been little more than a wagon track. They stomped and pounded it as they passed far more efficiently than any road-building crew could have done, yet all the turns made for slow going. At the last of these bends before the ports around Seagate, Phynagoras and Musa crested a hill, and all at once the horizon opened up before them.

It was a cold, mostly clear day, the fog for once blown away by the winds. The land beyond descended gently from north to south, then cut sharply down in a wall of white. Below, a rocky beach stretched into the Lacaryc Sea. Only a few paths were shallow enough to connect above to below. On top, the walls of Seagate were dwarfed by the cliffs, yet only the pointed tops of buildings and towers were visible, and King Osmund's flag flying next to that of the local satrap. Below was the port, and....

"Ships!" exclaimed Musa.

"Yes," Phynagoras said slowly, more suspicious than elated. "Lots of ships." The port was choked with them, in fact. He squinted at the tiny shapes, wishing he'd thought to acquire one of those ingenious glasses from Pelona that made distant objects seem near. "And lots of masts, rigged in the new style." These were no lazy fishermen or merchants caught flat-footed by the invasion. "Let's get closer."

"Shouldn't we send scouts first?"

"I want to see this for myself. I've no one left to trust now." He kicked his horse faster, ignoring the pace of the army behind him. Half a mile closer and they could make out sails. Black sails. A mile closer and they could see crews, ramming prows, arbalests, ballistae.

"Warships!"

"General of the obvious again, Musa," said Phynagoras with annoyance. "Fifty at least. But whose?" Then a cloud passed from in front of the sun, and one sail stood out in the light. Gold thread glimmered, and Phynagoras frowned. "Gods, they did it. The bastards really did it."

"What?" asked Musa.

"That down there is the entire defensive fleet of Holy Artamera. We're trapped."

CHAPTER THIRTY

Contravallation

The trio huddled around a small fire with one blanket shared among them to hold back a chilly afternoon drizzle. Linet continually held her amputated stumps near the flame, enduring the pain piled upon pain in a vague attempt to kill whatever foul decay might have taken root there. But the swelling and redness weren't going away, though Aerrus and Eyvind said nothing on the subject, only exchanging occasional worried looks.

"I still say it could've worked," Aerrus said as he passed them joints of cured pork to gnaw on. The man's characteristic edge of sarcasm was gone now, burned away by the Vrril fire and the season of slaughter they'd barely survived. "It did once before, after all. Dress up like them, walk in and deal some damage on the sly, then make a quiet exit."

"That it worked before doesn't mean anything," Linet countered. "Clever disguises, infiltration? Oldest tricks in the book. They might work once, but not too often. They'll be more wary now, paranoid. And this time their leader's no dupe."

"Either way, we're lucky we didn't try it," said Eyvind. "Even if we did get in that night, pinch some sloggers' kit and blend in or somesuch, whatever happened in their camp spooked 'em. We'd have been found out. It's good we called it off when the screaming started. But what *did* happen?" Whatever it was, they'd spent the night listening to wild howls, disturbing even from a distance. And soldiers searching for something in the dark. The next day the army moved on with their mass of followers in tow, and the three of them had as well, but keeping a good distance and going on foot to avoid attention. Now they camped just off the road in the wake of the ten thousand migrants who spread across the coast like a moving slime mold, hoping to remain ignored.

"I don't know or care much," grumbled Aerrus, "except it doesn't look like we'll get another chance like it. If Phynagoras takes Seagate it'll be a thousand times harder. You're right about two things: getting into Wengeddy was a fluke, and their general was a moron."

"But Seagate has good walls, and he's still got no siege engines," Eyvind said as he forced down a hunk of dry, salty pork. "Not even trees here big enough to make a ram." Indeed the scant growth they now hunkered beneath did almost nothing to hold back the stinging cold rain. "He's a smart bastard, though. Something tells me he's got a trick or two up his sleeve yet, and enough men to whip Osbren and the Polytheon's mob both."

"Not to mention his followers," Linet said with a nervous glance toward the nearest gaggles of them. "Gods, they're like a whole moving city themselves! Even if they don't fight, they can still make trouble...." Linet suddenly gave a weary chuckle, the movement adding to the throbbing in her abbreviated fingers. "Guys, what are we doing? This...isn't going to work, is it?"

Aerrus and Eyvind looked at each other, perhaps hoping the other would answer first. The silence screamed. Finally Eyvind sighed. "Maybe not. I don't want to imagine what odds Davenga would give us. I started this whole thing just wanting to run away, but someone caught me, gave me something to fight for, remember? I've watched too many good people die to give up now. I owe it to 'em—"

"I'm sick and tired of hearing what the dead are owed! The dead are owed nothing, they owe nothing! We've done...all we could. It wasn't enough." Linet broke into shallow sobs, tired to the bone at last.

"Hey," said Aerrus, "remember Dunsmere? It might be enough. Even if we're not around to see it, Osmund's coming."

"I'm not hanging my hopes on that fool," she sniffled. "I got no hopes left. I just want to sleep." She laid her head in Eyvind's lap.

With that sad pronouncement, and with all the debates and arguments finally aired out, they leaned against a wet log under their shared blanket to try to snatch some mockery of sleep. The poor fire hissed as the rain snuffed it out, and they shivered through the night.

They awoke late. In the gray dawn they could see scattered groups of migrants and a few army patrols moving southeast in haste. Shouts in foreign tongues that nonetheless communicated urgency echoed over the hills. In the distance Phynagoras's army was already moving away. "But why?" Eyvind wondered. "Unless...."

Eyvind hiked up a nearby hill to peer northward, along the road they'd traveled for nearly a week. To the right the foothills of the southern highlands rolled. To the left a frost-covered plain with a smattering of tree cover.

"What do you see?" Aerrus called from below, occupied with acting as a crutch for Linet, who'd seemed to grow weaker since the night before, not stronger.

"I see...." He squinted, peered through the lifting fog. "Ha! About time."

"What? Is it Osmund?"

Eyvind slid back down the slope and turned toward the road. "No such luck. Osbren. Little brother, little army. Someone must've scouted them coming and raised the alarm."

"Won't do much good alone," Linet said tiredly. Her face was pale and her eyes red, her wounded hand tucked into the tattered folds of the blanket draped around her shoulders. "But I guess we need all the help we can get."

"Let's go meet them," Eyvind said, "and hope we don't get taken for the enemy, filthy as we are."

They stood by the side of the road as the army approached. At its head Osbren's banner fluttered, and even then they might've been taken for hostile had not a familiar face been riding alongside the lord.

"Aunt Tess!" Eyvind waved, and when the woman recognized him she smiled.

"There ye are! See, m'lord, it's as I said!"

The mounted mountain of armor drew rein, and the helmet atop it nodded. "I see, madam. Hold up!" At a raised gauntlet the advance ranks of the small army halted behind him, and Osbren lifted the visor of his bascinet. "You three've been a thorn in my side lately, that's certain."

"How's that?" Aerrus asked, unawed by the pageantry.

"I heard about the Marchman attack on your little hideaway. I must admit I've wondered for years just where you lot made your warren, didn't press the issue since you proved so useful. Then this here cantankerous lady—"

"Oy, what's that mean, m'lord?"

"—barged into my command tent with the tale. I sent what aid I could spare up there, if it means anything."

"Thank you," Linet said, with the barest dip of a knee.

"And word of your little suicide pact. Three wounded rebels gone off to murder Phynagoras all on your lonesome, eh? Lunacy!"

"We've had that word tossed at us before," Eyvind said. "Didn't stop us then."

"Uh-huh. I intended to wait for my brother's arrival, but it seems you've inspired my captains into demanding action. So here we are. To do what I'm not sure, but the…what's it called again? Army of the faithful is just behind us. Unruly lot, but there you have it."

"You don't have to *do* anything. Just catch us up to him, let us get close."

Osbren frowned, looking more like his brother than ever before. "Hmm. Ferry you off to your deaths, is that my job? Maybe make a good example to my men against impulsive foolishness. But, you've done the impossible before, guess you just might do again. Very well, mount up. We don't stop until Seagate."

The flow of migrants scattered in terror at Osbren's march, even though they outnumbered him ten to one. He ignored them, pressing ahead. But Phynagoras's army was already far beyond, having stolen yet another forced night march. As Seagate grew into view from a dot on the horizon to a city perched atop the cliffs, they became aware that something was off. They could see the walls of the town, but something else.

"What is that?" Linet asked weakly, riding double with Eyvind, with him now the one holding her steady in the saddle. The grassy plain around the city lay scarred and broken. Thousands of soldiers toiled, stood watch or just milled about while a jagged white snake of earth seemed to encircle the city.

"It's…walls," Aerrus said uncertainly, "but…."

Osbren gave a loud guffaw of wonder and almost admiration. "Contravallation! The bastard's building a second wall around the city, with them behind it." The high mound encircled Seagate and also cut it off from the slopes that ran down to the sea. Phynagoras's army was camped in the space between, with the vast majority of his followers shut out.

"Won't he be attacked from the city?" wondered Eyvind. "Unless it's abandoned. But then why not just take it?"

"It's not entirely abandoned," said Osbren. "Trastavere's no doubt hiding up in his mountains waiting for Osmund to rescue him, same as Valendri, the cowards. But if the messages I received were true, there should be a garrison of Artameran marines holding the place. Not many, but enough."

"Artameran!" Linet, Eyvind and Aerrus all exclaimed at once.

"Of course!" Osbren answered with a knowing grin. "You didn't think the Polytheon'd break their precious neutrality only to leave matters to a gaggle of worshipers, did you? They sent a fleet here to hold it against capture. Most of their troops stayed home to defend the Holy City from land attack, but brought some here in their ships. Those should be in the port below right now, but they're cut off. Seems like a stalemate. Sorry, friends, don't know how to get you in there now."

★   ★   ★

Phynagoras watched the earthwork take shape while keeping one eye on the city. So far he'd spotted only the occasional figure skittering along the walls between the fixed catapult and arbalest positions, peeking at the contravallation work at one place only to disappear upon being spotted, then reappear somewhere else. He estimated no more than a hundred fighting men were inside. *Enough to hold the place, but not enough to drive me off. And I'm all out of acrobats.* A calculated response, one meant to achieve the maximum result with the least risk. Under other circumstances he might've admired the move.

The ground might indeed have been unsuited to earthwork-building, but Phynagoras had forced his army to build it anyway, and once again they'd worked their miracle, packing the loose chalk tight and high and wetted in place by the rain, enough to hold off the enemies without for a while at least.

"My lord," said Musa, jogging up to where Phynagoras stood supervising the last stretches of defenses. Phynagoras had already registered the man's tone, and knew he was about to bother him with some mundane issue that the young general yet felt without authority to tackle.

He sighed. "Yes, Musa, what is it?"

"Well, it's the camp followers. They want in."

"In?"

"Inside the defense."

"Absolutely not!" Phynagoras snapped. "We barely have space for the army."

"The enemy host we briefly fought before has arrived, and they're afraid. About a thousand are crowding the entry—"

"What do I care?" He fought to maintain composure, not let such insignificant matters rattle him. But it was getting harder and harder these days. "No one forced them to come along. They came all on their own. I was hoping their sheer numbers would be of use, but they've been only a burden so far. Let them squat outside my walls. They can be my shield for once."

"Erm, yes, lord. There's someone else who wishes entry as well."

"Oh, for...who?"

Musa winced. "It's Ordovax, lord. I don't know what he wants."

"Didn't I send him and his superstitious barbarians away?"

"Not really, you just stopped talking to him. He did manage to whip those terrorists in their own den."

Phynagoras waved dismissively. "Too little, too late. Damage was done. Fine, fine, let him in. Then get about plugging that entry. I don't want anyone else getting in. If we have to leave we'll dig our way out."

"Lord, we still outnumber the enemy in the field—"

"And if we fight we'll win. But how many will we lose? I still need this port and the city. Everything depends on it, and we're not leaving until that's accomplished. I've been careless before. I won't be again."

Ordovax was shown to him, and Phynagoras felt no surprise when the chieftain made no gesture of greeting or obeisance. He simply stood for a moment, watching the earthwork go up with arms crossed. Finally he spat onto the ground, then pointed out at the wall. "It is like our Tels. We build high in mountains. But round, and higher. Not so fast."

"That is incredibly fascinating to me, Ordovax," Phynagoras said in a monotone.

"Yes?"

"No. What do you want?"

"Enemies all around you. You make these dirt hills, though you are stronger. I do not understand this, but I understand you need friends."

Phynagoras laughed bitterly. "And exactly what friends do you see here? You? What use are you? You won't kneel before me, you won't fight at night. There are a few hundred of you at best."

Ordovax nodded. "All you say is true. Yet we have what you do not. We have places, in our mountains. Strong places."

"Your Tels?" Phynagoras mused with a sneer. "Piles of dirt are no use to me."

"No. Those are for the ancestors. We have strong places, what you

338 • ERIC LEWIS

may call 'fortress', or 'castle', no blocks but cut into the bones of the mountain. More than one, but few know them all."

Phynagoras perked up at that. This was new information. "Oh? Of a size to hold my army?"

"For a time. In the day of my third forefather we needed no such things. We were strong in muscle and spirit, and the sheep-men of Ar'Vaddhfa feared the sight of us. But times change. Now we need strong places. I think you do also."

Phynagoras rubbed his chin. *For a time. Time enough to send for reinforcements. Time to regroup, ride out the winter.* He might not be able to conquer Holy Artamera, but Barg-o-Bhanii was still possible. Not even with his demonic magic could Osmund blow a whole mountain to bits, surely. "Interesting. Very interesting. I need to think on this."

"Think? You think much, and look where it takes you."

"Point taken. Still—"

He was interrupted by a watch captain running up to him with something in his hand. "M'lord Phynagoras! A message."

"Message? Where could a message to me here possibly come from?"

"The enemy satrap," the captain huffed, holding out a slip of paper. "He sent a scout right up to the wall."

"A scout? And no one spotted him?"

"He must've sneaked real good, mixed in with the followers. Then straight off again—"

Phynagoras snatched the paper from the captain, and his hand shook as he unrolled it. The last note he'd received had been...distressing, after all.

To the invader, Phynagoras of Porontus,

You are surrounded. King Osmund is at hand with power to effect your most assured defeat. Your schemes against the Artameran Polytheon have left you despised and friendless. It would be wise of you to consider my present offer of a parley. Send word of your answer by messenger, and rest assured that I will use your deputation far more gently than you previously did mine.

From Osbren, High Lord of Kingsmarch, Duke of Thoriglyn, Disciple of the Polytheon of Holy Artamera, Voice of Osmund, King of Greater Argovan

"Ha! Confident prick, isn't he? Osmund must be weeks away at least. Of course he makes no mention of my own impaled emissary in front of Phenidra, but whatever."

"Do...you wish to send a reply, lord?"

Phynagoras tossed the note away and shrugged. "Why not? His puffing himself up tells me he's weaker than I imagined. Let's see what he has to say. Your sentries failed to catch the scout, so you can draw lots for who gets to be the return ambassador."

The captain gulped nervously. "Erm, yes m'lord."

"Someone find Musa! Tell him not to plug up the entry just yet."

Ordovax shuffled his feet, not completely comprehending the situation. "King, your answer to my—"

"You'll have my answer when I'm damn well ready to give it. And I am not."

CHAPTER THIRTY-ONE

One Briefest Instant

Linet looked out across the sloping plain, holding on to a tent pole to stay upright. Space was filling up all around with the press of humanity. It seemed here, at last, this city by the sea was to be the place where all armies converged: invaders, defenders, followers and faithful. *And us*, Linet thought, mind dizzied by the growing infection in the remainders of her digits.

The Polytheon's mob had caught up to Osbren, and now faced down the much greater numbers of migrants from Bhasa, Porontus and a hundred other places. Both groups snarled and snapped at each other and here and there skirmishes broke out, but they fizzled quickly with no one to lead them on.

Near sundown a figure on horseback forced its way through the sea of supplicants beating at the new earthwork barrier, bearing a banner of white with Phynagoras's sigil embroidered on it. Linet recognized the sign from Eyvind's ring, and Eyvind did as well from his reaction.

"There's our answer at least, whatever it is," he said with finality. Not excitement or fear, but just a weariness beyond his years, and a vague plea to make an end to things one way or another.

Aerrus tossed a bundle of twigs onto the fire outside the small tent the trio had been lent. "Figures, I just got this going. Hardly any kindling around here. What, er...." He looked left and right before lowering his voice, nervous perhaps, absurdly now, about being overheard. "What are we going to do, if we get close to him?"

"You have the Vrril?" Linet asked.

Aerrus nodded, patting the leather phial case at his waist. "Yeah.

I guess that's what I figured. But he'll be surrounded by guards, probably. How—"

"Best keep it loose," said Eyvind. "Don't plan too firmly. If you see a chance, if I see a chance…take it."

"Right."

The emissary approached Osbren's camp, a hundred and more bows and spears pointed at his head. Osbren himself marched out to converse. It seemed a slow palaver, for there was a bit of a language barrier. But at last a slip of paper changed hands, and Phynagoras's own terse reply was given. The man rode off, and likely more than one itchy finger burned to put some sharp metal in his back. Eventually Osbren found the trio and pulled them close, out of the hearing of his soldiers.

"He says yes. I get the feeling he thinks he has the advantage, as well he might. I'll try to keep him guessing, keep him off balance until my brother arrives, if I have to. If you three can accomplish anything more, erm, permanent, well…I got no problem breaking the peace of parley after what he's done. But I won't be the one to move first, understand."

Linet nodded as a wintery gust chilled her bones. "We understand. War and politics. Just don't stand too close to him."

*   *   *

It didn't seem real. Not after fighting so hard for so long and building it all up in Linet's mind, building *him* up into some supernatural demidemon. To simply walk into Phynagoras's camp, surrounded by his invading armies that their little insurgency had barely managed to irritate, it must surely be a dream. A nightmare brought by the fever of sickness and winter. But no, the pain and fatigue and burning hatred told her that it was all indeed very real. And all of them without the familiar instruments they'd used to work their will upon the world: no swords, no knives, no bows or arrows were permitted within the confines of the enclosure hastily erected just beyond the massive earthwork that encircled Seagate. *My bow would do me no good anyway*, she thought. *Not now, nor ever again*. She'd left it behind at the charred remains of the Lodge. Maybe someone else could make some use of it before the end.

The party also consisted of Osbren, his herald, his top captains, and a priest of the Polytheon. Not one so elaborately done up as those they'd seen in Pelona, but still a bizarre tattooed and pierced spectacle who spoke little. Linet, Aerrus and Eyvind were by contrast easy to ignore, and so bedraggled it could not even have been said by some sudden newcomer which side they hewed to.

There was no mistaking Phynagoras, however. She'd never laid eyes on him before, yet he had a wild intensity and presence of command that made all around him mere satellites orbiting his splendid sun. Linet imagined that he'd gathered so many followers to him simply so that they wouldn't have to worry about being on the receiving end of that intensity. As the party approached on foot, he stood with an easy grace, clad in saffron robes and surrounded by his officers. Overhead his panther and stag sigil fluttered. Next to him stood Ordovax, one-eyed and scowling and brutish. The Marchman scanned each face as they entered, perhaps suspicious of this odd notion of treating with the enemy instead of killing them. When his cyclopean gaze fell on Linet he grinned, and she shivered.

At several yards' distance Osbren halted, and his retinue did the like. He took his time unstrapping his bascinet and removing it entirely, the shining armor glimmering yellow in the firelight. A little red brazier crackled between them as a light snow began to fall, with one Bhasan soldier poking at the fire to keep it going.

While Osbren worked at the helm, Phynagoras laughed. His laugh unsettled Linet, not because it was sinister but because it was casual, friendly even. He stepped forward to warm his hands over the brazier, then said in perfect but heavily accented Argovani, "He keeps me waiting on purpose as a show of dominance. If this is what they teach you in satrap school this will prove a very brief conference indeed." He clapped the soldier on the back. "That'll do, Musa." The soldier put down the poker and left the fire to tend itself. Aerrus lightly fingered his phial case containing the last of the Vrril, but he was surrounded by enemy guards, and would never be able to get close enough.

The battle of words joined, Osbren rose to the task with a shrug. "Maybe I'm just clumsy. Been a long while since I had to put on harness. No one's been dumb enough to break into my brother's house and start breaking things until now."

Phynagoras laughed again, this time with what might've been genuine delight. "Oh, good! A self-professed wit. I was beginning to think the only thing the people of this country did well was die. Oh, not *well*, exactly, but at least in great numbers."

"Yes, I hear your famed General Boras set quite an example. Made a very pretty corpse. Too bad your men didn't get to see it, what with their turning tail and running from me at the time, along with *that* cowardly mountain of stupid." Osbren jerked his chin toward Ordovax. The man's understanding of Argovani might've been rudimentary, but he knew when he'd been insulted. The chieftain grunted and started to move forward before Phynagoras put a halting hand in front of him. Ordovax glared at that hand, but held his place.

"I see the pleasantries are over," said Phynagoras, his smile now evaporated. "Fine. I will accept your surrender now. Move your motley band of starvelings off and dismiss the fleet below, and I'll consider letting you live a bit longer."

Now it was Osbren's turn to laugh. "I apologize, my lord! Either your own wit is even greater than rumored, or your grasp of our language is lesser. Look around, you Porontan fop. You're surrounded, with no more friends. Osmund is coming with hellsfire, Pelona's not far behind. You managed to stir the hornet's nest of the Polytheon – the very gods are against you!" The priest next to him inclined a long neck slightly in agreement. "Quite an accomplishment, but now it is I who am here to accept *your* surrender."

"*Are you incapable of counting?*" Phynagoras shouted it, giving away more than a hint of his true state of mind. Half a second later, he recovered, but the damage was done. "I outnumber you, I have defensive positions, and my followers alone could swallow you up whole."

Eyvind chuckled bitterly. "You mean the brainwashed worshipers you locked outside your silly fort? How long you think they'll follow you when the king burns 'em all to cinders? That little chastisement I gave you outside Phenidra will seem a pleasant memory."

Phynagoras started at those words so like his own not long ago, his eyes widening for a moment. "You...you're the one, up on the walls...." He took a deep breath, then forced a smile again. "Well, you've miscalculated. I have yet one more friend. One you've been unable to subdue even after uncounted centuries." He reached out to his side and wrapped an arm around Ordovax, drawing the surprised Marchman to him.

Osbren made a disgusted sound. "*That?* You truly are desperate."

"Oh, no," said Phynagoras, "I'm confident. Why, these brave warriors have owned your highlands since time began, and still do. They have strongholds where I and my army may wait out the winter at our leisure. Fool, this was only the first thrust! I have a million souls at my command, and soon this entire pitiful country will belong to them. To me!"

Ordovax listened to this speech, paused a moment, looked between Osbren and Phynagoras, then tilted his head in a noncommittal gesture. "This may be."

Phynagoras turned beet-red. "*May be?*"

"You laugh in my face," Ordovax said to Osbren, "but this is proper. You are my enemy." He turned to Phynagoras. "Not so long before, you laugh also. What are you, then?"

"Ordovax," said Phynagoras, less confident now, "listen to me, please. I...have my moods, I admit. It's a side effect of believing my own myth. But we are so close now! Victory is just over the next hill, and it's a small hill at that. Forgive my mistakes, my friend, and look to the prize. Help me take the Ar'Vaddhfa from these sheep-men, and the ancestors will have this entire peninsula! I'll give it to you, all of it!"

"Lies," snarled Osbren. "You'll never take it. You'll freeze in those mountains until Osmund burns you out."

Ordovax squinted his one eye. "You swear? Before your ancestors?"

Phynagoras nodded. "Before mine, and yours!"

The chieftain nodded. "But one more thing do I wish."

"Name it!"

Ordovax extended one great meaty tree trunk of an arm and one gnarled finger...straight at Linet. "*That one.*"

Linet jumped at suddenly being made the center of attention. "W— What?"

"She is..." Ordovax said something in his own language that seemed to have no translation, but his evil smile left little to the imagination. "If she lives, she will give me strong sons. If not, then...enjoyment."

"Done! Ring 'em in, lads!" All at once Phynagoras's soldiers pressed in on the party, spears ready. Any gap that might've led to escape was closed off, and Osbren's captains shouted in indignation.

"You've made the right choice," said Phynagoras, beaming and shaking Ordovax's arm in thanks. "Musa! Bring us some of that wine we took from Ólo. There should still be a little left. We'll toast our bargain anew, and remember old Boras, gods rot the drunken lech."

"You bastard," Osbren huffed, "you can't do this!"

"I can do any damn thing I like, my walking corpse of a satrap. One of the perks of being a messiah."

Wine was brought, and Osbren's party stood and watched impotently as fine cups of colored glass were filled from a quarter-cask and Phynagoras, ever the showman, made great ceremony over the affair. Even to the point of swearing his oath to Ordovax on his own knees, a gesture no one present had ever seen. So rapt was his army that the wine cups sat forgotten off to the side, along with Aerrus, who'd neither spoke nor moved throughout the whole production. Thus no one noticed when, with a deft, dark little movement, he slid a hand to his waist to grasp his phial case. A flick of one finger, a twist of the wrist and it was done. Only Linet saw him do it, her eyes darting all around for any chance to escape whatever Ordovax had planned for her.

With the oaths exchanged, Phynagoras ordered the wine brought to them. He handed one to Ordovax and held the other aloft. "To friendship! To the ancestors of Ar'Vaddhfa, to the future, and the passing of Barg-o-Bhanii from the memory of the world." He drank deep with much drama. Ordovax drained his cup in one gulp, and Phynagoras laughed. "Just like Boras."

Ordovax stared at his cup, frowning. "Eh. Not very good."

"Maybe it's gone off during our journey. No matter, we'll have all the vineyards on the peninsula soon enough. In fact, we'll— What's wrong?"

Ordovax's face went white, and he doubled over. "Aargh!" He collapsed, clutching at his stomach, then began convulsing.

"What the hells? What's— Oh. Oh, no." Phynagoras grabbed his own belly, but managed to remain standing. "Ah, you...sneaky bastards! Betrayal! You've poisoned me!" He shattered his cup on the ground and looked across the gathered soldiers, his own and his enemies, the followers beyond, the few Marchmen attending. "But which one of you? Who? Who's done this?"

Musa ran to Phynagoras. "My lord, what is—?"

Phynagoras pushed the man away, laughing maniacally while Ordovax foamed at the mouth at his feet. "Get off me, fool! Whatever you've done, you failed! I am immune to poisons, I have made myself so long ago! You cannot kill me, I am a god. You hear me, a fucking *god*! I'll drown the lot of you in poison before you can touch me! Caerdig! Bring me Caerdig!"

This newest spectacle continued to hold every single eye, Musa and the soldiers watching in open-mouthed horror as their savior went insane right in front of them. The one tasked with holding Linet secure before being turned over to Ordovax now stood slack-jawed and slack-handed. Suddenly free, Linet felt time slow to a crawl. The snow seemed to stop its descent, all sounds muffled, all the shadowy figures around her still as marble. The fire in the brazier before them flickered at a snail's pace. And it was all so clear now.

She turned to Aerrus and Eyvind. They saw her. She made a single hand signal: *stay*. Aerrus shook his head sharply, jaw clenched, but she just held the sign. Looking Eyvind in the eye and seeing fear and confusion she gave a smile, but he did not return it. *Thank you*, she mouthed, *my mountain lord*.

Perhaps realizing what she was about to do, Eyvind tried to scream *No!* but to his horror it caught in his throat. Linet tore free of her captors and ran toward the brazier. Passing by, she plucked the poker from the fire. Behind her, Aerrus shouted at Osbren's party to get back. She ran – *oh, so slowly!* – at Phynagoras, still in the grip of his mad tirade.

He only noticed her in the very last heartbeat, and the two enemies locked eyes for the one and only time as the red-hot poker pierced deep into Phynagoras's flesh, into his stomach, where the Vrril yet remained.

"Eulalia, you've come back to m—"

All light and all sound and all everything enveloped Linet, and for one briefest instant, it felt like victory, it felt like peace, and, best of all, it felt like hope.

CHAPTER THIRTY-TWO

Kneel

In a moment a fiery hell surrounded Eyvind. Oh, there was actual fire, a searing wave of heat that singed his beard, but so much more than that. So much worse. Even before comprehending what had happened, the deafening Vrril blast coated him also with bits of flesh and their stench, and the screams of men on fire, running every which way with no thought but to get away.

He lay on the ground while snowflakes fell stinging into his eyes, and chaos dominated the periphery of his vision. Bodies in various states of being alive, horses, little burning bits of everything caught by the winter wind floated past while the ringing echoed. When it finally began to fade, he sat up. His head swam. In front of him Phynagoras's panther and stag banner lay burning.

"What," he coughed, "what happened? Where...where's Linet? Aerrus?" Aerrus lay beside him, slowly squirming to his knees.

"Aargh! Oh, gods. She did it. She did it." There were tears in his eyes.

"What did she do? Where's...?" His head began to clear, and memory of the horror returned. "Oh, no. Linet! Gods, no!"

Aerrus pulled Eyvind to his feet. "Come on, we have to get out of here."

Eyvind wept openly as they plucked through the pandemonium. They found Osbren, wounded but alive. The Polytheon priest was dead, and some of Osbren's captains. A whole host of the invaders had been blown to bits, and of Ordovax and Phynagoras nothing was left. The remaining army and their followers were quickly succumbing to panic, and Eyvind fought back the deepest pits of grief to drag Osbren the several hundred yards back to his camp before they were swallowed up by it.

He and Aerrus dumped Osbren, armor and all, onto a pallet in his command tent while Tess scrambled to find a physic for him. The two men lay on the ground, breathless.

"I...can't believe she's gone," said Eyvind. "Just like that, she's gone."

Aerrus nodded. "That's often the way of it. It's what we all knew could happen."

"Not her. Somehow, I always thought it would be you. Or me. One of us, but not her. Not her."

"Maybe that's how it goes in the stories. No one's safe in real life."

"How very practical of you," Eyvind spat bitterly.

"I didn't love her any less than you did, soldier boy! She made a brave choice, don't know if I coulda done the like. I won't dishonor it." He put a hand to his pounding forehead. "Oh...."

Some time later, after Osbren had been seen to and put into a dreamless opiphine-laden sleep, a strange sound surrounded the camp. It was like the hum of insects, but lower and much louder. Aerrus forced his aching joints into motion and stood to poke his head outside. "What in the hells is that?"

Tess came running up to them both. "We have to go, now."

"Why?" Eyvind asked, half asleep from exhaustion. "What's happening?"

"These foreigners," said Tess, "word's spreading among 'em about their precious leader getting blasted to jam. They're ready to riot, and I don't think they're too happy with us."

The plain around them had begun to close in, with thousands of dark shapes merging into colony creatures, like the arms of an octopus each with its own primitive brain. And they were all getting closer, the angry shouting of soldiers and migrants both all combined into that terrible hum. Osbren's men had put up what defenses they could, with sentries and shield walls and a thousand watchfires lighting up the night while Osbren himself lay insensible. But it wouldn't even approach enough to stem the tide should the mob choose to attack, even with the army of the faithful on their side. It was only the weeks of forced marching and digging that sapped their strength to do so straight away.

"We have to stop this," said Eyvind. "There's no way to fight our way out. Can we talk to them?"

"How?" Tess held her hands out wide in frustration. "They have no leaders. That's the whole problem!" One of the octopus arms now stretched closer to the camp, a group of several hundred followers who now had no one to follow gripping crude weapons or just rocks, yelling unintelligible curses in their own languages.

Aerrus grabbed Eyvind and rushed over to one of the captains nearest the mob. "Can any of you understand what they're saying?"

The soldier shook his head. "Nah, it's just gobbledegook! What do we do?"

"You're asking me?"

Then, one of the panicked rioters stepped forward, a Bhasan man who looked slightly less impoverished than the others. "You! You bastard! I understand. You killed our messiah, and now we will tear you apart!"

Enraged, Aerrus strode forward, dodging stones tossed out of the dark. The man was twenty yards away, and he had to shout to be heard, but by the gods Aerrus *would* be heard. "Are you insane? You invaded our country, not the other way round! Phynagoras was no god, just a man with a silver tongue and a big head. Of course we killed him! What did we owe the prick? What do *you* owe him, even now?"

The man shook his fist at him. "We owe him our loyalty!"

"The dead are owed nothing!"

"He was our leader! We had no life in our country, no future. Now we have no country again, no life, no leader. All we have is revenge, and we will take you to hell with us!"

"Sounds depressingly familiar," Aerrus muttered. "Hmm...."

"What are you thinking?" Eyvind asked suspiciously.

"Captain," Aerrus said quickly, "can you hold them off for a little while?"

"Hold 'em off? Are you crazy?"

"If you concentrate all your men on this spot, can you at least hold off this group?"

The captain frowned in confusion. "Here? I guess…wait, who are you to give orders anyway?"

"Stay here," he told Eyvind, then ran off into the dark without explanation.

They set up a shield wall, and built up the fires until half the plain was bright as day. The mob made some furtive advances, but without proper weapons it was a stalemate at best.

When Aerrus returned, he was holding a large piece of dark cloth under one arm. A cloak, it looked like. And he held a white rock in his other hand. "Here, lay this out on the ground."

Without comprehending, Eyvind nevertheless obeyed. "What are you up to?"

"The last thing I can think of. Here, pull each corner tight and flat." He stood over the cloak of dark blue wool. He cut off the hood and stretched it out until it was vaguely rectangular. "Captain, please find me a…I don't know, a spear or tent pole or something, the longest you can find."

"But—"

"Hurry!" The mob grew louder and angrier.

Aerrus took the rock in his hand and used a knife to chip it into a point at one end. It was soft local rock, the same white chalk as the cliffs beneath them. Standing over the cloth, he used it to sketch out a crude shape. Eyvind stood behind him, watching, and when Aerrus's plan became clear he shook his head in wonder. "You're crazy, that'll never work. It's folly."

"Then you best go make your peace with the gods. But they didn't light that priest's path except with hellsfire, so I doubt you have much better chances." Aerrus paused just long enough to take Eyvind by the shoulder. "Lin just blew herself to bits to defeat Phynagoras. I won't let that be for nothing. Now please, help me."

A long tent pole was brought, and a supply wagon empty of supplies except for one empty crate. Aerrus attached the cloth to the end of the pole at two places then climbed atop the wagon and crate both, standing stark in the surrounding firelight, suddenly an easy target. He hoisted the pole, waved the cloth back and forth and wailed at the top of his lungs. "*Kneel! Kneel!*"

The mob looked up in bewilderment. Fluttering above was a new sigil, flicking in the light of watchfires: A dark blue field emblazoned with the device of a castle atop a bridge, with fish below. The banner of King Osmund.

"Kneel before the King! Kneel and he will be merciful!" Aerrus pointed at the man below who spoke Argovani. "You! Tell them. Tell them to swear faith to King Osmund, and they will be welcome to stay in Argovan. As an agent of the king I pledge this in his name. You want a leader? You want life? A country? Kneel and you'll have it! Or else we'll use our magic fire to blast every last one of you. Die with us, or kneel and live with us. Make your choice. Kneel!" The banner kept waving as Aerrus kept shouting and the Bhasan man repeated the words.

At first, there seemed to be no effect. The mob's curses continued. Then, as more and more people noticed the madman waving a cloak above them, they grew less panicked and more curious. The translated command spread through the mob and, not knowing how much of the terrible weapon their enemy yet possessed, the threatening crush of bodies stopped its advance.

Finally, just as Aerrus's voice was grown hoarse and about to give out completely, someone knelt. A young woman holding a baby in her arms. Watching all this in wonder, Eyvind was reminded of the incident in Downhill that seemed so long ago now. Then another, an older man in bizarre Ghreshi dress, knelt also. Then two more. Then ten more. Then a hundred. A wave of knees falling to the ground spread out from the center, until the darkness obscured the edge of it. Silence began to fall across the plain.

Shocked, Aerrus wedged the tent pole between the crate and the side of the wagon so that it stayed aloft on its own, then climbed down.

"Incredible," said the captain, "absolutely incredible! How did you do that?"

"No—" Aerrus coughed, his voice scratchy and withered. "No idea. Didn't really expect it to work."

"I don't believe it," Eyvind said. "The stubborn arse who refused to kneel before the king convinced a whole damn nation to do it. From one messiah to another."

"Osmund's no messiah. And that's probably for the best."

★ ★ ★

In the morning Lord Osbren regained consciousness, and when told of what had transpired he ordered Aerrus and Eyvind brought before him. "Are you two out of your minds?! Who do you think you are, using the royal standard like that and making promises in the crown's name! That's treason!"

"What were we supposed to do?" asked Aerrus. "Go down fighting? I've tried that. It's not as heroic as you think."

"It was a last-ditch gamble to save all our lives," Eyvind added, "including yours. We're all out of Vrril until Osmund arrives, but they don't know that."

"But what am I going to tell my brother? You can't expect him to honor this, this…infamy! Legions of dirty foreigners settled all over his lands? He'll never accept it!"

"That's his concern, not ours." Aerrus leaned in close to where Osbren lay with wounds bound. "But I doubt even he has enough Vrril to prevent a bloody massacre on both sides if he wants to go back on the promise. Might be less trouble to let 'em stay."

"And encourage more to come! Where'll it stop?"

"Well, it's a good thing we've got good Marcher lords guarding the borders, isn't it?"

Osbren did not much appreciate that.

354 • ERIC LEWIS

Eyvind and Aerrus were kept under nominal house arrest within the camp until Osmund finally showed up. He had cobbled together an army of Argovani volunteers led by his household bravos, Pelonans, Marzahni, and even a few mercenaries. Ingenious devices made to utilize the destructive power of Vrril were driven before them that put the insurgents' clumsy efforts to shame. The migrants parted at the sight of the strange engines, fearful yet clinging to ragged shreds of hope. Osbren hobbled out of his tent to welcome his brother in a public embrace that gave heart to his own small, surrounded army.

When the cheers faded, the king with Essimis at his side and Captain Eimar one step behind as ever came to a small tent near the edge of the camp. The tent flooded with sunlight when it opened, and the two within squinted. When he realized their visitors, Eyvind sank to one knee. "My lord king." He looked over at Aerrus.

"What?" Aerrus sighed. "Oh, fine." At last Aerrus joined Eyvind in doing homage to Osmund.

"So," the king said, "it must be true, what my brother tells me."

Aerrus nodded, rose to his feet. "It's true."

It was not from Osmund that the deluge of indignation came, but Chancellor Essimis. "You! You had no right! That little badge went to your head, that must be it. How dare you! The indescribable arrogance—"

Osmund held up a hand, and Essimis fell reluctantly silent. "I heard about Linet, about her sacrifice. I'm very sorry. She was a remarkable young woman."

"She was."

"It's a debt that can never be repaid. So I won't try. I can understand why you did what you did. But it does leave a bit of a mess for me."

"Os—" Aerrus began to say, then noticed Eimar's eyes widening in irritation. "King Osmund, I'm no chancellor to make laws or grand decisions, but this might be an opportunity."

"Oh?"

"You live in palaces, in crowded cities, so maybe you don't notice it, but Argovan's been painfully empty for a while now. Even so long after your bloody civil wars, we're underpopulated, a tempting target. These people might be just what you need. You could be taking in twice as much revenue from the farms and mills if only you had the bodies to work them. And if you let 'em stay, I imagine they'd be mighty grateful."

"Grateful? They were in the process of exterminating us, if I recall. All in the name of their savior."

"I don't think it was really Phynagoras they followed, Your Grace," Eyvind said. "It was the promise he held out to them. He just wrapped himself up in it to use them for his own reasons. Maybe make them another promise, of a chance for better than they had. Less grand but more real."

"'Course," Aerrus said, "I wouldn't recommend trying to impose the old feudal order on 'em."

Osmund's mouth turned up at the corners. "Careful, Essimis, I think you might have a rival for your job."

"Oh hells, no! Just something to consider. Your Grace."

CHAPTER THIRTY-THREE

The Course of the Sun

Without Phynagoras's leadership gluing them together, the bulk of his exhausted army surrendered. All but the most fanatical and bloodthirsty accepted what was being called Osmund's Peace. Those who did not, mostly from the old Second Hazara, made a desperate last stand, attacking from the mouth of the chalk earthwork. The full force of Osmund's Vrril weapons was loosed against them, and they were wiped out in a matter of minutes. Explosions of almost divine intensity dwarfed even the sum total of all that had been seen thus far, and even the victors stood horrified at the easy annihilation. Not even pieces of the enemy remained. They were just...gone. Osmund took not a single casualty. Any doubts about the substance's power were put to bed with jaw-dropping shock. A few fools tried to storm the walls of Seagate, and though no one laid eyes on any of the Artameran marines supposedly manning the place, a number of bodies were hurled back over the parapets without ceremony.

Secure in the knowledge that he possessed, for now at least, the most powerful force in the entire world, Osmund began a lazy peregrination back northward. Word of the victory spread, and the roads were soon crammed with peasants, merchants, laborers and civil servants streaming back to whatever was left of their homes. For some it would yet be a hard winter, and a king nearby to dispense succor would help blunt the blow of the strange new migrants in their midst.

Aerrus and Eyvind were granted provisional paroles for their 'crime' of usurping royal authority, and as they accompanied the king's army north, Essimis spent much time in their company, though little of it in good humor.

"Babysitting us, is that it?" Aerrus asked as they rode near the way back up to the Lodge, where he would soon take his leave. "Afraid we'll give away the rest of the kingdom?"

"I wouldn't put it past you," the chancellor growled. "And what we've still got is in shambles. Riots in Carsolan, Thoriglyn. The panic in Lenocca at just the rumor of Phynagoras's approach caused almost as much destruction as a siege would have. It'll still be a long recovery. But in truth, I've been tasked with, well, evaluating you."

Eyvind patted the mane of the fine black horse he'd been loaned. "Evaluating? For what?"

"The world is much changed from what it was just a few seasons ago," he said almost wistfully. "New people, new weapons, and it's just going faster."

"Oh, no," said Aerrus with alarm, "you don't really think I want your job, do you?"

"I should think not! No, but His Grace is very aware that we'll need new blood to meet these challenges. This Vrril, for example. It can have employment in many areas other than war. Who knows what incredible inventions might spring from it, wrought by clever hands? And the Marches. We cannot continue simply holding the upland tribes at bay, forever fearing retribution for ancient conquests. We must reconcile with them. And lords who hide in their castles will be of little use now that they can be blasted to gravel. You, Eyvind. You wouldn't be such a one, now, would you?"

"You know I wouldn't," he answered.

"Good. Because you are now Lord of Phenidra and of the Northmarch."

Eyvind drew rein only because his limbs froze. "I am?"

"Well, hells boy, you have been in fact if not in name for some time now! That sit well with you or no?"

Eyvind looked at Aerrus, who just shrugged. "Erm, y-yes. Yes, it does. Thank you."

"Hmph. You can thank His Grace, when we've time to do a proper investiture. In fact we may have to bring back some small patents of nobility across the kingdom to keep order. With *limited* temporal power, mind you." Essimis turned to Aerrus, who rode a humbler beast that he'd been given to keep. "As for you...."

"You don't intend to make some noble hooplehead out of me, surely."

"No. But the loss of Rinalda was a terrible blow, in more ways than one. His Grace had hoped to offer the position of cryptarch to young Linet, but...of course that won't happen now. I don't suppose you want the job? You exposed the traitor, after all."

Aerrus shook his head. "No, I'm not for that kind of thing. We've lots of rebuilding of our own yet to do." Suddenly two thin people melted out of the brush by the roadside, waiting it seemed. Aerrus waved. "Thanis! Kay! Over here!" The two came alongside Aerrus's horse, glad to be reunited but sad at Linet's absence. "Right on time. And I didn't even spot you. Either I'm getting sloppy or you're getting better."

"Probably both," said Thanis.

"Gee, thanks. No, chancellor, I can't take that job either. But I think in time we could send you one or two likely candidates, teach you some of what we know. New blood."

"Fair enough."

"In time," said Kanessa dourly, "but not now."

"You're going back up there, then?" Eyvind asked. It was as close to goodbye as he could manage. That was fine, Aerrus heard it anyway. He clasped Eyvind's arm in his own and nodded.

"Aye, Lord Eyvind, for now. It's where I belong."

"But your Lodge is destroyed," said Essimis, "and no longer secret."

Aerrus nudged his horse to the side of the road toward the path uphill. "Maybe that's just as well. Can't hide from the world forever. We'll have to find some new place soon." He gave a wry grin. "But I ain't telling you where."

*   *   *

The Polytheon fleet sailed home to Artamera to deal with any foolish attacks from remnants of Phynagoras's home armies. But with the death of their messiah, old forces in Porontus fell to scrapping with each other to fill the vacuum. His Bhasan satraps suddenly found themselves little kings outright, with problems that now belonged to them and no one else.

The migrants were settled on lands that were neither rich nor the easiest to cultivate, yet it was still a paradise compared to the places they'd left. The remaining soldiers that had taken part in the massacres were given much harsher terms besides, but none dared complain. It'd be a difficult road assimilating them into Argovani society, with a lot of bad blood lingering long after the invasion. To discourage further waves that would overwhelm the kingdom completely, a cadre of border regulation officials drawn directly from the newcomers themselves was established, as was a charitable aid program for those still struggling in Bhasa and elsewhere. The Polytheon proved eager to help with this, keen to rebuild its reputation of strict neutrality. But the memory of the now-dissolved 'army of the faithful' would not soon fade.

The surviving Heron Kings salvaged what they could from the wreckage of the Lodge and stowed it among the various smallholds they operated. Aerrus recruited from among the insurgents who had nothing to go back to in order to rebuild their numbers. It'd be a hard task keeping the Marchwood safe without a base, not to mention shepherding the migrants until they were fully integrated, which Aerrus supposed was partly his responsibility now.

"It's a hells of a tough job you left me with, Lin," Aerrus said as he held her old bow and watched Thanis lead away mules laden with their charred archives. "Not sure I'm up to it alone. I'm dog tired. Gods, I miss you! But I guess we got no choice. Can't stop the course of the sun, and I think the Heron Kings just might have a role yet to play in the world before its ending."

The westering sun dipped below the cleft horizon, and under the old mountains the Heron King slept.

FLAME TREE PRESS
FICTION WITHOUT FRONTIERS
Award-Winning Authors & Original Voices

Flame Tree Press is the trade fiction imprint of Flame Tree Publishing, focusing on excellent writing in horror and the supernatural, crime and mystery, science fiction and fantasy. Our aim is to explore beyond the boundaries of the everyday, with tales from both award-winning authors and original voices.

•

Other titles in the *Heron Kings* series by Eric Lewis:
The Heron Kings

You may also enjoy:
The Sentient by Nadia Afifi
The Emergent by Nadia Afifi
American Dreams by Kenneth Bromberg
Junction by Daniel M. Bensen
Interchange by Daniel M. Bensen
Second Lives by P.D. Cacek
The City Among the Stars by Francis Carsac
The Garden of Bewitchment by Catherine Cavendish
Vulcan's Forge by Robert Mitchell Evans
Black Wings by Megan Hart
Stoker's Wilde by Steven Hopstaken & Melissa Prusi
The Widening Gyre by Michael R. Johnston
The Blood-Dimmed Tide by Michael R. Johnston
Those Who Came Before by J.H. Moncrieff
The Sky Woman by J.D. Moyer
The Guardian by J.D. Moyer
The Last Crucible by J.D. Moyer
The Goblets Immortal by Beth Overmyer
The Apocalypse Strain by Jason Parent
Until Summer Comes Around by Glenn Rolfe
A Killing Fire by Faye Snowden
Fearless by Allen Stroud
Resilient by Allen Stroud
Screams from the Void by Anne Tibbets

•

Join our mailing list for free short stories, new release details, news about our authors and special promotions:

flametreepress.com